WALT WHITMAN'S SECRET

WALT WHITMAN'S SECRET

A Novel

GEORGE FETHERLING

RANDOM HOUSE CANADA

www.randomhouse.ca

Random House Canada and colophon are registered trademarks.

This book is a work of fiction. Names, characters, places, and incidents either are the
product of the author's imagination or are used fictitiously. Any resemblance to actual
persons, living or dead, events, or locales is entirely coincidental.

Library and Archives Canada Cataloguing in Publication

Fetherling, George
Walt Whitman's secret : a novel / George Fetherling.

ISBN 978-0-679-31223-9

I. Title.

PS8561.E834W35 2010   C813'.54   C2009-905058-7

Design by Leah Springate

Printed in the United States of America

10 9 8 7 6 5 4 3 2 1

For Eric Marks and Heather Craig

ONE

I NEVER SAW THE MAN whose spirit-child I became when he didn't actively appear to be dying. He was a person who, for all the emphasis he placed on vigor and robust manliness, started his decline early and continued on the downward path during all the time I sat with him and listened and asked him to teach me. His descent into death was especially rapid during his final three and a half years, when I was preserving a record of his conversation. What I am about to say might seem cold-hearted to anyone else who might read these lines, but I know that you, dear Flora, will comprehend my message with the perfect and honest clarity for which you are known. The simple fact is that W was growing thinner and more feeble at the same rate as my manuscript of his table-talk (bed-talk might be a better term) got thicker, meatier and stronger—as though all things in the Universe were suddenly in balance.

I was not yet fifteen years of age when my father, Maurice Traubel, a lithographer and engraver with his own little shop, told me that a famous poet, a great man, had come to live in Camden and that we should be proud to have him in our city. My mother, Katherine, a native of Philadelphia across the river, had renounced the Christianity in which she had been reared, then married a Jew who himself had repudiated Judaism some time earlier. For Father had no special affection for the ways of the Hebrews back in Frankfurt or here in America. "Why should I be permitted to do one day the same acts I am then forbidden on another?" he would say. "I see no rational sense in it, and I reject it." He did not wish to be considered a German in the new land any more than he had wished to be thought of as a Jew in the old one. This attitude became part of my inheritance from him, though I was of course not considered a Jew because Mother wasn't one. Unlike most people, I recognize the revision of one's personal history as the necessary removal of an obstacle that cannot be overcome by other means. The longer I live, and as you know, I am approaching the end of the process, the more I discover how much I have resembled my father even while I was struggling to become like W instead.

The idea of a famous American poet, the most American one of all, as many said, right in our midst filled Father with admiration, for he never lost that love of art and learning that is supposed to be a traditional and some say almost mandatory part of Jewish life. In that spirit, he took me with him to pay our respects at the house at 322 Stevens Street. This was the home of George Whitman, W's younger brother by ten years, the one who had fought in the war of secession and suffered a wound, and who now earned his living manufacturing pipe.

W, who was to become the other half of my life, was seated in the parlor, wearing a comfortable suit of clothes. His shirt was open at the throat. His vest had rolled lapels, and an inexpensive watch chain, with no fob, stretched across one side. He had a sensitive mouth and a generous portion of nose, and his hair had retreated most of the way back, giving him a forehead like a cupola on some large public building. His white beard, though wispy in spots, was also long and fully shaped, obscuring the exact outline of the face beneath. He had the habit of combing his whiskers with his fingers as he spoke. His complexion was slightly pink, like a certain type of sea-shell, suggesting a level of health that in fact he could no longer claim to possess. He seemed impossibly old to me then, an antediluvian figure, some ancient god speaking with the authority of long and everlasting experience. In truth, he was fifty-four. Now that I myself am not much older than that, I understand all too well how illness can cause one to fade so quickly and prematurely, though his ill-health differed from my own. My own disease is knowable; it can be circumscribed. His could not be understood or even defined, not until the post-mortem examination that I attended almost two decades later.

Father asked W how he was faring.

"Middling, middling," he said, without real conviction and certainly without the sincere optimism he was to project in later times, worse times. "The left leg's gimpy." He stretched it out straight, then bent over and patted it once, treating it like a faithful dog. "The arm, not so bad." His speech was clear, unaffected by the episode that had taken place in his brain. It was one of those strong voices but was nonetheless soft and well modulated, rather than rough or raucous. He told Father that he was inclined to dizziness now whenever he rose, however slowly, though the problem was less acute when getting to his feet from a seated posture than from either a prone or a supine one. "The blood settles in pools," he said, "like petroleum collecting in the Earth." The words are exact, though of course they were uttered a number of years before I began to write down everything he said to me. Well, almost everything.

Looking back, I know he enjoyed our visit, the first of so many, because my family had come from Europe. W was infatuated with the idea of people forsaking the Old World with its timeless animosities and systems of tribute and packing up for America where they could fill their lungs with oxygen and make their own way without assistance or impediment. That Father respected the rôle of the writer was another attribute in the eyes of W, for he felt that he was an outcast among the literary personages of his own country, as on the evidence he often had been and to a certain extent continued to be. The fact that Father was a part of the printing trades also counted for a great deal. To W, writing and printing were two ends of the same stick, a connection not to be broken but rather to be celebrated. Most of all, he enjoyed having visitors. It seemed to me, in what is called the egoism of youth, that he was especially welcoming to me right from the beginning.

When I quit school, he said to me, "You have wisdom far beyond your few years to have done so," adding: "I was a schoolmaster myself once upon a time, on Long Island, and I know the deleterious effects of school upon young noggins." Soon afterward, when I told him that I was learning how to set type, he smiled warmly, knowing that I was aware how he himself had helped set up the first edition of *Leaves* after he had amputated his own formal education. Soon I was working in the job shop of the *Camden Evening Visitor* and indeed had become its foreman, promoted to the position when I was only sixteen (though I confess that the *Visitor* was hardly a big enterprise nor commercial printing its largest component by any means, to say nothing of the fact that the wages were not enough to have lured a married man).

W often remembered autobiographical details divorced from their place in the sequence of living. Perhaps he had been this way even before the stroke of Seventy-three, I don't know. Only in later years did I feel that I had a full command of what he had done and where he had been at particular times and of just generally how everything fitted together. At first I was aided in this process by *The Good Gray Poet*, which his friend O'Connor wrote in 1866, the year after the war, to protest W's dismissal from his clerkship at the Interior Department in Washington for having promoted immorality in the immortal *Leaves*. Ultimately, though, the knowledge, the understanding, the *knowing*, came to me slowly, grew inside me as I spent so many hours, days and weeks—years almost, if one were to string together all the time continuously—listening to him talk. W was by way of being a professional talker. I, by contrast, was his own professional listener.

When he was living on Stevens, I would make a point of stopping by after work, especially on warm sunny days that I knew might find him sitting on the front stoop. Then we would talk about books on and on. I was of the tender age at which we self-educators have a dire thirst for reading, one that cannot be entirely slaked except perhaps by decrepit maturity. I was happy to take in literary chat, which he could spool out hour upon hour, pleased to have his opinions regarded with such enthusiasm. For as I was not merely becoming self-educated but self-radicalized as well, my ears received with some satisfaction much of what he had to say. Unfortunately, I kept not even a simple diary in those early days, yet I recall a good many of his revelations and pronouncements, for they showed me that we were (or so I thought at the time) members of the same political congregation.

He said, for instance: "The persons who are interested in poetry alone, estranged from most other forms of useful expression, cannot explain why Homer and Virgil are as much different as they are alike. They can't see how the one man was moved to song while the other set out, with utmost calculation, determined to sing, the feelings of the heart be damned." Such utterances were part of W's more general dislike of the literary professors and literary professionals, a subject that could, paradoxically, occasionally drive his pronouncements somewhat beyond the limits of what he actually knew to be true. I once heard him say that he hated polite literature the same way Generals Grant and Sherman had hated warfare: because it was Hell. But the metaphor he chose required some clarification. So he launched into a kind of oral post-scriptum. "Unlike Grant, I am not a West Pointer," he explained. "That is, not the literary equivalent of a West Pointer. I have received no commission for I am not of the officer class, nor could I ever have become so. I have risen through the ranks to whatever small position I now possess (or possesses me)."

He said more than once that he favored books that were small enough for workingmen to tuck into their pockets (though this was not a principle of book manufacture he adhered to with respect to the immortal *Leaves*). Lately I have been remembering one of his book-thoughts in particular. It is his observation that as people get older, they can no longer stomach Shelley's romantic idealism, but nod in agreement with that poet's dislike of biography and history, knowing now that he was correct in thinking such books a bunch of bunkum.

He always said that I brightened his day. I see now, as I did not at the time, the extent to which the first crippling event in his brain, back in Washington, had harrowed his spirits. His mother was ill as well, and was living with his brother George and his wife in Camden. Her death, only four or five months after W's medical misadventure, might easily have propelled another such sensitive person into a deep crater of gloom. He was sorely tested all right, but he did not stumble into the darkness. It was at this time, finding himself first lame and then motherless, that he gave up Washington and moved in with George and his family, occupying his mother's former room. He was careful to leave everything just as she had last seen it. He slept in the bed in which she had died, under the same bed linens. These events were playing themselves out around the time of our first meeting. But other than noting his halting step, I knew little about his physical state, and not one whit about his emotional one.

Strange to say, it was as a result of another death in the always troubled and tragic Whitman family that our friendship achieved its next plateau. One of his nephews had died, Walter by name, called so not after his uncle but rather his grandfather. He was under one year in age. Such a tiny coffin to be sealed up in the ground that way, a thought that came back to me, twenty years ago now, when Anne's and my second child, born the year after our Gertrude whom you know, succumbed to the scarlet fever, months shy of his fifth birthday.

W didn't look especially frail at Walter's graveside service, though he walked with difficulty, like a ship listing slightly to port. I stood behind him in the small knot of mourners. He removed his old sloucher and held it in front of him with both hands as they also gripped the handle of his cane. He was in the same clothes he always seemed to be wearing. His bald head, which I had not seen from that perspective before, was like an old globe from which the continents had been erased. The service over, I expressed my condolences. Despite the melancholic nature of the event, he seemed, as usual, gladdened to see me.

"Horace, my boy, you must tell me how you've been keeping." His shoulders were stooped and his gait hindered, awkward and a bit unsteady, but his eyes were full of vitality. "I am having a rough passage these past few months, these past few years in fact. News of your doings would well right the balance."

I had no news to convey other than that I was leaving the *Visitor* to go to work with Father. He understood what I would gain by such a move as well as what I would be losing.

"I never regretted the time I spent on the papers," he said. "The best training there can be for a writer, in my view. Teaches you concision and sharpness. I had an excellent sit on the *Eagle*." He was referring to the *Brooklyn Daily Eagle*, which he conducted in the late forties. "You learn not to waste words, or ideas either. Everything gets used up properly, like the wood in a stove that's drawing well. It produces heat and leaves pure ash, no cinders, no clinkers, but only stuff that can have other uses later."

In time, I would come to understand that he parted company with the proprietors of the *Eagle* in an editorial difference of opinion, having turned the paper into a Free-Soil organ, fighting against the spread of slavery in the West as the territories acquired statehood. Yet later still I learned that during these early years of my acquaintance with him, he was at hazard with his former friend O'Connor over the matter of rights for the freed male Negroes. W did not feel they were yet ready to enjoy the electoral franchise. The issue was complicated to an extent young people to-day, and especially perhaps all you Canadians and those in the other places where slavery had a far shorter history, cannot warrant. Even I, simply by reason of being his junior by four decades, could not always locate the cognitive bridge-work I needed to understand how the nation's heart had been turned topsy-turvy. W was known to have once supported the theory that the black race would disappear eventually as a result of Evolution. As difficult as it may be for us to grasp, this view was regarded in its day as progressive by certain of the white intelligentsia. Nonetheless, I came to the view that W was more of a champion of the Negroes in theory than in actual practice.

When he quit the *Eagle*, W put out a little paper of his own in Brooklyn, then at the theater one evening, for W was an avid admirer of plays and especially of the opera, he met the proprietor of a New Orleans sheet, the *Daily Crescent*, and went down there to work along with his younger brother Jeff, though he did not remain too long there either. He was too sympathetic to abolitionism for Southern tastes, as in the North he was often too compliant with the slavery scourge to suit any but those who were ultraists on the subject. "Be radical," I used to hear him say, "but not too radical."

We differed as much as I dared. Often in the years ahead, I would attempt to nudge him toward Socialist Revolution, but he would have none of it. He used to say that he loved agitation but not agitators. He refused to hear strong unvarnished opinions that were at hazard with his own. He ever denied that the love of the People in his poems was connected to the political side of life. "But how can you have the one without the other?" I would ask. He would not answer directly. When confronted with a difficult rhetorical challenge, he would retreat into poetry, or the poetry of his conversation at least.

In any case, he had seen slavery with his own eyes along the Mississippi, he said, and I had not. When Socialism triumphs, I would remind him, whites and Negroes shall be as one, without distinction between the one and the other. I could convince him of nothing. He would alter the course of the conversation in a most easy natural way. "The Creole women of New Orleans!" he said to me on one occasion. "How they can make a young man's mercury rise in the tube!" He sometimes told inquisitive literary admirers, especially those from outside the United States, that he had fathered six children out of wedlock in his time. I was correct in scarcely being able to believe this true.

Leaving the funeral service for little Walter, we talked as we walked, with me keeping my stride deliberately short so that our steps would be in harmony. I left him at the spot where Fifth and Stevens intersect, where he said he would get the horse-car. Riding the cars always had been a favorite diversion of his, but now it was a sad necessity as well.

Later that day, I had to cross over to Philadelphia. Coming back, I saw W on one of the hard benches of the ferry, resting his clasped hands on the handle of his cane, enjoying the river air and the other passengers' evident health and abundant liveliness. W was even fonder of ferries than he was of the horse-cars, and could rhapsodize about locomotives as well. He said that each ferry had its own distinct personality and that his favorites were the *Wenonah* and the *Beverly*, though as a lifelong Camdenite I could see no difference between them at all and now cannot remember which one we were aboard. What I recall, rather, is an elderly Negro flower-seller who had evidently been unsuccessful in the city and was returning with visible dejection to the Jersey side with her stock of unsold blooms. I bought them all, for they were offered at distressed prices, and presented the entire bouquet to W. As I did so, I thought that I was probably being forward, and would be seen by him and anyone who was watching as a silly young man; but W pronounced himself delighted, and the worry fell from my countenance. He bade me sit with him as we chugged across the Delaware. We talked until interrupted by the sudden cessation of forward momentum and the reassuring clicks of the ratchet wheel as it swung the landing stage up flush with the deck and the passengers began to form a line, eager to return to their homes.

As we hobbled through Camden with our backs to the river, W suddenly said, "Spring emancipates me." He certainly always seemed or acted much younger in Spring than he had in the Autumn and Winter months preceding, as though the clock were running backward temporarily; but this may be true for all of us, especially those who are not entirely well. At such times W enjoyed watching games of baseball. He and I would sit on the unforgiving seats and become part of the crowd. "It is fitting and inevitable that our national game should have taken root during the war," he said. "It was played by the boys of both armies, you know. Another of those little proofs that the fight was not between two different peoples, as some charged in the excesses and weariness of the moment, but between siblings who had loved one another once and would do so again." He saw the essential democracy of the game of course, and watched attentively as the players bantered among themselves and every so often emitted little bursts of motion, and emotion. "To be out in the open air, in the free open air with the breeze on your skin, watching young comrades enjoying manly pursuits, is second only to being such a young comradely fellow yourself once more." He said this with enthusiasm and without remorse at the passing of time, though everything in its way reminded him of the past. At one ball game he returned to the connection, one that existed in his own mind at least, between the game and the war. "When I look out upon such vigor and virtue," he said, "I'm reminded of all the boys in Washington back then." During the war, he meant. Uniquely so for a poet of his day, he made the war and its immediate aftermath the central experience of his life and his later writings.

Of course, Flora, you, like all good members of the Whitman Fellowship, both on this continent and abroad, know the outlines of how the war years came to define him, internally and publicly. But as legend tends to abrade the subtleties, permit me to recapitulate what took place.

George Whitman, a stolid and conventional fellow, devoid of politics and parsimonious with words, had joined a Brooklyn regiment in the first flush of wartime zeal, and after the slaughter at Fredericksburg was listed in the papers as among the wounded. W gave up his life in New York to go to Washington in search of him, knowing that the wounded were sent to the capital for treatment whenever possible. As it happened, George had only a slight wound to one ear. W remained in the city, however, eking out a spare living as a government clerk and copyist while volunteering in the hospitals— visiting "my boys" as he called them, bringing them sweets and small necessities, writing letters for the illiterate ones and those who had lost their hands, reading letters to those who did not know how to read to begin with or had been blinded in battle—cheering them, listening to them, giving them his affection, trying to make their young lives a bit less miserable, taking only their regard in return. Apart from the immortal *Leaves*, this was the most meaningful work of his life: such is what I sensed he believed. Who are we to contradict him?

To someone such as myself, born just as the pot of politics was about to boil over as war, such stories were remote yet compelling.

It was hard to credit that such things actually took place when I was conscious on Earth, that such momentous events and such tumult were coming to pass as I pursued my childish games, oblivious to them (though I do remember the blue stream of soldiers flowing down the streets of Camden).

As you might suppose was almost inevitable given the attacks on *Leaves* and its author by moralizers and other censorious public men, W was as notorious in Camden as he was in the wider universe, and for all the same reasons. Had he not written, and then kept expanding, what so many considered an immoral book? The stories of his dismissal from small positions in government offices had brought his name before those who otherwise would never have opened *Leaves* and would not have comprehended a word of it had they done so. For every person who boasted of making his acquaintance, there appeared to be thousands who spoke of him in dire Christian whispers. My parents' neighbors, including some who were no doubt well-meaning, though most were malicious gossips, insisted on calling Mother's attention to my friendship with such a "lecherous old man." To her credit, Mother was alarmed only to the extent she thought was expected of her. Father, predictably, reacted in a similar fashion, and I, thus reassured on this point, privately enjoyed my association with W in a new and additional way.

When I reported some of these conversations to W, couching them in the least accusatory language of course, he replied with what I thought was practiced and perhaps not totally sincere sadness. "I am a prophet without honor in my own land, or indeed in any other." In truth, this was hardly the case. Later, as we began to spend ever more time together once he moved into his own place at last and I came by almost every evening to check on him, I got to know about the large following of admirers he had on the European continent and in England—and of course in Canada, England's loyal puppet. They appeared, many of them, to find in *Leaves* the qualities admired by readers here in America but also those that enraged petty officials and set the tongues of women to wagging over board fences in the back lanes of such places as Camden, New Jersey. Certain English adherents, brothers in the literary arts, were especially persistent in quizzing W about what they perceived as the real meaning of the many references, particularly of course in the "Calamus" section of *Leaves*, to adhesiveness between men. W always ignored or denied their suggestions.

In a way, I understand the frustrations they must have felt, because for my part, remember, I was never able to get him to own up to being the Socialist he obviously was in *Leaves* and other works and indeed in some of his actions as well. As he did not read German, W might be forgiven his unfamiliarity with certain texts, though translations of the major ones were available freely. Nor could I get him to discuss the English Socialist writers. He and I talked about books constantly, but the two subjects, politics and writing, never inclined toward becoming one, as I wished. He would tell me of his abiding affection for Emerson, who had done so much to ensure his early success. He talked of Tennyson and of his American opposite numbers whose faces are on the wall of every American schoolroom. But I could never get him to entertain the merits of the great William Morris or Edward Bellamy. Ruskin, being a strict moralist as well as a Socialist and, I admit, a stupefying writer of prose, was out of the question. So too was our own Socialist press here in America. It was as though the fiery abolitionist of the exciting antebellum days had lost his appetite for political theories after the exhaustion of the war itself, which had broken his health as surely as it had done that of soldiers invalided out with some camp fever of whose effects they would never be fully shed.

In short, whenever I would read the immortal *Leaves*, I saw the soul of a Socialist. W, however, would not admit the truth of my perception but only would gainsay it, almost vehemently at times, just as he did the inferences of those literary dandies in England and other places who, in reading the magnificent poems, perceived a philosophical connection to the ancient Hellenic civilization. In time, I came to believe that he was keeping a crucial secret from the world. My theory was correct, but I long misunderstood just what the secret was.

You know the rest of the story as well. How, after he had gone through periods of rising sap and ones of falling leaves, he settled into Mickle Street early in Eighty-four, preparing for his long slow descent. He bought the place for $1,750, the amount of his royalties from recent years plus a five-hundred-dollar loan from his publisher friend George Childs, one of the people who always seemed to turn up at crucial moments to help him through crises (as when he came to the rescue W's first day in Washington when someone picked the newcomer's pocket). And of course you know how, two years later, I determined to preserve W's conversation for posterity—and his papers as well. You see the results in the first three fat volumes of *With Walt Whitman in Camden,* the only ones for which I have thus far managed, with difficulty, to find publishers. I began accumulating an enormous mass of material: scraps of manuscript and copy, discarded proof sheets, letters and postals he had received, and drafts and sometimes even duplicate fair copies of some that he sent. In the years when he was bedfast and I served as his legs as well as his eyes and ears, I added greatly to the purely literary part of this devoir as I dashed about on our printing and publishing errands, preparing his works in prose as well as verse and overseeing manufacture of the books themselves.

Along with money gifts from admirers and friends, W lived, modestly but never in want, by the sales of his books and his contributions to the newspapers and magazines. He took delight in filling orders for single copies that arrived in the morning mail, wrapping and addressing them for me to take to the post office. "I am like the smith at his forge," he said. At other times he used the metaphor of the mechanic, the house builder (which he once had been, briefly and long ago) or the small freeholder.

When I went on with my own life's work, I fancied that I knew more about W than anyone else living except the man himself, but some of the most important pieces of understanding came to me only when he was on the very verge of death. If I could, I would make adjustments to the first three published volumes, but of course I do not have the privilege that W enjoyed of tinkering with and refining books once they had appeared, so great was the difficulty of getting them published in the first place. Even if I could do so, I no longer have the life-energy for such a task. It is all I can do to set down these reminiscences for you to read once I am gone.

Some of the notes and documents I collected and recollections I pried out of others increased my understanding only after I had reflected upon them more deeply. I had sorted through them to make the works you have there on your bookshelf. For example, when I saw W at his little nephew's funeral, I failed to comprehend that this was only the latest blow of many, what the French call a *coup*. It was as though it epitomized his relations with his family, which were all about love and loss. To be sure, it helped to show me, as I cogitated on the subject over time, how he must have felt to be living in Camden. To me, it is home and always has been. I have traveled the world in Camden, and have been happy to do so. W was of Mannahatta, as he called it, believing this to have been the usage favored by the original Red Indians there. From the farmland of Long Island as a youth and from the unceasing commerce of Brooklyn when he was a young man, he looked westward to Mannahatta, finally sojourning there with the unspoken intention to remain forever, until the war took him to Washington, with its government offices full of stifled air and its improvised hospitals reeking of horror and the aftermath of horror. He suggested to me many times that the lights of the capital were extinguished forever when President Lincoln was killed. His own began to dim thereafter. And when, later, the man who tended to the needs of the sick became one of the sick himself, he was initially drawn to Philadelphia, a stuffy place as he first believed and later knew it to be, and then just across the river to the family he was reluctant to let know him thoroughly but perhaps felt that he should do so now, given the circumstances—yet could not, not quite.

So the shrinking of his world is what brought him to Camden, a trick of fate for which I am so grateful, as I do not know what purpose I would have discovered in life unassisted by his ready example— that is, other than the cause of Socialist Revolution. Just as once, back in Brooklyn, his great heart had ached for Mannahatta to the west, visible on even the wettest, foulest day and attainable by the simplest ride on the ferry, so it was once more, down here. Philadelphia, on the western bank, is in similar relation to Camden on the eastern, two hemispheres, you might say, linked by ferries waddling back and forth like ducks both day and night. The difference was that Philadelphia was no Mannahatta. The view did not inspire his imagination; it merely reminded him of youth and health, both gone. Sometimes he spoke of the period immediately before Mickle Street as his Indian Summer, and I am glad he had one last warm spell before the Winter of his life began to blow. But we know that Indian Summer is an aberration. There is something artificial about it. It teases us with its tragic impermanence.

Old Philadelphia, believing itself to be the world's example of dignified commerce and exemplary probity in all matters, has twice held the world's complete attention: in 1776 of course, and again in 1876, the year of the Centennial Exposition, a period when W and I saw a good bit of each other. I guess that you would have been a young schoolgirl then and might not recall that Seventy-six was a presidential election year as well, the time of the great Tilden and Blaine controversy. I responded acutely to such matters, because I was now the Philadelphia correspondent of one of the Boston papers, earning a bit from my strings even at space rates. W, of course, was losing interest in elections as proofs of the democratic spectacle. I could not convince him to participate actively, much less take a glance at the writings of such people as Charles Bradlaugh, the Socialist parliamentarian over in England. He did read the papers, all of them in fact, and would sometimes respond to faraway events in poetry, as with his poem about the death of Custer (who did not seem much of a hero to me, but I demurred). I suppose he sometimes must have felt himself to be a bit like Custer, for only a short time had elapsed since he had once again been surrounded by hostile critics and publicists intent on massacring his poems. So in Seventy-six he whooped right back at them and rushed out a new edition (the sixth) of the immortal *Leaves*. He also published a combined work of poetry together with prose pieces, most of which had been in type before but were reappearing in different clothing. The new stock of *Leaves* was printed for him at the job office of the *Camden New Republic*. He attended at its birth there, careful to engage and reward the midwifery of the pressman, the binder and even the printer's devil. These were courtesies I later had to observe on his behalf.

The controversy about the supposed indecency of *Leaves* seems only to have flared up again with the so-called Centennial Edition but did much to enlarge interest in his work, especially in England, where many literary fellows defended him with public praise or wrote to him privately in support as they subscribed to the books. I say "fellows," but there was at least one formidable woman amongst them: Missus Gilchrist. She was determined to immigrate to our shores so she could become W's friend in person rather than by post. I think W was as much alarmed as flattered at the prospect of a woman crossing the ocean for his favor. She took passage anyway, bringing along her husband and two children and staying for about three years, setting up a sequence of households that W would visit, sometimes for months. In the fullness of time, the son became an artist and returned to America on his own, once painting a picture of W and his mother having tea together. The daughter, however, disliked W from the outset, believing he was a publicity-seeker, deluded by vanity. The aversion was mutual.

When I say that I eventually came to understand a part of W not visible to the generality of acquaintances, either on the page or in the flesh, I take into account the complex nature of some of his friendships, for W was an enthusiastic and considerate friend to those whose lives he took it upon himself to share and help protect. For example, Mister and Missus Stafford tenanted a farm south of the city. W enjoyed their company and especially that of their young son Harry, whom he took under his wing and sometimes called his honorary nephew. W believed the country air at the Staffords' bene-ficial to his health, as was evidently the case, though when his real-life nieces (the daughters of his brother Jeff) visited and he took them to the Exposition, he had to borrow a new device: a wheeling-chair, as people called it then. Later we needed to acquire one of his own. It had a wicker seat. At first he could propel himself by slowly spinning its two big wheels in such a manner as to strengthen his by then sunken chest. Later he required the assistance of pushers, including former patients in the soldiers' hospitals, the Stafford boy (who always wore a gold ring W had given him), a sequence of paid nurses and of course yours truly. The various parts I played in his life made me realize eventually that I must leave off lithographic work and find some sensible and unfulfilling position that would be regular as to wages and hours and thus, by its very rigidity, allow me the freedom to carry out my *real* job in life, one 'that carried no lofty title, or any title at all, and was made up of assisting the great man in any way that might arise.

TWO

I KNEW THAT BEDROOM better than I knew my own. You climbed eleven scuffed wooden stairs. They sagged in the middle from so many previous residents whose tread most likely was heavy from worry. As you went up, Missus Davis's damned mutt would always bark at you from one of the little parlors below. Sometimes her parrot joined in. Missus Davis was a sea captain's widow who did for W. He paid her nothing, but she got free room and board in perpetuity. Another part of the bargain was that she contributed all her furniture for their common use, as W himself didn't own any furniture when he moved to Mickle Street. Perhaps he had never owned any, or certainly not more than a work-table. Missus Davis's furniture was old and nicked and sturdy, rather like she herself.

At the head of the stairs was a small window that looked out on the backyard. The window had colored glass panes that turned the light red, blue and yellow. This was the only purely ornamental touch in the little place, and of course it was one I noticed only when I visited during the daytime, when attending to our publishing affairs or bringing W the papers. Mornings were often rough for him, but he usually seemed to feel better as the day lengthened. So I usually, but not always, went in the evenings when, although his physical energy was likely to be low, he became quite frisky of speech, especially after escaping from a nap. In fact I frequently disturbed him when he was still asleep in the small bed with high skinny posts with fancy lathe work.

"Throw your hat on the bedpost," was what he said heartily as soon as I entered the room on the night I've had it in my mind to tell you about as best I can. You see, he often hung his trousers in that manner, though his own hat, the soft gray sloucher with the high crown and the sweat stains, lay as usual on the round table by the windows, holding down a stack of loose documents. W often wrote on pieces of scratch paper and the backs of envelopes, then pasted the pieces together in a string, a practice he had picked up in the newspaper offices of Brooklyn and New Orleans. A paste pot and brush for that purpose stood on the big writing-table. He had taken off his boots of course but otherwise had fallen asleep fully dressed. The evening was warm and muggy, but he shuffled across the plank floor, struck a match on the side of the stove and tossed it in the firebox. I could see the orange flame shoot up.

"I fag early," he said, "but then I rise early to go downstairs and sit in the front room and await the mail." He wasn't good on the narrow stairs, particularly going down. He considered the postman a friend, knew his name and his history, and the stories about members of his family, talked with him at length. The same with the neighborhood boys. The younger ones were afraid of him, but often hid their fright in giggling when they passed on the sidewalk. Perhaps their parents had told them to mind whom they spoke to.

Missus Davis knew how to keep the little place clean and tidy, but W's room, the biggest by far, was a thicket, no, a blizzard, of disorder. Manuscripts, letters, note-books and photographs covered every flat surface, including the floor. Dead newspapers were a particular problem. Once his ability to be an active participant in public life faded, W seemed determined to remain a close reader of the New York, Philadelphia and Camden papers, morning and evening, and in this way maintain complete communication with the world of the fully alive. Once having read them, however, he seemed unwilling to part with them, as though by clinging to the news they carried he was clinging to that particular day, which meant holding on to life. In the corners especially, and in the area nearest the foot of the bed, the papers were sometimes strewn shin deep, like snow that had drifted. But it would be wrong to suppose there was no method in all this. By having all his papers of whatever type spread out at his feet all the time, he knew where every piece was to be found, or at least its general whereabouts. I could raise a thousand other examples to illustrate this practice but think now of a specific one, the night he began to tell me about the horrors of the hospitals and became aware that I was starting to become curious about so many other things as well.

"It's here all right," he said, "I just need to get a big stick and churn the waters. It'll float to the surface." He reached down and neatly extracted what must be one of the most famous and consequential letters in all literature, the one that Emerson sent him in response to the first edition of *Leaves* in 1855, before I was born: "I greet you at the beginning of a great career, which yet must have had a long foreground somewhere . . ." He allowed me to hold it and examine it closely for a few precious moments while he continued to prospect for the sheet of paper he actually had in mind.

He talked in a quite animated manner as he searched away. "Missus Davis insisted on redding up the room," he said. "Her meddling, though well intended, threatened to set me back *years*." He was smiling under his full gray beard, I could tell. "I had to enjoin her from coming in. Which is, in any event, a stipulation not to be despised, in view of her unblemished reputation in the town and my own pock-marked one—so lustful and unwholesome, you know." Many have remarked on what they believe was W's lack of humor, but I often heard him mock himself this way.

It was a very close Camden evening, when the fertilizer plant across the river had ceased sending its signature through the air for another day and with the railroad sometimes causing the room to tremble slightly as he moved about slowly until finding what he sought. It was on the work-table all along. He then sat down in the rocking chair where he liked to write during the day, putting a board across his lap as a desk and with an old-fashioned quill as his pen.

"It's from one of my boys," he said. "From the war. A fine youth, from Indiana. I remember him quite well. Sweet of temper and with something angelic in his appearance." I knew he kept in touch with quite a number of them.

He read the letter aloud in a slow, deep, careful voice. It told of small-town life in Indiana, of crops and children, and reminisced not about the war as such but about what was evidently a long conva-lescence in Washington and later.

"Was he badly wounded?"

"Oh yes. An amputation that didn't want to heal. We didn't expect he would pull through. But look, it's twenty years on, more than twenty, and if I imagine correctly and am reading between the lines in the way he intends, he is as full of health as I am empty of it, rich in the clean air of the country and the warmth of family." He paused for a fraction of a moment. "West," he said. Then he lapsed into a cough-ing fit. By the time that was over, the subject had changed.

"Was this at Armory Square?" I knew that was the hospital where W had done much of his nursing. I was nearly two generations younger than he was, but unlike most people my age, who had grown up with old men's war tales and were heartily sick and tired of the subject, I was eager to learn more. I wanted to know as much about

W as possible. At times, W and the war became, for me, one and the same thing—inseparable.

"I can picture him yet. An affectionate boy. How lucky to be sent there, if one can be called lucky to be lying wounded and chopped up in such a place. I mean that people called the Armory the model hospital. It was in fact as clean as a whistle, which was not the case with all the others, believe me. The walls were plastered and the floors well scrubbed and swept. There was a great rush to open new hospitals all round the District. The builders got rich fast, throwing up places where the poor boys could bleed and die of dysentery and such."

He rhymed off the names of the hospitals. There were so many, he said, that the newspapers printed directories of them for the benefit of people who came to town searching for their fathers, husbands, sons and brothers among what W once called the Great Army of the Sick.

"Ones like Finley Hospital and Campbell Hospital were for all intents and purposes like towns, with twenty acres or so of wooden barracks laid out in streets and alleys, numbered and lettered like the capital itself, whole communities of the diseased or badly burnt, a market town for thousands, except that there wasn't the bustle of a market day, only the motionlessness of the truly mortal, stoic and manly, largely silent, except for the occasional moan that couldn't be suppressed any longer.

"Carver Hospital really *was* a kind of city, with city walls and sentries. Oh, there were so many. Lincoln Hospital and Emery and Harewood and Mount Pleasant—lots of them. A fight on the scale of Chancellorsville and they would fill up quickly, the way a good show fills up the theaters and the opera houses."

At the peak, he said, there were seventy thousand boys and men being put up and cared for in some fashion, as best as could be done in the circumstances, far more people than the whole population of the city before the war. Imagine!

"The convalescent camp might have ten thousand at any one time. The city ran short of the new Wheeling ambulances, so named after the place where the factory for them was. Some people called the vehicle a Rosecrans ambulance, for General Rosecrans, knowing conditions in the field the way he did, had suggested the design."

"What the French call an *hôpital ambulant?*" I interjected.

"If by that you mean a two-horse affair with two rows of shelves in the cab, then that's what it was. They could slot twelve boys in there, six on either side, but it was a tight squeeze. They were far better than the enormous wagons that the army had to hire when the numbers kept rising, letting the freighters and even their teamsters get rich too. You'd see long trains of wagons waiting at the steamboat dock to pick up the stretchers and litters coming over from Virginia. They'd haul 'em up Seventh Street. After a while people didn't pay any attention. It got so folks in the street didn't give a glance at the strings of Rebel prisoners coming back either, terrible worn-out and bedraggled boys, flaxen-haired and good-looking, many of them, with ill-matched pieces of uniform, in fact no two dressed alike so not really in uniform at all, sometimes so dirty you couldn't tell what color they'd been wearing when they set out.

"Rebel wounded, too. We took them in and they were treated. I used to visit boys from North Carolina and Mississippi and Alabama, country boys far from home, and I'd give them the same care and cause for hope as I did the others."

Before the war, W wrote in a poem that he was the poet of the master and the poet of the slave, of the North and the South equally, the one the same as the other. I wanted to ask him now if he still had such feelings, if he remembered them, when he was nursing the Secessionist wounded. But what left my mouth was a more specific and direct question, for in his chronology he was about to begin a new chapter, about which I had been wondering for months.

"Is that how you met Pete?" I asked, trying to show my nonchalance.

He knew that I meant Pete Doyle, for there was only one Pete. I was fascinated to get some biographical particulars about this mysterious individual who, I understood, was an Irishman who fought on the Rebels' side, making his friendship with W an improbable thing, I believed. I had heard his name mentioned by others a few times around Camden, only briefly and sometimes in a hushed or knowing tone.

W's eyes could not conceal what his whiskers hid. He was not the sort of talker who pauses once his conversation is in flood, but he stopped this time for a moment, noticeably.

"No, Pete the Great came later." He found a little chuckle to go with the words, coating them lightly in chocolate. "I'll tell you about him." He meant: "—someday." And then: "Good old Pete!"

Thereupon he rose from the rocker and went to the corner of the room where the discarded but carefully preserved paperwork was deepest at that moment. In using the imaginary big stick to stir up the piles, he came up with something else that he wished me to see. It was a crude little bibelot of a thing that he had fashioned by folding sheets of stationery in two, cupping each one inside the others and putting a few stitches through the gutter to hold the pages together. He had glued a paper label on the front cover. The whole thing was dog-eared, worn and soiled, as though it had gone through a war. It had. This was one of the homemade memorandum-books W had carried in Washington. It was full of things he jotted down about the soldiers. He would scribble their names, ages, where they were from, the nature of their wounds, and what they wished or badly wanted or needed—postage stamps, horehound candies, underclothing.

"My method," he said, "was to first of all get a good night's rest. In the morning I'd bathe, give my clothes a brushing and try to work myself into the best frame of mind. Singing bits from the great arias seemed to give me the extra push I needed. Then I'd set off to the

Army Paymaster's Office to do my bread-work. The job there was steady and not taxing. Some days there were long lulls when I could lift the top of my desk and work on the Blue Book."

This was his nickname for the 1860 *Leaves*, bound in blue cloth. He kept a master copy in which he made his revisions for the next edition. His emendations were methodical in the sense of being constantly ongoing. "Clerks had to pay attention. In my case, I had to be very careful to keep from letting my best copybook hand slip into the quick scrawl you're all too familiar with, as are compositors everywhere who have cursed my penmanship for years."

It's true, his script was slanty and jagged, with some strings of letters run together like a row of slum dwellings collapsing into one another. Many people confronted with it found it difficult to decipher. But this was usually the case only with intimate associates, for the issue of legibility arose mostly in connection with quick notes to himself or to others or in hasty fragments of verse—ideas and literary images caught on the wing, as you might say. The more formal sorts of letters were generally quite readable. The more important the stranger to whom they were addressed, the more they seemed to have been laid out not by W the venerable poet but by W the long-ago schoolmaster or W the short-lived house carpenter. That is, they showed either the clarity needed for the slate on the schoolhouse wall or the precision of pencil marks showing where the saw must cut.

(In any case, his hand was far better than my own, I hasten to say. I have observed, however, in going back over early papers, that mine was better in extreme youth, rounder and more perpendicular, but steadily descended into crabbedness as I became W's friend. To the point, as you can see, Flora—at least I hope you *can* see, and make out the meaning beneath the poor appearance of the words on the page—I now scribble like a physician instructing his dispenser to prepare some poultice, potion or elixir.)

W went on. "Then, with the day's labor done sometime in the afternoon, I would take up my haversack and be off to make my rounds." The haversack was a black canvas bag on a long strap, like the ones common soldiers carried, stuffed with the requested items for that day, plus whatever special foods, books &cet. he thought they might like. W used his own salary to these ends, less only what he put aside for his room and board and what he sent home to his mother. More importantly, he was a master of shaking contributions from the prosperous and patriotic citizens, so that sometimes he would arrive at the hospitals with food baskets and flasks of brandy, and even cash itself. "I brought them the brand-new ten- and twenty-five-cent notes, all crisp and clean, thinking used bills might remind them of that which they needed to forget." Looking back, it is little wonder he was so successful publishing and selling his own books, as for so much of his career he was forced to do. He threw his energy and talents into a good cause. Sometimes the cause was the plight of the wounded; at other times the cause was the immortal *Leaves*.

"I would dress wounds," he said. "I had to learn not to show my shock at what awaited beneath the bandages, which oftentimes were yellow from the infection they covered up. Some of the boys wouldn't permit anyone but me to change their dressings. They trusted me. I purposely kept my hair long and my whiskers full and bushy; the farm boys and woodsmen and sons of the frontier among them were less comfortable with people too citified in their grooming. And I talked to them as an uncle would whom they were especially close to. Conversation was the essence of my medicine. Sometimes I even got one of them to let out a laugh, but I didn't turn away from or ignore the ones who wept. Many times boys asked me to hold their hand. Many others didn't need to ask. When I came in to find someone new in a bed where I had known a familiar face only the day before,

I discreetly inquired of the details and later wrote to the mother or wife, or sister, using my notarial hand of course, for I knew that what I sent would be saved and be passed along through the family in years to come."

W was not one to treat his war stories as yard goods. He did visit the past quite often, though, and when he did so, there were certain topics that could be counted on to transport his emotions. One was the Patent Office both as it had been early in the war, before the losses mocked everyone's worst expectations, and as it became again later, near the end. You may know the building. It is in the manner of a Greek temple, and it is huge. W said: "Its rooms had echoes, and the echoes were the cries of the dying." Around the great hall were tall glass cabinets where the scale models of new steam engines and other inventions were displayed as proofs of Man's imagination, creativeness and talent at resolving problems. Between these cabinets, beds had been set up for young men with wounded bodies, many of whom were dying—proof of Man's *lack* of skill at resolving problems. The Patent Office was only one of numerous public structures taken over temporarily for the use of the sick and maimed. (At one point, though not for very long, there apparently were cots in the aisles of the House of Representatives. Good God.)

"The Patent Office was an especially poignant place," said W. "The smell of death was strong there." Why it should have been more obvious there than at the other hospitals he visited I cannot say, unless he meant that it was one of the last government properties converted for use as a warehouse for the dying, not one of the first, so that its patients were mostly those who had managed to escape injury until the end of the fighting was nearly at hand. But I dared not interrupt him, as he was about to tell me a remarkable tale.

"There was a soldier named Billy Prentiss, nineteen years of age. The surgeons had taken off his right leg, but the stump never healed properly. His eyes were like glass marbles in the days that followed, and I knew by looking into them that he wouldn't pull through. I sat with him many an evening. He was very weak. We talked, though his speech was not always logical, owing to the morphine they gave him. One night he was sweating something terrible. I mopped his face with my kerchief and he took my hand and brought it to rest on his cheek and kept it there. He wished me not to go. When he released me, he suddenly spoke, clearly, coherently, and in a stronger voice than before. I remember his exact words. 'I hardly think you know who I am,' he said. 'I don't wish to impose upon you. I am a Rebel soldier.'

"'You tell me something I did not know,' I answered him. 'Be assured it makes no difference. Rebel and Union men are as one to me.'

"He pulled on my forearm and I bent low, thinking there was something more he wished to tell me, but in a whisper. But when I was near, he kissed me on the lips. I kissed him in return.

"The story becomes still more tragic. Young Prentiss had an older brother, a young Union colonel. Officers ran young in those days. I found him in one of the other wards. He spent much of his time there praying with intense passion. Both had been struck down in the siege or stalemate at Petersburg that dragged on for ten months in all and at a horrible cost. I visited Billy daily for two weeks, and then he died. It was May of Sixty-five, a month after the war ended. The life went right out of him before he could be reunited with his brother, who was in horrible pain as well but was discharged, as the fighting was over, and transferred to a more permanent bed in my dear Brooklyn. There he too died shortly thereafter, sometime in June. They hailed from Baltimore, where their situations and then their reunion can scarcely have been unique, for perhaps no other state than Maryland supplied a higher percentage of its men to the two opposing armies.

"In March, only two months before Billy left us and less than three before his brother followed suit, the Patent Office, that place of Billy's death and so many others', had been the scene of President Lincoln's second inauguration ball. Down below were the rooms of the Office of Indian Affairs where I had found a new position as a clerk, after failing to get work at the Treasury despite a letter recommending me from Emerson himself, the Secretary saying that my writings had put me in a bad odor. I thought I would be safe in this corner of the Department of the Interior, safe in my cellar of the Patent Office, below where the wards, with *their* bad smell, now were, beneath the floor that the hems of ladies' gowns had swept clean on the night of the grand celebration. On the last day of June, however, the new Secretary, part of President Johnson's cabinet following Lincoln's murder, ordered my dismissal. Someone had riffled my desk and discovered the Blue Book and evidently shown it to the Secretary, who was a pious and God-fearing Methodist man."

W had a faraway look. "Eighteen sixty-five. There's never been a year with more excess emotion and greater public tragedy. Seventy-three, with Mother's death and what the doctors kept calling my ictus, was as much as I myself could bear, or so I thought at the time. But Sixty-five was a stroke of the soul rather than one of the body."

I presumed he was referring to the assassination and not merely to his dismissal, which actually brought him significant and long-lived sympathy and gave a boost to his renown besides. But I didn't know the half of it, and couldn't have imagined then what I now understand. The secrets he carried with him, I mean; secrets he transferred to me, as though they were a strange bequest and a legacy that was stranger still.

The night I am telling you about here was only one of times beyond number in the Mickle Street bedroom I shall never forget, if for no other reason than I have willed myself to remember, thinking there may still be more to learn from them.

It was around noon on one of the days when W was feeling good enough to get out. I knew the moment I climbed those narrow steps that he was feeling spry, for he had opened the shutters on all three windows. When he was feeling poorly, all of the windows would be covered and the room darkened; when he was somewhat better and had been working in his rocker, the western-most window would be dark and the other two not. This, however, was the first time I'd seen all three simultaneously being put to the use for which they were intended.

"I've bought us the makings of a lunch," he said. From the pine shelf he took down a small loaf, one little parcel wrapped in oiled paper and another done up in what I recognized as a page of the *Camden Daily Post*. He took out his penknife. This was like any other small folding knife carried in the pocket and given the name penknife except that W actually used it on occasion for cutting off the tip of a fresh quill, into which he then inserted a steel nib. In this way he made a concession to the modern-day pen without abandoning at least the look of the instrument that had all but faded from use by, say, the time of the *Leaves'* first appearance. Moving about the bedroom, he sometimes bumped into a mountain of books and newspapers, occasioning an avalanche.

"I haven't felt this good in five or six years," he said cheerfully, "not since I went on my big travels and saw the true America stretched out in every direction, there for us to bathe in."

He was referring to one of his only two long journeys, if you don't count the sojourn in New Orleans. The first came in Seventy-nine when he was asked to be the official poet of a small group of dignitaries invited to visit Kansas to help mark the silver anniversary of the Kansas–Nebraska Act of 1854 by which the two places became states.

"My brother Jeff, whose wife, Mattie, had died a few years earlier, was still settled in St. Louie, an engineer in the waterworks, and I paused there for a family powwow before moving on to Lawrence, where the martyred John Brown fought the pro-slavers in the Fifties. Now, some people tell me they find the Plains monotonous, but I thought every mile fascinating. The time flew by as quickly as the landscape out the windows of the brand-new palace-car, but then it's always that way when you're going west, following the possibilities, racing the sun to day's end."

"That must have been your first time west," I said.

"Well, Jeff and I came back from New Orleans by way of Chicago, but yes, I know what you mean."

"Did you have the urge to go all the way, to California?"

"Had the urge but lacked the means. Or even the opportunity. Events intervened. Made it as far as Denver, though, a town a mile up in the sky, very lively. But the air's so thin there that I started having spells, some of them quite bad. I retreated back to St. Louie and forted up. There I had the worst spell since Seventy-three. I don't mind telling you, I thought it was time to pour the coffee on the campfire. I didn't get back home"—it pleased me to hear W refer to Camden as his home—"till January. I'd been gone two months."

As I piece together the fragments of past events, I see that when W returned from that trip, a new chapter in his life was about to be initiated. I refer of course to the way that his health, having improved enough to permit such an excursion at all and seeming to have stabilized at that new level, plummeted treacherously, putting him on the downward slope he was never to leave. But I also mean that this was the beginning of important new friendships and of existing ones deepening and becoming more meaningful to those involved. Around this time he made the acquaintance of William Sloan Kennedy, a local writer in Philadelphia, who would ferry over to spend time with him. You of course know the book he published after W died, *Reminiscences of Walt Whitman*. Bob Ingersoll, the famous agnostic and rationalist, came into view as well. Maurice, your own friend and mine and one of your leading countrymen, Doctor Richard Maurice Bucke, whom people long thought a genius but under oath couldn't explain just why, came down from Canada to gather information for the biography *he* was writing, with W's assistance, and the two of them attended one of Ingersoll's fiery orations. W always attracted helpful admirers as easily as stubborn detractors, so that his life was a litany of both favors and gross disservices done for him or to him, respectively. Now, though, is when a strong international circle first formed, made up of figures dedicating themselves to W's work and thought. So W had to carry less of the daily burden himself, which was just as well, given how his condition kept declining, albeit jaggedly so, with many periods of hope and even laughter during the protracted and relentless slide along the gradient. I suppose you could say I became the sergeant of the army of W's admirers, an army otherwise made up mostly of officers.

In the summer of Eighty, after he had spent half a year righting himself from the exertions of the West, W made his second big trip, to Ontario to see Bucke and stay with the Bucke family at their home on the grounds of the insane asylum in the town of London. Bucke was only three or four years into the position as the institution's director, an appointment that, as you know, saw him through the remainder of his life. This was the only time W ever stepped outside the United States. You know as well as I do the extent to which Bucke saw great mystical significance in W, believing that in him there was some hint of how the human race might evolve in future times, indeed calling him one of the rare figures such as Jesus Christ of Nazareth who prove up the high potential of the mind and spirit. "Prove up" is a phrase our friend Bucke might have used, for as a young man he had prospected for silver in Nevada, before finding himself in medical study and becoming, we're always told, one of the world's leading alienists and an expert in the various diseases of the mind.

W used his penknife to cut the bread into four thick slices. He unwrapped the first paper parcel, containing some cooked beef, and then the second, which housed a block of hard cheese. We discussed Doctor Bucke as we ate our sandwich lunch. "Canada was as America used to be when I was young, long before the war, as long ago as to be nearer Creation than our own time, when city and country lived in harmony and the sky was blue with promise."

He went on in this vein, and mentioned how on his trip home to United States soil he arranged to meet up with Pete Doyle at Niagara and traveled with him, via Montreal, back to Philadelphia, where before too long Pete found a position as a baggage master for the Pennsylvania Railroad. I think W was testing to see if my ears would prick up instantly. They did so, of course.

Once we finished our luncheon, having consumed all the bread, meat and cheese, W swept the bread crumbs into the wrinkled piece of brown oiled paper, made it into a ball and wrapped it inside the page from the *Daily Post*, then tossed the result into his little barrel stove. He rubbed his palms together as though to say, "There! That's done, then!" What he actually said was: "No trace remains. The flames erase." He wiped his penknife on his trouser leg, folded the blade back up and stuffed the thing into his pocket.

❧ THREE ❧

THE DESIRE TO DOCUMENT and the need to conceal. That the tensions between these two urges propel Walt's life on Earth is so obvious now, as we look back from the vantage point of the twenty-first century. He knows there is no heaven and no hell and won't even dignify them with capital letters. There's only a state that your lifetime of dreaming has been preparing you for without your quite realizing it (though some of you have at least suspected). No time as such, but only a long discontinuous story. One never becomes tired of it because, having no body any longer, one never becomes tired of anything at all.

Let me illustrate my thesis about our Walt. Never has there been a writer more concerned with leaving a complete archive of himself. He was so devil-may-care, so indifferent to posterity, so willing to take his chances come what may, so totally unconcerned with the space he would free up by dying, and in the meantime so alive in every moment, that to prove it he left behind a warehouse-load of notebooks and letters, diaries and journals, manuscripts and jottings, all carefully worked up or worked over to reveal the untrue and conceal the true when necessary. In private writings he wrestled with feelings. Reviewing these sentences in later life, he decided they were too indiscreet for others to read after his death. He might have burned them in the stove. Instead, he scratched out letters, making *he* into *she* and *his* into *her*, but fooling no one, about as sophisticated as the number-substitution code a child could crack: 16.4, the sixteenth letter of the alphabet and the fourth. One can hardly expect others to believe a lie one doesn't believe oneself.

It was the same with likenesses of himself. He missed no opportunity to go before the lens. Nearly a hundred and fifty photographs are known, about the same number as there are ones of Lincoln, for example. He was one of the most photographed figures of his day, and certainly the most photographed artistic one (though Wilkes, if he hadn't died at twenty-six, might have matched him in the end). Such was Walt's obsessive pride in his own humility that he needed to spread the doctrine of his modesty by visual means for all to see.

Everyone knows the story of the famous butterfly picture. It was the frontispiece of *Leaves*, the 1889 edition. Walt wears his soft high-crowned sloucher and a big thick cardigan and sits outdoors, supposedly, in a rustic chair inside a photographer's overheated studio in 1883 in bucolic Ocean Grove, New Jersey. Having complete trust in the poet, a butterfly has landed on Walt's forefinger. Not even Francis of Assisi has equaled that. Walt said later that the picture showed "an actual moth" that was his friend. When Walt died, his three executors, Bucke, Horace and Horace's brother-in-law, Tom Harned (for you need a lawyer in a group like that), cleaned out that hovel of a room on Mickle Street, grabbing papers from the floor by the double-armful and stuffing them into hogsheads from a cooperage. Under one wodge of carefully planted detritus they discovered a cardboard butterfly on a wire ring.

Following the custom of his time, Walt gave photos of himself to callers and admirers, using only the most recent of his sequential personae, as Walt the young rough metamorphosed into Walt the democrat, good gray Walt the tender but manly caregiver, and Walt the sage, practically Confucian in his ancientness and wisdom. He also donated his photograph to charitable causes. When a visitor requested it, he would inscribe the picture with an appropriate and practiced sentiment. When he went to date pictures, however, his imagination took wing. Up to his old tricks again, fooling only himself except in one all-important area.

Here I am thinking of two photographs of Walt and Pete Doyle together. The better known shows the pair of them facing each other in two chairs arranged like a love seat. Tall Walt slumps a bit, stares into space purposefully, arms folded, while little Pete the Great, hair swept back so his hat will fit, tan coat, arms hanging loosely at his sides, stares at his soul mate. So handsome just a few years earlier, strong of chin and piercing of eyes, dangerous, trouble, he's now begun to turn jowly, pasty-skinned, someone who's started to keep count of how many times he can cum in a single night, both with a snoot full of whiskey and without—compare and contrast. Walt fixed the photo as 1865, the year he said they met, or 1866, when what proved to be the path of the future already had made itself known. He had good reason for wanting you to think it was then and not earlier.

The other photo, which is commonly considered to be postwar, was taken over the winter of 1864–5 by a photographer in the District, and shows Walt seated, hands in coat pockets, looking away, toward the West and Democracy no doubt, and Pete, left arm on Walt's right shoulder, full moustache, staring straight ahead like the soldier he had been so recently, determined, wiry and strong, a real example of what Walt Number One sold himself as being: one of the roughs, not a "kosmos," to use his word, but certainly one of the roughs.

Pete comes from Ireland. And "times are bad in Ireland," people say. This was one of those timeless statements, comparable with observing out loud that the weather has been unsatisfactory of late. His parents marry five months before the first baby is born. Elizabeth and Mary, his sisters, perish in the Great Hunger, which starves a million Irish to death and drives away a second million. As they enjoy doing, the Doyles and their neighbors blame the b——dy Proddies, the godd——ed English. Pete's father, a blacksmith, emigrates first, taking John, who's been promoted to eldest child on the death of his brother, also named John. Pete and his mother plus an assortment of three other brothers follow in time. Each easterly gale makes off with another piece of the ship. Pete's mother keeps her rosary in her hand the whole time, every hour, every day; the beads impress themselves on the skin of her palm. After copious prayers, this second load of Doyles arrives largely intact on Good Friday 1853 and immediately gives thanks to the Blessed Virgin—or everyone does except Pete, who only moves his lips. He is taught by the Jesuits of St. Mary's in Alexandria but shows no aptitude for what they desire him to learn. He is a scrapper.

The Doyles thought they could fool the hard times simply by changing continents, but they are mistaken. The hard times track them down and visit them like the Flood, so the family removes to Richmond, much farther south, in the heartland of Virginia rather than along its tawdry top. Father finds work in the Tredegar Iron Works, where many immigrants from Ireland and Germany labor along with the slaves. The Tredegar works will become the Confederacy's major source of cannon, virtually the only one in fact. By that time Pete, seventeen, is in the Fayette Artillery of Richmond, most of whose guns are graduates of Tredegar, though two are esteemed relics, as they saw service in the Revolution, which indeed makes them almost holy. They were gifts to the Americans a generation earlier from the elderly Lafayette on his nostalgic tour of the Republic. It was on that trip that the old marquis, reviled in France, revered only in America, made a stop in Brooklyn to lay a cornerstone. As part of the ceremony he is introduced to a gang of Sunday school boys. One of them is Walt, age six, a curious child.

By the time Pete's unit fights in the Peninsula Campaign, Pete has become a corporal, rewarded for his useful temper and fighting spirit. At one point he is detailed to help track down deserters from the ranks. At Antietam and elsewhere, he and Walt's brother George face each other across the field of battle. His comrades help to cover Lee's withdrawal to Virginia and are the last to cross the river. Pete himself is one of the lucky ones at Antietam, as he is merely wounded.

A few documents survive. "This day personally appeared before me a Notary Public for the Said City in the State aforesaid, Peter Doyle, and made oath that he is not a Citizen of the Confederate States, that he was born in Ireland, in the Kingdom of Great Britain, and that he came to the Confederate States of America in the Spring of 1860, that he came from the City of Washington, D.C., where he had lived for three or four years that being the first place he stopped at after arriving in the United States. That he came to the City of Richmond, Va. in the year 1860 in search of employment, and remained in the said city until 1861 when he joined the Fayette Artillery (Capt. Cabbell) for one year, and was mustered in the service of the Confederate States where he has remained ever since. That he has never acquired domicile in the said Confederacy, that he owns no property, never paid taxes nor voted in said Confederacy, and that he has no family. He asks the Hon. Secretary of War to discharge him from the Army of the Confederate States."

A fortnight later, "the affidant, Peter Doyle, further states on oath that he joined the Fayette Artillery (Capt. Cabbell's company), on the 25th day of April, 1861, and that he does not intend to acquire a permanent residence in the Confederate States of America and that he intends to return to his native country (Ireland), as soon as an opportunity will afford his doing so. Sworn and Subscribed to me this 31st day of Octr. 1862."

Four others from his unit, including Poitras, a Canadian, and Baccigal, from Sardinia, receive discharges as aliens. Pete's attempt too works like a charm, the way lies frequently do. Thirty-five others desert. Pete is out of the army by the time those who remain fight at Fredericksburg, where George Whitman gets his wound from a fragment of a Southern artillery shell. Pete, with a bad fever, is in a hospital in Richmond when, having failed to leave Virginia as promised, he is arrested as a deserter. Four months after that, he has quit the South for Washington when he is again arrested, by Union troops this time, for "entering & attempting to enter our lines, from the insurgent states, without a permit from the Federal authorities," him a penniless and benighted subject of Her Majesty, whom he despises, a refugee fleeing the war. The British legation asks William Seward, whom most Americans hate worse than Pete hates the Queen, to investigate. The judge advocate rules that Pete is one of a number in the Old Capitol Prison who are "poor Irishmen who fled from Richmond to avoid starvation [and] will not take oath of allegiance, but will give sworn parole," which they do.

Pete gets work as a blacksmith's helper at the Washington Navy Yard. His brother Francis, whom he lives with now on M Street in the Island section, home of immigrants and freed Negroes, was a smith at the yard earlier in the war but is now in the Union forces. After the war, he becomes a Washington cop, dedicated to keeping an eye on miscreants like Pete. The yard is where the ironclad *Monitor* is fitted and launched. Their father, who helps armor the *Merrimack* at the Tredegar works in Richmond, soon disappears, presumed drowned en route to New York, presumed dead drunk in a gutter somewhere, presumed anything you like, but indisputably absent. Eventually, most all the surviving Doyles end up in Washington, city of brothels and pawnshops, whiskey stews and gambling hells, pickpockets and profiteers, cradle of democracy.

⚜

To hear Walt tell it, any year qualifies as his worst one ever, but 1863 is different in that his problems, and they are genuine, are psychological as well as physical. He ardently hopes he will not have to continue past the Spring in the Army Paymaster's Office, but even intercession by powerful acquaintances does not shoehorn him into another position. He is shocked finally to realize just what a thick crust of prejudice has formed around his name and his *Leaves*. He finds that what takes place in the hospitals is heartbreaking. Having a crush on a nineteen-year-old Rebel in the wards does not prevent him from being choked with emotion when a Union sergeant he has nursed returns to the fighting. Walt writes to the sergeant often. "My love you have in life or death forever." But he seldom receives a response. Such is the disadvantage of young men. They are callous. If this were the future and there were telephones, they would promise to phone you the next day but never follow through.

When the hot weather comes, living in Washington is like being suffocated with a wet pillow. At the same time, the president, for reasons having to do with the pressure, the weather and the first lady, cannot stand to be in the Executive Mansion longer than necessary, and every evening when he can do so rides to the Soldiers' Home just outside the city, accompanied by only a few troopers. Their sabers are drawn and the scabbards jingle at their sides in answer to the clicking of hooves. Walt comes upon the scene by chance on Fourteenth Street as he is leaving the office for his rooming house. He gets quite a good look at the president in his tall hat, mounted on a gray mare that must be sixteen or seventeen hands high. No horse, however, will ever seem in the right proportion to him. He looks overwhelmingly sad: the face with its rugosity, the eyes with their mournfulness, everything. Without quite admitting to himself that he is doing so, Walt contrives to be at the same spot every day at the same time, even if he has to rush through paperwork or slow his pace once he's picked up his hat to go. The president is robust, virile, manly, strong—almost supernaturally strong, with the long knurled muscles of a wrestler or a wolf. Yet vulnerable, compassionate, bereft, beset by trouble that words can never convey as well as his face does.

The president grows accustomed to seeing the white-bearded gent standing on the pavement. The president has received a literal drawerful of mortal threats, some dating back to well before the inauguration. He does not fear the persons who write such letters, and there is certainly no need to fear the man on Fourteenth Street, for he is merely a particular example of a large species, like a bird one gets to know in the woods or a fish one has come to expect seeing in the pond. Sometimes, as he trots past, the president touches the brim of his absurdly high hat in silent greeting and the man in the plain rough suit and the whiskers like white stalactites returns the courtesy, lifting the sloucher off his old pink head until the president and his little blue toy soldiers have passed by.

It is the summer of Gettysburg and the hospitals reek in the heat. There's only so much good that gifts of tobacco, fruit juices and playing cards can do. A few of Walt's network of donors begin to waver in their generosity as new rumors reach them of the poet's immoral propensities.

Walt's family problems refuse settlement, especially at long distance. In the Autumn he gets his hair cut and his beard pruned back— he looks like a different person now, years closer to his true age—and goes to the Executive Mansion to ask the president's secretary, a well-known dispenser of alms, for railroad passes so that he can return to New York to assist his brother Andrew, who is dying of throat cancer, his brother Jesse, whose mental condition, never strong, continues to deteriorate apace, and a third brother, Eddie, who labors under physical as well as mental handicaps and must live with their elderly mother, a strong woman but feeling much put-upon by the tragedies of life, the personal, individual ones that have nothing to do with politics or the news. While in the outer office talking with young Mister Hay, the secretary, Walt catches a glimpse of the president behind a partially open door, talking to a much shorter man, his head lowered, holding a sheaf of papers at his side, before stepping out of sight across the room, slowly but with the enormous stride of those obviously powerful thighs. That night Walt records in his journal that the president's face is "inexpressibly sweet." He goes on to say, "I love the president personally."

New York is a familial hell. His one consolation is the opera, in which he immerses himself. *Il Travatore, Lucrezia Borgia, La Sonnambula.*

***

Pete's own family troubles are many and complex. Some have to do with the Almighty, others with the Devil. In response to the simpler ones, arising from nothing more complicated than poverty, Pete takes on a second job. At night, after his shift at the yard ends, he reports to work at the Washington and Georgetown Railroad. The horse-cars run along Pennsylvania Avenue from the Capitol. One evening in that Winter of 1864, when winds are slamming rain sideways against the coach, a passenger climbs aboard and pays his nickel. His hat and clothes are soaked, and he has an army blanket draped over his coat for added warmth. He takes a seat in the middle on the right-hand side and drips water on the velvet. He sports white whiskers. He keeps eyeing Pete as though he knows him from somewhere, or wants to. Pete thinks: Looks familiar. From the army? No, he seems "like an old sea-captain." The man is sitting so near the oil lamp that its red globe gives his face a rosy tinge. "He was the only passenger, it was a lonely night, so i tought i'd go in and talk with im. Somethin in me made me want to do it and something in him drew *him* that way. He used to say there was somethin in me that had the same effect on im. Anyway, I went into the car. We were familiar at once—I put my hand on his knee. We understood. He did not get out at the end of the trip. In fact, went all the way back with Me."

They arrange to talk more another time. Pete doesn't read much, and when, later, he opens Walt's book, the copy Walt has given him, he's unable to make out what the Hell the author is trying to do and therefore doesn't know whether he's succeeded. He's a bit better with the prose pieces in the newspapers, but of the *Leaves* he can't make heads or tails. But when Walt talks! How the words pour out of his mouth like thick erotic syrup. He could almost be Irish. Pete wants to know everything about Walt and Walt wants to know everything about Pete.

Hard to say who is the more vulnerable, the prison-scarred Rebel deserter living in the enemy capital or the poet of freedom who's the slave of his own infatuations. Early indications are that for Walt this is a much deeper attraction, far beyond adhesiveness. Love makes him feel manly, healthy too: illusions, of course, he knows, for he is in fact unwell, as he has picked up many bad humors at the hospitals. The illusions, however, are necessary ones seeing that his emotions are so thinly stretched already. He has watched, through a door ajar at Armory Square, as a dear young soldier-friend has a limb amputated, and has tended him quietly through the long recovery. He is even more confident that the war will end soon as the glorious General

Grant pursues the president's angelic mission, the noblest one ever devised in These States, that of holding said States together. But while this may be, the maiming and suffering and death must continue, and he must continue to live surrounded by it all.

He crosses over into the pacified part of Virginia, visiting the hospitals there, which are places to store the wounded temporarily until the goods can be freighted to Washington, mother of the Republic, the most heavily fortified spot on Earth, people say. For weeks he even camps with troops in the field, the not yet wounded and the not yet dead. Later he goes to hear a famous spiritualist, wondering, at the back of his mind, whether there might in fact be some way to receive messages from all the young men whose cots have suddenly become free after a quick scuffle with the angels in the middle of the night or simply from defeat of a spirit weakened by pain and a broken heart. He would like to believe, but he cannot.

He realizes with greater and greater certainty just how the hospital visits are affecting his own health more and more. He complains to himself and others of poor circulation, tingling sensations in his fingers, toes and reproductive extremities, and mysterious headaches that seem to come from the center of the brain, not the front or the temples. In time, the doctors can see what is becoming of him. They order him to stay out of the hospitals until he has recovered. Some days war and family are not separate things. Rebels in his bloodstream are in a secessionist frame of mind.

Every day the evening papers are full of war news, some of it accurate. An item says that George Whitman's regiment, the Fifty-first New York, will pass through the city with the rest of General Burnside's army. Walt stands among the parade watchers for three hours as the current of blue uniforms ripples past, on and on to the point where people might suspect that the head of the column had circled the city block in a flanking maneuver, forming a continuous loop. But no, the regimental flags are always different. Then he sees one such flag, for the good old Fifty-first, and there he is, George, flushed with sunburn though it is not yet May and looking perfectly hale. Fortunately, he is marching at the head of his rank and Walt rushes out to surprise him. He walks along at his brother's side, keeping pace but staying out of step, and brings him up to date on news from home, none of it particularly refreshing. Walt tires, but the marching does not. He clutches George's right hand in farewell and soon the two sets of fingers slip away from each other and the army pushes on, disappearing up the street as though into a tunnel.

"Tell me about the men in your life before me."

Walt is surprised, for he would never make the same demand of Pete, who for all his general cockiness is most guarded about his own affections. His actions always speak more loudly than his words, for he lives in the sway of the present moment, not the stillness of the past.

"They have been several. More than a couple but fewer than a multitude."

The two men are in Walt's room in a boarding-house on Pennsylvania Avenue close to Third Street where he has relocated, believing that a change of environment might do him good, not to mention regular meals of better food.

"All right, who was the first one? Start with him." Pete says this in a tease.

"The first important one was a driver." Walt is actually skipping a few decades here, not letting on that he is transposing Pete's immediate predecessor to a point far back in time.

"You fancy all the drivers, don't you?" Pete is smiling. He has a fine smile, though his teeth are in poor repair.

"Pete, I swear it, you are the individual and not the symbol, yet I can't deny the suggestion. Transportation-men are the most modern. They're always heading westward, for that is the way the roads, the rails and even many of the greatest rivers ultimately run. They see life as it is to-day and see it up close and at first hand, not through a gauze curtain. They see it in bright sunlight. On the other hand, they—maybe I should be saying you, all of you—remind me of the ancients, the Greeks, how they take things at their ease and are robust."

Pete sees that stevedores, deckhands, carters, brakemen and teamsters do have something in common, but the talk about Greeks eludes him, its meaning undisturbed.

"What was his name?" Pete has the fingers of his left hand on Walt's upper thigh and is mimicking a piano player's motions on the keyboard.

"It's now long in the past."

In fact, though, Fred Vaughan up in New York has written letters to Walt until just a little while ago, usually moaning that he so seldom receives a reply. Still, his letters have been full of good humor. In Sixty, when a Boston publishing concern took on Walt and his plans for a bigger edition of *Leaves*, relieving him of the chore of selling his own book, he tells Fred of his plan to go up there for a couple of months to see the work through the press. In response comes a letter back offering suggestions. "If you want to form the acquaintance of any Boston Stage men, get one of the stages running to Charlestown Bridge, or Chelsea Ferry, & inquire for Charley Hollis or Ed Morgan, mention my name, and introduce yourself as my friend." The Boston publisher went bankrupt the following year and the plates of the greatly expanded *Leaves* were acquired by a notorious book-pirate. Recently Fred has been writing again, not knowing that Pete has appeared on the horizon and indeed now consumes the foreground, like a big tall figure taking up all the space in a narrow doorway. Walt neglects to respond even more adamantly than in the past.

Fred is from Canada. Eventually, after many long years in America, he will return home. He will marry there, only to grow restless and footloose in his native jurisdiction and die in a place called Vancouver, a town too new to have history but only opinions.

Pete becomes still more mischievous. "Was his robertson as good a thing as my own?" he asks, looking down at himself. Pete's dick is not long but nonetheless enormously thick even in repose, nearly the circumference of a silver half-dollar.

"I'll not answer that," Walt replies. "But I have had the sad duty to give bed baths and such to many a young man in the hospitals. I may very likely have seen more phalluses than the majority of doctors, and while some are sweet and others sassy, none is more outstanding than your own."

Pete purses his lips in satisfaction, receiving the compliment for what it is: generous but not exaggerated.

❧

Having already told Walt to keep away from the wards until his own health is more certain, the doctors suggest he go north where there are no noxious swamps and where, by seeing that the other Whitmans are all right, he might relieve at least one major source of the anxiety that has caused him to become so run-down. The nurse who has now in effect become a patient has hesitated, undecided as to what he should do. The fighting is intense, the reports in the papers still horrifying. If George should be wounded again, would he not be sent to the capital once more? Walt should be there for him. And yet the family is coming apart. Jeff is all right, always has been. But Andrew is in the grave now, Eddie the slow one still lives with

Mother, and Jesse is not right in the head either, just as before, except that now he is prey to violent outbursts against Mother and Jeff's daughter (who is called Hattie because her full name, supplied by Uncle Walt, is Mannahatta). Jeff wants Jesse committed but Mother does not, just as she also holds out against confining Eddie (who thus runs free until her death). Jeff writes Walt asking for his support in the Jesse matter. In the circumstances, the boys' sister Hannah, living in Vermont with her husband, a painter, refuses even to come near Brooklyn. For her part, Mary, the other sibling, seems strangely sane though she resides at Greenport, not far away from the scene of the chaos.

When Walt tells Pete he must go to Brooklyn, not sure for how long, the news is not well received.

"God d—n you," Pete says. "What would you have me do? i've got family too and a work that goes a long way toward keeping em fed and shod. i can't go running off. But then i suppose you understand as much, don't you? Will you forsake my affections for them you get from other people?"

There's no talking sense with him. Walt slowly repeats his reasoning about the doctors, Mother, brothers and sisters, the soldiers in the hospitals. The discussion, if it be called that, continues late and keeps returning to its place of origin, like some elliptical river unknown to the science of geography. Walt can barely concentrate, given developments. It is as though the pair of them are part of some company of touring actors in which assigned parts are performed by different members of the troupe in different cities on certain days of the week. Despite the roughness of his manner and speech, Pete is not usually the demonstrative one but most often the jaunty one who goes along. But now he's moved from being a playful and only sometimes slightly troublesome dog to being a snarling, unpredictable one, gums drawn back to reveal sharp teeth. "I've given you everythin i got to give," he says, "and you treat me like i'm an irish serf boy who don't have to be spoken to about important matters." And a little later: "You just want to climb up on the tops of omnibuses! I know you. Who knows better than Me? That's what i say, old fool."

All this while Pete tramps the room, scraping chair legs against the floor, and at one point, but only one, banging his left fist on the wallpaper. He is like a little boiler letting off steam so it won't build up pressure to the point where it ruptures. "Eternal damnation!"

Walt thinks to say that, although the Doyles live so close by, he doesn't really know them any more than Pete knows his own relations up in Brooklyn. But he stops himself. That could lead to accusations that each is so ashamed of his love for the other that he thinks it best if family members are never introduced into the life the two of them have together. Besides, Walt is always so weary now and sometimes too deficient in spirit to climb out of his gloom. Pete's anger will pass, he knows, but his own mood appears to show no sign of elevation. Sometimes he feels a bit angry even with himself. But then he is low-down all over. So much so that he entertains unfriendly thoughts that he does not even bother trying to express yet is somehow pleased to have at hand. They at least prove that he's still capable of normal animation.

At length Pete stalks off home. The two don't meet again before Walt boards the train for New York in a few days' time. Walt writes a note of reconciliation, reiterating his deep affection for the greatest and closest of all his comarados down through the years. But he doesn't post it, concluding that the better course is to let time work its wonders. He hopes that a temper that comes up without warning will withdraw with equal quickness.

In Walt's absence, Pete's anger finds expression in behavior rather than words. He goes for angry strolls in President's Park close by the

Executive Mansion, where indeed the president does take some air from time to time in the afternoons before darkness gives the place a different character, a different complexion. Men and near-boys— soldiers, deserters without papers, farmhands feeling lonely in the unfamiliar city, all the various types drawn to the capital by the opportunity the war affords them—take their nocturnal exercise there and oftentimes fall into conversation. Pete wanders slowly up and down the footpaths, his boots in need of blacking, his hat level with his brow. There on a bench is a nobby-looking gent in a full cloak of some fine dark material. He looks up to see if he recognizes Pete or, more to the point, whether Pete recognizes him. At close quarters, one can see that his eyes are every bit as dark as his moustache. He has an aristocratic face and a sensitive mouth. One can tell at a glance that he is lithe and athletic under all those clothes. The inevitability is startling.

≋ FOUR ≋

S YOU SEE, I have many imperfections as an author.
Believe me, I too am piercingly aware of them, though only
now have I gained the knowledge that eluded me for so
long without my being conscious of its absence. I refer to how it has
been only in the past few years that I have come to accept that my
gift was never for making even minor literature but only for reading and appreciating the literature of others. Would that I had comprehended this before publishing those collections of my verse and
prose. All of them were failed attempts to work in the manner of
W—under the spell of W, one might as well say it—while lacking his
invention and authority. The wise student is the one who absorbs the
lessons his teacher has to give with no wish to become his instruc-
tor's *Doppelgäenger*. I have learned this too late in life.

Only partly by his design, W's instruction gave my existence much
of its purpose and more of its tone, but his passive example provoked
an itch for literary expression that I've never been able to scratch and
so have abandoned—except for these pages I am writing in as much
haste as my failing heart permits me, without resort to any research
beyond a few diaries and an uncertain memory. I have waited too long
to begin the ending of the story and still I prattle on at too great a
length. Like you I am sure, I much admire Bernard Shaw for his

dramas and comedies that are in essence both Socialist and, to use Charles Fournier's original term, *féministes.* I am given to understand that Shaw is known to offer apologies to his correspondents for writing such lengthy letters, explaining that he doesn't have the time to compose a postal. I am in much the same situation here.

What I am getting at is that I have no reputation, no credible one at least, for writing or any other art. At this point I am not concerned with this lack, despite the way some of W's old enemies, or sons of his enemies, try to calumniate against me injuriously by charging me with being overly confident to the point of arrogance, vanity and narcissism, or at the very least braggadocio. Perhaps their criticism was partly true in times past, when I seemed to be the primary bearer, often without much assistance, of W's banner. It is hardly so now, when I am a vessel that is so nearly empty.

The point I am trying to make in my rushed yet long-winded way is that I don't know why exactly I am writing all this for you rather than for a wider readership, even one as small in the world's eyes as the Whitman Fellowship. The only plausible reasons are that you are one of the last few people I am likely to meet on Earth and are a woman of advanced progressive views. As you have gathered if you've read this far, I wish to pass along, to someone who will truly understand, the fact that the skeleton in W's closet was not the one outsiders suspected, for the meaning of his Uranianist and adhesive propensities was obvious to anyone, anywhere, familiar with such terms or to those less knowing who probably couldn't define the words but recognized in their own being the things his words described. Meaning that the supposed revelation W was at such pains to hide from the public while being compelled to reveal it in his work was actually not a secret in the least, but a commonplace truth for limited circulation.

This manuscript is composed in such haste because the hour grows late. I implore you to receive it kindly even when it contradicts (never deliberately) your own vision of W's work and thought. I have no wish to come back as a ghost and haunt you (a gentle joke, dear Flora, and not a threat, especially since, as you know, I am not like yourself a follower of spiritualism and never was, though I try to avoid prejudging others' beliefs—or are they only hopes?). No, I am seeking your patient reading of this because you have worked so hard and long for the rights of women, are an acknowledged leader of the movement in your own country through writings, speeches and most of all actions, and will understand me, supporting yourself with the tools of the seamstress as I have done with those of the writer and printer. Specifically, I pray that you will understand and not be offended by, or be careless with, the story of my marriage to Anne, who would be well within her liberties not to forgive me for saying what comes next: the fact I have finally located the courage to admit what I've known in my heart all along—that I am and always have been far more in love with her than she is with me. Can such a union truly be one of equals? Until this moment, all of your male co-religionists, so to call us, have considered ourselves to be your partners in striving for change. We have assumed as your own gender does that all inequality in marriage flows in only one direction, *ex* the dominant husband and *pro* the subordinate wife. While of course this is so in virtually all instances, it is not the case in every last one. I cannot illustrate the point for your knowledgeable consideration without being somewhat indiscreet.

How long now have all of us been reading in the papers and periodicals about the phenomenon of the New Woman, so labeled, who speaks her mind, bobs her hair and strides with utter confidence through the business world and all other such domains to which her mother was denied entry—in fact, was magisterially assumed to have had no interest in being part of? My single contribution to the pool of insight into this matter is to point out that Anne Montgomerie was a precursor of to-day's New Woman and remains, though the field is crowded now, a genuine original and a marvel besides. I have loved her so dearly for such a long time that I have enriched my merry soul even while abusing my mere body. I silently challenge you, when you again observe Anne and me together in a few weeks' time, to look into these dilapidated green eyes of mine and say that this is not the case.

I first espied her in the Spring of Eighty-five, and what a sight she was. W was well settled into Mickle Street, after spending a few years in accommodations he rented farther along on Stevens Street once he had quit, amicably enough, his brother's house a few blocks away. Our acquaintanceship, mine with him and his with me, was growing steadily, and I guess I was slowly coming to the realization that I should make its furtherance my principal activity. This is when I sought a job that would afford me food and cover but consume fewer hours and less energy than the invariably hectic and often unpredictable life of a printer. I accepted the offer of a *very* part-time position as an assistant bookkeeper at a small factory, a place of such little importance as to be unworthy even of description except to observe that one Anne Montgomerie was a supervisor there and a most proficient one. She was twenty-two, five years my junior, born in 1863, the year of the virtually simultaneous victories at Gettysburg and Vicksburg, and of the great defeat at Chancellorsville that equaled either in savagery, but also the time of Lincoln's declaration granting freedom to the slaves.

Anne's own emancipation was self-proclaimed and, like that of the Negroes, not fully implemented for reasons outside her control. As I need hardly tell you (of all people), few young women back then labored for wages or salary other than those who taught, nursed or worked behind counters in shops, particularly establishments selling goods of a feminine character. To say the least, there were even fewer women working in manufacturing, much less helping oversee a noisy, smelly plant where men sweated freely and were fluent in profanity. I soon gathered that she had no urgent need of the income. Her father, Peter Montgomerie, a well-known *homme d'affaires* in Philadelphia, enjoyed more than sufficient prosperity. The family did not live on the Main Line with the filthily well-to-do in their unseemly mansions. They merely inhabited the upper register of the wide and complacent middle swath of society, occupying a large, pleasant house in an equally pleasant neighborhood lined on either side with trees of good parentage that seemed smugly satisfied with their station in the plant world. The Montgomerie place was of the Queen Anne style still popular at that time. It had a high turreted room to one side, facing the street, which was balanced for the eyes' benefit by a large dormer on the other front corner, indicating the room where the maid and the skivvy slept. Anne, whom the whole household doted on and admired, never *wanted* for anything but *wished* to undertake some activity that only cigar-smoking men had done. And she did so, and did it supremely well.

She was my boss, but I was, in the romantic rather than the Confederate sense of the word, her slave; was so from the moment I first spoke with her. You know her now for the still-slender straight-backed woman of fifty-five whose intelligence penetrates to the heart of whatever subject she addresses. Would that you had seen her as I was privileged to do. Then no more or less than now, her silhouette was tall and elegant, and she was somewhat athletic in her habits. Her face was the ground where fiery determination met exceptional kindness. It was presented as a perfect isosceles triangle decorated with a delicately rounded chin. Her unusually large eyes are blue, as you know, and neither too light nor too dark. They seemed to symbolize her warmth and understanding. She appeared to be the effortless leader in any serious conversation, though she never gave the impression of taking charge. She did not whisper (that was not her way) but had, as you cannot help but know though you might not phrase it quite this way, one of those fleecy feminine voices that leads men, old as well as young, to a mild form of insanity that would have been worthy of study by our departed Doctor Bucke. When I would see her in her partitioned-off office on the factory floor, her almost-flaxen hair would be gathered in the back, giving prominence to her wide forehead of course but also, in some way, I don't know how exactly, adding emphasis to her aquiline nose and her lips. In other surroundings, her hair was evenly distributed, framing her face so softly and artfully that one (I, in any case) constantly had to resist the temptation to stroke her cheek for the sheer tactile pleasure of doing so.

Flora, I hope you will not take offense at the way I've expressed the facts about Anne's appearance alone, exclusive of all other significant considerations. But I feel I should at least describe, if I cannot scientifically account for, the effect she had on me. And not on me alone but, as far as I know but wouldn't be surprised to see confirmed by independent assessors, on every other male adult who fancied himself, deservedly or not, to be smart, intellectually and culturally developed, and gifted in one of the creative arts. As you will see, I do not exclude from this category one celebrated old Uranian adhesivist whose friendships with women before this time had covered the spectrum from limpid fiction (those Creole ladies of old New Orleans) to well-hidden trepidation and even fear (Missus Gilchrist) to a puzzling prurience that was in great measure adulterated by an even more intense regard for male members of the same household (Susan Stafford, young Harry's mother).

I am trying to write of her as seen through a young fellow's eyes in the former century that is rapidly being forgotten, and perhaps in the process writing better than I could do were I not so inspired by the topic, back then just as I am to this day. But I will leave you to decide whether Anne has made my prose jump as high as my now-ailing heart. You, the former Missus Flora MacDonald *Denison*, have experience in these matters. As you remain a sophisticated woman conversant with the world, you appreciate science and cannot be in doubt as to the biological forces hard at work in the situation I describe. We are, all of us, indentured to biology, especially at the ages she and I were. I trust I won't repel you when I say baldly that when I saw her rise to her feet in her modest glass-fronted office across the way, as viewed from the even smaller closet-like cubicle I shared with two others, I was overcome with silent speculation as to whether her ankles and calves could truly luxuriate beneath that skirt and what exactly her shirtwaist hid.

Throughout my three half-days of work each week, I made a point of engaging her in conversation. I forged urgent questions about some invoice or misplaced payment so that I could run with it to her side of the shop floor, stepping around the mysterious clanking machines. She was always patient and even-tempered, though I have no doubt whatever that she saw right through my pathetic ruse. Anyone would have done. I like to think she smiled inwardly at my clumsiness, which was at once so helpless and so hopeful. Here I was, far shorter than she, dark to her fair, an American-born foreigner without a family of long-established Yankees to ratify my existence. My hair had yet to droop this way or even to begin graying en route to going white. It was obvious that I had not quite grown into the moustache I wore, which of course was in those days dark as well and had yet to turn downward at the corners of my mouth, making me look sorrowful and unkempt even when in fact I am at my happiest and most dandily groomed. In short, I was annoyed that here I was, not a Jew according to Jewish law, enjoying none of the uplifting cultural, ritualistic and, yes, religious benefits of Jews as I have come to appreciate them in old age and following Father's death, but a Jew nonetheless in her eyes, as I was sure must be the case.

She betrayed nothing of the matter, but I thought I could almost hear her mockery. I need not say that this first appraisal, of someone who after all is even more of a democrat than I, proved absolutely mistaken. I discovered all this only after I had marshaled my skill with the language, a smaller one than her own, as I learned to my chagrin, and secured her agreement to have dinner with me. She had first countered my invitation by suggesting a luncheon instead to discuss the firm's finances, saying that she couldn't possibly step out with me socially as I was an employee. So I immediately gave in my notice and repeated my proposal.

If she found my priorities a bit startling, she found my persever-ance flattering in a way, though I feared it would potentially give her ammunition for even greater disdain in the future should I turn out to be the same awkward dullard at table that I appeared to be when seated at the cluttered desk covered in the ledgers and a monstrous German device called the Arithmometer. This mechanical innovation had ranks of keys, more like a lilliputian Linotype than what in those days, I'm sure you remember, we called a typewriting machine, for *typewriter* was the term for the operator, not the thing on which she performed—another sterling opportunity having opened up for independent females not averse to the menial, the repetitious and the ill-paid. There was a large black handle on the side of the infernal Arithmometer that one pulled, causing the addition or subtraction to take place and get recorded. Three times out of four I couldn't get it working properly.

I digress because I believe I clearly hear what I imagine you are asking: "How did the person as he describes himself here ever win her hand?" The answer is that I did not; it was won for me. As I was deter-mined that the first meal we shared should be on her native terrain and not my own, we went to an establishment in Philadelphia that served a great deal of roast beef, cooked Yankee-style, which is to say without discernible flavor. We exhausted whatever chat we possessed about the factory almost before reading the bill of fare, and were talking about the other part of our lives. She told me about her family, and I, cautiously, told her about my own. She said that Camden seemed the most surprising yet most familiar of places, being little more than an arm's length from Philadelphia but separated from it by something more fundamental than a mere river. "When I was growing up here, I never had reason to cross," she said. Then she told me about a remarkable old poet known as Walt Whitman who had been living in Camden for years, and how "his poetry is just like the city, invigorating in ways you thought were familiar yet had never experienced, or been able to experience, until seeing what he himself saw through his own eyes." I was flattened and flabbergasted, almost literally unable to speak.

While my hands fumbled and my brain roiled, she proceeded to tell me of the first time she laid eyes on him. He was lecturing, sitting up on the stage in a plain chair that seemed too small for him, waiting for the convener of the event to finish his introduction. "Walt rolled up his old felt hat and stuck it in one of his coat pockets while extracting from the other a few crumpled pieces of scratch paper—his notes. He wore plain black clothes, not of recent birth, and a big floppy black necktie, possibly velvet, tied like a great bow girdling his throat, as though he were about to make us a gift of himself, which I suppose in a way he was. He adjusted his beard and was about to rise to thank his introducer and begin telling us about President Lincoln. But in the second before he got to his feet, a bright yellow light, as yellow as a lemon rind, lit him from behind, blurring the edges of his contour and making him appear to be from some other world. Some world better than this one."

She looked around at the dining room I had selected with such consideration. "I have no idea what caused this effect, which lasted only a second. The part of me that believes in science mocks the part that doesn't, saying I am a careless and inconstant girl. But I believe some event occurred that permitted me—I don't know whether others saw it—to see him from the inside out, you might say, to catch a glimpse of the essential spirit that resides just inside his physical body, like the lining of a coat."

If at that moment I had had a mouth full of roast beef, I might well have choked to death. I recovered my breath and, entreating myself to speak calmly, told her the entire story of my friendship with him, my attachment to him, my entanglement, some would even say my inculpation. She took in every word separately as well as collectively, sometimes looking directly into my eyes. I knew then that we would be lovers eventually. What I did not foresee—for who would have done?—was that W would always seem to be present at the foot of the bed, writing a poem about us in his mind.

Anne had read his poetry in the newspapers and wherever else she could find it. Buying a copy of the most recent edition of *Leaves*, complete with the pleasure of knowing that the parcel had been wrapped in butcher paper by the author himself—"The hand that holds the pen," I told her, "also knots the twine"—was out of the question. "Father would never allow it, and you can imagine how angry that makes me." The anger existed only because she said it did; there was no trace of it in her voice (which is not made for anger) or her face (ditto).

There was no mystery about how knowledge of the book's unspeakable salaciousness and debauchery might have seeped (but did not) into the Montgomerie household. In such situations it is customary to terminally suspect the servants, always the simplest course of action when there is blame to be apportioned. Then as now and forever, Anne was a capable and ingenious woman. Our meals together became frequent, and at one of them she told me how she had gone to one of the rare-book dealers' shops off Chestnut Street and placed an order for a copy that she could then pick up there in person to deliver secretly to herself. The proprietor had grown prosperous and pompous selling long sets of books to matrons who wished bindings that matched their draperies: the Waverly novels, the Life and Letters of this or that famous personage, the more pretentious and generously gilded the better. The bookseller pretended he was unacquainted with the work, and gently, gingerly, questioned her about its contents, in order to discover the—how might he have expressed it to himself?—*sophistication* of the young lady's taste in literature, for however much he might look askance at the request, he did not look down his nose at a paying customer, not one of such filigreed manners and obvious pluck.

"The compromise," she told me, "was this, which he was able to have sent by a colleague in London."

Out of her bag came a rather well-used not to say unhygienic copy of *Poems of Walt Whitman*, the harmless selection that W.M. Rossetti had edited back in Sixty-eight for English consumption. W of course never cared for it, and indeed tried to suppress his memory of it as ardently as others suppressed the book itself, or would have done if Rossetti, knowing the strictness of British law in this respect compared to the American, had not sidestepped the contentious poems in the "Calamus" sequence and some other "indecent" writings entirely, leaving not a bowdlerized pastiche exactly but one suitable for the hardier sort of female reader or the curious male one with a wife at home.

"This is actually quite difficult to find," I told her.

She laughed. "And was accordingly expensive. But my book-smuggling friend and I had entered into a criminal pact."

A few months later, when we were alone together, I took down my own copy of one of the American editions and began to read her the entire *Leaves* over the course of many nearly consecutive evenings. I betrayed no change of inflection when we came to the disputed verses. I remember reading to her such lines as:

Here to put your lips upon mine I permit you,
With the comrade's long-dwelling kiss, or the new husband's kiss,
For I am the new husband, and I am the comrade.

Or if you will, thrusting me beneath your clothing,
Where I may feel the throbs of your heart, or rest upon your hip,
Carry me when you go forth over land or sea;
For thus, merely touching you, is enough, is best,
And thus touching you would I silently sleep and be carried eternally.

I made bold enough to say that I didn't know what person W was addressing when he wrote this but that I for my own part now thought only of her when I read it, showing the power of poetry to provoke such individual responses and thereby prove its own urgent utility, independent of the poet's intentions. She kissed me warmly and cradled my head. In a later session, I moved right along to the most candid poems, the ones that the most naive of church wardens could instantly see (that was the problem) concerned phalluses and more phalluses. Afterward I reported to W that she did not wince even a little when I reached the passages that the world has outlawed, nor will she.

"Admirable, admirable," he replied. "For us fellows, what claim short of that can we ever make?"

As my trips to Mickle Street assumed an almost clockwork regularity, often extending into a second visit each day and sometimes even a third, Anne quit her job. Being in the factory, she said, only reminded her that I was elsewhere. What's more, she said, it reminded her that we had been supervisor and supervised, a fact she wished to forget as she desired us to be equals in life not in the present and the future but retroactively, back to our very beginnings. She then suggested that I begin to keep verbatim memoranda of all my meetings with W, or ones as nearly verbatim as possible. I immediately saw the beauty of the idea. His wonderful table-talk, both melancholy and fixed on the moment, often mixing lofty language with the slang of soldiers and transportation-men, was its own sort of poetry and a priceless gloss on the other kind. I am no biographer, no Boswell, but he could become his own, as General Grant, whom he so admired, had done in his own way and with a style, and a candor, that W thought so worthy of envy.

It is not enough to say that my exhaustive and exhausting project of recording W's conversation for posterity was Anne's idea, for the labor that followed was in some measure a collaboration between us. In the earlier stages particularly, whenever I came away with an especially fulsome or meaty stack of W's papers, she would sit with me to read through the material and analyze it. She read everything closely and offered up suggestions as to what should be in type as part of the text or else, in several instances, tagged for eventual shipment to the engraver's one day for reproduction in facsimile. When I was writing of events at which she herself had been present, but not at other times, she would help to rejuvenate my memory or offer gentle and seemingly casual suggestions about some of my phrasing. She was a better editor than I am an author. She was and is a natural.

"You should be writing this, not I," I told her more than once as I contemplated the growing miscellany of papers on the table. "Barring a few months here and there, I've spent the entirety of my working life to date in printing and publishing. The pattern does not appear as though it will be broken. But you have better . . ." And I searched for the words: " . . . flair, instinct and economy in many such matters than I possess." (She herself never had to search for the right words, for she already possessed them all.)

"Nonsense," she would say. "I bring to the task only what an avid reader does." She said this in a self-mocking way, suggesting that she had only a head full of nothing but the sort of novels published to entertain women and keep the subscription-libraries in business. This jest of course showed how different she was from most other women, certainly from most of those known to me, or known to people who were known to me, that she could speak so lightly of what she worked so hard to relieve: the plight of women.

Both of us were young, I was healthy enough to tax my body with absolute impunity in late nights of work, and these were some—many—of our happiest times. I miss them, but find comfort in the memory of them, just as W did in his war stories, horrible though some of them were, and his dwindling number of old reliable friends and his mostly private recollections of young men who vanished as they grew up. I see this so clearly now that he has been gone all these years, having taken his personality with him or left it in the open, uncovered, to evaporate. But then he left it to all of us in the pages of books, his own that he made from the dialogues with his heart and the discourses in his mind, and my own, pasted together from whatever he said aloud.

Anne's and my first years together were full of love and laughter. I recall the time she seized mischievously upon some of the incongruous juxtapositions in the unusually large load of papers I carried home from Mickle Street. She closed her eyes meaningfully and laid her right palm flat atop the pile of paper and mimicked the tone of a spiritualist in a trance (forgive me, Flora, perhaps I should have written "a mind-reader in a carnival show").

"I am receiving a strong impression now," she said, imitating a disembodied male voice. "An image is being transmitted. And a second one, and now yet another. I see two sheets of costly linen stationery. Beautifully worded messages—questions?—are written on them in equally beautiful cursive hands. They are from—yes, from esteemed and revered poets who despise each other cordially in a land far away, across an ocean, I think. I perceive plainer ones as well, written with a pencil stub, from boys who disappeared into the uncharted spaces of the West, gobbled up by Democracy. Then, what is this? A manuscript, mayhaps? No, a laundry ticket? Ah, it is a receipt from a livery stable. The date comes into focus now: Eighteen sixty-one. The Other Side is communicating with me quite fully now. There is a page torn out of an unknown book, a woman's recipe, an advertisement from an unidentified newspaper turning dry and yellowy, and some hard object, small and round, with perforations. Oh yes, I see, a button from the fly of a gentleman's trousers. But the energy—the energy dissipates. And is gone."

Then, the psychic power having drained her earthly strength, she pretended to swoon, one languid wrist draped athwart her forehead. She actually feigned a collapse to the floor. As she did so, the hem of her skirt blossomed outward in a circle, like the petals of a flower. She pulled me down with her and we laughed. We rolled on the rug a few times. Flora, am I telling more than you wish to hear? Well, it is less than I need to remember.

Her other imperishable contribution to what is now *With Walt Whitman in Camden*, volumes one through three, with the others, still in rough note form, to follow eventually if at all, is that W was so taken with her—and she allowed him to be. As a result, he was even more voluble with her than with me, whether she and I visited together or she on her own. She had the knack of elevating his spirit when he had cast himself down into the dark pit of his imagination. I wondered whether these changes had to do with the natural desire, evidently found in him as much as in all men differently inclined in their leanings, to emit or discharge charm, or attempted charm, in the presence of many if not all or even most women of a certain type.

One day he gave me one of his books that my collection lacked, and then generously offered to sign it with a sentiment of friend-ship. I said I would prefer that the inscription be to Anne. He smiled about as broadly as I believe a very sick man can do and wrote, "Anne Montgomerie from the author WW" followed by the date. I instantly perceived why he wrote out such a *pro forma* dedication, the kind one would send to a complete stranger who asked for a signature in a copy sent through the mails. He did not want to risk embarrassing me, of revealing me to some later owner of the book, far in the future when all of us are gone, as the emotional equivalent of a cuckold. The phrase is completely overblown, and I would scratch it out if the act would not make a mess of the page. But I cannot come up with a more telling metaphor right this instant. He blew on the wet ink to dry it and handed the book back to me, still open at the flyleaf where he had written. As he did so, he let me know what he felt but, for the best of reasons, dared not put on paper.

"She's as sweet and dear as an unsoiled flower," he said, sounding for a moment like a different type of poet entirely. "I am sure she comes first." And in this way he released me from whatever concern I might have been nurturing and, so to speak, tipped his old sloucher at me as well as her, wishing us both well—together. Although he was by now quite an old dog indeed, perhaps he had learned a new trick anyway, simply from seeing so much of Anne, who could defuse awkward situations with the same ease with which she enlivened drab ones.

Inevitably, I keep casting my mind back to my first meeting with W, when Father called him a great man and a great poet and introduced me to him. While hating to be thought of as a European immigrant,

Father never seemed more European than when he spoke of W, whom he admired for precisely the qualities from which W worked so hard to dissociate himself: the idea of literature as a rarefied and genteel occupation, the conduit of philosophy and high ideals, carrying forward the noblest traditions of art and beauty almost older than history itself. Father didn't understand that W was the enemy of literature thus defined and that, at least in his version of events, it was the enemy of him. Father wouldn't have listened to me if I had tried to explain. He had turned away from the Talmudic scholars in his misguided and of course utterly unsuccessful attempt to be perceived as some type of four-square Yankee (in the manner of, to use an example easily at hand, Anne's father). Accordingly, he redirected his admiration to Authors. Yes, in his imagination the initial letter was deserving of the upper case.

Behind my straight face, I was quite amused when W asked me how Father was and then painted what struck me, privately, as a wonderfully comic scene.

"He was here the other day, sitting where you're sitting now. He spouted a great deal of German poetry to me: Goethe, Schiller, Heine, Lessing. I couldn't understand a word of course, but I could understand everything else. Your father has the fire and enthusiasm of a boy. He would have made an actor. I was never so struck with the conviction that if everything else is present, you do not need the word. There he was declaiming away in a language strange to me, yet much of it seemed as plain as if it was English."

I looked deliberately impassive, and he continued. "Now I understand how people can go see Salvini on stage and not be ignorant of what he is saying in Italian."

The reference is to the famous Italian actor Tommaso Salvini. Do you know his work? He was much in the news down here then because he made a triumphant return tour of America, playing

Othello, in heavily accented English indeed, to the Iago of Edwin Booth, W's theatrical hero.

Another of our conversations had a similar commencement, but an ending so poignant that I restrained my tears as earlier I restrained my laughter.

"Your father was in the other day," he began. "We talked about Goethe and Schiller, mostly about Schiller's sickness, his victory over sickness."

This remark perplexed me slightly. Goethe's friend and brother poet Friedrich Schiller suffered from lunacy and is said to have died of syphilis, conditions over which he conspicuously did not in fact prevail. When W was under way, reeling out things I knew I must keep in my memory until I got home to record them, I was reluctant to interrupt his flow. Perhaps this speaks to a weakness of mine. I believe that Anne, with her innate finesse, could have done better.

"That always impresses," he went on. "A man's victory over his sickness. I have thought something very interesting, valuable and suggestive might be written about the influence, good or bad, of disease in literature. I mean 'disease' more than 'sickness.' The influence of drink in literature might also be written about. It has so many sides, noble and devilish both, that it would need to be rightly interpreted, not by a puritan or a toper (the puritan is only another kind of toper)."

Toper, you may not know, is obsolete American slang for a drunkard.

"I have almost made up my mind to make some use of the themes myself, though I don't know as I'll ever get to them. So many physical obstacles have dropped onto my pathway in recent years."

Now he was doing just what he ought not to do, pushing himself in the direction of despondency. He saw the danger and backed away.

"Take my love to your mother," he said as I prepared to leave after doing my best to lure him away from despair. "And how about Anne Montgomerie? She has not been here for ten days. When she was here last, she brought me a bunch of roses. They were very beautiful, though not so beautiful as she herself. She has cheeks like the prettiest peach in the orchard."

How had fate permitted me to find this woman who had both the power to keep me enthralled and the power to make America's greatest poet sound like a schoolboy in the first flush of desire?

FIVE

W HAD BEEN HAVING considerable success getting
his poems printed in the newspapers, weeklies and
monthlies, including all or most of the best places. He
was always skilled at that. Yet since *Drum-Taps,* published the month
following Lincoln's murder (as he always called the assassination),
his heart had been inclined more in the direction of prose. It seemed
to me that around 1865 something important had taken place to
change him profoundly—in addition to the end of the war or the
murder, I mean, something unconnected to public events. I wasn't
certain what or just how. Such was my feeling at the time I enthusiastically accepted Anne's suggestion, resolving to commence a
record of my Mickle Street visits. Practically every day, usually
after dinner but sometimes in the morning as well, I found him in
either the front parlor or the bedroom.

The downstairs room was furnished with a davenport and chairs
and decorated with two busts, one of Elias Hicks, the other of W
himself. Hicks was the Quaker divine who farmed on Long Island and
whose common-sense democratic theology led to a great schism
amongst Quakers. When W was a young boy, he heard Hicks, who
must have been about eighty years old, preach a lesson, an event that
had gained some powerful hold on W's imagination and philosophy.

"Hicksite-ism may be found on every page of the New American Bible," he said. This was the name he sometimes gave to the immortal *Leaves* in candid conversation, whether in jest or not I can't say. The other conspicuous object in the front parlor was a model of a sailing ship, which I believe had belonged to Missus Davis's late husband.

Although I did not mention that I was now resolved to keep a daily memorandum of his conversations, I was aware soon enough that our relationship had changed on that Wednesday when I jotted my first such entry, trying to find a style that would capture the cadence of his speech, for W's bump of intuitiveness was one of the most remarkable of all his gifts. If he was his own critic, using his experience as a news-paperman to write anonymous praises of *Leaves* and see them pub-lished in the press, then his friends were his biographers: his wartime associate O'Connor, whom he hailed for his "Keltic" qualities, and of course Doctor Bucke. Now, knowing that he was in steep though not unchecked decline, he instructed me what to do after he was gone. "When you write about me one day, tell the whole truth," he would say, unaware—no, I mean "with no proof"—that of course I was writing about him already, every night, as prelude to my reading in Socialism and other subjects, sometimes until the dawn announced itself. He began handing me newspaper cuttings to read and discuss. He extracted letters from the bottomless midden of paper. One was a letter from England more than a decade old concerning some small Whitman controversy of that place and moment between two of his many admirers there.

As he received letters from abroad, so too did he receive visitors from all over, visitors high and low. One pilgrim from the British Isles declared that his two ambitions in America were to meet W and see Niagara Falls, both sites being conspicuous wonders of Nature. Others of the first rank among writers and artists, such as William Michael Rossetti, brother of the more famous Dante Gabriel R., took W to be a man of high literary standing, but of course they were not American. In any case, W once spoke of them as "the tribe of the Oxford-Cambridge Israel who have felt that, despite their great scholarship, layers on layers of erudition," they had something in common with him or at least with the immortal *Leaves*, as though the two could be viewed separately.

Soon he was giving me such letters to take away, knowing, without the subject being raised, that I would transcribe them into the nocturnal journal of our conferences. He always claimed that he'd come upon a certain letter by chance while "mousing" in the hillocks of paper. "I clean house from time to time," he said, sitting in the bedroom, which in fact showed few signs of such activity. The best Missus Davis could do was to work around the considerably smaller stacks of newspapers and letters in the parlor. At least this way she prevented it from resembling too closely the room above, whose door was always closed and often locked, even when W was inside, a habit that would prove worrisome later on, as his periods of comparative health gave way alarmingly to ones quite different. He went on: "Give you bits—hunt them—that I think might be of service to you. Service or interest. The rest—most of the things—go into the fire." His gaze floated toward the little round stove. "I know you are jealous of that fire. Well, that stuff is trash, notwithstanding your appetite for it. Trash, trash, trash." This was mousing in a rather different sense. We were playing a cat-and-mouse game, and I was not the one that purred.

He would speak a brief preface to each piece as he passed it to me. "I want you to have this letter of William's for your archives," he said one day, giving me one of the letters from O'Connor that he cherished. "It would be valuable enough if it was only William's, but it happens to be more than that. You see the date—1865." The letter dealt with the defense of W that O'Connor was writing following his friend's dismissal from the Interior Department, the manuscript that became *The Good Gray Poet.*

For the most part W seemed perfectly at ease giving me his treasures. The exception was the famous Emerson letter of 1855. I kept asking if I could take another look at it. He would then claim that he would lay it aside to show me the next time it turned up, which it never seemed to do. This was a further illustration of how he found it necessary to be wily in certain matters. And then there was one instance in which he was only provisionally generous. "Take this away," he said, thrusting a letter from Tennyson at me. "But take good care of it. The curio hunters would call it quite a gem." Several times later on he asked for the temporary loan of it. He even sent visitors to my place with requests that they be allowed to read it on the premises.

<hr />

Four years earlier, shortly after W moved into Mickle Street, thirty of his admirers had banded together and surprised him with the gift of a buggy. The donors included Oliver Wendell Holmes, Mark Twain, John Greenleaf Whittier and Edwin Booth. Holmes, the famous physician and writer, was one of the doctors who always appeared to take to W, perhaps because he was such a good case for study. As for actors such as Booth, W counted himself an omnivorous watcher of plays, both comedies and drama, though this was most true in his New York days before the war, for in Washington he was far too preoccupied with tragedies, the kind performed in the hospitals, and in Camden too limited by the encroachments of age and illness.

But the soothing effects of his many friendships could not make up for the cumulative effects of all the public abuse he had endured, which marked him for the rest of his life. The critics, he told me that Spring of Eighty-eight, had given him a devil of a time, and he was "even to-day not accepted by the great bogums," though it could be easily shown that the statement was less true, *far* less so, than in the past. The disapproval he had accumulated over the years naturally disposed him well toward some writers but not others, and membership in the one category or the other was not determined by literary criteria.

He presented me with the correspondence that passed between Booth and himself in which he sent Booth a likeness and asked if in return he might have one of Booth's father, Junius Brutus Booth, the great Shakespearean whom he had often seen on stage. A long time passed before I ever heard him speak of the patriarch's middle son, John Wilkes, except in connection with the public lecture on the Lincoln murder, which he was asked to give at various times.

Regarding John Greenleaf Whittier, well, some poets adhere to one another and others mutually repel. It is in the nature of poets to be this way. Whittier was one of the New Englanders everyone read in school. No one would ever think to look there for W, whom you might expect to feel no sympathy for Whittier; but because Whittier supported him, though apart from the buggy fund more passively than actively, W responded warmly. But writers who were safely dead had the strongest claim on him. He read and reread the novels of Sir Walter Scott, who had been born almost two decades before W's father (who died in Fifty-five, the same year that *Leaves* first appeared). Not only was Scott safely in his grave, a figure from benign antiquity unable to slander anyone even if he wished, but the grave was on the other side of the Atlantic. Writers closer to W in both chronology and geography, usually ones much younger than himself, could rile him by their existence, most especially if they were more literary. Henry James was "only feathers to me," he said. But then, whereas Scott was a Scot, James was an American who pretended to be English. When Matthew Arnold, slightly W's junior, died that Spring, W said to me, "He will not be missed." Later, when the subject of Arnold came up, he put it this way: "There is no gap as with the going of men like Carlyle, Emerson, Tennyson." Of Arnold's work he said, "As poetry it is fragile. It lacks substance."

Emerson of course was the one author he admired with almost no qualification, Emerson who had given *Leaves* such a hand-up so long ago and who, while he never repeated the tribute, never revoked it either. W thought him "in ways rather of thin blood," this man who brought the mind to Nature, but I know how important to W their few meetings were. W thought the great New Englander "was born to be but never quite succeeded in being a democrat." He was, however, an American through and through, the greatest of American idea-men and philosophers, and this was no unimportant thing to W; essential, in fact. He urged Emerson on Anne as a vital subject for study. He was forever advising her and doing little kindnesses for her.

The distinguished subscribers to the fund for W's buggy didn't seem to know that W was sufficiently prosperous to have bought his little frame house on Mickle Street mostly with cash on hand. Still, he was never (as he liked to phrase it) flush with money, and stories about his penury and want appeared in the papers occasionally (sometimes only to be disputed by others). He may have been embarrassed by these appearances, but he gladly accepted the benefits, including a purse collected by poets and authors in England (including Feathers James). The buggy was very much appreciated. All agreed that W should get more air, even if it could no longer be country air except when he managed to visit his young friend Harry Stafford on the Stafford farm.

W had concluded reluctantly that he was no longer up to hitching and handling a horse himself, so he acquired a young driver named Bill Duckett, to be paid by a yearly subscription from friends. Later, Duckett moved into the small bedroom next to W's big one, but he came and went. When going the last time, he owed Missus Davis a not insignificant amount of money, for which she took him to court. He was succeeded as a driver by Missus Davis's son, Warren, like his late father a mariner, whom Walt forever called "a lusty fellow," one of his highest-ranking compliments. By the time I became so involved in his life, W was out driving only about once a week, despite the fact that another friend had secured a ferry pass for both him and the vehicle.

"I am getting more and more satisfied by my bed and my chair," W said. "Which is suspicious." Yet there were still times when he had greater mobility than usual, and might be said to have resumed being spry, at least for a few hours.

You expect that most elderly sick people, and I proffer myself as an example, are crotchety when they're in pain or terribly frightened. This is perfectly understandable but still tests the patience of those who are caring for them (again I confirm, sadly, that I speak from experience, though Anne has never complained out loud). As W was often uncommunicative even on good days, so too was he prone to strong emotion on his bad. Or, rather, there were certain subjects that roused him to praise or condemnation regardless of what type of day he was having when the trigger was pulled.

One of the touchy subjects was Thomas Eakins, the artist. "Eakins is not a painter, he's a force!" W said when talking to me about the portrait of him that Eakins had done. They appeared to put up with a great deal from each other. For example, Eakins always addressed W as "Mister Whitman," much to the latter's bemused intolerance. W considered even the use of "Walter" an affront to democratic values.

I wondered whether this bond between Eakins and W might have been rooted in a shared propensity for scandal. Eakins was an exceptionally serious individual, slender but muscled, and had steely eyes that must have terrified his students as they did me. He had been the director of the Pennsylvania Academy of Fine Art in Philadelphia before being discharged or asked to resign following accusations of improper conduct. The gossip was pretty thick for a while. It centered on the story that Eakins outraged morals not merely by having female and male pupils together in one class, drawing from the figure, but by yanking off the model's loin drapery in pursuit of some point or theory, leaving him nude before all.

Once freed of the position, Eakins was able to throw himself even more into his own paintings, including a portrait of W from life. W sat for painters and sculptors many times, and usually was much pleased to do so. Still, the fact that the results of a painting were so much more difficult to anticipate than those of a photograph was one of which I imagine he was keenly aware. Certainly the Eakins picture, showing W facing to the viewer's right in three-quarter profile, was difficult for its subject to embrace at first. Eakins's use of color was different from most people's, muted but daring, certainly complex— sophisticated, I suppose you would say. Also, W's mouth looked odd, the lips pursed a bit perhaps under his moustache and whiskers, maybe in a little knowing smile. It was the mouth of a man with secrets; I often saw the expression in real life. In any event, W did come to admire the portrait enormously, calling it the best &cet. Eakins let W keep it at Mickle Street when it wasn't being shown in a gallery. When W had it in his possession, he sometimes moved it around the bedroom, following the track of the most advantageous light.

One evening, when he was lying next to the Eakins portrait as though to elicit flattering remarks about either it or the model, he greeted me by saying, "I am growlin' with a bellyache. What is the use of poetry or anything else if a man must have a bellyache?" Some days he complained that he was tottery when he stood up. Other times he used a different phrase, saying the dizziness had made him feel "uncertain on my pins." At still others he said nothing of the legs but told, more ominously, of problems with even simple tasks of memory, of difficulties "on the top." Certain days he appeared quite hard of hearing too.

Although I might be making it sound as though he bemoaned his fate, he was actually bearing up bravely or at least dispassionately, as though he could distance himself from his ailments and diseases and look at them through another's eyes. "My blood is so sluggish," he would say. "My pulse is so slow. But what's the use of grumbling? Everything don't come my way, but lots of things do." When he uttered those optimistic words, however, he was too weak to leave his bed, that is, too weak to work on the book that was bedeviling him.

He showed me a parcel of newspaper cuttings, copies of old letters &cet., tied with twine. He wanted somehow to translate this careful if carelessly wrapped accumulation into a new book of prose and poetry combined, to be called *November Boughs*, for he was in the November of his time on Earth, he said. I feared that the calendar might have jumped ahead to early December.

He struggled to work on the manuscript. "I get up mornings and say: 'This is the day,'" he told me. "But somehow, before the day is over, I see this is *not* the day. Yet it will come out, and before long, God—and you too, Horace Traubel—willing, for I shall need you to help me through with this expedition. If you go back on me now, I might as well fold my wings."

There was no chance I would go back on him of course. It was part of my job and my duty to serve as the proxy for his pins, just as at other times I had to be a diplomat, gently prodding him to finish writing what he had begun.

He wanted to compose an essay on Elias Hicks, a task he had been attempting intermittently for about forty years. He said that this was the last piece of *November Boughs* still not complete. The organization of his thoughts on Hicks, while firm enough in his mind, had yet to be fixed on paper. On several occasions he promised the piece to me the following day, all the while blaming his infirmities and apologizing for how, he said, they had added to my burdens.

"I thought you said it was ready yesterday," I would chide him.

"So I did. So it is. *About* ready. But sometimes that covers a multitude of cautions."

Very soon afterward, news of the imminent book started appearing in the newspapers. "That ought to spur me on," he said, "though as you know, I am not easily spurred." I presumed that he himself (though possibly my brother-in-law, Tom Harned) had brought the information to the editors' attention. I held my tongue. W naturally was anxious that *November Boughs* appear "before I light out." I was in favor of whatever would contribute to its speedier birth, while understanding that he himself was the only obstacle to its appearance. As the weeks went by, he was fully, repeatedly and deservedly apologetic.

"This will mean a lot of extra work for you," he said. "It will tie you down every day to some routine. Are we to make a regular arrangement? I haven't much money, but such money as I have I ought to share with you."

"I would not be interested in doing the work for money," I said.

"It's not hire. It's only a sort of Communism." He knew how to flatter my principles. "Why shouldn't we arrange that amiably together?"

"The arrangement was made long before money was mentioned," I said, for we had achieved a silent understanding of my rôle long before.

When he heard this, he drew me near him, wrapped me in both arms and kissed me. "This is a solemn pact to be ratified by love," he said. "You have saved my book. Of the people I know, you are the most fitted to help me just now. You know books, writers, printing-office customs. Best of all, you know *me*, my ways and what I need to be humored in." His gratitude was joyous and childlike.

As a rule, Tom and my sister Agnes, whom everyone called Gussie, confined their entertaining to Sunday supper parties beginning at about one o'clock so that Tom, who needed to be sharp in court Monday morning, would not be kept up late. But toward the end of May Eighty-eight, when W would be turning sixty-nine, an exception was made. The Harneds invited W, Anne and me, along with quite a number of others, including a big helping of Tom's fellow Republicans, to one of their Sunday affairs. Having done so, they then turned around and threw W an ambitious party on the actual anniversary of his birth, the last day of the month. That after all was the milestone that most or all of us, not excluding the patient himself, had been by no means certain he would reach.

They invited forty-five people. As long as he could establish the time-table, Tom loved having guests in for a meal; I believe it reinforced his sense of being a paterfamilias, in a particularly Republican sense of the word. But poor Gussie. Tom had discharged the cook. Was he experiencing money troubles? I didn't know; we were never able to speak of such things as men do, because he regarded me as a mere Bohemian. With no one on hand to assist her, Gussie had taken on the cook's rôle herself. And not only did she do most of the work in preparing the meal, she had the duties of hostess to perform as well, though Anne helped out as needed in the second capacity, and did so very well indeed and without apparent strain or special effort. There's nothing like growing up the way she had done to teach a person how to put some oil on the waters when the conversation goes awry or, with the remaining oil, lubricate parts of the event where squeaks have developed. The birthday party should properly have been held in a house the size of the Montgomerie residence, or at a banqueting hall or restaurant (my own preference had I been asked). Tom and Gussie had a fine home to be sure, with more than enough room for them and the children, but the size of the celebration put the place to the test.

Sometimes in these recollections, Flora, two or more parts of the past will run together in my mind, for as I have filled these pages with my scribbles, first in New York and then Connecticut, intending to finish on your side of the border, I am always aware of just how very long ago these events took place. There is no danger, however, that my recollections of W's two sixty-ninth-birthday meals will elide, for to say the least they were of different characters.

On the day of the pre-anniversary get-together, Anne and I waited with the others for W's buggy to draw up outside the house on Federal Street shortly after one. W came in, helped by his driver. Some of the guests were seated in the parlor, laughing and talking, loosened by the drinks Tom was making them. W looked pale, even deathly, and had the usual problems of locomotion. He eased himself down into a comfortable chair, announcing, without preamble, "I feel miserable, as the darkies say." His choice of words disturbed me, and Anne as well, I could see; but I stayed silent and made a point of only smiling weakly. Tom began to concoct a drink for him, but W said no, no toddy to-day. "It would finish me." Then he went on to tell a joke about "darkies." Again Anne and I refrained from laughter. I often had to reassure myself that these terms he used for Negroes were those commonly uttered by most everyone in his own younger days.

Tom then asked if W would like to sample the stock of local "champagne" he had laid in (another economizing measure?). W declined politely but finally let himself be poured "a little less than two fingers" of the vile but undeniably democratic stuff. He took only a sip or so. Tom asked him what he thought of it.

"I pronounce it authentically lunar," he replied. "Moonshine has its importance and place too."

The other guests chuckled.

Normally, W didn't drink at all, and had scarcely done so since the big stroke in Seventy-three. Yet there were days when he was feeling at his best, as circumstances had redefined that state, when for a brief period he could drive bodily worries to the hindmost part of his brain. Then he might hoist a glass and recapture for a moment the presumption of immortality that is the right and privilege of the young and healthy. That was as much as the former beer-quaffing Bohemian from Brooklyn—one, it might be noted, who wrote a Temperance novel in his twenties—could engage in without endangering himself any further.

His talk that day was animated but jumpy. One minute he was speaking about Elias Hicks. This pleased me, because it signified that he was trying out on us the ideas and no doubt the very phrases he would soon, I hoped, get down on paper. The next minute, with no concession to transitional niceties, he was going on about Doctor Bucke.

Now, as you know as well as I if not better, Bucke was a big man and an unstoppable one, strong in the way that cripples often become as they try to make up for the cards that have been dealt them. W was telling everyone the story of how Bucke had lost one leg and the toes of the other foot when, as a young man, he strode down from Canada to prospect in our western states but became trapped in the mountains when the big snows came and almost perished—an unusual beginning for someone who became such a figure in what W often referred to as the "medicine-men" fraternity. He graphically described the frostbite that his valued friend endured after being, in W's own words, "'froze out and starved out,' as the n——s say." I was shocked, and instinctively looked across at Anne, who seemed just as taken aback as I was, though I was the only person who could see through her fine tranquility and perfect etiquette. Reflecting on the matter later, she and I concluded that we had been horrified all the more because the offensive statement did not reflect poor antebellum slaves in the Deep South, where temperatures low enough to freeze anything were unknown. Rather, it illustrated the abiding habit of Caucasians even in the present time of derogating and humiliating the entire Negro race, whose cause, as you know, I have worked hard on over the years.

Just when W's talk was taking its unfortunate turn, Tom and Gussie's front door swung open dramatically and the resulting aperture was instantly filled by—speak of the Devil—Doctor Richard Maurice Bucke himself, as though a prompter in the wings had given him his cue. "I see I have got here just in time," he said heartily. "Wouldn't have missed it for the world. First took the train to Toronto and continued on from there, changing at Montreal. Wonderful journey, marvelous, scenic, but tiring." He neither looked nor sounded fatigued in the least. Then, turning to W with not just rapt attention but the kind of concentrated energy that could cut through steel: "My dear fellow. *Jolly fine* to see you about in these preliminaries to your birthday, as though I could believe that you could actually have been born like the rest of us, in naked obscurity, rather than sent down from Parnassus fully formed!"

Caught up in Bucke's long-legged enthusiasm, Tom tried to persuade the guest of honor to have another digit of the *soi-disant* champagne. "Where are my manners?" he said, but W demurred.

No sooner had the hubbub of Bucke's arrival subsided than W, in another gaucherie, allowed himself to indulge in an argument about mere business, one such as might suggest that such matters are important. The specific subject was the tariff issue about which everyone was excited in those days. The conversation at the table assumed this direction when another guest, the retired United States consul at Liverpool and a political ally of Tom's, began going on about the high tariff protecting American industry. W remained an advocate of free trade, though in other respects his politics doubtless changed with age. Now his views were sometimes puzzling, at least to me, as they were not always so clear-cut and unambiguous as his opinions on, for example, the tariff question.

W, you see, often accepted gifts of clothing, even of drawers. A female admirer in England had sent him a waistcoat, the delivery of which had been delayed by Customs. He was certain that duty would make it the most expensive waistcoat on record. "The whole tariff business is an insult to our good sense, besides being a palpable impertinence and invasion," he said, nearly fuming. "The spirit of the tariff is malevolent. It flies in the face of all American ideas. I hate it root and branch."

At this time, W's *bête noire*, and that of all other free traders, was James G. Blaine, President Harrison's secretary of state, who made high tariffs a key point in his own run at the presidency. "I am for free trade, absolutely free trade, for the federation of the world!" W said. In his mouth the name Blaine became a jagged oath. "I am all for getting all the walls down. All of them."

His antagonist, the former consul, condescended to ask whether W wished to strike down even the barriers between planets as well as those between nations.

"If I could, yes. That's what the astronomers are working on all their days and nights, especially the nights, to do."

They bantered on like this, smiling through their animosity. Once again I glanced over at Anne. She was beginning to look worried by the exchange, though my sister, as is expected of a hostess, showed no trace of disequilibrium. No doubt she had already learned the trick of being wife to a young lawyer with ambitions for public office.

I assumed that Anne would save the day by casually saying something that everyone would adjudge to be charming. Before she could do so, however, one of my nephews clambered down from his tall seat, saying, "There's too much old folk here for me."

W laughed and replied, "For me too. Let's all get young again. We are all of us a good deal older than we need to be, than we think we are." Thus was the tension broken.

Seeking common ground, the way a diplomatist must do, even one appointed as reward for his contributions to the Republican Party, the consul proposed a toast to the memory of Abraham Lincoln. From where he was sitting, W could see the portrait of Lincoln that hung on the opposite wall. He raised his barely touched glass of alleged champagne in a gesture of homage and said simply, "Here's to you, here's to you." The moment was a moving one in ways I cannot convey. Here was the author of "O Captain! My Captain!" and "When Lilacs Last in the Dooryard Bloom'd" confronting the source of his inspiration on those occasions, someone with whom he never spoke but with whom he might be said to have had an intricate emotional relationship that was strongly resistant to understanding by others not acquainted with the construction of his mind.

Perhaps Lincoln was especially in his thoughts on that particular Sunday. When I had called on him only a few days earlier, he told me he had "been making a few notes to-day on the subject of my removal from the Interior Department" after someone discovered the "Calamus" poems and showed them to the Secretary, James Harlan. W said: "I was told by a man then very close to Lincoln"— John Hay, the president's secretary? I was too surprised to ask—"that this obtuseness in Harlan had gone a great way toward nullifying his ambitions for the vice presidency."

Can it really be that the gods brought about Harlan's downfall in retribution for his rebuke to W? Was W perhaps permitting his desire for justice to influence his recollection? I don't know. That he was read by people in Lincoln's circle, including Hay, seems clear enough.

Over the last few courses of supper, W resumed entertaining and educating us with talk of Hicks. He placed special emphasis on how

Hicks applied Quaker principles to the routines of daily existence. One example concerned how, despite his small income, Hicks was able to put money aside against lean times and misfortune. Of course I thought of W, the freehold owner of Mickle Street despite having a poet's income.

Then he said: "I want to take a vote on an alternative of titles for the poem section of *November Boughs*. Should it be 'Sands at Seventy'"—for W was looking ahead to his seventieth year—"or 'Sands on the Shores at Seventy,' or something in effect the same?"

He urged us to vote on the choices. When polled, we were all of one accord: "Sands at Seventy."

"I was a good deal unsure about the title until your unanimous vote removed my uncertainty."

"That's a big concession for you to make," Tom teased him.

"Never mind, it's the truth."

When inevitably there were further observations about the war years, I grew apprehensive, but needn't have. W simply wished to expound on some of the Union generals, including Sherman, his almost exact contemporary; they were separated by only a few months in both their births and their deaths. "It is necessary to see him in order to realize the Norse make-up of the man," W said. Sherman's Norseness came as a surprise to me, as I suspect it would have to Sherman himself. "The hauteur, noble yet democratic, a hauteur I have always hoped that I too possess." He went on: "Try to picture Sherman—seamy, sinewy in style, a bit of stern open air made up in the image of a man. I can see him now, at the head of the line on Pennsylvania Avenue the day the army filed before Lincoln, the silent Sherman riding beyond his aides." W had high regard for the military virtues and sometimes used military terms in his speech, as when he suggested that young writers would do well to "stay beyond my pickets." I did not feel the admonition was directed at me, for I was hardly young and had yet to become a writer even to the extent I did later.

Not long afterward, during one of my daily visits, W held up to my eyes a document he had discovered in the great job lot of stuff on the bedroom floor, the way he enjoyed doing. "Here's a letter from John Hay written to me years ago—twelve years ago. I laid it aside for you. It illustrates the friendly basis upon which our acquaintance rests. When Hay was with Lincoln, I used to see a great deal of him. He has been loyal, has always watched my work, has inevitably appeared at the right time with his applause." There was a screen of formality erected behind the note's friendly tone. The message expressed thanks for a cutting of one of W's new poems.

As close as W and I became—spirit-father and spirit-child, than which no other bond is closer—I could never bring myself to ask for explanations or to give voice to the possibility that his memory might possess variant versions of past events, though privately then, and less privately now, that is what I supposed. People of my age and medical circumstances know that memory resembles the art of mosaic-making more than the science of archeology.

"I like to cross-examine," W said to me once, "but I don't like to *be* cross-examined."

⁕

Then, in a week or so, came the main event, the birthday banquet itself. By this time I had made another move, a definitive one, in my continuing search for a job that would let me devote hours each day to my manuscript, which I was calling *With Walt Whitman in Camden*. Anne had stubbornly pledged never to accept any of the Montgomerie money (even though she received its fruits, as she still lived at the family home and had long since left her factory job to be with me—and W). As she and I were becoming a single dimorphic entity, I needed a situation that would provide a bit of financial stability combined with the fewest possible hours and the lightest labor. So it was that I accepted a minor clerical position at the Farmers' and Mechanics' Bank on lower Chestnut Street in Philadelphia. It was repetitious work that provoked tedium, but it didn't tax one's mind or even demand too much attentiveness. I stayed there for the next dozen years.

Late on the morning of the banquet, I stopped by Mickle Street en route to work to offer W my congratulations and give him a celebratory kiss. The anniversary, he said, was being observed "by young women in Camden and elsewhere," though he gave no names and displayed no telegrams or letters, not even a postal, though various male friends did write and one of them in England had arranged for delivery of a floral tribute and two bottles of champagne, definitely not of the lunar variety. The list of young women for whom he felt significant affection had only two names: Anne's right at the top and then Gussie's. The latter had sent over a birthday cake shortly before I arrived. In one of his characteristic little acts of charity, W had me deliver it to a woman in Arch Street whom he knew was sick.

His disposition was not buoyant that morning of his sixty-ninth birthday, as he leapt to contemplate the next one. "Seventy years," he said. "Seventy failures? Seventy successes? Which do you say?" But he managed to rouse himself to quite a hearty and energetic state for the local well-wishers who gathered that evening.

Unfortunately, I didn't arrive at the dinner in time for the toasts, having been delayed by the press of book-making business, so Anne was representing us both. When I did turn up, I found grand high spirits all around, to be followed, after Gussie's fine meal, by much singing and piano playing. W talked at length about why he believed that Bacon had written the plays of Shakespeare (whose name he liked to spell without the final *e*, a style I too affected for a while). This was one of his favorite topics, one he spoke of with the type of animation he must have radiated routinely in his much younger days. I was delighted, having thought he had none left. I imagine it was quite an effort, but he impersonated his younger self gloriously. He lingered until eleven p.m., a later hour than I had ever seen him stay out, and made a touching speech at the end. I have my memorandum of it here. "This has been a calendar day for me," he told us. "It has justified itself throughout, chiefly by your courtesy, consideration and love. You have been good to me all day. Now I am going. Be good to yourselves. Go to bed; get a rest."

He told me that he had more copy for the printer and would ask Missus Davis to hand it to me the following day on the ferry dock so I could take it across. Bucke was among the guests, and so was William Kennedy, the Philadelphia writer and future W biographer whom W called "one of my most ardent—I often say 'granatic'—admirers. Indeed he outbuckes Bucke" (but of course no one could do that). Kennedy and I helped W up onto his buggy. As the elderly mare bestirred herself, W called out a reminder to me. "This side. The ferry. Tomorrow. Twelve o'clock sharp."

The book, then, was never far from his thoughts. I imagine that was how he was with each of his works, and each successive version of *Leaves*, though *November Boughs* he may have worried over to an unnatural degree. He confessed to me that the Hicks piece wasn't "sufficiently rounded up yet," adding, "I am a slow piece of machinery. I do not seem able to muster myself for duty on call." Then he added an uncharacteristic confession. "It needs some finishing touches. I do not seem to be equal to them." He was thinking of either not including it in the book or publishing it as a separate "volumette," one of his coinages.

I was going over to Philadelphia consulting with the printer who was putting the pieces of *November Boughs*—virtually all of them except the Hicks—into type and giving me the multiple sets of proof sheets W demanded. This was exacting work, because W had very definite ideas about how the eye would respond to typography, which should therefore be "open" and "democratic." What's more, he liked to correct proofs quite heavily. Aware of this, he made certain that I took a silver dollar to the lad who pulled the galleys, one of the lowliest tasks in a job-printer's shop. So it was that I went to Mickle Street shortly before noon the following day to report on such matters and deliver a large installment of proofs, rolled up under my arm like the bills and posters one sees men pasting onto board-fences and hoardings.

I was greeted by a distraught Missus Davis out front. As she tried to shush her loudly barking dog, she told me that W had come down to breakfast, hobbling a bit more than usual on the stairs perhaps and looking terribly ill. She feared the celebration had been too much for him. She related how he went into the front parlor, put on his spectacles and, sitting near the window with strong light coming over his shoulder, began to read the morning papers the way he liked to do, but was having difficulty. He had experienced a brain attack during the night, and it was followed by two others later. Fortunately, Missus Davis was nearby, and got to him in time to prevent him from crashing to the floor. She in turn called Warren, and together they manhandled him into a reclining position on the davenport. W came round and told Missus Davis she needn't stay with him but to go about her domestic chores, coming in every once in a while to "take a gander" at him. I rushed into the front room and found W supine on the sofa, with Tom and my nephews looking on. As luck would have it, they had come by for a morning chat. Seeing this scene, I immediately feared the worst, but in this I appeared to be quite unlike the patient, who did not seem to be especially downcast.

"I have had since last night," he told me, "three strokes of a para-lytic character. Shocks, premonitions." His voice was strong and its tone seemed untroubled, but some of the words themselves were slightly slurred. "That's all there is to it. Don't worry about it, boy." He reached out and took my hand and held it tightly.

He explained that, after leaving the feast, he had had himself driven with Bucke to Norristown, the site of the New Jersey asylum and of the medical business that had brought his friend across the border this time. That done, W asked to be driven out to the seashore for some clean night air. Then he returned home, where he collapsed to the floor while bathing himself with a sponge. He believed he lay there for some hours. I asked why he didn't shout for Missus Davis, who was in her room at the end of the short corridor. He replied that he had had many small attacks in the past and had always recovered without assistance. This time, the stroke was followed by another in the morning, then yet another. I asked if his ability to speak clearly had been impinged upon back in Seventy-three.

"I never suffered that entanglement in my former experiences," he said with a bit of difficulty. The formality of his utterance struck me as unusual coming from this man who relished slang and often cultivated poor grammar to set himself at a distance from what he called "the literary class." He had dissuaded Tom and Missus Davis from summoning the medicine-men, saying, "I shall not only have to fight the disease but fight them, whereas if I am left alone I have but the one foe to contend with."

Now he sent the others away and, when he and I were alone, asked me eagerly for the batch of proofs. I was skeptical of this being the right time to go over them, but W said, "This attack is a warning to us to hurry the book along as we can." He unfolded his eyeglasses so as to begin correcting proof, reminding me to bring four sets of the other "matter," as printers call it, when I returned that evening.

He was shooing me out. So after only a half hour I left with Tom, who had a telephone at his home on which he said he would attempt to contact Bucke. On finally being located, the Doctor rushed to the bedside in the company of William Osler, the fellow Canadian who ran the medical department at Johns Hopkins University in Baltimore (how you Canadians stick together).

They were there when I turned up about eight with untitled proofs of what was now to be called the "Sands at Seventy" section. In exchange, W gave me copy to take across the river the next day. Although Bucke kept up a façade of relative unconcern with the patient present, W was not fooled, telling the medicine-men: "There are earthquakes which shake walls, chandeliers, and, yes, there are earthquakes which destroy cities." When I was alone with him, W said: "I know myself. I know my peril. I am on shaky foundations. It cannot be concealed. So let us push the book along—get it done—before anything absolutely disqualifying occurs to me."

He gave me a couple of old letters that had recently floated to the surface in the bedroom upstairs. "Curios" he called them, as though he viewed them as unimportant, which obviously they were not. Some days later he showed me another letter, dated 1870, from a physician at the asylum in Brooklyn, informing him that his brother Jesse had died from the rupture of an aneurysm and was being buried the next day. I expected him to comment, but he didn't.

Finally I said, "Do I understand that I am to take this?"

Yes, he said; I should see that it is preserved.

His speech was not yet returned to its original clarity, but he was happy to chat anyway. I made a passing reference to Anne.

"I have my suspicions about you and Anne Montgomerie," he said in sly fashion, pretending to be more innocent of the details than he actually was.

I had to go over to Philadelphia on W business, where I ran into

Bucke, who started by saying that, although he couldn't determine exactly why, it seemed to him "as if the old man is dying"—as though W were simply another patient. I suppose medicine-men must learn to steel themselves against emotional responses. Later in the day Bucke turned up at Mickle Street with Doctor Osler once again. When I returned from the bank, I found W full out on his sofa in the darkened parlor, with Bucke taking his pulse at the wrist. Tom was there as well. W had obviously taken another step in his descent since I had seen him earlier.

When I entered, he called out, "Who's that?" I said my name. His response was, "Ah, I thought it might be some other particular friend of mine."

Tom, Bucke and Osler agreed that W needed a resident nurse. W overheard the discussion and weighed in with his own idea. Missus Davis had been so kind, he said, "but if I am going to be more than ever helpless, it will not do for me to impose on her for more service." He thought "a large man" should be engaged as the nurse, "no slim or slight fellow." Before dashing across the river to recruit one of this or some other description, Bucke took me aside with instructions to engage in long-drawn-out conversation to keep W awake, saying that the patient was mentally confused as well as in physical straits. But in fact his mind had cleared a bit since my morning visit. I pulled a chair up to where he lay. "Someday there will be a final spell," he said, "and then . . ." He trailed off. "But then, we are not going to discuss that final spell until we have got out *November Boughs*, are we, Horace?"

Later he showed me a note he had sent to the printer without telling me. It advised the shop to put "two good men" on the job, hard-working ones. I didn't know what to think. Was he afraid that I wasn't forceful enough to see the book done right? Or put another way, did he feel that his signature would add forensic force to my instructions to the back-shop? No, I concluded that, having turned sixty-nine, he was at the age where he sometimes distrusted the abilities of the young—ones younger than I myself was, for at least I had been born before the war.

Sitting there, engaging him in the long elliptical conversations that Bucke had prescribed, I already was thinking how I might raise money from W's admirers to pay for the nurse that Bucke would return with. As I did so, I looked down at W's sweet upturned face. He had become my own wounded soldier boy.

Over the next several weeks, I continued to bring him proof after proof, thinking that was what he desired, but he found his memory had gone haywire. He complained of "jelly-like sensations in my skull." He settled back into the cave of the bedroom above, where Missus Davis carried all the books and papers that had been in the parlor. He refused to see visitors, even, for example, Eakins. But despite his condition, he still kept on with his small acts of kindness toward others, as when, for instance, he gave me a quarter-dollar to pass along to a particular newsboy who worked the ferry dock on the other side.

He redirected some of his unease into worrying about writing a new will. He applied himself to the chore with a discipline he could not muster for what seemed to me, putting his physical problems to one side for a moment, the incomprehensibly difficult task of finishing the Hicks. He showed me the resulting document. Family members were to be the primary beneficiaries, with a bequest of two hundred and fifty dollars to Missus Davis and his silver watch and chain to Pete the Great, about whom he spoke from time to time—of how, for example, the two of them used to walk together all over Washington in a spirit of ease and were sometimes hailed with greetings by the late martyred president, James A. Garfield, then still a mere member of Congress. As he passed, Garfield would shout out a couple of lines from one of W's poems.

One day he surprised me by saying, "Pete was in yesterday and brought some flowers." Pete, he said, had been his salvation after the first attack back in Seventy-three, serving many of the functions now performed by Missus Davis and me (and by then a medical student taken on as a nurse, ensconced in the tiny bedroom next to W's). W could not walk any longer without the use of the cane he had had for years and had been using only sparingly.

"It was Pete who gave me the cane with the crook in it," he said. "I always use Pete's cane. I like to think of it having come from Pete, as being so useful to me in my lame aftermath." Then he asked, "You have never met Pete?"

He knew full well that I had not.

"We should arrange it some way sometime," he said. The promise was quite as insecure as it sounded.

SIX

THE CELEBRATED THESPIAN known to his friends as Wilkes, one of Baltimore's favorite sons but one who is frequently away, appearing in plays in all the major cities and a great many minor ones as well, must continue to move around from city to city as though he were still acting. At the Holliday Street Theatre in Baltimore he meets his old school chum Sam Arnold, the one who joined the Southern army early but was invalided out. Arnold found work as a clerk in the Confederate government, though he gave it up after a short while. Wilkes invites him to his hotel room and regales him with stories of his exploits offstage and on. As they talk and drink, there is a rap on the door. It is Mike O'Laughlen, another old friend, who served in the same regiment as Sam.

A generous host, Wilkes orders up more wine from the bellman. When all three of them are fluent but none drunk, Wilkes turns the conversation to the rumored plots to capture Lincoln and trade his freedom for that of Southern prisoners.

"Much is chattered about some such course of action," Arnold says. "My suspicion is that those who talk, only talk, and that those who would act never say a word. But I don't know."

O'Laughlen pipes up. "Whether rumors in the newspapers cause the talk or the other way around, I cannot say."

They drink a great deal more wine. There is more tobacco too, and more brandy. Independently of each other, the two Baltimore men come to the simultaneous conclusion that Wilkes is not engaging in mere badinage. He is a serious operator, whether sanctioned or not (he is coy on this point—as someone who is sanctioned would be). He is obviously well financed (by his own speculations in shares, he insists, though his listeners know he may be saying this to account for money that actually comes from Richmond, perhaps via Montreal). He inspires confidence, for now. They agree to help him realize his hostage scheme in whatever small ways they can, not knowing exactly what these could be, only that they will be called on for some competent service in the District where, accordingly, they will have to resettle. The two young men, neither of them prospering in the world, resolve to keep down expenses through shared living accommodations.

⁂

"Where is your sentimental friend?"

The man from the President's Park is of medium height, not a six-footer like Walt, and his complexion is dark. He is brooding whereas Walt is open by nature, albeit with the particular kind of bonhomie that is sometimes a nursery for secrets.

"He's still up at New York," Pete the Great replies, not disguising his bitterness, "but he Has written up a Letter to me sayin he's returning soon enough."

"I must go there myself shortly," Wilkes says. "I am engaged in a great enterprise that requires my presence there and other places."

In a vague way, he has spoken to Pete of his plans earlier, more than once in fact. The first occasion began with war talk of the sort everyone engages in. Wilkes then drew attention to the matter of the prisoners.

"You, dear heart, have been in one of their foul dungeons. I do not preach to you, for you were converted already by your own experience."

"I can lay claim to havin been a Prisoner of both armies," Pete answers. "I have no preference for the one over tother. I tell you though that the yankee prison here in their capital is a barbarous Place. It is God's truth."

"I have no doubt of that at all," Wilkes replies.

Wilkes possesses the gift for making others feel the emotions he wishes them to experience. Such is the way of actors. He is such a well-proportioned man, not muscled as with a farmhand but strong all the same, and most of all vital: lithe and athletic, as though he could bound into the saddle from a standing position beside the mount, without reference to the stirrups or the pommel and without losing his breath. His jaw is firm. His hair is so thick that curls tumble over the precipice of his forehead. He is a clean-shaven man but for his moustache, which adds to his flamboyantly distinguished bearing. The voice is magnificent, and Pete the Great is vulnerable to voices.

In their conversations, the two of them have touched on Pete's romantic situation. "The ting about it is that it ended before it really picked up a full head of steam," Pete says.

Wilkes appears sympathetic. "Why did your friend go back up north? What precisely is he doing there?" The actor certainly knows how to make the inquiry sound casual. "Do you know?"

"The people that he does the job of work for at the Hospital got concerned about his nerves," Pete says. "They told him to get away for a time. So he goes to New York to see his kin. Course, he takes in the hospitals up there, too, so as to seem to be carryin on with business. He does write-ups about em for the Newspapers. Sent me one."

"I read his views on the prisoner exchange," Wilkes says. "I must say, I approved, if from different motives."

Early in the war, each government repatriated prisoners in return for the release of its own from the enemy camp. As the Confederacy has grown weaker, the practice has been steadily curtailed.

"The cold-hearted tyrant and freak!" Wilkes is referring to President Lincoln. His sympathetic manner has slipped away, like a piece of painted scenery slid off the stage.

"That was what walt and me was arguing about just before he upped and departed," Pete says. "He's always goin on and on about St. Abe, like he's comparing me to him to my disadvantage. About how Lincoln is tall and stately, so manly, and how he's come up from his beginnings in some shanty on the prairie, meaning that I have done no such ting. Course, he's twice my own age at least. To hear Walt tell it, if the Proddies had a calendar of saints, Abe would be on it all right, one of the most important ones."

Wilkes is careful not to smile, careful not to point out that the first requirement for canonization is to not be among the living.

Just as, early in the Struggle, men in the District predicted the imminent fall of Richmond and a quick termination of hostilities, so now they speak of an end to the war at the very first breath of Spring, if not sooner. The Struggle cannot stagger on much longer with so few men in the ranks and many of those not much better fed than if they had been prisoners on Johnson's Island or any of the other notorious pesthole prison encampments.

Pete fulminates against St. Abe a bit longer, his jaw locked and his gaze ignited. When he finally winds down like a dollar watch, Wilkes offers him a diverting evening.

"There is an establishment in this benighted town of which it is unworthy," he says. "It is one of the District's most closely held secrets, known to only a few, who guard the fact of its existence as though with their very lives. Clean yourself up and we shall go there, and you will be amazed."

It is nearly Christmas.

On the twenty-sixth of December, a drayman arrives at the family home in Brooklyn to deliver a battered trunk with G. WHITMAN 51ST N.Y. painted on it. As the others watch, Walt pries off the hasp with an iron bar and lifts the lid. Inside is George's uniform, a Colt revolving pistol, a mirror, a comb, a tin mug and various other such articles, and George's war diary. There is nothing to indicate why it has been sent or even by whom, if not by George himself. The family members gathered in the small parlor don't ask out loud whether the owner might be dead, but this is what they are thinking.

In the ensuing days, Walt seeks out officials, former colleagues and acquaintances, and old contacts from happier times when he was a newspaperman, hoping to learn at least where the regiment is camped, that he might go there. But there is no information of this sort to be had through such channels. He remains diligent. More than three weeks later, a Union officer returned to New York, one of the trickle of captives still being exchanged, arrives in Brooklyn with fresh news and a letter he has promised to see safely delivered to the mistress of the house. He informs them that George is being held in Virginia. The letter tells of his capture more than three months earlier at Poplar Grove Church, a nearly invisible pimple on the map of Virginia. George puts on a brave front: "I am in tip-top health and spirits, and am tough as a mule and shall get along first rate."

The next day's mail brings a letter from George giving the family what he thought would be the first news of his predicament. It should have arrived before the trunk but has not. It tells of being one of three and a half hundred officers held under guard in a tobacco warehouse at Danville.

Walt arrives back in the District, knowing that he can plead, cajole and bargain for his brother's exchange more effectively from the capital than from Brooklyn, going as high as young John Hay in the Executive Mansion if need be. Only days after his return, he is able to have a wooden box of proper foodstuffs sent across the lines to Danville. He doesn't know that George is falling ill and will soon be too sick to finish off the contents.

❈

The room is enormous, its walls papered in red felt with velvet trim. The bill of fare begins with mock turtle soup and proceeds to "to-day's New York oysters in variety" and entrées both boiled (salmon, turkey with oyster sauce, leg of mutton with caper sauce) and roasted (pork, duck, mongrel geese). The array of puddings, custards and pastries is staggering (sago, mince pies, lemon and squash pies, and so on), the relishes likewise. The register of them extends all the way to syllabub. The lengthy wine list is a bit confounding, as most of the wine Pete has drunk has been at Communion, for he is a spirits man. "Truth to tell, i'd be happier looking at a pitcher of this grand Set-up than sittin here," he says.

Wilkes smiles—almost laughs—at his young friend's artless candor. "You needn't feel out of place," he says. "The public rooms of a fine hotel such as this are in the essentials a type of theater. The lighting is identical, as you see. The same sconces and plaster work and carpets, the same soft white clouds painted on the ceiling for when you glance upward—look."

"Same uncomfortable seats as well," Pete says.

This time Wilkes does laugh, appreciatively. "And we are at once the players and the audience, strutting across the boards while all others watch us and we watch them watching us. Everyone's eyes are fixed on the costumes while waiting for the action. You do *enjoy* the theater?"

"Walt's the big one for the plays and things. He likes all kinds. Comedies, tragedies and such. He is a Glutton for it. He is that way with music too, and can sing whole operas."

"In any event, I hope you will enjoy what I have planned for us this evening." The first course begins to arrive, the waiters moving as though they themselves and not just their tunics have been stiffened with heavy starch. "With this fine dinner under our belts, and both of us in a relaxed state, I will make you a gift of my promised surprise. It will have to last for a time, as I am going to New York as I mentioned, to be gone a number of days. I'm unsure just how many."

They leave the hotel and begin walking through the snow, Wilkes taking long strides, Pete with shorter legs taking occasional catch-up steps. They go to a row house in a street of row houses in a neighborhood of such streets. Number Seventy-five is three from the corner, a three-story brick house with large twin dormers set in a fish-scale roof and a modest bit of stained glass in the fanlight over the thick black front door. Wilkes, wearing a heavy cloak against the wet snow, raps on the door with his stick rather than use the knocker. Pete, after blowing on his hands, has stuck them deep in his trouser pockets. Recognizing a distinguished gentleman, the Negro who opens the door graciously nods Wilkes to the double parlor on the right-hand side, where another man, white, pulls apart the oaken sliders.

"Welcome," says the second man.

Nodding toward his companion, Wilkes says, "This is a young friend of mine, Peter, whom I would like you to meet."

"How you do, sir?" the man says to Pete, who answers with a quick modest smile, showing two blackened teeth in the bottom row. "You will find a warm haven here on such a night," the man continues, speaking to Wilkes as another Negro, a youth, takes the visitors' wraps and hats.

"Whom do we have this evening, then?" Wilkes asks.

Two young men sit at opposite ends of one of the deep blue sofas. The taller one, the one with the very pale skin, gets to his feet on some subtle signal from the person in command.

"I am Thomas," he says. His brown hair has been cropped abnormally short.

The other one then rises in his turn. "Francis, sir. A pleasure to see you again, sir." He is skinny and refined-looking, with hazel eyes and long fingers like a musician's.

"Peter, I believe Francis and you will find you have something in common."

"You Irish?" Pete asks.

"No, sir," replies Francis, who was a private in the Rebel forces only recently. "Unfortunately," he adds, smiling.

Pete is not accustomed to being addressed with an honorific.

"You should compare experiences," Wilkes says.

A bit uneasily, the two strangers, whose combined age is rather less than fifty, move to another of the sofas, near the grate, where the fire replaces the wall globes as the source of illumination.

Later, Wilkes ascends the wide staircase with Thomas several steps to his rear. He pauses on the first carpeted landing and leans over the well-oiled banister to speak to the proprietor. "If a man you've never seen before should call for me here, asking for Doctor B, please tell him to meet me on the fourteenth," he says softly. "He will know where."

⁂

Wilkes has stood more or less where Walt has stood—they easily might have seen each other—waiting for the president to canter out to the Soldiers' Home with his little Praetorian guard of troopers. Wilkes has been told that on occasion the president is accompanied by no one at all, though this is only gossip; he has not himself seen the solitary and unescorted figure on a mount: a ridiculous spectacle even to contemplate.

The plan inspired by the ritual and the rumor is not lacking in boldness or daring, but is brilliant in what might be called its flamboyant simplicity, as the actor's admirers might have expected. He will arrest the procession (if there is one), abduct the president at gunpoint, spirit him away and free him only when the demands are met. The demands are to be the release of all Southern prisoners—the emptying of the prisons and the prison encampments.

Walt and Wilkes may also pass each other in the streets of New York: Walt hurrying along uncharacteristically, not seeing much beyond the spots on the pavement where his feet will land next, so concerned is he about the fate of his brother; and Wilkes doing an important chore, appearing both righteous and shifty, like a player not certain whether he has been cast as hero or villain. The errand is the purchase of ammunition and firearms. Specifically, of Spencer carbines, short enough to fit in his trunk. As George's trunk makes its way to Brooklyn, Wilkes's trunk travels to Baltimore. There, Mike O'Laughlen carries it by buggy to the District, helped by Sam Arnold.

<hr />

The idea of abducting the president may have derived from a suggestion by one of the local Confederate operatives, a plainspoken and unsmiling man who might be mistaken for the owner of a feedlot with a couple of thousands in the bank and some more in the mattress ticking. He has been assigned either to assist Wilkes or to keep an eagle eye on him. In practice, the two tasks are interchangeable, for assisting Wilkes is in fact the best way of maintaining a watch over him.

The two men don't care for each other, the foppish actor dressed in immaculate style, well connected, suave, handsome, at close range always smelling of lilac vegetal as though he has just emerged from the barber's, and the other fellow, hale and well met but deceiving no one, a shady but not entirely sharp-witted jasper who believes in the Struggle to be sure but might not continue to do so if sorely pressed, for he lacks passion.

The two of them go shopping for a boat and a boatman, and in this way come upon the ignoramus Atzerodt. His forename is George, but he calls himself Andrew. Wilkes calls him Port Tobacco, for that is the miserable village on the river where they find him. There he scratches out a livelihood of sorts as a wheelwright. Less exaltedly, he also does general repairs to carriages and other types of rig. He is short and grotesque-looking, as though a monkey's head has been stuck atop a man's body. He has a permanent stoop, so that his figure in profile suggests a barrel stave. He wears his hair untrimmed and oily to the touch, and his eyebrows come within half an inch of meeting in the center of his overhanging forehead. His clothes never fit properly, and he always looks as though he is dirty not from working with axle grease and the like but merely from absence of mind.

Much or most of the time there is no trace of Prussia in his speech, such as it is. His voice is low and guttural, his talk simple and constantly interrupted by a lunger's cough, the sort that starts out like a hellhound's growl and increases in spasmodic ferocity until you think it might begin rattling the globes on the lamps and the panes in the windows. Wilkes is told that Atzerodt has run the Union blockade. That is difficult to believe. But he does have a boat and can get other ones if needed, on short notice and with discretion. More important, he knows every marshy appendage to the river and every copse of waterlogged trees where a person might secrete himself until he could cross to the opposite bank undetected and step ashore on the glorious soil of Virginia.

Wilkes's manner of speech is too complex, his sentences too long and cadenced, for Atzerodt to comprehend fully. This is where Wilkes's companion is useful. He knows how to converse with such people. And so conversing, he reassures himself and Wilkes that Atzerodt too is a patriot, albeit one who prefers to be paid for his services, for the war is sputtering to its inevitable and ignoble conclusion and in such a situation a young man does well to look to the future, uncertain though it is.

Wilkes returns to the District, where he has a tryst with Lucy, a young woman of abundant charm and intellect. She is a skilled lover and the daughter of a senator who is a devout abolitionist. As for her own views, they are outrageously advanced, encompassing the nature of relations between male and female. She has no objection to her beau's ill-concealed adventures with other women "so long as it is I with whom you take breakfast." She gibes him with allusions to her own several admirers. One of them is a young officer assigned to General Grant's headquarters staff, a position that his powerful father has secured for him. His name is Robert Todd Lincoln.

<hr />

Walt has returned in a state of qualified relief. George, though imprisoned in the tobacco warehouse in Virginia, is alive and, in his own telling at least, perhaps for his relatives' benefit, well. The District is a city of soldiers to be sure, but it is just as much a city of landladies. Walt has a new one, a Southern woman who serves good meals. Prices for everything are criminally high, but the price of lodging especially so. Still, his clerkship at the Indian Affairs office at Interior covers his meals and room and the coal and wood to heat it, with some left over to satisfy his obligations to the wounded and to send more food and clothing to George, wondering if the parcels actually get through. Of course, with such wartime prices, he has no spare cash but is able to spare hours, which he devotes to two causes. The first is his campaign to convince those in authority to effect a special prisoner exchange for George. The second is the regeneration of the relationship with Pete the Great.

The reunion is warm and rewarding, but can the feeling be sustained? That's the question. Pete seems even more crotchety than before the trip north. He is a low flame simmering politely along a prescribed path until, every so often, he stumbles upon a new piece of fuel to consume, causing sparks to shoot up all of a sudden.

Now that everyone can see and feel the war coming to its conclusion at last, the nation, Walt thinks, will soon seem to have been decontaminated and sanctified, not simply reunited. He believes he is sympathetic to the thicket of contrary emotions that the looming finale provokes in Pete, whose allegiances, while not always acted upon, are certainly obvious enough. To him, the Yankees are the English and the Rebels are the vassal Irishmen. His position becomes still more apparent when he says to Walt that the North started to win the war when it made sure England sent no aid to the Rebels and didn't attempt to rend the blockade though it was in the British interest to do so. Walt, however, questions the special significance of those particular facts. His doing so leads to an argument, a rather one-sided one, with Pete storming about, puffing up what Walt considers his beautiful little chest and throwing his head back like a rooster.

Now comes another such battle, and like so many ugly events it arises from innocent remarks whose potential for inciting combat no one could possibly have foreseen.

They often tell each other stories about their families and recount what has happened in their work that day. Pete speaks of the strange assortments of people who patronize the horse-cars—women with small children, workingmen coming and going, and always some officer reporting to somebody somewhere, one hand reining in the polished scabbard of the saber belted around a scarlet sash at his waist. Walt, for his part, tells Pete about the Red Indians who are received at the office. "They pass the clerks' room when they come to call," he says, "and you know, Pete, they have a dignity you would not expect any petitioners to exhibit. Even a nobility."

Pete is eating a peach as he listens.

"They are not tall men, but they look to be well made under all their finery and feathers," Walt goes on. "There is much sadness in their faces, relieved only by the wisdom in their eyes. They are strong and unhurried and fully comprehending, you might almost say accepting, of the tragedies all around them." Walt makes one observation too many. "In these essentials," he says, "they put me in mind of the president."

Pete just stares for a moment—stares and squints. Then he lets loose a barrage of invective, Christian and secular. Lincoln the tyrant and torturer, Lincoln the invader and desecrator, nay Lincoln the murderer on a terrible satanic scale. "you'd have *him* in your Bed if you could!"

Statements are contradicted and denied, oaths uttered and returned. Pete's face begins to go red as though a rosy shadow were passing over it quickly. His upper lip straightens and his neck muscles tighten. He sweeps a lamp off the crude chest of drawers. Fortunately, it is not lighted and only the chimney breaks, though lamp oil spills out onto the rug and splashes the unpainted baseboard. Walt stoops to gather the broken glass. When he rights himself, all he sees is an Irish blur of brown clothing and all he hears, after the door is slammed, is the hard flat-footed tread of two boots stomping down the stairs, some muffled questions from the landlady and someone running out the front door into M Street, where all trace of him is lost amid soldiers, strollers and loafers, wagons, buggies and the occasional barouche.

❃

"Come, I'm taking you to a hotel to meet some friends," Wilkes says.

"It's not another of them big dinners, is it? I couldn't Stomach another such one." Pete grins at his clever play on words, possibly his first deliberate one.

"No, no," Wilkes says. "We won't be dining. This is just a meeting with two of my Baltimore friends. An important meeting. Historic, in fact."

Pete doesn't know how to respond to that except to wish that he were a little better dressed.

Like Wilkes, Lucy Hale lives at the National Hotel at Sixth and Pennsylvania, and shares a suite with Senator Hale. This proximity makes it a simple matter for Wilkes and her to carry on their *affaire*. He is a patron of numerous other such hostelries as well, using them for meetings and conferences related to his patriotic endeavors. Generally, he does not use the same one twice. To-day's is splendidly nondescript. As though it were a much grander place, Wilkes puts one boot and then the other on the cast-iron scraper outside to clean the mud off the soles before stepping into the lobby, and Pete follows suit. They go upstairs.

"Who's this with you?" asks one of the men in the room.

Wilkes is usually careful to employ only their forenames, but in this case thinks it safer to go another way. "Mike, Sam, I would like you to meet a young friend of mine." He always relies on this locution though he is only four years older than Pete; O'Laughlen and Arnold are getting close to thirty. "I call him Irish. You may do so as well."

"A pleasure to make your acquaintance, Irish," says O'Laughlen. Arnold nods warily. Both men have sad eyes that make them look forlorn even when they are not.

"Irish too is a veteran of our forces," Wilkes says.

Arnold, a *rara avis* as he was actually born in the District, has been living in Maryland, where partisans of both sides exist cheek by jowl and one never knows the truth of one's neighbor's allegiance. As for O'Laughlen, he is a bigger fellow than Arnold and handsome in a different way, broad of shoulder and with a high forehead. He wears full moustaches with a small goatee that looks as though an artist has painted it on with a camel-hair brush. He is a Confederate deserter but doesn't brag about it. Prior to relocating in the District, he used as his place of residence the Baltimore feed barn and livery stable that employed him.

"Gentlemen, I have asked Irish to participate in our interview to-day because he is, in his heart, one of us and has faith in the right-eousness of our mission." Sometimes Wilkes's speech becomes a trifle too well enunciated, as though he were trying to make the words reach the family circle at the rear of the hall, but even when speaking softly he speaks clearly. "Simply, I wish him to join us, as I intend to inform all of you of a momentous development that will cause us to alter our plans thus far, which by your leave I will now recapitulate not only for his benefit but our own mutual refreshment."

Pete realizes that his eyebrows have shot up in surprise, but he has the presence of mind to stay completely silent for once. He looks first at Wilkes and then at the others as Wilkes presents his summary, talking of the North's refusal to continue large-scale prisoner exchanges, the Confederate operations in Canada, his own purchase in New York of arms brought into the District secretly. Sam and Mike try to hide their impatience at the long recitation, especially as it is, despite the speaker's preamble, clearly only for the new boy's benefit.

In recounting the plan for the president's capture, Wilkes describes how he has kept a log of the days and precise times that the president passes along Seventh Street en route to the Soldiers' Home and back. He explains how he himself has carefully traveled every foot of two escape routes, the alternate being in reserve should it become necessary to abandon the first one at the last minute.

There he pauses half a beat to heighten the drama. "Gentlemen," he says, "now I must tell you of a startling development, as I have been informed of it by Mister Watson." Jack Watson is one of the names used by his old friend John Surratt, the courier who transports documents between the office of the Confederate secretary of state in Richmond and that of the Confederate commissioner in Montreal. "He has told me reliably that for some reason the president will no longer be traveling to the Soldiers' Home or anywhere else in the countryside, and I have confirmed this independently and then, just to be sure, confirmed it a second time."

Sam and Mike give each other quick glances to assure themselves that their reactions are the same.

"As a result, I have had to conceive a new plan," Wilkes says. "Given that the president is such an ardent lover of the stage"—he sneers a bit as he says this—"we shall abduct him from the theater!"

More looks are exchanged as Pete for his part tries to puzzle out what is taking place.

"That's ridiculous." Mike is first to put his reaction into words. "Seizing him on a public highway or in open country is one thing. Doing it with hundreds of people watching and then having to escape through crowded streets—scarcely possible."

Wilkes answers their objections individually. As the president patronizes the theaters often, his presence in and of itself, though it always draws the usual gawking curiosity seekers, will not seem to anyone a singular event. He will occupy a grand box wherever he is, be it Ford's or Grover's or even one of the lesser places, but human guard dogs do not accompany him there. In the usual run of things, the president will have no entourage beyond a messenger, ready to run news to or from the War Department or the Executive Mansion or any other official place.

"In contrast to Seventh Street, he will not be surrounded by troopers," he goes on. "Of course, there are almost certain to be many bluecoats in the audience. Who can say that a few of them might not be quick-witted and one or two of them armed with their pistols?"

Pete is struck by shock and excitement but says nothing, for now he is unsure whether he *can* speak. As Wilkes continues with his outline, he appears to be smiling slightly. He explains how he of course has free run of all parts of the theaters and can slip unnoticed, or at least unremarked on, into the entrance of any box and immobilize the president with a blow or simply a handkerchief (his are silk) soaked in chloroform. "I would hold the other persons in the box to stay still and be silent, using my pistol for this purpose, out of sight of the rest of the audience. You will enter and together we will truss the tyrant and lower him to the stage by rope and whisk him away through the stage door."

The conference is thrown into chaos as the room becomes a shambles of emotions and resentments. Arnold and O'Laughlen have lost confidence in Wilkes. For certain this time, he must be mad. For his part, Irish isn't altogether sure what's happening except that he is now part of a world different from the one he inhabited seconds before he crossed the threshold of this hotel.

O'Laughlen sputters a single word: "Impossible!"

Arnold is less dismissive. "How would we get him across the lines?" he asks.

"We would not. Yankee soldiers would infest the countryside like a plague of blue locusts. All the while our prize would be safe in a cellar not far from the spot where we sit this instant. I am preparing the space now."

To differing degrees, Sam and Mike are at once both dumbfounded and extremely skeptical. The two reactions engage in a gladiatorial combat to see which is to prevail. As for Pete, he thinks he might actually be sick with excitement, remembering the guards at the Old Capitol Prison where they had him incarcerated, and of course thinking of Walt as well.

Wilkes seems pleased with himself. He looks his listeners in the eye and rests his left hand on his hip. "You will allow, gentlemen," he says, "that I do my best work in the theater."

⚜ SEVEN ⚜

THE FIRST COUPLE OF MONTHS following W's strokes were particularly difficult. It was a time of strong emotions all around. I was fully engaged in my courtship of Anne, though courtship isn't a word she or I would have used (it is not a Socialist word). Seeing her, or seeing the two of us together, or simply hearing me mention her from time to time, always brought some animation to W's face. He would smile slightly, and for a second the smile seemed to cover the creases and declivities that ran up and down his face before taking cover beneath his whiskers. It didn't do much for the condition of his skin itself, which, on the days when his natural complexion couldn't make itself seen, was alternately patchy and pasty. But it made him look, for just a moment, younger than his years. This was remarkable because for all of his adult life, judging from the photographs taken at various times, he looked older than the chronological aggregate. No doubt this was mostly deliberate. In any case, he was fond of Anne, fond of how she addressed him and how she behaved in his company, but fond also of her youth.

So long as they were not writers, which is to say competitors, young admirers generally reminded him of his own salad days, which were now moving rather speedily into deepest history. But he put a great deal of thought, you might say, into how he could display his thoughtfulness to Anne in particular. I'll take an instance almost at random. He was invited to attend a meeting of the Contemporary Club to hear a discussion of hypnotism. He would have liked to go, for though he held no brief for the subject, he did enjoy gathering ammunition for his views. But he was too sick and so signed the invitation card over to Anne, encouraging her to attend not in his place but as a lively intelligence with positions of her own. Such was his renown that she was admitted, making her perhaps the first woman allowed there. The distinction was one that she liked to consider true, so of course it pleased her mightily.

Sometimes he went a bit far in ingratiating himself, as when he gathered some of his own works and asked me to take them to Anne's father when next I went to the Montgomerie place. "It is not as careful a selection as I should have made had I been given more time, but I hope it will do," he said. "I have never seen the old man, but I wish you would tell him Walt Whitman sends his love." Lucky for me, Mister Montgomerie was out the evening I called with the goods under my arm, so I could leave the bundle with a straightforward note that couldn't be misinterpreted. The stack did not include *November Boughs*, which was not yet through the press, but shortly afterward W gave me a proof of one of its essays, the one on Robert Burns, which he signed "To Peter Montgomerie," on the hopeful assumption it would be met with interest when I delivered it to its adoptive home.

W's thirst for writing, in the months after the strokes when he was nursed back to at least a semblance of occasional and relative health, returned even more aggressively than his appetite for food. He had always loved newspapermen and especially the Bohemian character that many of them displayed, for he himself had been a prominent (or do I mean notorious?) New York Bohemian in his day. He cherished the notion that they were laboring men no matter what their shirt collars might say. They loved him in return and often boomed his books for him—that is, when he did not boom them himself, either pseudonymously or anonymously. In later years I've heard criticism of this practice by people who chose not to understand how he thought of himself as a rebel cast out of the literary elite and needed to make sure that others thought of him that way as well. The audience of those who admire outcasts is far smaller and usually less well-off than the one of those who do not, but it is easier for a person such as him to win their affection. "Many stray dogs are rounded up from the streets and shot," he said to me, "but some are so wretched that families with little enough to eat decide to take them in, regardless." I thought he was about to wink at me as the words emerged from his beard.

All this is in support of the idea that he was honest but shrewd, often very shrewd indeed, in his literary dealings. As soon as he was well enough, he directed some of his energy to keeping up the bargain he had made earlier with the editor of the *New York Herald* to supply fresh poems on a regular basis, so many each month, on topics taken from the current news. He also published fairly often in the *Daily Graphic*, a paper in the same city but of the lowest stratum, and the local sheets in Philadelphia and Camden. The *Herald*, however, was a different order of things. He received regular monies for poems commemorating the anniversary of Lincoln's birth and the death of the Kaiser, or the burial of General Sheridan, or ones that described calamitous events in the weather or evoked New York scenes from long ago. They widened his audience no doubt. Being regularly spaced, they came to be expected as a natural component of the paper. They also lifted him a bit, giving him another reason to rise each morning, though always his conversation, and his expression of discomfort and weakness, returned him to the inevitable.

One summer day I mentioned that Anne and I had been on a romp to Wissahickon Creek, which is a smallish stream, about twenty miles long, I suppose, that empties into the Schuylkill River at Philadelphia. A pretty place.

"That reminds me that years ago I thought some of pitching my own tent out there, squatting, loafing the rest of my life in that vicinity," he said. Then he added in a different tone, "I cannot be said even now to have wholly given up the idea, though I don't suppose that it matters much where I happen to spend the rest of my days."

Bucke had found a young man who knew enough of the medical arts to answer all the questions put to him by W, but he stayed only a brief time. Whereupon Bucke dispatched us one named Musgrove, whose primary asset was his size and strength, for he was fully able to carry his patient in his arms if necessary. I thought him a dark manner of man when I first met him and never had reason to revise that impression. He was sullen and often deflected conversation.

When W asked what medications he was being given, Musgrove replied curtly that he did not know, though whether this was because he lacked the knowledge or merely wished to discourage talk, I can't say. Probably both. W refused to swallow what he was offered blindly, and this led to a general suspicion of the younger man by the older. I could see the added damping-down of W's mood as a result. I had no choice but to report as much to Bucke. He soon sent a replacement from his own establishment in Canada, and W picked up a little bit after that.

He made another will to reflect the new realities, leaving his money and goods to his brother Eddie, who was nearly mute and had a mind little better than an infant's, and to their sisters, that they might use the inheritance to help take care of him. W asked me and my brother-in-law, Tom, to be the executors of his literary remains, along with Bucke. The will named young Harry Stafford and Pete Doyle among those marked for bequests. The former was to receive W's gold watch and chain, though it was not a terribly good timepiece.

The latter would get only the silver one, inferior in all particulars as to both appearance and mechanism.

No doubt in acknowledgment of the document's eventual consequences, Eddie was brought to Mickle Street for a visit while W's niece and sister-in-law were moving him from one asylum to another. Through the courteous patience of Missus Davis, he was to stay the night.

He made a sorry spectacle. His eyes looked dead and stared out from a face even deader. He could not support his head on either side at will, as you and I do. "He inclines heavily to starboard" is how W put it. He had but a single expression, one of absent disinterest, and did not pick up his feet when he walked but slowly slid the soles of his shoes across the plank floor. I had observed how W kissed his brother Jeff when they met, kissed him fully. With Eddie he merely held the visitor's hand. Eddie spoke few words and they were not always easy to comprehend. They were either simple nouns or infinitives, widely spaced. "His conversation, if that it is, is well leaded," said W, slipping into the jargon of the composing room as he often liked to do. From such grunt-like sounds one was left to deduce the drift of Eddie's thoughts.

The two Whitmans sat up until late evening in the company of Missus Davis, until W asked her to escort Eddie to his bed.

"Good-bye, boy," W said. "I will send for you soon again. You shall come whenever you choose." But it wasn't to be.

Later he remarked this to me: "Eddie appeals to my heart, to my two arms. I seem to want to reach out and help him."

Not that these two situations could be compared, but this was the way the small band of us felt about W.

Eddie apart, W was cheered by visitors, both those in bodily form who climbed the concave stairs and those whose corporality was exclusively postal and were slid under the front door rather than walking through it. One of the second sort enlivened me even more than it did W. It was a copy of one of the British journals with an essay headed "Walt Whitman as a Socialist Poet." W said he read it to see whether he was being slagged (he admitted there was no disrespect intended) but also to see how he looked "to one who views all things from the standpoint of a Socialist." He looked at me impishly from over his reading spectacles as he said that. That night, when I added the day's memoranda to the manuscript I had begun, these were his words as I reconstructed them: "I find I'm a good deal more of a Socialist than I thought I was, maybe not technically, politically so, but intrinsically, in my meanings."

I found this utterance a great relief and affirmation. I would have urged him to expand upon it, but somehow, I'm not sure how, this exchange led smoothly to one about poetry instead. The question will sound asinine, but I asked whether there will be more poets coming along (I knew there could be no more quite like him).

"I am neither the first nor the last," he replied. "There will be more and greater poets than have ever been."

"What kind? Your kind?" I was refining my question.

"I don't know about that," he said. "Some *free* kind for sure. The stylists object to me, but they lack just what Matthew Arnold lacks. They talk about form, rules, canons, and all the time forget the real point, which is the *substance* of poetry."

He went on that he has never sought the big audience because he knows that the message of *Leaves* will spread. "The book is like the flukes of a whale: if not graceful, at least effective, never superrefined or ashamed of the animal energy that imparts power to expression. Even Goethe, in loving beauty, art and literature for their own inherent significance, is not so close to Nature as I conceive he should be. I say this with all due respect to Doctor Bucke, who reads Goethe in the German and declares to me that I have but very little conception of Goethe's real place in the spiritual history of the race. Well, maybe I have. I care less and less for books as books and more and more for people as people."

He told me that he never kept diaries. But as I would learn, he did in fact do so for various periods, especially his summer in Canada with Bucke. Rather, he said, he maintained a thick day-book wherein he jotted thoughts and lines of verse. Just as he always found excuses for not showing me the famous Emerson letter again, so he refused to let me read the day-book. It lay temptingly out of bounds, each day at a different spot in the room, an indication he was still using it daily as both a place of deposit and one from which to make withdrawals. He had a habit of patting its binding. This was the raw material of his writing, and without writing he would be nothing, as he well knew; he was aware that I understood this as well. Still, the stuff he *did* let me see was often remarkable enough.

The presents he enriched me with! For example, a photograph, taken in New York during the war, of his brother George in what W called "his sojer clothes." It caused me to remark that I could not conceive of W himself in any army. He reared up, adamant almost to the point of violence on the subject of his pacifism.

"Yet they say you condoned the war," I interjected softly.

"They say that, do they?" He sounded angry.

Sometimes he took this disputatious tone. I put it down to the ache of his infirmities. Tom once brought up the debate about restricting immigration. He pointed to strong opposition to the proposed limitations, not only among businessmen in need of cheap labor but also among many ordinary citizens who nonetheless chose to remain silent in public. W, who opposed the limitations, flew off the handle. "Well, here's someone who spit it all out," he said of himself, accusing those who did not so expectorate as being lacking in courage. "Contract labor, pauper labor: I have no fear of Americans. Not the slightest. America is for one thing only—and if not for that, what? America must welcome all: Chinese, Irish, German, pauper or not, criminal or not." He went on at length, becoming quite heated.

He was not a man in conflict with his own contradictions on such subjects as this or the war. I was obviously too young to fully understand the second of these. Always would be. That is, I was the wrong generation to comprehend how it must have been, great armies, tens of thousands, scores of thousands at a time, each man with his rifle and his blanket roll, moving by foot or by train across great distances to places none of them had ever seen to kill fellows such as themselves. W said he felt the growing obligation with others of his own vintage to set down recollections of the period even if they are not memoirs of the war itself: "evidence of the curious things thrown to the surface in an era of major disturbance."

The phrase has stuck with me as an apt description of how he fed me material from the museum of himself that was his bedroom, workshop *cum* office. The letters from Bucke (the earliest a book order from 1870 from someplace called Sarnia) were interesting of course, as were those from Burroughs and all the other nearest-and-dearests. But the most curious were those from British admirers who, I see now, in light of developments in my own journey through life, guardedly sought absolution for inverted thoughts they would never confide to anyone except this stranger whose openness in *Leaves* made them trust him. I speak of obvious Uranians such as John Addington Symonds and Edmund Carpenter, writers who once had had a literary movement that they openly called the Uranian Circle. These were men who had been educated at Oxford or Cambridge. W was suspicious of them and annoyed at their persistence. Yet he had all the time in the world for members of the *other* little Uranian group, up in Bolton, in the North of England.

Was it their lack of artifice he liked? Certainly. But in my view he indulged them because they were all fellows from the laboring class, or at least aspired to be. W didn't have many readers in America among the workers whom he was so often addressing in his poems. He'd had such individuals as lovers, to be sure: his "transportation-men" especially. Yet among his readers he could point to few, leastways few he knew of for certain, who fell in that category of workers that does all the country's monkey jobs. The workers returned his love, but they didn't memorize his poems. With their "betters," it was the other way around. This was one of the frustrations he endured with what, all things taken into account, was saintly patience and forbearance.

Which might well explain his enormous affection for Anne. It was not rooted in carnality, to be sure. So it must have come from the fact that a young woman from a background at least somewhat privileged, by the high standards of a country such as this, admired him, it seemed then, almost as unhesitatingly as a handful of respectable authorial figures and (a different form of admiration) a great many youngsters from the coach yards and docks.

The more I came to understand the *erotische* side of W's life, what now would more likely be called his *Sexleben*—that is to say, the more I followed leads that Bucke was to suggest—the better I understood that I had no cause whatever to be jealous of him even if he had been a healthy man of my own age. Yet for a while I was concerned.

I can still see him as he took leave of his birthday banquet, thanking Gussie, shaking Tom's hand emphatically, hugging the Harned children—and giving Anne such a protracted and, I thought, lascivious kiss on her mouth as one would never expect to see at any public event but a wedding. Was this a sincere expression of how he felt about her? Or was it intended to reinforce the perception of him as a fellow with bastard children still to be found in the tap-rooms or convents of New Orleans? Perhaps neither. Perhaps a bit of both.

For my part, I was love-smacked, as I imagine many intellectual, progressive and literary men would have been had they found Anne before I did and somehow allayed her unspoken hesitations as thoroughly as I was able to do. Over time, I became more comfortable with W's affection for Anne, and vice versa. Until then, I was prudent to be worried.

Back in the early days, the candor I and so many others admired in W's utterances and writings had a different effect on me when directed toward Anne as an individual. Even in the first precarious weeks following the attacks on his brain, when his grip on the world's assets was obviously so slippery, he managed to be his old self where she was concerned. When Tom was leaving after a ritualistic visit to the Mickle Street sickbed, he was asked to bring no other callers than himself the next day "except for Horace and Agnes"—he never called her Gussie—"and Anne Montgomerie." That would be innocent enough were it standing all alone. But when Anne had not appeared for two or three days, he asked me to tell her "that if she don't come to see me soon, I shall think she has gone back on me. I know I have said I won't see visitors, but she is not a visitor, she is one of us." Or, most flirtatious of all—and this, mind you, from a man way too ill to impersonate the male equivalent of a coquette—"Kiss Anne Montgomerie for me even if it is not lawful!"

Despite my rational nature, I naively saw a dilemma where there was none. Anne believed that the way W spoke of her and behaved toward her was a touching expression of his advanced ideas, proof of a progressive ideology, one that I, at least, knew existed as much in W's memory as in the realities then current. When he said, for example, "Tell Anne that I am alive yet, though not lively, and that I may survive the work we laid out to do" and I relayed the message (though tempted not to), she reacted by thinking he was applauding her spirit of independence and compassionate but self-sustaining heart. I was alarmed but not surprised, anxious but not eager, to hear of her visits to Mickle Street at hours when I was at the bank. I did not mention this subject to her lest she question the sincerity of my own commitment to the new face of women's position in civic, social and political affairs. I did, however, bring up the topic with W after the third or fourth time he mentioned in passing that she had stopped by. I did so casually, and he responded casually.

"Yes, she comes sometimes, brings flowers, kisses me," he said, "but she doesn't come enough. You're always harping on her." By which he meant that I was playing cupid in my own romantic interest, not someone else's. He liked running together her forename and her family name, as though it were a compound or were hyphenated in the English way. "What's Anne-Montgomerie to you, or what are you to Anne-Montgomerie, that you should love each other as you do?"

That quite floored even as it reassured me. Before I could respond in an articulate fashion, he took up the slack with a weak jest.

"A boy can do a sight worse than to have a girl. He may *not* have a girl. *That's* a great deal worse."

I had reclaimed my speech but not my wits. "And that from a bachelor!" I said.

"Not too much of a bachelor either, if you knew it," he replied, a bit archly.

The skylarking was at an end and so was conversation. I first thought he was going to say something more on the subject of love or romance. Instead, he shut his lips tightly. He spoke nothing further, so I said good night and went home.

Except for the one missing element, its essay on Elias Hicks, *November Boughs* was ready to go. I kept nudging him to finish. When nudging failed, I gently implored, gingerly prodded and discreetly begged. He replied with excuses that were altogether sincere, saying that his brain "could not cope with it, gets tired, takes my pen out of my hand. Reading only passively tires me." Other times he placed blame not on the topic, but on himself. "Hicks is entitled to my best, not my worst," he said. "My best would be too little, my worst would be an insult."

That he could not grapple with Hicks on days when he was at his weakest was natural enough. "It now takes all my energy merely to get to the chair and back to the bed again," he told me.

My sense was that he feared I might grow impatient. In this he was incorrect. Another "young" man might have done, but not I. Instead, I encouraged him to talk about Hicks, hoping he would find it easier to rewrite his own conversation as prose rather than tackle composition straight on.

"I knew the habitats of Hicks—my grandparents knew him personally so well—the shore up there, the whole tone of life at that time and place. All of it is so familiar to me. I have got to look upon myself as sort of chosen to do a job as the Hicksite historian. I have seemed, to myself at least, to be particularly equipped for doing just this thing and doing it as it should be done. Now it threatens to go up in smoke." He sighed not with his lungs and voice box alone but with his whole silent body.

"Do you know anything about the method of the Quaker meetings?" he asked. He didn't give me time to answer. "Well, if you do, you know that they never take a vote. They discuss questions, one this side, one that. Or sometimes most of them on one side and only a few on the other. Then the moderator—I believe they call him that, at any rate the man who presides—announces the result, yes or no, as he sees it in the balance of feeling. It is remarkable, I think, that in the history of the sect these decisions have never in a single instance been appealed. If there is not a pretty ardent leaning one way or the other, the moderator reserves judgment. That is the only guard. They seem to select their most judicious men for the place, men who cannot be swayed by momentary passions, interests, prejudices, or even sympathies.

"What all this comes to is that just that sort of a debate is going on in my mind now, whether to condemn or save the Hicks, whether to send it to the printer or throw it into the stove." For just a second he flicked a one-eyed glance at the old round stove. "A debate not to be put into figures or votes, but real, with a decision pending which I must abide by at last. Tell the printer to give me until Monday. This is Thursday. Till then it will be a life-and-death struggle. For all these years I have had it in my plans to write a book about Hicks. Now here I am at last, after all the procrastinations, stranded, with nothing but a few runaway thoughts on the subject to show for my good resolutions. Well, if I can't do all I started off to do, maybe I'll be able to do some little toward it, give at least some hint, glimpse or odor of the larger scheme."

The following day too, he was once again drained of energy, complaining of "great languidness, feebleness, weariness." Fortunately, the languor did not affect his talk, which as delivered was that of a healthy man. He limited himself to a single visitor besides myself: Susan Stafford, mother of Harry Stafford, who had come and gone in his life several times but of whom I never got a fixed impression as I did of Pete Doyle. Missus Stafford, he said, was "not literary. I account that one of her merits." Literary or not, she knew the *Leaves* and in fact had read all his books.

The subject of swimming came up when I saw him that evening, and he told me about his boyhood exploits as "a first-rate aquatic loafer." This led him to ask if I knew the painting *Swimming* by his friend Eakins. As he put the question to me, he seemed to motion with his head to Eakins's portrait of him, which that day occupied pride of place on a plinth of books stacked upon the writing-table. I confessed that I was not familiar with it.

"It is not one of his large pictures," he said, "but it is magnificent. It shows a scene toward the close of a long hot summer's day. Four or five boys are swimming in a river—no doubt our own river, here."

I was pleased whenever I heard evidence that he had come to think of Camden and its environs as *our* rather than *your*.

"They are gloriously but unaffectedly nude, nude in their brother-hood and their humanity, as they dive from some rocks by the shore and frolic with one another. They are slender and muscled. They remind us how like a piece of fruit the body is, reaching the perfect state of ripeness that is all too brief. Eakins caught them at that moment, before they had any awareness that the ultimate end of the process is to rot and fall from the branch."

He looked sad. Sadder than his norm, I mean. I imagined he was thinking not only of death but of the loss of so much freedom that was prefacing his own.

"Eakins painted himself into the picture, I think. He is the mature figure, also nude, swimming toward them with a certain determina-tion. He works a great deal from photographs, you know. He is him-self an excellent photographer in the sense of not being too artistic about it."

Such talk, whether to himself or aloud, was doubtless another factor deflecting his progress on Hicks. He did, however, manage to complete small clusters of new paragraphs about Hicks and feed them to me for putting into their proper places. *November Boughs* was still growing, but sometimes sideways rather than up. The following Saturday, for instance, he added further new material for the essay but ended up excising more than he put in by vaporizing all the references to George Fox, one of the founders of the Quaker faith back in England. Later, he restored the Fox material to the book but stuck it in a different place. I persevered with aggressive good nature.

Possibly to disguise his lack of progress, he kept making sidetracks to discuss the war, a subject that always had my interest but was coming to seem longer in the retelling than it could ever have been in reality. On this occasion his recollections had what struck me at once as an unnecessary mysteriousness, a fact that was itself mysterious to me at the time. He spoke a bit disjointedly. He said, "My place in Washington was a peculiar one, as were my reasons for being there and my doing there what I did. I met no others there who shared my own motivations, but then I could not at that stage articulate them to myself, so how I could expect others to do so? People went to the capital for all sorts of reasons: to convert, to proselytize, to observe, to do good, to sentimentalize, from a sense of duty or from philanthropic motives. Women preachers, emotional gushing girls."

This sounded like the beginning of one of the long lists he made so much and so magical a part of his poetry.

"I honor them all. Knew them, hundreds of them, well, and in many cases came to love them. But no one, at least no one that I met, went just for my own reasons, from a profound conviction of necessity, affinity, coming into coldest relations, relations so close and dear, with the whole strange welter of life gathered to that mad focus. I could not expect to do more for my own part at this late day than collect."

The extremity of his fatigue made him ramble beautifully this way, as though he were trying out the one faculty, speech, that remained to him whole. But I sensed a greater coherence in it than perhaps he intended. He seemed a bit weaker for all the effort, so I was reluctant to press for qualification, should I have known how to do so. I had the suspicion, however, that he was telling me something about Pete Doyle. I say suspicion. That is the wrong word. I mean instinct.

"I haven't cast out all my devils yet."

W was referring to his health, though I don't think he honestly believed that illness could ever be cast out, not at this late stage. Some other type of devil, yes, to be sure; for he did in fact rally to finish the Hicks piece. He did not declare an end to it arbitrarily and then, in resignation, send it out into the world to fend for itself. He lowered his original expectations in line with the restrictions imposed by his condition, once satisfied that these actions were reasonable in the circumstances. Then I was able to turn over *November Boughs* to the men with ink-stained fingertips.

Tom usually stopped by to see W each day, just as I did in the evenings. Normally he brought one or both of the children with him. W doted on them and they on him, though his beard proved scratchy whenever he hugged and kissed them. Being in the law, Tom was also perforce a man of affairs. He suggested that the publisher, W's old friend McKay, who had lent him some of the money for Mickle Street, price *November Boughs* at one dollar and fifty cents. W, always eager to reach the readers with little income (those who, in his phrase, were "not holding"), thought one dollar and twenty-five the correct amount. He argued that the quarter-dollar was the boundary between ordinary readers—people who were not bookish and whom he valued for just that reason—and the writers, journalists, businessmen, doctors, officials, lawyers and others for whom the price difference was not a determining factor in whether to make the purchase. He also knew that a thousand copies was the right number to print. He had acquired a sure feel for such matters, he said, and it had helped him to survive in the world.

He was so pleased when, in the last week of August Eighty-eight, two months after the disturbances in his brain, I brought him a stack of the finished books. He held one in his hands, a squarish book of a hundred and forty pages. He flipped through it and took the edge of one page and rubbed it between his thumb and index finger. He held the volume to his nose and inhaled deeply, as though sampling a fine wine or a tasty stew in a hotel dining room. When asked the question, he answered that he calculated the venture would bring him no more than he had laid out for it. I didn't know how literally to interpret this statement, as I had seen with what dexterity he negotiated his way through literary commerce.

Around this time, he showed me the letters from three or four years back that had passed between him and a man who was operating a sort of syndicate for fine prose writing. His correspondent had signed up several important monthlies and a number of the bigger newspapers to print contributions on certain topics he would solicit from writers of note—in his words, "from famous men whom newspapers cannot reach—nor afford to pay separately even if they did reach them." He was commissioning war reminiscences from certain figures who still trod the Earth, and he wished W to write on Lincoln and of course on the wartime hospitals. He evidently labored under the impression that W had actually been acquainted with Lincoln in the usual sense, not just on the spiritual plane. W did not disabuse him, not that I saw, reading the letters. W got twenty dollars per thousand words, the very highest rate, but later came down substantially, and shrewdly, I think, in order to get his copy into still more of the bigger papers and increase his profit in that manner. W asked me to read all the letters aloud so that he could relive his small commercial triumph. Some of the correspondence related to a memoir of the Bowery Theatre in New York and Edwin Booth the tragedian (both onstage and otherwise).

In his newspapering days, W was a prolific reviewer of books, plays, concerts, lectures and all types of exhibitions, as well as of politics and crime, those staples of journalism. Now, at the other end of his life, he found it difficult if not impossible to stop pronouncing on the merits or deficiencies of what fell before his eyes every day. For example, he could seldom let pass without commentary the old letters and other documents he had salvaged from the unswept corners of his bedroom to put in my hands. Whenever he was being particularly charitable this way, I would ask once again to see the Emerson. He would find some excuse or change the subject. In time I almost came to believe that on the next occasion he would inform me that Missus Davis's dog had eaten the thing.

Talking was his last pleasure. Fortunately, all of us who were his friends loved to listen to him. Beneath his discursiveness and casual language, he was discriminating and sharply critical, no less of himself than of others. About this time, someone began producing a calendar that featured quotations from W's work on each leaf (a venture that in a way seems now to have presaged the later appearance in the marketplace of Walt Whitman Cigars). W called the calendar "a dubious experiment. I don't shine in bits. There are no 'gems' in *Leaves of Grass.*" He meant rather that the book was a life being lived, a process not an object, a river not a pond or lake.

It was my duty to keep the out-of-town leaders of his loyal circle informed about his condition, as when I would write to Bucke up in Canada, as the doctor had insisted I do. This correspondence was related partly to the nurses who would always be present in W's life. The patient knew that his friends were paying for them, but I didn't want him to know that I was orchestrating the effort, trying to get various people to pledge small monthly sums for as long as necessary.

I didn't want to keep secrets from him as he did from me, but neither did I wish him to feel that he was even more dependent on me now than before. So he became distant with me when Bucke stupidly mentioned to him in a letter that I had been discussing my spirit-father's health in my own correspondence.

"I don't want Bucke to know the worst until the worst is frankly hopeless," he said to me when I pressed him about his reaction. "He worries over bad news. Write him in a cheerful vein."

"Lie to him?" I asked.

"Well, lies don't help, I suppose. But don't tell him the evil until there's no more good to talk about."

One day he showed me letters from the great actress Ellen Terry and from Bram Stoker, the right-hand man of Sir Henry Irving, the actor-manager, and other new discoveries: two more of the home-made note-books he carried with him to the hospitals. I asked him if he had the letters he no doubt had written to his mother back in New York during his years in Washington. Surely these would be a valuable source of understanding about his experiences, even though he might have wished to withhold certain scenes and descriptions from her. Yes indeed, he replied, saying that he retrieved them, hundreds of them, following her death. Using Pete's old cane to steady himself, he led me to a door that I had supposed, if I had thought about it at all, was a closet. He asked me to remove the large mound of stuff that blocked it: the usual documents and old newspapers. Once I had shifted all the treasured rubble, he let me into a small room, once perhaps a dressing room, full of books and files. This was the musty warehouse of W the writer who so often had had to be his own publisher as well. There were long identical rows of his own books and below them open cartons of unsorted papers.

He began to draw aside some of the contents by the handful. He passed me a photo he had found. Although only a couple of years old, it was a tintype, not one of the many more modern types of photograph, showing W seated, legs crossed, behatted and holding the very same cane. Standing behind him, one hand resting on either W's back or that of the chair, was Bill Duckett, the thin young man who had not yet achieved his majority and left Mickle Street under a cloud.

"A sweet boy," W said. "Eakins was very fond of him, you know. Used him as a model not long ago."

"He painted him?"

"I can't say. But he took photographs of him, for the benefit of his art students."

"You mean photographs of the figure?"

"Oh, yes. Even for a painter, Eakins is especially unblushing with respect to the nude, as you know. This has provided the two of us with some interesting conversation, particularly when I too submitted to his lens."

"You posed undraped for Eakins?"

He didn't answer but found a picture to show me. "It is one of a series and he allowed me to keep a print. You see, he would photograph his anatomical models in six or seven different standing poses: hands atop head, facing the camera, side view, back to the camera, and so on."

It was W all right, from his bald dome to his crooked feet, and wearing not one stitch in between. He stood looking right into the lens with one arm behind his back.

I was shocked, for though I had frequently seen him in *déshabille*, I certainly had never lain eyes on his generative appendage. I was shocked in another way as well. Although the picture could not have been more than a few years old, it illustrated all too vividly how W had deteriorated—decayed.

He saw me thinking this and beat me to the gate. "This is what a man of sixty-five or so looks like, my young friend, as you will come to know all too well. Note the involuntary tonsure, the sunken chest, the flabby belly and spindly legs. But is it not a beautiful piece of machinery all the same?" He put the photograph back in its box. "This I believe I shall hold on to, if you don't mind."

That was in August of Eighty-eight. The following month he determined that he was no longer able to go about as he had done before the strokes and so made arrangements to sell the horse and gig. A clergyman of all people, a moralizing, book-burning firebrand no doubt, paid a hundred and thirty dollars and promised he would treat the horse well. W didn't leave 328 Mickle Street again until the following May.

EIGHT

HOW DID THINGS EVER get this far out of control? Here's how.

Like all societies, like all of us who comprise them, the South is good at some things, not so good at others. For two full generations it has contributed its young martial geniuses to the national pool of military talent, where they accounted for a greatly disproportionate share of the whole. Now the Southerners are in business for themselves, and it is a desperate affair. They sweat glory and are soaked.

In the fight they are in now, there are none better. None better at the fancy card-trick flanking maneuver, the clever feint, the holding action that suddenly gives way to suck in an enemy that will find itself trapped and confounded. Certainly none better at the mad daring gesture, however futile it may be. But strangely, for all the cosmopolitan ease and buttery charm, those who make up the small stratum of educated and wealthy Confederates are not so skilled at diplomacy. They speak and dance beautifully. You'll never catch one of them making an error in French grammar or leaving an engraved calling card with the proper corner not turned down. But they don't have a Ben Franklin to romance the courts of Europe. If only Prince Albert had lived, many have been saying, our British cousins (often literally) would have come over here and broken the asphyxiating blockade of our ports. If only the French, who've always hated the Yankees anyway, for the sheer perverse enjoyment of doing so . . .

As an obviously immoral person may be a splendid human being who happens to be missing only a single essential component of his character, so might a society be so full of accomplishment yet lack one necessary aptitude. If diplomacy is a retail trade, the selling of public policies in foreign capitals, then espionage is diplomacy that is made to measure by secret tailors. So they're not very good at espionage either.

Military strategy and tactics are where they excel. Robert E. Lee's overriding ambition is to relieve pressure on his beloved Virginia and somehow move the war northward. Let the enemy see what war's like for a change. For their part, his political masters think a victory on Northern soil might be just the ticket for getting recognition abroad, and thus outside help. Lee's first attempt ended in Maryland, the state that interposes itself between Virginia and the North and supplies men to both sides.

Lee, being the underdog, has had to be bold as well as tenacious. Invading the invaders—imagine. He crossed into Maryland and met an army twice the size of his own and fought it to a standstill, but in the end had to fall back to Virginia. The North frequently names its battles after population centers, while the South, a more rural society, often chooses the names of nearby rivers, streams or other natural features. This case, however, was one of the exceptions that prove the rule. The North calls the battle Antietam, after Antietam Creek; the South calls it Sharpsburg, after the nearest town: an engagement with two names, as both sides claim the naming privilege that belongs to the victor. In truth, it was a draw; in truth, everybody lost. This was the bloodiest battle ever fought in North America up to that time, with 23,000 dead and wounded in forty-eight hours.

The next year, 1863, Lee tried again. This time he made it to the middle of Pennsylvania, to a place no one had ever heard of, written as Gettysburg, pronounced Gettisburg. The armies fought for three days, two of them touch-and-go, back-and-forth, in the biggest battle ever fought in North America. The third day was a decisive Union victory, the turning point of the war, people are still saying. Again, Lee pulled back to Virginia. Again, a new record: 51,000 dead and wounded. The North can rebuild its ranks with more conscripts. The empty spaces in the Southern lines aren't so easily filled. The population isn't large enough. And while the South has a draft, it awards no medals. Southern men know what the stakes are.

For the South, every decision is a life-or-death one. Boldness and daring are the tools of underdogs who don't give up and can't afford to be more conventional. Their ideas are costly when they fail, as they usually seem to do, but if they were to work—you never can tell, a big-enough kick could well prove fatal to the enemy or, at the very least, ensure that a peace candidate would take the presidency from Lincoln, though that might happen anyway (with George McClellan, whom Lincoln fired as commanding general, the likely successor).

The next Summer, 1864, Lee (West Point '29 and eventually its superintendent) tries one more time. General Jubal Early (West Point '37) is a misogynistic lawyer who has been protecting Richmond. Like Lee, Early had opposed Virginia's secession, but unlike Lee, he believes in the slave system. He loves a teeth-wrecking fight. Lee orders him to leave Richmond's fortifications (a brave gamble in itself), push north into Maryland and, if victorious there and conditions are favorable, attack Washington. The moment is right, because the capital's sixty-three forts are under-garrisoned and many of the troops stationed there are old or wounded or both, serving out their obligations with passive duty. Attack Washington. At the very least, that'll put the fear of God in 'em.

Early has only twelve thousand troops, albeit tough ones. When, however, he meets resistance in Maryland, at a place called Monocacy Court House, only a few miles south of Frederick, it is from fewer than half that many Federals. They are commanded by General Lew Wallace, the military governor of Baltimore, whom history will remember not for the battle resounding through the fields that day but for being the author of *Ben-Hur: A Tale of the Christ*, the best-selling American novel of the nineteenth century. He will write it while serving as governor of New Mexico Territory in the days of Billy the Kid (whom he meets).

Wallace's casualties are heavy when this, the Confederacy's northernmost victory, is over. Of greater importance strategically is that the fighting has put Early behind schedule. He circles around to Fort Stevens, at the northwestern extremity of Washington, uncertain about whether to proceed farther. There is just enough time, barely, for General Grant to hurry some of the troops he has menacing Richmond to relieve the pressure on his own capital. The two commanders fight fiercely before Early pulls back to Virginia— essentially trading places with the enemy troops who have come to rescue Washington. During this confrontation at Fort Stevens, President Lincoln insists on leaving the Executive Mansion and the District to go see the battle for himself. He ignores advice and stands on the earthen breastworks to get a better view. He is totally exposed and makes an unmistakable target, what with his absurd height, so exaggerated by his famously tall hat, also absurd, and of course that face—there can't be two people in the world who look like that. Finally, the soldiers around him defy their commander in chief and pull him back down to safety, but not before he becomes the first and only president to come under enemy fire while in office.

Wilkes is not around either capital city during these events, or indeed for much of that summer. He is on the road, but not touring with a play. He's acting all right, but there are no stages, no lights, no audiences and no applause. When he pays a visit to his sister Asia, she tells him that a man has come by the house asking for him, calling him Doctor Booth. Oh, Wilkes explains, the man makes that assumption because I am smuggling to our valiant troops one of the most valuable commodities being denied them by the Yankees: quinine. He then raves on about politics. She knows to let him rant until he runs out of rage, like a horse that must be allowed to exhaust itself before it will accept the bit.

The war is certainly grimmer than it has ever been. Indeed, everyone knows in his or her heart that it is hopeless now, that absent the English or the French, divine intervention is called for. But God—sometimes He works in ways that aren't so mysterious as Scripture would have us believe, for however bad the military situation, the political one looks as though it may start running in the South's favor. As this election year progresses, it is increasingly felt that Lincoln, notwithstanding enormous unequivocal successes on battlefields both east and west, has as much chance of winning a second term as he does of being elected the Pope in Rome.

His life is threatened routinely. He is burnt in effigy as a matter of course. Such members of the cabinet as are still loyal nonetheless consider him a buffoon. Large numbers of people who voted for him now regret having done so, believing him a tyrant, a betrayer of the Constitution, a man with an insatiable thirst for blood. Additional prisons are constantly being built to house the people who dare disagree with him. The army sets up extra-constitutional courts to try civilians whose loyalty is considered lackluster and to frighten everyone else. In one terrifying instance in Indiana, such a commission has sentenced freely elected opposition politicians to death. Some of the more studious commentators express regret that the fathers of the nation tossed out the parliamentary system that would have seen the government fall on a vote of non-confidence long ago rather than have the country stuck four years with a dictator. Well, let it not be eight. In any case, never again.

The president's best hope is to press the mounting advantage against the crumbling enemy as hard and as quickly as he can— before the ballots can be tabulated. The two nations have a combined population of only thirty-one million; in the end, six hundred thousand will have died in the war. Lincoln calls for another million men to be drafted. Now he will take the war into Southern parlors. Now there will be war against children and women and cattle and pigs and chickens, against railroads and telegraph wires and crops and pastures and public buildings and food stores (such as they are), against houses and books and artworks and pianos: against everything that moves and a great deal that does not. Hell, cut off the head and cut out the heart at the same time. A young cavalry officer named Dahlgren, son of the man who designed the Dahlgren gun used to pound Southern emplacements from ships far out at sea, is sent on a raid to Richmond to kill Jefferson Davis and his cabinet in their own lair. He is himself killed along the way. He has stupidly carried his signed orders with him, and his killers find them on the body. Now the metaphorical gloves are off, if in fact they had ever been on.

The Southerners fight the way poor people who lack the enemy's numbers, money and technology always fight when the lives of their families and their homes are on the line. They fight the way people fight against invaders, the way people without powerful friends must fight when it's either that or give up and die. In time, there will be reports of Southern soldiers actually going into battle stark naked, as there are no stores for them and no means of resupplying them if there were.

The problem, however, is not merely how poorly they're equipped and fed, but how few they are. The South decides to release a great mass of its Northern prisoners. This goodwill gesture, coming at a time when simple rancor has turned to murder all around, could well give further encouragement to the Democrats up north, who, when elected in November, might accede to the growing peace movement and seek some sort of settlement that would at least leave many still alive who will otherwise soon be among the dead. It also of course may lead to the release of prisoners on the other side, a resumption of the old accord that would let the South reinflate its ranks, at least a little. Besides, turning the prisoners loose means that the South doesn't have to feed them anymore, as it has been largely unable to do for quite some time. Many of those sent on their way home are little better than skeletons in rags. Instead of encouraging moderation, their appearance enrages people in the North and makes matters worse. In Washington, Edwin Stanton, the secretary of war who many say slickly manipulates the dull-witted Lincoln, orders Southern prisoners be kept where they are. Then he orders their rations cut.

Britain's refusal to take sides in the war is owed to more than simply the South's failure to persuade it to do otherwise. It comes also from Lincoln managing to do something right. Britain came closest to getting involved early on, after the United States boarded a British ship at sea and took off two Confederate diplomats. Later, by keeping Northern belligerents away from the Canadas, Lincoln has ensured that Britain will be nothing more than a distant observer. Of course, there have been moments when Britain has been wary nonetheless, doing what it always does in these colonial situations, sending out some leisured aristos to inspect the fortifications and write reports on the state of Canada's defenses. In the normal way, such reports are followed by the reinforcing of the main garrisons. Montreal is now home to the Household Brigade, consisting of the First and Second regiments of Life Guards, the Royal regiment of

Horse Guards and three regiments of Foot Guards—the Grenadiers, the Coldstream Guards and the Scots Fusiliers. They drill and peer over the border both anxiously and impatiently, and amuse themselves as best they can.

AMATEUR PRIVATE THEATRICALS,
At No. 9, Prince of Wales Terrace, Montreal.
Her Majesty's Servants will perform the *Comic Drama*, in 2 Acts,
by J. STERLING COYNE, Esq., entitled
THE SECRET AGENT!
Performances to Commence Precisely at Eight O'clock.

In Britain, there is wide support for the Confederacy, especially in commercial circles and among the intelligentsia. In Canada as well, to the extent that Jefferson Davis will be greeted as a hero when he visits Toronto almost immediately after getting out of prison once the war is over. Such a show of support for the South is not an endorsement of slavery, which was outlawed in Britain long ago, even longer ago in the Canadas. It is mostly a wish for a humbler and less menacing United States, which has not yet become the world's most powerful nation but is perceived as the most dangerous. The Empire isn't pro-slavery, it's anti-Union.

The Confederacy has set up a mission in Montreal, and the city instantly becomes a nest of Northern spies, freelances and mercenaries: interesting people. Because Britain does not recognize the Confederate States (no one does), this is not an official embassy but only a commission, run by a commissioner. There is a branch in Toronto and another in Halifax. At first, the primary business of these commissioners is the remote cultivation of the so-called Peace

Democrats and Copperheads. But the extent of true antiwar sentiment in the North is difficult to gauge and easy to misinterpret,
for the administration is always able to shut the mouths of opponents
simply by calling them unpatriotic. In any case, the commissioners
operate independently of one another, indeed are answerable to
different parts of the Confederate cabinet—War and State. Later
that Summer, too much later in fact, they switch to hatching plots:
plans to free Southern prisoners by force, plans to strike at Northern
civilians as Lincoln had struck at Southern ones, plans to have third
parties donate clothing infected with the yellow fever bacillus to
Union hospitals.

The Democratic Party will be convening in Chicago to choose its
candidate to run against Lincoln. Camp Douglas, nearby, houses
eight thousand Confederate prisoners. What if the eight thousand
could be freed, and armed? What if an uprising could be organized
in several American cities for the opening day of the convention? The
logistics are of course insurmountable and the very logic is wobbly,
as many of the poor prisoners are weak from sickness and malnutri-
tion. The conspirators fall to arguing but agree to postpone the plan
until the general election in November.

Having failed to win the support of Britain, the government in
Richmond—paradoxically, just like the one in Washington—aspires
at least to keep it neutral. Yet it hopes to open a sort of second front,
harassing the Union from Canada, a tricky proposition in several
ways, given the neutrality laws. Necessity triumphs over caution.
Richmond is so desperate that it sends a great deal of money it
cannot afford to spend, an enormous sum for the starving nation-
state that shrinks every day like a summer pond, to finance its
Canadian operations. The people in place there, however, can't agree
on who's in charge. The commissioner in Toronto, who before the
war represented Alabama in the United States Senate, operates from

the Queen's Hotel on the north side of Front Street between Bay and Yonge. He becomes involved in spreading rumors about a proposed peace conference to be held in Niagara Falls. The plan is to lure Lincoln into participating and then expose the event as a sham, thus making the odds against his reelection even longer. The invitation comes when Union losses are particularly appalling, and Lincoln knows he must pretend to be interested. Horace Greeley, the editor of the *New York Tribune*, acts as intermediary and general busybody. The commissioner sets himself up at the Clifton House, a hotel in Niagara Falls, and grants audiences to all sorts of strange characters from both sides of the border. Nothing happens.

As all this is playing out, the celebrated actor with the black hair, black moustaches, black piercing eyes and finely tailored black suits of clothes checks into the best hotel in Montreal, the St. Lawrence Hall on St. James Street. The Confederate commissioner lives and works there. Wilkes is counting on the fact that all comings and goings are observed by Union spies.

❧

The election and the end of the South's ability to fight are both getting close when the Toronto commissioner has another idea. There are three thousand Southern prisoners on Johnson's Island, near Sandusky on the Ohio side of Lake Erie, not far from Windsor and Detroit. A Southern spy has ingratiated himself with the crew of the Union gunboat that guards the prison camp. His mission is to disable or scuttle it. His colleagues hijack an American passenger steamer to help spirit the freed prisoners to the safety of Canada. Alas, the Southern spy, the same person charged with carrying out the yellow fever plan, is a double agent, and reports the Confederate plot to the American consul in Toronto. Finding themselves betrayed, the insurgents beach their pirated ship on Canadian soil and seek refuge. The United States demands they be extradited and Canada agrees, but Britain overrules the order.

Wilkes has been earning as much as thirty thousand a year as an actor. From this he has invested six in the petroleum boom that is sweeping Pennsylvania. Until just a few years ago, the substance was used primarily as a medicine, both human and veterinary. When ways were discovered of extracting it cheaply and then refining it, it was turned into kerosene, making whale-oil lamps a thing of the past. Many fortunes are being made as refineries get built (though within six or seven years all of them will be owned by one man, this young Rockefeller chap in Cleveland). Wilkes, however, actually loses money in oil. He either sells his shares in Dramatic Oil and Pithole Creek at a loss or signs them over to his family and friends, for he is putting his affairs in order.

Wilkes and many of his friends are Marylanders. Maryland is indeed the perfect location for them to be from, a bizarre world unto itself. There is no other place where people change sides with such alacrity or play both sides against the center with such ease. There is probably no other where the political divisions among members of the same family are starker or more fractious. Maryland has slaves, because Lincoln's Emancipation Proclamation applies only to the eleven Confederate states. Now, in October, Maryland's voters go to the polls to endorse or reject a new state constitution put forward by Lincolnite Republicans that would outlaw slavery there and bring the state into line. The Democrats work hard to defeat it and at first blush appear to have succeeded, albeit by a margin of a mere two thousand votes. For only the second time in American politics, however, absentee citizens are eligible to vote. In this case, the majority of absentee voters are Union soldiers. When their ballots are tallied, the new constitution is upheld by the skinniest of margins. The

Democrats cry foul. Lincoln's enemies add election rigging to their list of his heinous sins.

The Montreal that Wilkes visits for ten days or more can probably boast the world's densest concentration of spies, government detectives, informers and double-crossers. Many local businessmen see an incomparable opportunity to cash in on politics. This is especially the case with Montreal shipowners, who have a lucrative business carrying passengers who can enter the United States or set foot on a U.S. vessel only at the greatest possible peril. Canadian vessels can sail down the St. Lawrence and head south for St. George's in Bermuda or Nassau in the Bahama Islands. There the travelers connect with still other vessels, some of whose owners provide only the simplest documentation and whose loyalties, whenever any must be shown, are tailored snugly to fit the occasion.

Such men are distinct from actual blockade-runners, usually Americans, loyal either to the Struggle or to money, possibly both, who enter Southern ports by stealth and trickery. Some of their steamers, low and fast, are painted the color of slate. They await a night when the air currents are perfectly in their favor, with banks of fog drifting in and out. They burn especially carbonaceous coal so that a huge plume of black smoke forms above them. Then they close their dampers and allow the fog to carry the black cloud away, hoping Union gunboats will chase the smoke and not the ship, which slips into Charleston, let us say, under cover of poor visibility.

The work is obviously dangerous, and many of those who practice it are, just as obviously, untrustworthy. One of them, a Baltimore man now operating out of Montreal, is such a questionable fellow that the Confederacy keeps just as close a watch on him as its adversaries do. Wilkes befriends him, befriends his family, and entrusts him with his entire theatrical wardrobe—his bread and butter—which he has brought with him, no doubt as part of his cover, and now pays to have shipped back to Maryland by way of Nassau. The two men go to a Montreal bank, where Wilkes opens an account, trades gold for pound sterling, which he gives the man in payment for his service, and gets a draft for four hundred and fifty-five dollars, which he then takes back to the States himself.

While this is going on, the Montreal commissioner launches another scheme to disrupt the Union. He assembles a band of raiders, former prisoners of war who had escaped to Canada, to recross the border into Vermont and rob banks and set fires in the town of St. Albans. This time the Union feels the pain and reacts with boiling anger. The raiders make their way back to Canada but are pursued by U.S. authorities, who arrest fourteen of them on Canadian soil, where of course they have no authority to do so. An international incident ensues. The United States surrenders the men, grumpily, to Canadian officials, who try them for violating the neutrality laws. They are found not guilty on the grounds that they are foreign soldiers at war. Only the leader is treated more severely, but he is saved from the gallows by the brilliant legal work of John J.C. Abbott, a professor of law at McGill in Montreal. Thus propelled into public life, Abbott later becomes prime minister of Canada. By this time Wilkes, back in Washington, finds, at a livery stable, another conspirator, Davy Herold, a twenty-two-year-old pharmacist's assistant who, though quite a bit brighter than Atzerodt, is nonetheless distinguished by his lack of mental vitality.

A Confederate lieutenant and a group of his men set out to snatch the governor of Maryland but scrap the plot at the eleventh hour; as they flee southward, the mastermind is killed by locals during a robbery. Such kidnapping schemes are not uncommon, and some talk goes far beyond mere abduction. The newspapers in Richmond speculate openly about how Lincoln might be assassinated. General Lee keeps vetoing the crazy schemes that people put to him. Meanwhile,

Wilkes continues to make a point of being seen with people he knows are being closely observed, so that word of his movements will be noted in reports sent to Washington. In this way he reinforces the supposition that he has Confederate credentials. But in a world of double agents and others who are not always (perhaps "not often") what they appear to be, he comes to the attention of Richmond as well. Wilkes is famous and he certainly *looks* as though he is well funded, and so Lewis Powell is sent to insinuate himself into the conspiracy, or whatever it is.

Powell, who now calls himself Lewis Payne (or sometimes Paine), is a professional, trained to be clever, and his cleverness, like other people's, is often ruthless. He has been a soldier and was wounded at Gettysburg. He has been a prisoner of war. He can talk his way out of most messes and fight his way out of the others. His best trick was the time he escaped custody after getting a prison nurse to fall in love with him. He knows how to do such things. He knows equally well how to kill someone by quietly wringing his neck as he would a chicken's.

The raid across the Canadian border into Vermont is the only Confederate operation planned in Canada that has come close to succeeding. Wilkes has low regard for the Southern operatives up in Montreal but knows that giving voice to such a view is dangerous to one's congeniality. The commissioners, after all, are representatives of his country's government, a legitimate constitutional authority born of necessity. People will be more likely to join him in his mission if they believe that Richmond is winking at him approvingly or even paying him for his efforts.

Wilkes's sister Asia and her husband have moved to Philadelphia. He stops by on his way back to the District after one of his mysterious visits to New York and carries on predictably. He paces as he fumes, perhaps the natural extension of his violent emotion, perhaps the residue of his long training on the stage. He tells his sister that Lincoln is no less tyrannical than Napoleon and "is overturning the republic and making himself king": a common theme of his talk. He sputters on about how Lincoln, the simple country lawyer and man of the people, accepted a fortune as his fee for getting the Illinois Central Rail Road out of paying its taxes.

Asia knows that her brother becomes angry when he is depressed, and she is glad that he feels he can purge himself of fury in her calming presence. She believes that this is how she can be of value to him, and hopes he is saving his rage for when he can calumniate in her front parlor, banging into the furniture, going wherever emotion takes him, not tossing it about recklessly in public. Secretly, for he is a man of secrets, he feels the same way, but cannot always prevent certain surges of impulse from overpowering him. Because of the difference in gender, and also despite it, they share a bond he does not enjoy with his other siblings, a couple of whom, particularly Edwin, he has come to despise.

That he is not in Edwin's presence on the day of the national election is undoubtedly for the best, for that is when the well-nigh impossible comes to pass. When Grant unclogs the Mississippi and then moves east, the Confederacy finds itself truly surrounded. But then Grant gets bogged down in the long siege of Petersburg, near Richmond, just as the butcher General William Tecumseh Sherman is himself brought to a halt outside Atlanta. Voters in the North know of course that the South is losing day by day, though they are more concerned with the fact that the North is not exactly winning, as enormous armies sit on their haunches, conspicuously stalemated. The Democrat, George McClellan, who has war credentials and, to many, including himself, the status of a neglected hero, is anticipating a new life in the Executive Mansion. But then, in September, Sherman breaks through to the center and soul of Atlanta. This is the city where all the railroads converge, pumping blood into a Confederacy that is still alive somehow, miraculously so, however limited its time on Earth. He destroys the city more thoroughly than any city has ever been destroyed before. He does so just in time for Lincoln to nab fifty-five percent of the popular vote, the first president since Andrew Jackson to win a second term: the greatest last-minute comeback in the history (and perhaps the future) of American politics. As in all such miracles, the winner's enemies charge fraud. This time eleven of the thirty-five states allow absent citizens to exercise the franchise, and the troops in blue cast their votes for the boss. Wherever he is when he reads the results, Wilkes gasps with barely suppressed violence until green and yellow bile seems to run from his nostrils and the corners of his mouth, dripping onto the costly carpets.

Maryland. What a place. The Baltimore oriole is the state bird, the white oak is the state tree, and Wilkes's distemper is the state personality. It is a place that takes politics personally. In one obviously Democratic county, the only known Republican has been lynched. Curiously, this does not deter Republicans from multiplying exponentially. In the southern reaches of the state, rivers are outlined by swamps and low-hanging vegetation. Virginia is just a spit away. A paradise for smugglers, political as well as commercial, despite the efforts of one Lafayette Baker, a self-inflated runner of spies who has slowly taken control of the Union secret service from Allan Pinkerton and is vowing to root out the evil-doers from whatever swamps they have hidden in.

Pretending to be interested in investing in local real estate, the perfect cover for all otherwise unacceptable forms of curiosity, Wilkes goes down to the riverine boundary with Virginia, then to Philadelphia once again, where he entrusts Asia with a sealed packet of documents, watching her as she locks it in her husband's iron safe. Wilkes is not fond of his brother-in-law, largely for the same reason he is also not fond of Edwin: they are Union men. Another brother, Joseph, is of the opposite inclination. As for Junius, the eldest, named after their late and sainted father the famous tragedian, no one is sure, not even Junius himself. Their mother is frightened of the discord, which is making her ill. The children and in-laws must avoid discussing the news or politics when she is present. All the more remarkable then that Wilkes and Edwin, who oftentimes have difficulty speaking to each other in private, agree to do so onstage. There will be a performance of *Julius Caesar* at the Winter Garden on Broadway in New York, a benefit to raise money for a bronze bust of Shakespeare to be installed in Central Park. Wilkes, clean-shaven for the occasion, portrays Marc Antony. Edwin plays Brutus. In retrospect, it should have been the other way round. Mother sits in the audience. At one point incipient panic runs through the house on the rumor that the theater is on fire. In fact, it is the hotel next door that is the target of arsonists. It is one of a dozen structures, including P.T. Barnum's museum of freaks and curiosities, that Confederate agents from Canada have tried to set ablaze. To that end they have employed Greek fire that a local chemist has concocted for them using phosphorous and paint thinner. He has, however, cheated them by utilizing inferior materials and pocketing the difference in price to maximize his profit. Wilkes is disgusted when he learns of the bungled exercise in official pyromania. He wonders whether he is the only competent person other than General Lee trying to bring the United States government to its knees.

⁂

He feels pretty good about bringing people like Dave Herold into the kidnapping plot. He makes bold enough while on another visit to New York, and again a little while later, to approach a former acting colleague, Sam Chester, first talking in loaded generalities, then subtle hints, finally in veiled blatancies. Chester is used to reading texts for their concealed meanings and deflects the silent demands for a response. When Wilkes continues to feel him out at other meetings obviously contrived for this purpose, Chester finally expresses his horror at what his friend is suggesting. Wilkes reacts as though he has been wounded in battle. He has to be careful, more careful now than ever, more careful every day, yet he finds he can work things out only by resort to pencil and paper.

"There will be many in this enterprise," he writes in a memorandum to himself. "In the end I am unsure what the number will be. Dozens will be necessary, even scores, I have no doubt. I shall recruit as the need arises and opportunity allows, but I must not lose sight of the fact that this is a conspiracy of one, by myself, and therein the danger, for there is none who can measure a mind-storm such as that which has caused me to assume incorrectly that my old acquaintance of the boards has the intellect to see the solution to the problems that command the urgent attention of us all."

The mind-storms that sometimes overtake him, often seeming to come from nowhere, always trouble him after the fact but are invigorating at the time. They speed the mechanisms of the brain. He sees with perfect clearness and celerity the actions that are necessary and their consequences. Sometimes, when the condition has swept up and obliterated the predictable thinking of the workaday world, he finds *all* of his senses grow instantly sharper and his faculties enlarge. Once, at Asia's, he looked across the parlor and suddenly saw the spines of all the books in intaglio relief, as though they had been carved out of stone like inscriptions on classical monuments, but colored brightly. He has come to cherish these moments of transcendence. (Is there another word? He doubts that there can be.) They provide him with enormous advantages in making decisions, though other powers are oftentimes demanded to clean up the unintended minor consequences. This is his advantage over others. Anyone can acquire simple information, even secret information. The ability to analyze it both before and afterward is given to few. Its absence is notably apparent in, for example, the dullards assigned to Canada.

He keeps appearing in rural Maryland. Still using the pretense of wishing to invest his oil profits in farmland, he continues to scout all possible routes by which Lincoln might be transported to Richmond through the enemy's lines. A local doctor who might have property for sale is kind enough to introduce him to another such person, Samuel Mudd MD, whose place the actor later visits. The bottom has fallen out of farm property in Maryland because of the devastating ban on slavery in the new constitution. The doctor and the visitor discuss this. Wilkes raises some questions about easy places to get across the river into Virginia unseen. He is a professional actor, after all. He knows how to use his voice to project innocence or whatever other state or emotion he wishes, regardless of the lines in the script. He is, however, unsure of his audience this time. He doesn't know whether his own voice is too subtle for Doctor Mudd's ears. He is in the market for a horse as well. Mudd recommends a neighbor with an animal for sale. Wilkes makes the purchase.

You can't deny it: Wilkes does have a thespian's knowledge of how to plumb the meaning of daily life, with all its comedies, dramas and curtain-raisers. He lingers in the area, making the acquaintance of a Lincoln-hating local who is expert at getting people into Virginia without being seen, using his intricate knowledge of the smallest marshes and waterways. Within hours, Wilkes takes the man aside and confides his intentions. Like Chester, the fellow is alarmed. "Why," Wilkes writes in his notes, "have the beautiful mind-storms begun to betray me so? I do not understand. Do I misjudge others or do they wish to betray me from their ignorance of the importance of what must be done?" Shortly, however, he brings the man around. Even so, that night he burns the notes to himself. He must do so every night, he tells himself. However circumspect I am, he says silently, I cannot allow myself to be caught with notes more than a few hours old, if indeed with any whatsoever.

He collects equine accomplices as well as human ones. Back in the District, he asks Sam Arnold to acquire a horse and gig while he himself asks people at John Ford's theater, where he often gets his mail, to recommend a boarding stable. The theater's carpenter suggests one in Baptist Alley, which runs right behind the building.

✻

Wilkes's acquaintance John Surratt is a slender young man with the serious, ethereal and most of all bloodless look of the divinity student he recently was and would like to be again were he not intent on becoming a spy instead. When his father died in Sixty-two, he had to abandon his studies and go to work tending the tavern and hotel (it is also the post office) that the family owns in Surrattsville and for most purposes *is* Surrattsville, ten miles below the District, on Maryland soil. All the residents nearby knew Surratt senior. Now all of them know the junior one.

Surratt looks even younger than his twenty years, but Wilkes knows full well that there is more to him than meets the eye. He knows that the Surrattsville tavern is a safe house for Confederate couriers passing north or south, and for who knows what other skulduggery. The information is so common that the authorities in Washington have sacked Surratt as the village's part-time postmaster upon hearing of his politically unsavory longings. Wilkes and Surratt have not been in touch of late, but then Fortune and necessity reunite them. Two days before Christmas, Surratt meets Wilkes in

Washington, where they then run into Doctor Mudd, who has come into the city for last-minute shopping. With Surratt is another young man, a former classmate who now boards at 541 H Street, the house that Surratt's mother inherited and has turned into a rooming house. As Missus Surratt knows so well, Washington is a city with too few beds. It is also one with strange bedfellows. The boarder with Surratt is Louis Weichmann, who is wearing blue trousers with a stripe on the legs. They are part of his uniform as a member of an infantry unit made up of War Department employees. Weichmann used to work there for the general in charge of feeding Confederate prisoners. Wilkes does what he does so well and invites everybody to join him for a drink. Surratt, Mudd and Weichmann end up in Booth's room at the National.

The next day, Wilkes dashes to New York again in the grip of another mind-storm. Confronting Sam Chester once more, he tells him bluntly of the plot against Lincoln, tells him that he must take part or be blackmailed, or even risk being shot with a small but heavy-caliber pistol that Wilkes says he has taken to carrying for just such occasions. Chester naturally thinks Wilkes has gone mad.

Running now with all engines burning, Wilkes returns to the District by way of Philly. There he pays two calls, the first on his sister, the other on a theatrical manager he has known for years. He gives Asia another packet to put in the safe: evidence incriminating Chester in the plot. Such tactics are an essential element of his plan, for evidence of someone's association with Wilkes's efforts, however flimsy the claim, will, under the rules in use at the time, preclude that person from testifying for the prosecution. From the theatrical manager he begs a favor: persuade John Ford to hire Sam Chester for his stock company in the capital. He suggests to Surratt, a good patriot, that he follow his own example and sign over all his property to others so that it cannot be confiscated by the federal government should matters go awry.

March 1865. Family troubles and publishing details back in New York will soon truncate Walt's brief return to the District, but while he is here, he must not forsake the spectacle. The crowd is certainly the largest he and the others have ever seen. Certainly it is the thickest, the most dense. How many thousands? The newspapers' estimate is fifty, all jostling one another, waiting for the president to leave the Senate chamber of the Capitol, where he has renewed his vows, and come outside onto the giant east portico to speak to them. There are a few hundred Negroes in the throng below, and many thousands, perhaps tens of thousands, of white men in blue uniforms. It is shortly after noon on a cold day, Saturday the fourth, and it is raining. An uncountable number of hats, of every type and variety, seem to bob atop the mob like blossoms tossed upon the ocean. The dome of the great white building has finally been completed and seems all the more impressive against the endless and dispirited gray sky.

The president is delayed at the Executive Mansion by last-minute paperwork and arrives at his inauguration just as the new vice president, Andrew Johnson, is addressing the assembled dignitaries prior to his own swearing-in. The vice president is Southern-born, a tailor from Tennessee who has been taught to read and write by his wife, and at the moment he is as drunk as a monkey in a monkey-tree. He gives an incoherent speech that embarrasses all who listen. As **Lincoln** leaves the chamber to step outside and deliver his own **oration,** the soldiers who have protected him on his journey down Pennsylvania Avenue are superseded by the Capitol police. Along the way, these officers must subdue a "bibulous lunatic," as they later describe him, who breaks free of the crowd and makes for the president with fairly obvious intentions.

The president's remarks have already been set into type and copies printed for distribution to the press. He has cut up the galley proofs with scissors and pasted them in two columns on a sheet of stiff paper. Even without his ludicrous hat, he still towers above the others on the platform, but is towered over in turn by the enormous fluted columns in the Corinthian order that are lined up behind him like marble bodyguards. His voice is high-pitched and somewhat squeaky, a fact that always surprises people hearing him for the first time and expecting more sonorous and dignified sounds. But this afternoon few in the crowd spread out below like the mightiest of his armies can in fact hear Lincoln at all. Instead, the acoustical conditions carry the sound upward, where a tangled knot of important onlookers strains behind a wrought iron railing. As the president begins to talk, the sky suddenly clears and sunshine strikes the crowd in a wide beam. This causes Walt, unseen somewhere in the colorless multitude down below, to widen his eyes in an almost mystical awe, while Wilkes, who stands above the president and to his left, surprisingly close to the action, rolls his own eyes in disgust. The man everyone has come to hear is only a few yards from the dignitaries' perch where Wilkes and his friend Pete stand with Lucy Hale and her father, thanks to the senator's skill at scaring up two more of the much-coveted tickets. Pete looks uncomfortable.

The speech is so short that thousands of people are still arriving as the president concludes it. Wilkes, however, is positioned to hear every word. The president speaks of the war as a divine punishment meted out to a society that allowed the continued existence of slavery for so long. He belabors the point about God's rôle in the nation's affairs. Then he changes tone and is conciliatory: "With malice toward none; with charity for all . . ."

Wilkes knows that at the previous inauguration, four years earlier, there were Yankee sharpshooters on the roof of the enormous alabaster building. He presumes they are there this time as well, and when he turns around and looks straight up, he sees that the top-floor windows are, rather pointedly, wide open.

The crowd is dissolving now. Booth says good-bye to Lucy and her father, who is dragging her away to prepare for another official function. Booth doesn't speak for some time thereafter. When he does, he addresses his overwhelmed and bewildered companion in a sad but exultant whisper. "I could have gotten him," he says. With that, he takes Pete the Great's left hand and places it lightly on the right-hand pocket of his expensively tailored coat so that the younger man can feel the pistol.

✦ NINE ✦

MANY IN THE DISTRICT are drinking champagne on the evening of the inauguration. This fact gives Lucy an opportunity to tease Wilkes about why he is not doing the same. She is perhaps the only person who can tease him without risk of repercussions. In any event, he drinks copious amounts of brandy instead. They are in his room at the National, downstairs from the suite she shares with her father. Wilkes is quietly livid as well as morose, muttering into his glass—obscure oaths and what must be lines from old plays. She understands his first emotion. She understands the second as well, for she shares it.

"He has done this to destroy us by dragging you away," Wilkes says. The accusation has been building for a while. The man whom he likes to call "the human baboon" and other things has nominated her father to be ambassador to Spain. Now, in the light of the reelection, the appointment is certain to go through without opposition or complaint.

"Why must you serve your father and play the hostess?" he demands once again. "There is nothing more absurd than the spectacle that is in my mind of you curtseying to a papist court and wasting your charm on fat old men from whom your father seeks compliance with the Baboon's wishes."

She is especially patient, as she knows to be when Wilkes is drinking heavily. "You understand, dear one, that the situation could be different only if Mother were alive."

Wilkes nods in recognition at a well-worn explanation, but this time adds a refinement of his own. "Why could he not ask his mistress to bear the burden, as an honest man might do?"

Knowing not to accept the provocation, she laughs instead: the laugh that she understands without being told can change his mood sometimes. She ices it with her impression of a young Southern lady of high degree and great hypocrisy. "Why, suh, you dishonor me with such a suggestion, for that is no way to speak to a Georgia maiden."

He looks up from his glass. There are black demi-lunes under his eyes and his lovely thick curly hair is mussed. But his voice smiles even if his mouth does not. "My darling, the stage is poorer for your decision to avoid its unhealthy air and its immoral suasion of the innocent and instead to pursue your fortune as a Yankee senator's daughter."

Then they are silent for a moment. They have stopped play-acting now.

"Wilkes, I don't know how I can persist without you. Not knowing exactly how long before I will see you again is another impossible burden to be lain atop the first."

"Four years, I should think," he answers. He sounds matter-of-fact. "That is, presuming that the Beast and his litter can be defeated after that length of time. Some are optimistic, others not; but no one knows for a certainty. Everything is so much conjecture now. Of course, an act of God could alter the course. Or indeed, an act of Man." He mentions "four years" not to dampen her hopes but to bolster them. He has confided his plans to the men necessary to help him carry them out, men who in any event he does not care about, but he has never intimated more than the subtlest indication of his thinking to Lucy. Because he loves her? because she is a woman?

because she might tip her hand to her father if she knew the secret? He is in no state to dabble in the mathematics of the emotions.

She looks into those black eyes, like the cinder-eyes on the snow effigies that playful children make each winter back in New Hampshire. She always has been the careful coquette, the rounded intelligence that smooths the edges of his own more angular presence. But now she draws her words from a deeper source.

"Wilkes," she says, "I would love you no less were I a man and you a woman. It would change nothing."

He seems slightly taken aback, but for only a second. Recovering his stage presence, he asks, "And if we were of one gender between us?"

She says nothing.

From his left-hand breast pocket he withdraws his billfold, lays it on the table and begins to remove its contents one at a time, as though to itemize them. There are several calling cards given him in New York and Montreal. These he must remember to burn. There is a generous but not ostentatious sheaf of banknotes, including two or three of the Confederate States with portraits of Jefferson Davis or Judah P. Benjamin. They suffer from the most casual comparison with the Yankee currency by the poverty of their engraving and printing. The South long ago ran short even of paper. He has seen notes printed on the verso of old wallpaper of a rather parlor-y design. There is also a note from one of the Montreal banks, and a variety of postage stamps.

A flap comes down to reveal a special pocket from which he extracts six photographs. He puts them on the table linen face down, then flips them over one at a time as though he were playing vingt-et-un.

The first three are the cartes-de-visite of young ladies she has never lain eyes on before. None of them is what you could call plain, though several are prim or aspire to give that impression. The photographs are well thumbed.

The dealer then flips over the fourth photo and then the fifth. More of the same, but all different. These last ones are not simply photographs of young women with straight mouths but of young women showing the viewer how they are having their likenesses made in some photographic gallery (the District is full of such establishments now).

The final image he leaves cupped in his hand for another moment before revealing it with a flourish. It is, as expected, the image of herself that she has given him to carry on his travels. Now, she knows, it will have to support him during her own long absence.

"In my profession, I'm sure you know, it is easy for people to confound the character they see on the stage with the man behind the mask. They find it easy to be attracted to the one and mistake him for the other."

"I myself, in the first instance . . ." She trails off rather than interrupt.

"Sometimes young ladies one meets in social company will present one with such things." He taps his right ring finger on the image of the lovely Lucy. "This is the only one that I carry next to my heart."

His speech has lost its slur. The drink has not affected him to the usual extent. He has stopped drinking at the moment of maximum clarity. But he knows that this will not prevent the headache.

⁂

Anne and I were married on the twenty-eighth of May Ninety-one, a Thursday. Our friends took our motivations as being obvious to all, but the actual decision to make the abstraction real—that came upon us suddenly, like the most benevolent Summer storm you could possibly imagine.

Our first thought was that the ceremony should be conducted, as Father so enthusiastically wished it to be, at the Traubel family home (as none of us thought that the Montgomerie one would be so welcoming). This plan changed, however, when it became clear that W would be unable to attend. His numerous ailments—the word is hardly satisfactory—which previously attacked him in an orderly sequence, a few each day or each week, had now joined forces and were massed on the border. Every part of him seemed to be afflicted. He said, as he did quite often by this point, that he feared most for the condition of his heart, which he always called his "pump," though the list on which it appeared was a long one indeed.

About six weeks before the wedding, he took one of his by then infrequent voyages in the wheeling-chair. Less than a year had gone by since a carriage ride down to Haddonfield from which he had returned overtaxed but also, so it seemed to me, exhilarated. This says nothing of the bad fall when his left leg gave way under him, a reminder of the paralysis he had now been struggling against, somewhat discontinuously but only somewhat, for the better part of two decades. And all his problems of digestion and disposal were worse than ever. What's more, his respiration was seriously impaired. I remember seeing him napping one time and noticing that the thin blanket that covered him scarcely rose and fell at all, so insubstantial was his breathing. He took measures to preserve his eyesight, which declined on a sporadic basis, as did his hearing; but he could not accommodate himself to a pair of new spectacles—or the pair after that. He complained of headaches and of heightened sensitivity to sound, especially the voices of visitors with whom he was not on terms of intimacy.

The Great War in Europe has brought us a fiercely strong central government but one completely devoid of any of Socialist impulse or influence whatever. One, on the contrary, that is more bellicose, more immoral toward its own people and less democratic than any since the one whose horrors were the making—I mean the perfecting—of W's welcoming heart. In size alone its bureaucracy terrorizes, quite apart from policies of materialism and fear that it enforces on behalf of this administration.

It is almost impossible for people to-day to comprehend how much smaller the country obviously was during W's own war—smaller in everything except its armies. Lincoln's Executive Mansion, for example, employed only two secretaries, as they were known: all-purpose civil servants who crossed all departmental and public lines in supporting the president and made certain that everything ran smoothly. John Nicolay was one of them. The other was W's budding friend, young John Hay. They both ended their careers as ambassadors and such.

These men, who had worked for Lincoln back in Illinois and were with him for hour after hour every day at the Mansion until late at night, became his joint biographers. Astoundingly, they produced a life of Lincoln in ten volumes; and I am doubtless one of the few living—barely living—authors who can appreciate an effort so Herculean. The difference is that mine is the story of a great artist and philosopher of democracy and theirs that of the martyred president whose horrible death within days of his ultimate victory made his story as indelible to my countrymen as that of Adam and Eve or Jonah and the Whale. My own books stalled for want of broad interest on the part of both the public and the publishers while theirs became an almost peerless totem in patriotic parlors across America. I never read the entirety of it, but I well recall plowing through some of the volumes as they materialized and discussing my response

with W. After all, he was the friend of one of the book's collabora-
tors and the close observer and loving admirer of its subject.

I had skipped ahead to the assassination, and told W that I considered that part of the work a neglected opportunity.

He agreed. "Yes, it is absolutely without the vivid touches that
belong to the event. Hay ought to have been excused from the writing
of it at all if he could do no better than that. Besides, as you say, it
lacks entirely in perspective and is far too partisan to boot."

I said that the authors could not concede that Booth, however
misguided and however criminal, was obviously driven by more
than scoundrelism and derangement. I may have appropriated the
comment from Bucke, but I'm not certain. If I did commit a plagiary,
I apologize now to the Doctor's shade—or would you prefer I say
his spirit?

"You hit another nail on the head there!" W's ready endorsement
of my observation surprised me a little. "The authors are not in the
least Greek or Homeric. Old Homer, as long ago as that, had the
good sense to make Hector a great man, to fill him out, make him
expansive—indeed, so remarkably so as to incline some to demur. But
it was a true instinct, as necessary at this time as at that one. I think
I see through this *Life* of Lincoln a tendency to blackguard the
South and the Southern."

This was a literary way of addressing the problem. But I knew he
also spoke from his civilian heart. He looked at me intensely—at me
or through me. "This meanness of spirit against old adversaries
ought to be altogether gone by this late date."

Here was my dilemma encapsulated in a few brief sentences. W
often spoke of "Booth" and on a number of occasions wrote of him.
In the great majority of such instances, however, he was referring to
Edwin, the great interpreter of Shakespeare's tragedies. Otherwise,
when alluding to "Booth" he meant either the assassin's other

brother, Junius Brutus Booth the Younger, a much lesser figure in the acting profession, or the patriarch in both the familial and the theatrical senses, the original Junius Brutus. He had come from England when W was only a small boy. I am told that he was truly a madman if any of them was (though not dangerous).

Of W's familiarity with the work of the future murderer I knew nothing, but supposed that W must have watched him somewhere, sometime, and so further supposed there was nothing of the experience he wished to communicate or remember. Years later a cutting from a long-ago New York daily turned up in one of the hogsheads of papers we gathered up after his death: a critique he had written of the actor's interpretation of *Richard III*. That play is said to have been the actor's favorite of Shakespeare's works and was most certainly W's as well. W's almost proprietary feeling for it may help explain—who can know?—his uncharacteristic dismissal of the performance. He wrote that Booth's Richard "is about as much like his father's as the wax bust of Henry Clay"—you may not know the reference, Flora: Clay was a Southern senator and perennial candidate for the presidency—"in the window down near Howard-street, a few blocks below the theater, is like the genuine orator in the Capitol when his best electricity was flashing alive in him and out of him." The piece dates to Sixty-two. I found it crumpled together with one taken from *La Revue Européenne*, evidently a Parisian paper of the period. Its title was "Walt Whitman, poète et 'rowdy'"—which even W could have translated with precision.

His standard lecture on Lincoln, especially popular on each year's anniversary of the cataclysm at Ford's, was like a miniature annuity for him, the way a sentimental Christmas story, reprinted every year for a few fresh dollars, might be for a very different kind of writer. When *performing* had become difficult for him, he would read it from notes as he sat in a simple chair at the center of the stage. The effect was especially powerful, because he was alone on a nude stage as Booth had been and occupied the type of chair that old-time theaters such as Ford's arranged in concentric circles and screwed into the floorboards. The fact that W was obviously not a professional actor, nor even, numerous others have opined, a very good reader of his own work before an audience, only added more to the entertainment's evident sincerity, I have been told. He did not imply that he had personally witnessed the assassination, a difficult thing to have achieved as he was up in New York at the time, but he did allow people to infer that he had seen it happen if they were so disposed toward that brand of credulity. In actual fact, as I once heard from his own lips in what he hoped I would take as a casual aside, he had drawn much of the detail from a particular friend of his. The friend, he told me later, was Pete Doyle. He confided this because he knew I already had come to that conclusion.

❧

Nobody, perhaps not even Wilkes himself, understands what his plan actually is.

To O'Laughlen and Arnold, he is unstable and often exasperating but unswervingly loyal to the Struggle whose death rattle he, they and everyone else can hear growing louder by the hour.

To Surratt, who also goes by such names as Harrison and Armstrong, among others, Wilkes is a person much like himself, though a more perfect representative of their rare type. The others are plodders, but we are plotters, he says to himself. That Richmond has never rewarded us properly for our cunning, intelligence and bravery speaks ill of those in charge there and their entire conduct of the Struggle these past four years.

Payne, the name under which they know Powell, who as the situation requires also carries on business as Wood, Kensler or Hall, is more difficult to gauge. He is tall, broad-shouldered and square-jawed, like an heroic statue slightly larger than life, and, like any statue, he keeps mute. The way he says little about himself or anything else creates the impression that he knows a great deal, as indeed, Wilkes believes, must be the case. The cliché about keeping one's cards close to one's vest does not apply to Payne. He has memorized the entire deck. The information is safe inside his brain, to which he alone has the combination.

As for Herold, people have been telling him his entire life that he is slow-witted. He can't rule out the possibility that they are right, but isn't really sure. Certainly his is not a lively imagination. He first goes by the name Smith. Wilkes suggests he try harder, but that's the best he can come up with, so he is assigned a name: Mister Boyd. Whatever his limitations, though, he is more prepossessing than Atzerodt, who rechristens himself Azworth. When told that this is too similar to his actual name, he panics. Eventually he alights on Atwood, a name he recalls hearing somewhere. Maybe someone of that name came in wanting a carriage repainted, a wheel greased or an axle replaced. He can't remember.

Mister Atwood is one of those people who appears as though he has tuberculosis when he doesn't and looks at a distance as though he must smell bad, which at close quarters he actually does. The uninitiated can't really tell if he's been drinking or not because he acts slightly drunk even when sober. He can't help it. But his colleagues know that when he has in fact been bending an elbow, his speech sounds slightly German in a way that it does not otherwise. He's never quite clean-shaven and never quite bewhiskered, but perpetually looks as though he hasn't been near a razor in several days and hasn't been to sleep either.

Herold knows Wilkes is not just rich but famous. That's what everybody understands. That's what people say. He is proud to be acquainted with such a figure. When he is with Wilkes, he is with an important personage and wonders what it would be like to be his uncommon friend. Yet Atzerodt harbors no such illusions, has no capacity for speculation. Wilkes generally treats him no better than he would a mongrel dog foraging in the street, yet also gives him small sums of money from time to time. Wilkes is a moody man. When he is moody onstage, he is taken to be an artist. When he is moody at other times, he can frighten even those who know him best.

Most of these people, and there are many others—dozens or maybe scores, in more minor roles, whose names, real or made up, will never be known—are prevented from meeting one another unless and until such becomes absolutely necessary. That is essential in such an operation. The trick is that they be kept on a string of just the right length, like Irish Pete, knowing in advance what their job will be, perhaps, but not how it fits into the big plan.

Yet they are members of a gang, or a company of players, in a way that none of them quite realizes. Wilkes is busy all the time, running between cities, meeting people, reconfiguring his plot as the texture of events changes. One of his activities is buying horses, trading horses or getting others to do so for him, then stabling them at various establishments. Aside from himself, so resplendently handsome, and Payne, a virtual giant (much like the Baboon), and of course Atzerodt the troll—aside from such examples as these, the generality of men tend to look alike, but every horse is different. Wilkes is now the owner of a small and high-spirited bay mare, blind in one eye, with a mane as shiny and black as his own and a perfect white star on her forehead. No one ever forgets such an animal. No one remembers the rider. Let me see, Constable, I should say he was a man of average height and physique and oh yes, one other thing: his clothes were either black or brown, and he may not have been wearing a hat when I saw him.

Wilkes's various horses pass through the hands of many members of his group, with several of whom, including Pete, he has found reason to exchange notes. They are not exactly please-come-to-tea-on-Tuesday notes, but they appear equally innocuous in their rightful context. Later, however, much could be read into the very fact of their existence. Wilkes knows full well that blackmail is the surest form of insurance, and moreover that the most effective means of eliminating potential turncoats is to blackmail them without their being aware of it at the time.

Ten days have gone by since the ceremony on the Capitol steps, and Wilkes invites Surratt, along with one of Missus Surratt's female boarders and the woman's young daughter, to accompany him to Ford's Theatre. Payne goes with them. The play is English, *The Tragedy of Jane Shore*, an early eighteenth-century piece written, so its author believed, somewhat in emulation of Shakespeare. It is best enjoyed from the upper box that hangs over stage left: a big treat for mother and child. They enjoy the experience immensely for its story and its costumes respectively. Wilkes and Surratt keep stealing all-consuming glances at the entrances and exits, each taking measurements in his mind. Payne, however, while alert to everything around him, betrays no reaction whatsoever.

The evening ends with the men alone, contemplating where they might go to drink. The logical places are the competing establishments that stand on either side of Ford's and are dwarfed by it—the Star and the Greenback. But they go to a restaurant, not a saloon. Wilkes has stocked a private dining room there with liquor, oysters and cigars. Arnold and O'Laughlen arrive soon afterward and are surprised to find others present. They drink until most of the staff have gone home for the night, leaving only a watchman to lock up. Then Wilkes finally lays out all the details of his carefully revised scheme. Wilkes, Arnold and Atzerodt will overpower the president, handcuff him and lower him to the stage, where Payne will be waiting to help whisk the parcel out the stage door and into the night, with Surratt and Herold meeting up with the others well outside the city.

Everyone has questions about this great unacted drama, and Wilkes answers them with athletic contortions of language and logic. The session goes on until five in the morning. Later in the week, most of the principals will meet, without Wilkes, at Missus Surratt's, where Payne and Surratt have been gathering weapons and other tools of the trade. The landlady, who seems to most people to be a pious widow-woman whose entire life had been her family and her Church, has been keeping her rooms fully rented. Some boarders, such as Louis Weichmann, who is too nosy for the others' taste, live there permanently. Others come and go. One of them, for example, is a mysterious woman who speaks French and is never seen, even indoors, without her face veiled. She has no part in the meeting. The following day, however, she leaves the District for Montreal.

❧

W's conversation had always meandered. *Loafed* he might have said in earlier times, for this was among his favorite words before the war. I consult my notes—I fear they will forever remain mere notes—for July of Ninety-one. It seems I paid my call a bit earlier than usual, at five-fifty. As per custom, W first asked after my own health and doings before kindly filling me in about his own. He was terribly polite and cordial (quite different things). He did not complain as much as I may have suggested elsewhere by my inadvertent reliance on quotations that often sound like so much bellyaching. It was a case, rather, of his always having much to report, and so much of it being bad news that he usually expressed himself with reportorial dispassion, though not on the altogether random day I have chosen to examine now.

Speaking of his breathing in particular but with a more general tone as well, W said, "I have had a couple of bad days. Yesterday especially. Horrible. Wretched. And to-day bad enough too. I do not seem to amount to much anyway."

I remember that the last statement was made without any attempt to woo pity, though this is not apparent when the same words are set to paper without accompaniment.

Flora, this is why you are my perfect reader: you understand and do not judge. I assume this is true even of the fact that as regards spiritualism W was probably something more of an agnostic and somewhat less than an atheist. My enormous respect for you and the work of your Toronto group contains much praise for your loyalty. I sense that W would have had to commit worse misdeeds than we could possibly imagine, including perhaps the deliberate destruction of as many young lives as he instead saved during the war, for you loyal Canadians even to raise an eyebrow in reproach.

If the two of you had met, I daresay he would perhaps have come, under your guidance, to the same opinion as yourself. Although there are few significant female players in the drama of his life beyond Anne and his sainted mother, and to a lesser extent his sisters Hannah and Mary, this is only to say that he gave first honors to what he considered manliness, to camaraderie, and to the more deeply felt but less well articulated and so much misunderstood quality of adhesiveness. I don't even mean to say that women of the second magnitude of importance in his mostly masculine orbit, such as Missus Davis, necessarily felt they were denied his sympathetic attention. Yet none of them, at least not in his final years, came nearer his heart than did Anne, who in fact seemed almost to colonize it. The statement is the product of my close observation over a long period and not merely an expression of a husband's pride. I made precise notes of what passed between them in my hearing. In one of these memoranda he spoke of the roses in her cheeks and "the fresh air sent flowing" by her arrival. When she and I called at Mickle Street together, she would sometimes wait downstairs in the parlor when it appeared he might wish a private moment with me or might require my assistance finding a comfortable position. But he would always, regardless, summon her as soon as possible. "Bring her up!" he would say. "Bring her up!" As we made ready to leave, he would kiss her on the mouth.

On the day that I am calling to mind now, W and I chatted about Bucke, a constant subject at these times we had together, and then somehow got onto the topic of an especially unpleasant landlord of W's acquaintance, long dead by the year in question. I was writing so quickly then, much more so than I am able to do nowadays, though I am composing this manuscript for you at the limit of my boilers (another of W's expressions that suddenly comes to mind, a phrase I presume he picked up from the transportation-men). The landlord was a man named Quinn. "He was a mean Irishman," W said. "I do not intend by that to reflect on Irishmen in general, or to say that Irishmen are mean, but rather to indicate that Irishmen are so rarely mean that when you meet one of the real stripe, he seems to make up for all the rest."

The path leading away from this unanticipatedly diplomatic utterance took us somehow to architecture, particularly that found in Washington. He said he could well remember the Capitol before the completion of its famous dome late in the war. He described being in its shadow as he watched Lincoln's second inauguration there from a throng gathered down below the speaker's perch. He told how stark and erect and without purpose the monument to George Washington was before it was topped off with its stone cap. He mentioned the public buildings and natural vantage points from which one enjoyed the best views of the city.

Somehow making a marriage of Irishmen like Quinn and strolls through the wartime city, I mentioned Pete Doyle so that I could note how he might react involuntarily to the name, for a poker player's countenance was one of the assets that W was losing to fatal old age. But he responded with the customary platitudes: Dear sweet Pete, a good boy, we shared such good times, I regret how we have fallen out of touch, &cet.

"As you know, he has not been here for a very long while," he concluded without special inflection of any sort.

Subject closed, at least for the moment. The drawbridge to the past was squeaking its way shut now.

In fact, it was October before I had another such good opportunity to ask my question again with the same combination of casualness and compulsion. I told him that the Bolton group of Whitmanites in England, who seem determined to flush out many of the major witnesses to his life, had located Pete in Baltimore. W clearly had known all along that Pete was there but had perhaps misspoken earlier, for his memory was beginning to tease and trick him a bit, which of course made me keep my question on the docket. Pete seemed to have been employed for some time as a railroad brakeman, dangerous work indeed for a man of about forty-six or so, walking the tops of moving cars and leaping from one to the next.

In any case, W gave the familiar response, as though I were some local reporter with whom he could have his way by wearing the hat of the legendary Good Gray Poet when he spoke, rather than that of W the man. "The noble Pete!" he said. The exclamation point is not only another evidence of my poor writing style but an emphasis I heard in W's voice, unusual because he spoke most often in a raspy whisper now. That was all he said. His voice was (conveniently?) giving out on him, precluding any more bromides for the moment.

I must have been looking at him with my head tilted to one side and a countenance full of disappointment. (Anne has always said that I somewhat resemble a hound, with a hound's inability to disguise what it is thinking.)

W looked me squarely in the eye, commandingly. Leaning forward as best he could, the better to have his words travel the few feet that separated us, he said, "Be patient, Horace, dear Horace, my boy. Be patient . . ."

The message was cut short by an eruption of wheezing.

TEN

WILKES IS A BUSY MAN. In the afternoon he drops
in at Missus Surratt's boarding-house. This being Good
Friday, she is making preparations for Easter, the most
solemn of holidays. Federal employees receive the afternoon off,
so Lou Weichmann is there as well. Bumping into Wilkes revives,
as though such incitement were necessary, his curiosity. The emotion is a combination of suspicion that the actor is up to no good
and knowledge that he, Weichmann, is being deliberately excluded
because the others dislike him, he doesn't know why. For his part,
Herold is in town securing a roan, for he is still prepared to ride with
Wilkes on an escape through Maryland to Virginia, as though Virginia
too were not enemy territory now.

At the same moment, employees of the theater, including the
stagehand Ned Spangler and the dogsbody known as Peanuts, are
carrying out orders from Harry Ford, the co-owner with his brother,
to remove the partition between the two upper boxes to form a
single enclosure. When they finish, they are to decorate it with
flags borrowed from the Treasury Department. Out back, Wilkes
is riding quickly up and down Baptist Alley, practicing. Spangler
and another man come out to converse with him when their task
is completed. Wilkes treats them to a round at the Greenback,

and then announces he is going over to Grover's Theatre to deliver a letter.

A short distance away, the first batch of high-level Confederate prisoners taken since the surrender, eight generals among them, is being marched through the city for the people to jeer at.

In fact, Wilkes is going less to deliver a letter than to compose one. He asks for pen and paper and writes as follows:

"For a long time I have devoted my energies, my time and money to the accomplishment of a certain end. I have been disappointed. The moment has now arrived when I must change my plans. Many will blame me for what I am about to do, but posterity, I am sure, will justify me. Men who love their country better than gold or life." He lists them below: himself, Payne, Herold and Atzerodt. Admittedly, he scribbles in haste, and omits the pair of cowards Arnold and O'Laughlen, who are still probably sitting somewhere shivering with a fever of fear. Neither does he mention the Irish catamite with a stable hand's manners and the mighty robertson, nor any of twelve or twenty others of whom the planet's second and third rings are composed. So many names he cannot remember them now in the midst of the greatest mind-storm of his life. So many potential names that they might detract from the plan's heroic proportions were he to recite the roster, making himself seem in the eyes of history a simple organizer, a theatrical manager, a businessman.

Leaving, he stops to gaze at the poor prisoners being shuffled along some distance away and to glare at the small blue figures of their new masters. By chance he has met up with John Matthews, a stock-company actor of no great renown, currently cast as the drunken butler in *Our American Cousin* at Ford's; and the two of them take in the sight together.

"Great God," Wilkes says, "I no longer have a country."

He asks Matthews if he will please do a friend a favor and take this sealed letter to the editor of the *National Intelligencer* "if you don't hear from me by ten tomorrow morning." Matthews agrees. Just then a carriage passes by bearing General and Missus Grant out of the city.

Wilkes is still busy busy busy. He goes to the Kirkwood House but not to see Atzerodt, who already has been cast in his supporting rôle. Taking a card and a pencil from the front desk, he writes a note to Andrew Johnson: "Don't wish to disturb you. Are you at home?" He hands it to the unsmiling day clerk, who turns with a studied minimum of exertion and pops it into the vice president's mailbox, already full of various messages and reminders. Then it's back to the National Hotel, thinking of dearest Lucy upstairs, thinking of the assignment he has given himself that awaits completion. Again he asks for paper and something to write with. Two acquaintances happen to be in the lobby. Wilkes turns to them.

"Is it 1864 or 1865?" he asks.

They find it odd that he doesn't know which year it is, but they don't understand, cannot understand, how forcefully his mind is concentrated on the task before him, bearing down on it like a narrow beam of light on the carpet of an otherwise totally darkened room. He always has kept a scrapbook, the way theater people do, but has begun to keep a diary only now. It is a cheap one for the pocket, cheap because it is for the year 1864, and thinking of it just now, he has become confused for a second, hence the query. He finishes his letter, takes a postage stamp from his billfold and drops the letter into the mail slot on the counter.

✦

The president presides over the usual cabinet meeting. The agenda is taken up with questions surrounding the surrender of Lee (while

Joe Johnston's army, such as it is, is doing its fatal waltz with Sherman's in the piney woods of North Carolina). Outside the cabinet room, the president is laid siege to by a couple of the petitioners and favor-seekers who always have the effect of showing how seemingly infinite his patience is. He pleads, honestly, that he is already late for the theater and is going to be very late indeed if he tarries.

The presidential carriage stops en route to pick up a youngish officer, Major Henry Rathbone, and his fiancée, Clara Harris, who will be filling the two seats originally intended for the Grants. The party arrives twenty minutes after the opening curtain. The orchestra strikes up "Hail to the Chief." The audience is excited. Once in the box, the president acknowledges their affection with a bow then settles into the rocker that the Fords, knowing that he finds such chairs easier on his long legs, have kindly provided. The idiotic play resumes.

Missus Surratt has been to Surrattsville to visit friends, driven there by Lou Weichmann, but returns home to H Street to find Wilkes, nearing the end of his long and frantic day. They exchange pleasantries and Wilkes rides back to Baptist Alley and asks Ned Spangler to hold his horse. When Wilkes has gone inside, Spangler hands over the reins to Peanuts. Wilkes is pacing in the lobby and out front in the street, waiting for the minutes to tick away until the actors arrive at the perfect scene for the deed about to be done. To speed the process, he nips into the Star saloon for a whiskey and branch water. Thus fortified, he enters Ford's Theatre one last time to perform his greatest rôle. He walks up to the dress circle and flashes his calling card to the lone guard and goes into the dark passageway leading to the boxes, closing the door behind him and then barring it. The door to the president's double box has been left ajar. Through it he can see Major Rathbone but not the others. His right hand is in his right pocket, touching Mister Deringer's pistol. His left hand holds his dirk, guarding it jealously.

Wilkes is the only one with an overview of the whole affair. He will strike at Lincoln at virtually the same moment Atzerodt kills the vice president, Andrew Johnson, and Payne and Herold do in, not the next in line to take over the presidency according to the Constitution, but rather William H. Seward, the secretary of state, who is recuperating at home following a dreadful carriage accident. Seward is a career politician, age sixty-four, who for many years has been a loudly animated and influential opponent of slavery.

⁂

Payne and Herold are sitting in Lafayette Park opposite the Executive Mansion awaiting the familiar nine o'clock call telling patrons that the park is closing for the night. The call comes promptly. Without speaking to each other, the two men walk across to Secretary Seward's house. But the plan, for Payne to gain entrance by pretending to be a delivery boy from the chemist's shop, falls apart. Seward's doctor, the one who supposedly would have written the prescription that exists only in Payne's imaginative cover story, is leaving the house just as the two men approach; it must be him, for he carries a doctor's satchel and climbs into a carriage. There goes the idea of simultaneous attacks on the intended victims. Thinking quickly, Payne tells Herold to ride as fast as possible to tell Atzerodt and Wilkes, while he continues with his portion of the plot regardless. He is, after all, a soldier, and he has been given an order.

The servant who opens the polished front door sees an enormously tall young man in a distinctive long overcoat of some unusual light gray material.

"I am delivering the Secretary's medication," the man says.

The recipient of this remark thinks it out of the ordinary as the doctor has just left, and tries to turn the caller away. With almost no visible effort, Payne pushes him aside and bounds up the staircase two steps at a time in the direction of the master bedroom on the third floor.

❧

Knowing his recovery will be a long one, Seward has had his son Frederick made an assistant secretary of state, charged with keeping minutes of what goes on in the meetings that he himself is unable to attend. Frederick has been living in the house to be close to the patient during this agonizing recuperative period. He is studying his notes of the cabinet session held earlier that day when he is startled by a commotion and steps into the corridor to inquire. He doesn't recognize Payne, doesn't know that Payne has knocked over the servant two floors below, but is naturally suspicious of him all the same. He opens the door to his father's room to see if the secretary is still awake. That seems not to be the case, for the secretary is motionless and his eyes are closed; his sixteen-year-old daughter sits by the bedside, holding his hand as he slowly drifts into the promise of drugged and dreamy sleep. Frederick gently closes the door behind him as he leaves the room. But in a moment he hears the latch open again. His sister contradicts him: "He is awake now," she says.

Payne pipes up. "Is the secretary asleep?"

"Not quite yet, but almost," Frederick's sister says before disappearing back into the bedroom.

Knowing that something is amiss, Frederick takes Payne's paper parcel and tells him that he himself will give the medicine to his father. Payne accepts this and turns as though to go down the stairs. But in turning, he pulls a revolver from somewhere inside his long coat, puts it to Frederick's temple and squeezes the trigger. The revolver misfires. So he brings the barrel down on the young Seward's skull.

Miss Seward and a Negro, an invalided army private who is helping to look after her father, open the door again and peek around it to see what's going on. Frederick is on his feet, but barely. A cascade of blood is falling over his face. Payne has drawn another weapon from the voluminous coat: a bowie knife. He uses it to knock down the soldier and rushes past the daughter to where Seward lies, immobilized by his shoulder cast and the jaw splint holding his mandible in place. Payne crosshatches his victim's head and neck with deep cuts. He is pulling him over on his side to expose the jugular, which the jaw contraption obscures, when the wounded soldier jumps on the back of the much bigger man and hangs on his neck like a child playing piggyback. Payne loses his balance and the two end up wrestling on the carpet.

Another of the Seward children appears. Taking in the scene in an instant, he runs to fetch his own revolver. Whereupon Payne rises to his full height, tosses the soldier aside like a small piece of furniture and tears down the stairs, encountering a messenger coming up. Payne knocks him down and then stabs him before dashing into the street. In a moment the servant who first opened the door, on his feet once again but terribly dizzy, flies out of the Seward house crying, "Murder!" Some soldiers lounging nearby see a tall figure in a long coat mount a horse tethered to the now-locked iron fence of Lafayette Park. The unknown man rides off to the sound of hooves rapidly striking the paving bricks. Being on foot, they cannot catch him.

"Murder" turns out to be an overstatement. Seward is alive, though barely. His jaw hangs from the rest of his face by a strip of flesh. Payne has once again shown his daring, but this time he has failed. He has, however, come far closer to success with the secretary of state than Atzerodt who was delegated to kill the vice president. Andrew Johnson is not molested this night because his assigned assassin is too drunk to act, standing in a barroom, where Herold is unable to locate him. Indeed, after achieving a certain level of in-ebriation with his own funds, he is wondering if he can spot a famil-iar face or a kind-looking stranger who might stand him another drink, as such charity is his only conceivable source of credit.

***

The president, two women and a Yankee officer. The last of these is the only one who might—might—be armed. Wilkes watches the officer closely as he steps into the box and plants the barrel of the pistol right against the back of the president's skull. There is a deaf-ening report. The blast propels Lincoln far forward. The runners of the rocking chair tip violently, and the victim falls to the right, landing on the not particularly well swept floor. Not taking any chances that he himself could be shot from behind in turn, Wilkes leaps at the young major with his dirk and slashes him badly. He is moving so quickly, an infinity lasting only a few seconds, that his eyes do not even take in Missus Lincoln and the major's fiancée. He steps neatly between the empty rocker and the first lady's chair, grabs the rail and steps out onto the edge of the box, catching one of his spurs in the damned Treasury flags as he launches himself into space. He is five foot seven, mean-ing that once he jumps over the rail and straightens, the soles of his riding boots will plummet less than seven feet before hitting the stage. The problem is not height but rather the fact that the foot tangled in the flag comes down an instant later than the other, causing him to land awkwardly. He sprains his left ankle, though not seriously enough to impede his escape. He faces the audience for a second, hold-ing the blade aloft like a trophy, and utters an histrionic slogan. Most of those who hear it believe he says "Sic semper tyrannis," the motto of the Commonwealth of Virginia. Others whose hearing is just as acute interpret it as "The South is avenged."

Not too hastily but hastily enough, he crosses the breadth of the stage and goes out through the wings stage right, favoring his left leg only slightly. He whips into Baptist Alley, takes the reins out of Peanuts's hand, throws himself into the saddle and spurs the horse to a gallop, disappearing into the streets of the District, into the darkness and into history, just as per the plan.

In the theater, there is disbelieving silence. Then Missus Lincoln screams and wholesale panic breaks out. People are jumping to their feet, among them Pete the Great, who says to himself, "This ain't no Kidnap." Several members of the cast are still onstage but seem paralyzed. Many figures are running toward the presidential box: several doctors, some soldiers and also Laura Keene. Knowing that the fame of actresses lasts only so long for what they have accomplished onstage, she elbows her way into the box, kneels on the floor and, with difficulty, gets hold of the president's slippery head and nestles it in her lap. She stays until her costume is drenched in blood and speckled with tiny fragments of brain tissue and she can glide through the remainder of her life on a reputation for heroic selflessness.

Suddenly the theater is full of men in blue, and these ones are armed. Pete has left his seat and is making his way through one of the galleries en route to the street, slowly and with what he hopes is deadly earnest casualness. "I Suppose i lingered almost to the last Person," he informs Doctor Bucke many years later. "a Soldier come into the gallery, saw Me still there. Called out to me, 'Get out of here! We're going to Burn this d——ned building down!'"

"If that is so, I'll Get out," Pete replies, sensibly enough, and strolls out into Tenth Street and keeps walking, not too fast and not too slowly, until he can't hear the hubbub anymore. "I went out the same Way I come in."

He instinctively reverts to his military frame of mind, determined to reveal none of the fear he feels washing over him even as his carotid arteries pound like the long roll the drummer boys use to summon men to battle. The sound in his ears is the body's emergency supply of blood being rushed to reinforce the brain. He is, at that moment, too busy fleeing for his life in an orderly fashion, too busy escaping as unobtrusively as possible, to be fully conscious of his movements.

There is no curfew within the city itself, but no one is supposed to enter or leave after nine o'clock at night. That's the rule and everybody knows it. So a sergeant guarding the wooden drawbridge that crosses the Potomac, near the Navy Yard in the eastern part of the city, is surprised to see a rider approaching at twenty to midnight. The rider is calm and polite, but his horse looks exhausted. Wilkes gives his real name and explains that he's returning to his home in Charles County. He apologizes for not knowing about the rule but says that he was waiting for the moon to rise because the road beyond the city is so dark. This sounds plausible. The soldier notices that the gentleman's nails have been manicured recently. He shouldn't let the man pass, but he does anyway, grateful though he is to have another human being to talk to. Wilkes walks the horse over the bridge, as the regulations require, and then remounts and is quickly gone.

No sooner has the first rider vanished into the blue-black night than a second one draws up to the barrier. Herold says his name is Smith. He too is headed down to Charles and claims to know nothing of the restrictions in force. The sergeant is getting mightily suspicious now, until the stranger takes him into his confidence, man to man.

"You see, I was with this Dutch girl," he says. "I couldn't pull out in the middle. I mean, I couldn't tear myself away."

The sergeant smiles and lets him proceed.

Minutes after Dave Herold gets back on his horse on the other side of the bridge and speeds off to catch up with Wilkes, a *third* traveler appears. This is a real circus tonight, the soldier thinks. The rider says he's trying to catch the man who just passed through.

"I can let you go, but you know the rules: you can't come back into the city until the morning."

The latest rider is disappointed. "The son of a bitch stole my horse!" he says. He turns back toward the city.

Then, as always, comes the unexpected, for which no insurance can ever be underwritten. Across the river the road is dark, the two men are moving as fast as they can in the circumstances. Wilkes's mount lands with one hoof in a deep mud hole and rears up, throwing the rider. Herold takes the reins and calls out to see if his friend is hurt. Wilkes knows at once that his ankle is broken. The same one he injured in the theater. As it was already weakened in the escape from the president's box, it was begging for something like this. He curses his luck as he gets back into the saddle with difficulty, and the two men ride to the Surrattsville tavern. There they retrieve one of the carbines, a box of ammunition and a pair of binoculars, and buy a bottle of whiskey while they're at it.

At four in the morning, Herold wakes up Doctor Samuel Mudd and tells him there is a man outside—the dark silhouette sitting not quite upright in the saddle some yards away—who needs a surgeon bad. They ease him off the horse and into the doctor's front room. Mudd has to cut Wilkes's left boot to get it off the swollen leg. Mudd determines that the fracture is not in the ankle but the lower end of the fibula. It is a clean break. He puts on a splint and finds a pair of crutches. The injured man stays in bed all day, wearing a beard that has served him well in various stage rôles. Mudd later testifies that, despite their meetings the previous winter, he didn't recognize Wilkes (whom Herold, or Smith, was now calling Tyson).

By this time, all approaches to and from the District have been sealed off and the authorities are frantically looking for Wilkes and Herold in all the wrong places, believing at first that they have gone to ground in Baltimore. But there is progress in the blossoming investigation nonetheless. While the public and the newspapers wallow in information, wildly inaccurate gossip and preposterous rumors, the authorities prove themselves far better policemen than the plotters are criminals. Edwin Stanton runs the investigation from the War Department, right across from the Executive Mansion, and his brisk no brusque efficiency has never been shown to better advantage. Fourteen hours after the shooting of the president and the stabbing of the secretary of state, a thousand men, mostly cavalry, are racing through southern Maryland and the northern parts of Virginia.

When the newspapers identify Wilkes as the assassin, John Matthews opens the letter he was asked to deliver to the *Intelligencer.* He quickly destroys it, horrified at reading Wilkes's arrogant confession and the list of his main accomplices. Yet the lack of this information does not hinder the case that Stanton and his detectives and soldiers are making. One clue leads to another. Atzerodt's name keeps recurring in interviews and interrogations, and a search of the clothes in his room at the Kirkwood House turns up Wilkes's bank book in a coat pocket (right where Wilkes has secreted it, like a pickpocket in reverse)—but no actual Atzerodt, not so far. For on the morning after, Atzerodt has sold, for ten dollars, the revolver with which he was supposed to dispatch the vice president, and leaves central Washington for one of the outlying District communities. O'Laughlen for his part gives in to his fear in a different way. He goes on a champion bender, touring saloons, bordellos and leg shows. His friend Arnold is being hunted as well, but isn't immediately located either.

Troops go to Missus Surratt's and arrest her. While they are there, Payne arrives, wearing workman's clothes. As always, he has a believable alibi; he never leaves his bed in the morning without one. But the lady of the house refuses to back him up, and they are both taken in. People present at the attempt on Seward pick him out as the assailant, and he is transported in shackles to an ironclad lying at the Navy Yard. He always has a cover story, is not too vain to hide his intelligence, tells inquisitors nothing and shows no fear. There's a person inside the long overcoat, but no one knows him. It is as Lewis Payne that Lewis Thornton Powell will go to the gallows, a gifted pupil of whoever taught him the craft.

Getting a photograph of Wilkes isn't difficult. His image is everywhere to be found, including no doubt the bottom of the most privileged drawer in the bedroom chests of romantic schoolgirls. Likenesses of the others are obtained as well. The area for hundreds of miles is papered with circulars offering big rewards for those still at large, and they are illustrated—a Stanton innovation.

Within days the federal government has Arnold and O'Laughlen in custody under the strictest precautions, along with Payne and Missus Surratt and the unfortunate stagehand Ned Spangler, the only employee of the Ford brothers to be charged. Spangler's principal offense was that he held the assassin's mare for a few moments in the alley before turning the reins over to the clearly innocent helper called Peanuts and then perhaps leaving the stage door open. There were still no reliable leads on the whereabouts of Wilkes and Dave Herold, though they are now known to have headed south and not east. Atzerodt has yet to be hauled in, and there is no sign at all in what jurisdiction John Surratt may be. A colonel grilling Missus Surratt demands she answer the question. She replies that he is very likely in Canada.

The colonel explodes. "No man on the round Earth believes he went to Canada!"

But she is telling the truth. Her son was making for Montreal when the news reached him in Elmira, New York, and he crossed the border as soon as he could (it was not a difficult matter). He lands in Canada West but does not rush eastward to glittering Montreal. He knows, and his mother knows that he knows, that a devout young man who has studied for the priesthood can find sanctuary among priests across the borderline, particularly those serving rural parishes.

All this while, psychics, visionaries, people with the gift of either telepathy or of the gab, and all manner of other such individualists, bombard Stanton's department with news of Wilkes's whereabouts, some claiming that he too is to be found in Canada.

Wilkes's tactic of incriminating others by having them use horses with which he himself has been associated comes back to haunt him when the singular mare with the white star and the one blind eye breaks her bridle and wanders off while he and Herold are resting in the woods. The troopers crisscrossing southern Maryland, clambering and clattering all the way to the Potomac and soon enough beyond it, undoubtedly have full descriptions of the mounts as well as of the riders. A Wilkes sympathizer hears the two men making a racket in a thicket. He brings the mare back but advises the fugitives to get rid of their horses and find replacements, which they do. The man helps by taking the animals to a swamp—there are swamps everywhere—and shooting them. Herold's horse dies, then Wilkes's, whose head sinks last, the white star vanishing forever. The man has brought with him some newspapers telling of the assassination and its aftermath. Wilkes is hurt, alarmed and puzzled to read that he is being denounced editorially even in the Southern press. The dead president, the editors say, would have been easier on the vanquished states than his successors will be. In this, they say, they are simply putting into type the received understanding of the people.

"The fools." Herold isn't certain whether Wilkes is talking to him or only to himself. "Does it mean nothing that I have brought down the father of our country's misery?" Eventually his sentences turn into mutterings and mumbles whose substance he confides to posterity via his diary. The mind-storms become more frequent and perhaps more intense, but each lasts only a short while.

Pushing south, the fugitives come upon the house of a man named Swan, who is of mixed white, African and Indian blood. He sells them whiskey and bread and for an additional payment leads them to the other side of the great swamp full of water snakes and lizards, to the farm of a Southern gentleman whose views have made him famous in the area and infamous to the federals. He sells them a meal at his table. Herold then threatens their host's life if he ever tells of the visit. Despite this, the wealthy farmer helps them find their way. They are now forty miles south of the District but are still in Maryland, not yet in glorious Virginia.

The logical place to cross the Potomac is closely watched, and they wait, hidden by the riverbank, for several hours. Finally their guide, another local farmer, gives them a skiff he has hidden for just such a purpose after first misdirecting a band of cavalry. The wind is high, countermanding their progress, but the river is nonetheless in thick fog. The two fugitives have nearly made their way across when a Yankee gunboat appears. They sit as still as possible and hope that the fog and the darkness are their friends. In the morning they reach the homestead of another Rebel farmer, but they still haven't set foot in Virginia.

Mistakenly believing that the great swamp could not be crossed, soldiers and government detectives are working in tandem first at Surrattsville and then close to Doctor Mudd's farm even as substantial bodies of opinion point toward Baltimore, Canada and several other places. At the Mudd farm, a big break is served to them like mashed potatoes. The doctor's wife says the left boot that her husband had cut off the stranger with the broken leg got lodged under the bed and forgotten about on the night in question but has now come to light during routine housekeeping. She hands it to the soldiers. Inside is the inscription "H. Lux, maker. 455 Broadway. J. Wilkes. " Doctor Mudd is unceremoniously arrested. Now those in authority know positively that Wilkes has headed farther down into southern Maryland and will be crossing the Potomac once again, at a place where it is much wider than at the Navy Yard Bridge in the District.

Wilkes and Herold have overshot the fording place. To make a second attempt at landing in Virginia, they first paddle back the way they came and round the little neck of Virginia that juts far out into the river and forces it into the shape of a letter U as it runs to the sea. Federal gunboats are nearby, though they are proving no match for the wily locals. Wilkes and Herold aren't locals of course, but they manage, with only one close call, to blend in with all the other small river craft going about their business. On the morning of the ninth day after the events at Ford's Theatre—April twenty-third, Shakespeare's birthday, a fact hardly lost on Wilkes—they step ashore in Virginia and go in search of Elizabeth Quesenberry's place. Quesenberry is a minor aristocrat from a family of politicians connected to some of the Founding Fathers as well as the crowned heads of Mexico. She is living in such a benighted place because, until the loss of Richmond and the surrender of Lee's army, she had been using the modest home as a safe house for Confederate agents. When located, she is highly suspicious of the two visitors but delivers food to them through intermediaries, who suggest that Wilkes might find treatment for his leg at the Summer home of a Doctor Stuart, a few miles distant. The fugitives pay ten dollars for the privilege of doubling up on their informant's horse. Their compatriots are bleeding them dry.

Stuart is even more aristocratic than Missus Quesenberry, being connected, through the marriage of his cousin Robert E. Lee, to descendants of George Washington himself. And many others besides. He refuses to put the pair of men up for the night, much less provide medical help to the one who is hurt. He has sometimes been tricked by Yankee spies posing as Confederates in need of assistance. At one point he had been arrested and held for months on a river barge being used as a makeshift jail. Still, he would not turn away hungry men without a meal, not even these dirty and obviously disreputable jaspers. He also grudgingly gives them some advice about accommodation.

"I have a neighbor here, a colored man who sometimes hires out his wagons," he says. "Probably he would do it if he is not very busy."

When Wilkes and Herold locate the man's home, they find him unhelpful as well.

"I have no right to take care of white people," he says. "I have only one room in the house, and my wife is sick."

The strangers refuse to take such treatment from a member of the other race. Wilkes pulls his dirk on the man and forces him and his family, including his sick wife, to remain outdoors until morning, when they intend to make off with two of the man's horses.

Armed with the evidence of the boot, detectives are now pursuing the theory that the wanted men either are holed up in the woebegone swamp or have crossed into northern Virginia. If the former is the case, the searchers will have to wait until hunger and disease drive them out of hiding; if the latter, the fugitives will be running fast but out in the open, where cavalry could ride them down. On the hopeful assumption that the second idea is accurate, they cross the Potomac and renew the search.

To prevent the theft of the horses he needs to make a living, the black man, whose name is Charlie Lucas, agrees to take the two white men in his wagon down to the Rappahannock River. There the two can cross by ferry and penetrate much deeper into Virginia, where they may find a better welcome. At the dock, Wilkes and Herold meet two threadbare former Confederate soldiers making their weary way back home at last. Calling himself David E. Boyd, Herold states that he and his brother, John Boyd, who walks with crutches because of a wound incurred at Petersburg, are in the same position. The Confederates are mighty suspicious of these claims. So Herold blurts out, half bragging, half confessing, that he and his friend "are the assassinators of the president." For this is the problem that has been facing them: Wilkes knows that he lacks the common touch and will betray his education if he tries to engage such people as these in conversation. For his part, Herold, though by no means the mentally disadvantaged person that people in the District believe him to be, has none of his partner's acting talent. He always continues to talk and talk until he gets them into difficult situations. The ferry makes the crossing in only a few minutes, before either man can get them both hanged.

In Washington, Lafayette Baker, the disingenuous and self-promoting head of the secret service, is one of those who believe his prey are heading south through Virginia, not coughing with swamp fever in Maryland. He puts together a small but select band of twenty-five horse soldiers to scour the sections of northern Virginia that, however many times other troops have passed by, through and over them, have not been so thoroughly investigated as they might be. As its leader, he picks a young Canadian, a lieutenant named Edward Doherty.

The ferry's southern terminus is Port Royal, where Herold tries to find beds for himself and his injured friend. One landlady agrees but changes her mind when she sees Wilkes, who now looks like the hunted animal he is. She points them in the direction of Richard

Garrett's tobacco farm some miles distant. Meanwhile, the cavalry-men arrive at the ferry dock on the other side. They have photographs of Wilkes, Herold and Surratt. A black man tells them that he has seen the first two pass through but has never laid eyes on the third.

Without knowing the specifics, Wilkes and Herold certainly understand that the odds of their getting away are growing slimmer and slimmer. Eleven days have gone by since the killing. The locals they meet are no doubt betraying them to the Yankees as soon as they are out of sight. They decide their best chance is to split up and go in opposite directions; at least one of them might get out of the country and survive. Herold heads out alone toward the west but has second thoughts and returns to Wilkes's side. He is not a leader but a loyal assistant, not a star of the stage but a member of the audience sitting in one of the cheap seats. They proceed together to Garrett's farm.

The horsemen had been twenty-four hours behind those they have been pursuing, but as they are on fast horses and their quarry on foot, they quickly close the gap. They find one of the Southern veterans who had been on the ferry and knows the territory well, and from him learn that the figures they seek are most likely at Garrett's by now. The night is moonless and they ride hard for two hours. On arriving, they surround the farmhouse and wake the owner, whom they threaten to kill on the spot if he doesn't tell them where the wanted men are hiding. Garrett says they have gone, gone into the woods.

"What? A lame man go into the woods?"

"He went on his crutches."

Now the bluecoats produce a coil of rope and threaten to hang the farmer without further ado but give him one more chance.

"I do not want a long story out of you. I just want to know where these men have gone."

To save his father, Garrett's son tells the soldiers that the men are in the barn. The building is already surrounded, and Lieutenant Doherty forces Garrett to enter it and return with Wilkes and Herold. Garrett says they should surrender now, as Doherty calls on the two plotters to give up their weapons or the barn will be set alight. Wilkes promises a fight to the death, like a character in so many plays. The soldiers carry out their threat and set the building on fire. Herold says he is surrendering, ignoring Wilkes's vow to kill him if he does so, and walks out to deliver himself into custody.

The structure is old and dry. As in most such buildings used to cure tobacco, there are wide gaps between the slats for maximum air circulation, and the resulting cross-draft maximizes the speed and height of the flames. The soldiers closest to the scene can see Wilkes hobbling round inside with the repeating carbine taken from the stash at the Surrattsville tavern. One of those peering in is Sergeant Boston Corbett, a curious customer, born in England and a hatter by trade. He is a fervid and fervent born-again Christian. So much so that to help him overcome sinful temptation, he has castrated himself with scissors. He aims his revolver through one of the openings and fires. Wilkes falls flat on his face with a wound to his neck.

Soldiers carry Wilkes to the front porch of the farmhouse, where his hold on consciousness rises and falls. Garrett's sister nurses him (and clips a lock of his hair for a souvenir when no one's looking). A doctor is summoned. He realizes Wilkes has incurred spinal cord damage. Booth's body is like a nocturnal city that is going dark one block at a time.

In the moments when he can speak, Wilkes says, "Tell my mother that I did it for my country—that I die for my country."

He is paralyzed, and at dawn he asks someone to hold up his hands so that he can see them. He says, "Useless, useless." Those who hear him assume he is referring to his hands. Then he dies.

Pete the Great has fled the District and is lying low outside Baltimore, where he reads of Wilkes's death in the newspapers and shivers a bit until he remembers the horrors of prison and the worse horrors of battle and the tough hayride that has been his life so far. "i figured I ought not ta be cowed by whatever trouble there was to be," he tells W many years later. "I made a Decision. i decided i was scared a Yankees and englishmen about the same amount a pig is scared a mud." W thought those were poetic words, but he didn't know how true they were.

❧ ELEVEN ❧

ONE DAY IN THE SUMMER of Eighty-eight W gave me
a packet of correspondence, some of which was only three
years old—three years almost to the day. It was an exchange
with James Redpath of the *North American Review* concerning publication in its pages of W's piece called "Booth and the Old Bowery,"
about seeing the great actor perform in New York long ago, before the
Lincoln affair discolored that talented family. The gist of the letter
was that W originally asked a hundred dollars but was prepared to
bargain. The last item in the little pile was W's receipt for sixty, given
with the proviso that he be allowed to reprint the article in his own
book. For by then we were hard at work on a new project, one almost
absurdly ambitious for a sickly author. It was the *Complete Poems and
Prose of Walt Whitman, 1855–1888.* The former date was of course the
year of the first edition of the immortal *Leaves*. The latter was not only
the year of the book's most recent piece but also the year in which he
expected the whole nine-hundred-page affair to be published! Given
his diminishing energies and his tendencies both to revise and to pro-
crastinate, I thought this a difficult proposition. I also believed that
including the whole of *November Boughs* in the new book was a poor
idea, given that the independent existence of *Boughs* was so recent
that the market had yet to digest much of the inventory.

"Is this not competing with yourself?" I asked him.

"Not in the least," he replied. "You have yet to sharpen your sense of these matters on the whetstone of long experience."

As I was silently going through the letters he had given me, he asked me to read them aloud, as his eyes were bothering him that day. As I did so, he interrupted to reminisce about Redpath, recounting how the man he called Jim had offered to lend him money and sometimes did so.

"He was one of your radical crowd."

"Why don't you say 'our crowd'? Don't you belong with us?"

"Yes, yes, I do," he said, laughing a little. "But sometimes I think some of you fellows have outstripped even me in the way you flaunt your red flag of revolt."

"Do you mean that for a rebuke or a blessing?"

"For a blessing to be sure," he said.

I went along with him for harmony's sake. In his old age just as in the days of Lincoln, W was a Republican. Mind you, toward the end of his life I did hear him criticize the Republicans, but only in the sour process of itemizing events in the day's news. No doubt he voted for President Arthur but against President Cleveland. Personally, I saw no difference between them and voted for neither—nor anyone else, ever, until Eugene Debs came along. As we had such important work before us, I had no intention of speaking up in such a way as to lower his admiration of my curatorial talent. Later I came to realize that he had no choice but to try to please me. I was all he had, and he was old and sick. I understand these things so much better now.

⁂

That Summer was particularly hot and bothersome. Keeping the windows closed meant stifling. Keeping them open meant letting in the smell of the fertilizer plant and the racket of the railroad. One night W complained of having been "melted." All day he had been unable even to read proof, so that the *Complete Poems* was already behind its admittedly optimistic schedule.

"As to the ordeal of this book, perhaps of any of my books," he said, wiping the sweat from his forehead as he did so, "I feel on the whole like Abe Lincoln, who would not growl over the scars and the losses but thought that the government was lucky to come out of its troubles alive."

Lincoln seemed to come up in his talk with ever greater regularity. When he again told me his Lincoln stories, I didn't know if he was unconsciously repeating himself or merely trying to lay particular emphasis on what Lincoln had meant to him, and continued to mean. One day we fell to discussing his Lincoln lecture, which was to be included in the omnibus edition. I remarked that it was still very vivid after all these years, as though in his mind the events surrounding the assassination had taken place only yesterday.

He stared strangely for a second and then spoke slowly. "As you know, Pete was in the audience, watching the play. He heard the report of the pistol, saw the younger Booth drop from the box and land, paws down, on the stage, heard his arrogant slogan and watched him scurry across and disappear into infamy." He met my eyes when he added: "I have never been shy on the matter of Pete's attendance."

In actual fact this was one of the most remarkable mentions of his friend that he had ever made in my hearing. Pete was never in the present tense but seemed always to be hovering in the distant background of W's recollections. Here, however, was a statement about a time long ago that suddenly seemed remarkably alive. Then W retreated, falling once more into recounting their innocent friendship. "We were the closest of comrades," he said, "during the war, in Washington City, and later." This sounded like something one would say in the witness box, trying to clear oneself of a criminal charge.

I have no experience of war myself, but I understand that the pressures of wartime do often invest friendship with a special degree of intensity. Perhaps it is born of fear, or at least uncertainty. Loneliness may play a part as well, as might the simple excitement of living even a passive part in that which the news comprises.

I was still as determined as ever to get him to tell me more about Pete. By the counterfeit equanimity in W's voice whenever the name came up, I suspected that his Rebel friend was some sort of key to another aspect of W's life, the part that we all live out when dropping off to sleep at night or lying newly wakened in the morning with our minds racing but our feet not yet ready to be planted on the floor. That is, I believed I knew what the secret must be but had almost none of the details. In the end, my suspicions did not prove wrong but only woefully incomplete.

❈

Some days he was languid. Most days he was in some degree sick. But there were others, however infrequent, when his blood was beating its way around the body's racecourse. On those days, he wrote. He wrote his news-poems, as I called them, the ones about public events and the passing of national heroes, for which the newspapers compensated him quite well. Other times he wrote prose, albeit with more difficulty. Writing poetry seemed to add to his temporary vitality whereas writing prose seemed to subtract from it.

However discontinuous his literary output, his flow of wonderful talk was unimpeded. I remember one evening in particular when my visit coincided with a magnificent rainstorm that seemed to energize his body in somewhat the same way poetry did his mind. I was about to turn the knob on the door of his room when a loud celebration of thunder began. I had no sooner entered, expecting to find him in his sickbed, when a great jagged bolt of lightning revealed him standing at the center window instead, his bald head silhouetted against the northern sky as steel sheets made of rain beat against the pane and went splashing over the sill. He knew I was behind him, for his unspoken thoughts were suddenly given voice. I heard him conclude, "—one-thousand-three. The lightning struck very close, my boy, very close indeed. How sweet it is!"

I went home regretting even more than usual that I could never have been acquainted with him in his prime. I know that I had seen a remarkable but, alas, a momentary change come over someone who at that time was often unable to do so much as venture down the stairs. He was a prisoner now. He mainly talked about the past, as I imagine all prisoners do, reminiscing about when they were free.

Not long before, he had made still another will. I could see it sitting out in the open where it was sure to get mislaid among the poems, scraps, self-rejected bits of prose, yellowing newspaper cuttings and open books, both face up and face down, that tottered in piles or were spread on the floor but that might have been jammed into boxes if all the boxes weren't already stuffed. He had few possessions other than this poor little house, but he was rich in pieces of paper. As time went on, he became even more extravagant in unloading so many reams of stuff. He gave me or at least showed me many personal family letters, but not the correspondence with his mother. He spoke of her frequently and in reverent, yes, that is the word, terms. I asked if he wrote to her often back in Brooklyn during his Washington days, when he was so busy with the wounded and maimed (and with Pete, I said only to myself). Yes, and he had all those letters, he said. "They're here. I've got 'em. They came to me after she died." His eyes, both his droopy one and the other, still flickered whenever he spoke of her being dead. "A hundred or more," he continued, "scrupulously kept all together, still about somewhere with my manuscripts." I was certain that he kept them, possibly in a casket made for that purpose, behind the blockaded door, in that room where his treasures were housed with such care as to contradict what I came to believe was the studied disorder of his living quarters.

"The reality, the simplicity, the transparency of my dear, dear mother's life was responsible for the main things in the letters as in *Leaves of Grass.*" This was a surprising revelation if not merely rhetoric and grieving. "How much I owe her! It could not be put on a scale. It could not be weighed and it could not be measured or even be put into the best words. It can only be apprehended through the intuition.

"*Leaves of Grass* is the flower of her temperament active in me," he went on. "Mother was almost illiterate in the formal sense but strangely knowing. She excelled in narrative. Had great mimetic power. She could tell stories, impersonate. She was very eloquent in the utterance of noble moral axioms, was very original in her manner and her style."

I can only say that the fruit had not fallen far from the tree.

"I wonder what *Leaves of Grass* would have been if I had been born of some other mother," he said.

❧

From his asylum in Ontario, the alarmingly forthright yet mysterious Doctor Bucke wrote to make inquiries of his faraway patient and hero. "I should like to hear that you are gaining strength," he wrote. "I do not hear that. How is it?"

This was not on one of those days when W was able to write, so he asked me to reply for him. "How is it? I don't know," he said. "Do you? Tell Maurice we've given up guessing here. Let him make a guess in Canada." He said this with a trace of contempt.

Flora, you should know that W had a two-sided relationship with your country. He put the geographic Canada on a pedestal, praising the frontier freshness of its air and water, not to mention its Indians and wild animals. Everyone who knew him must have heard him recount the Summer he spent with Bucke up there. It was pointless to contradict him with the supposition that Canada must have a great many localities very much like Mickle Street, tucked away in some place such as Montreal or Quebec City, where there was a railroad within one's hearing and a fertilizer plant within the range of one's nose. He would not be budged.

Yet he could become rancorous about Canada's society and government. He seemed to believe that Canada is not a democracy. He once told me this was so. I suppose he meant that it is not a republic like America. He was suspicious of the Queen and her ministers, who he believed were plotting against the United States in some way.

I didn't disagree with him often, but I did mention that people from our nation had tried to invade Canada, not the other way around.

"The Fenians, yes, that is true, but they were Irishmen hoping to strike at England at one remove to win freedom for their own land." He added, softly: "I have on occasion wondered whether Pete was not involved with them in some way. He was drawn to secret societies, you know, and had seen so much violence that the habit of violence never became a stranger to him."

"I didn't think of the Fenians," I replied. "Did not the United States itself invade Canada once or perhaps twice?"

"Once certainly, in the Revolution. I know of no other. Ancient history in any case. Remember whom we were fighting then, and for what."

Only much later did I recall what little I knew about the War of 1812.

This conversation that day took on a piquancy because President Cleveland had just given a speech, a very harsh speech, about our fierce dispute with the Canadians over the fisheries. When I brought this up, W asked me to explain to him what I understood of the matter. I was surprised, for he still read the newspapers as an almost religious observance, and there was a time when he could have passed a daily examination on their content.

I outlined what I believed from my own reading of the papers to be the crux of the controversy, and he spoke on the opposing side. "Well, let them go on. Let them push it as hard as they choose. Let them run up their walls, obstructions, laws, as high as they choose. In the end they will settle for the best results. We will in fact pluck the flower of free trade from the nettle of protectionism. As an individual I feel myself imposed upon, robbed, trampled over, but I can still urge patience, patience. Let them push their theory to the breaking point. For break it must.

"I myself once fell afoul of an experience with Customs officers on the Canadian border. Happily, Bucke was along and extricated me. He took the officials aside and seemed to settle it that my baggage was not to be disturbed. Gave them a few dollars for their trouble. The whole thing was quite a source of wonder to me—intrusive, baffling. What struck me most of all was Bucke's ease, suavity, composure, négligence, a sort of taking it for grantedness coolly expressed in the way he assumed the manner of a born, tired traveler."

Then he slid from admiration of Bucke to anxiety about the circumstances. "It seemed to me then as it had before, and always has since, that here lay one of the worst evils of the system: its encouragement of lying, bribery, misrepresentation, hypocrisy, just as in the Temperance prohibition and other special cases. Yet this is a side of the situation no one considers." He spoke of corruption as "not a fiscal problem, it is a moral problem, and one that plagues the largest humanities."

It was somewhat unusual for him to get wound up in this precise way, rather than vent his fear and displeasure in brief staccato bursts, and it probably was not altogether good for his health, which I could measure by referring to nothing more than the new lines and ruts in his kind old face and the way his clothing now hung on his frame. This time, however, he went on and on, along a conversational path with many twists and turns. For example, he was fuming about the inequity of the British Empire's copyright laws. He described them as evil, for this issue of course was one that affected him, and prominent American writers generally, in the pocketbook.

I was now a mature man of about thirty, more thoughtful than before and more settled. I was beginning to ponder questions that my nightly visits raised. It was certainly true that W had endured considerable calumny, particularly of course for what he called the sex-poems in the immortal *Leaves*, yet he always had had his helpful admirers, of which I myself was one, but only at the workshop level, for I could aid him only by running his errands and performing his literary chores. He was not solely reliant on either his literary friends or his non-literary ones, for he had a gift for remaining in the public eye. He exercised it not out of glory-hunger but rather from an admirable refusal to be shunted aside simply because he was not genteel in word or manner and wrote about comradeship, adhesiveness, manly affection—he gave it many names. For years I wondered whether the practical need to keep his name aloft had, paradoxically, made him more secretive than he would have been without it. Or was the opposite nearer to the truth? Was he so open in order to conceal his secretive nature? I could imagine myself in such a position, because it is one not unfamiliar to Socialists in this country. In any case, it was clearly the war that changed him into what he became. Now that you and I have lived through (in my case, just barely) a time of far greater war, on a more awful scale than previously could ever have been imagined, I believe we can conceive of what those years in Washington must have meant to him.

One day, when he had allowed me to root around on my own in the decaying heaps of documents on the floor, searching for a certain sheet of paper we needed in our work, I found a letter written *by* him. The salutation was the affectionate but impersonal one of "Dear Friend." If it was a letter that had been returned to him, there should have been an envelope, for he was meticulous in the calculated mess he made of his quarters and always managed to keep all constituent parts of a document together. Perhaps the letter was never sent. Perhaps it was a draft, though it had no emendations and scratches. Perhaps it was a fair copy that he had made for his records. I scanned it quickly and asked to whom it was addressed. He claimed not to remember, and he asked me to read it to him, slowly, as he lay abed, that he might begin to recall. Doing so, I realized that this was a circular letter sent to acquaintances, soliciting money to help him care for the wounded and the dying in the Armory Square hospital. He described the horrible scenes there with the dispassion that I suppose comes in time from seeing so much and caring so deeply.

He let me take it away with me later. I shall quote from it now.

"I seldom miss a day or evening," he wrote. "Out of the six or seven hundred in this Hospital I try to give a word or a trifle to everyone without exception, making regular rounds among them all. I give all kinds of sustenance, blackberries, peaches, lemons and sugar, wines, all kinds of preserves, pickles, brandy, milk, shirts and all articles of underclothing, tobacco, tea, handkerchiefs, &cet &cet &cet. I always give paper, envelopes, stamps &cet. To many I give (when I have it) small sums of money—half of the soldiers in hospital have not a cent. There are many returned prisoners, sick, lost all—and every day squads of men from the front, cavalry or infantry—brought in wounded or sick, generally without a cent of money. I select the most needy cases and devote much of my time and services to them. Some are mere lads, seventeen, nineteen. Some are silent, sick, heavy-hearted (things, attentions, &cet. are very rude in the army and hospitals, nothing but the mere hard routine, no time for tenderness or extras). So I go round. Some of my boys die, some get well."

Then the tone changed abruptly. "O what a sweet unwonted love (those good American boys of good stock, decent, clean, well-raised boys, so near home). What an attachment grows up between us, started from hospital cots, where so many pale young American soldiers lie. For so many months I have gone among them, having long ago discarded all stiff conventions (they and I are too near to each other, there is no time to lose, and death and anguish dissipate ceremony here between my lads and me). I pet them. This does some of them much good. They are so indistinct and lonesome. On parting at night sometimes I kiss them right and left. The doctors tell me I supply the patients with a medicine which all their drugs and bottles and powders are often unable to match in efficacy."

I looked up at the time-worn countenance of the poet who presented himself to the world as someone as manly as any soldier, or iron puddler, or cow-boy on the plains of the western territories, and who talked much of his numerous illegitimate children, whom no one has ever seen or heard from. Tears were running down the channels of his face. I suddenly sensed what his British correspondents and acolytes evidently understood with their more refined European perceptions. I realized that he had been in love with all those boys.

TWELVE

Ｉ SUPPOSE Ｉ WAS BECOMING an even better listener, for I
began noticing, as I believe anyone would have done, that certain
traits were showing up ever more frequently in W's everyday
talk. For instance, when he spoke about the war, the subject of
Lincoln would always come to dominate the thread, though I came
to see that W wasn't serious about politics. For him, the subject
seemed to consist of a few abstractions, the same ones found in the
immortal *Leaves*, such as Freedom, Democracy and Liberty, which
he believed that America could spread around the globe only once
all obstacles to trade were pulled down. Predictably, this often led to
the despised tariff and the foreigners who wouldn't listen to America.
Usually this meant the hated British Empire, either in whole or in
part—the part closest to hand being Canada.

"Canada is a country of characteristics," he said. "The landscape
has characteristics, the people have characteristics."

I didn't know what he meant by this. Then he spoke more clearly.
He went on to say: "Canada has been injured by its colonial adhesion
to England."

Was his mind noting the kinship of *adhesion* and *adhesiveness*?

"I used to walk about when I was up there with Bucke and talk
with the people. Canada should be on its own feet, asserting the life

that properly belongs to it. I should say we on this side of the border are too much inclined to minimize its importance. It is good to get about among other peoples, to not take too much for granted in our superiorities, to take a little off our prejudices and put a little of our admiration there, just so's we may finally establish ourselves on the right family basis among the nations."

At the time, I took all this at its face value. But I hear W's words differently now, thinking of them in light of the late war in Europe and the way our government imprisons, deports, lynches and shoots down Socialists and labor people, or sanctions those who do so, trying to rid the land of anyone committed to change for the better rather than the worse. Canada divorced from Great Britain would be in need of another big friend. Don't you agree?

Another trait of W's over this period was that whenever he was feeling particularly unwell, which unfortunately was more and more often as the Winter of Eighty-eight–Eighty-nine drew near, he would urge me to work faster on the *Complete Poems and Prose*. "Better hasty than posthumous," he said one day.

⁂

Sometimes the ink on the armfuls of galley proof I brought to him was still a bit wet. He would look them over and, all too often, tinker with as well as merely correct them. I always made sure that he had a batch of them on his work-table or at his bedside, for the task aided his concentration and distracted him from his condition. I was used to such chores and half a hundred others, but sometimes his requests astonished me. For example, he decided that he needed a new stove. The old one, which it seems was given to him by one of his sisters after the first stroke in Seventy-three, was not functioning well, and he saw the necessity of keeping his bedroom as warm and snug as possible. I was to keep an eye peeled for something suitable.

"I am likely to be tied right here in this room the whole Winter if I live at all," he said. "Some days I get doubtful about myself, but I have a notion now that I may drag on several years at my present low level of life. It is a conservative level, conservative to the last degree, but suffices for some purposes, of which we will make the most we can."

The Spring of Eighty-nine was a particularly mild one, when the seasonal pleasantness eased ocean travel and seemed to bring an unusually large number of individual British visitors. In their company W kept his views of their Empire politely tucked away and received their veneration with a modesty I believe was sincere. One caller, a professional soldier, had developed an intense admiration for *Leaves* while in the British army. He was so stiff and bristly that I expected the conference between them to be difficult. But W was able in this case to extend his easy rapport with common soldiers, the younger the better, to a serving officer of great age and higher station, for flattery is a highly effective lubricant. And you might suppose W to have recoiled from knowing that one visitor, Edwin Arnold, was actually Sir Edwin and had one of those accents that cannot help but make a listener feel like a manservant or chambermaid. But nothing of the kind; W was as charming as a no longer terribly strong person could be.

To that same period belongs the visit by Doctor John Johnson, another member of the English race, who had been in correspondence with W for a couple of years. You must know him, I'm sure. I use the present tense, for he is still alive and therefore carries every promise of outliving me, I'm afraid. He is a physician in Bolton, which I am informed is a grime-covered city known for woolen mills and other no doubt horrid establishments. With his friend J.W. Wallace, of the same place, he founded what they mischievously called Bolton College. It is no college at all, but rather an organization of

Socialists who identify a major mystical strain in W's work. I know this interpretation is amenable to you and your own ardent group there in Toronto. In my observation, the spiritual connection to be found in W's poetry takes root most deeply in Canada and in the British Isles and other pink portions of the map, possibly because they are some of the most Protestant of cultures and lack much of what they believe W was able to provide. Doctor Johnson had come over to meet his hero, gaze upon his birthplace and see as many as possible of the sites associated with his subject's other biographical details. Although the Bolton Boys, as W and I called the group, had had some slight contact with the inversionistical literary chaps in London, the two circles were of such different characters that they might almost have been the products of altogether separate countries. Hence their different treatment.

The oddest and certainly the most troublesome of the visitors was the one W referred to as "the Japanee," though in fact only his mother was from Nippon whilst his father was a German. His name was Carl Sadakichi Hartmann, though he dropped the forename before the end of the old century, as on the title-page of his history of American painting, with which you and your friends might be familiar, or perhaps ought to be. When he first presented himself at Mickle Street, he sought my favor by addressing me in German. His effort was worthless. Although I comprehend the tongue as spoken (and read it rather better), I do not speak so much of it as you might suppose. Father always believed that the old language, like the old religion, should be jettisoned in the New World. Hartmann was a dandy and an aesthete (one of those), not a serious political man in the least. He was tall and so unnaturally thin that when he stood, he arranged his limbs artfully as though they were flowers in a vase; when he sat, he folded in on himself like a pen-knife. His talk was colorful and artistic, but he used a loud cackle for punctuation. In the presence of his host, he performed a sort of dance of attendance, clutching at every word from W's mouth.

Shortly afterward, unfortunately, he published his memorandum of the encounter in the *Herald*, which had commissioned many of W's poems about public events and had so often been kind in booming his books and platform appearances. He quoted what he contended were W's disparaging summations of other writers. Emerson and Hawthorne, two of the victims, were dead by then. But others, such as Oliver Wendell Holmes, outlived their supposed libeler. W of course refuted these untruths, as I believe it was proper for him to do. He may often have resorted to booming himself, as the leaders of literature had long forced him to do by excluding him from their Pantheon, but he was not a man to cowardly deny something of which he was guilty— a different matter from the instinct for self-preservation that caused him to be misleading about the origins of the sex-poems. In any case, Hartmann published subsequent articles feeding off his slight acquaintance with his elder and better, then had the audacity to gather these together in a small book. This time the author was identified simply as Sadakichi, no surname. Such trials of course did nothing to steady W's wobbling health. Certainly W lacked for internal peace when Hartmann turned up in Boston as founder of a Walt Whitman Society there, through which he began to solicit monetary contributions that never benefited W because they never left Hartmann's pocket.

The visitor with the biggest personality of all was of course Doctor Bucke, who arrived in Camden slightly in advance of Spring itself, for 1889 would see W's seventieth birthday and Bucke naturally wanted to be fully on hand for it, bringing all his energy, intensity, inscrutability and, at times, incomprehensibility—and certainly his singular limp, which I once heard someone say made him look like a person walking sideways up one of those very steep streets in San Francisco (whereas he always made me think of a side-wheeler with only one paddle). He took his medical education in the U.S.A. but had what seems to us Americans one of those curiously modulated Canadian voices.

Bucke was W's first true biographer if you allow that *The Good Gray Poet* by O'Connor, who wrote with great confidence indeed, better than I do at any rate, and *Notes on Walt Whitman, as Poet and Person* by John Burroughs, who wrote (and still writes) quite well for a scientific man, were more in the nature of pamphlets than actual books. Both were brought out after the war. Observe that after first making the acquaintance of my spirit-father—a term that Bucke could have defined much better than I can, though his explanation would have been hobbled by jargon known only to himself—I began calling it "the war," *the* war, as though there was no other and it was the doing of people my own age. I have always associated with persons older than myself, being interested in serious adult matters, not the nominal things of youth, which I found asinine. Anne aside, I dealt with my elders exclusively. I felt this gave me an advantage in developing as a person, but I was then unaware of the negative effect: the fact that most of them were to die when I was still at least active in body and completely alert in mind, leaving me feeling bereft and friendless. Now that my own end is in sight, at what everyone agrees with me is an insufficiently ripe age, I appreciate how many who might have been my companions will now outlive me without our having communicated in a meaningful way, if at all. I suppose that this could be seen as the wheel completing its revolution.

Of all my distinguished elders, Bucke was certainly the most difficult to get a handle on, and often the most difficult even to comprehend. He was an exporter of ethereal, spiritual and mock-religious talk. Not at all the personality of a scientific Socialist, though he was of a scientific bent of course. He was forthright in sharing his views, if not always helpful in explaining what he was talking about. He once told W that *Drum-Taps* was a big step down from *Leaves,* allowing one to infer that at least some subsequent books were in turn steps down from *Taps.* I did not agree with such statements, because *Leaves* belongs to its category on an exclusive basis and there are no other books that even brush against it. I'm sure such honest diagnosis is a virtue in a medical man talking to his patients, but it does no credit in dealing with a literary friend.

When Bucke was not saying such things, he was perhaps going overboard in the opposite direction. Put another way, his praise, though not his unanimous reaction to all things, could be, to say the least, fulsome. When, after the usual struggles, the *Complete Poems and Prose* saw the light of day, he wrote to say that "it will be the sacred text by and by. The First Folio of S is valuable but I guess after a little while that an autographed *C.P.P. of W.W.* will lead it in the market." Bucke was interested in Shakespeare, but not in the somewhat conspiratorial way that W and many others were. The Bard is not one of the god-like mystics in Bucke's *Cosmic Consciousness,* which places W alongside not only Jesus Christ but also Buddha, Saul-who-became-St.-Paul, Plotinus, Mohammad and William Blake. Will from Stratford-upon-Avon was a top student of human behavior, the doctor would say, but hardly a visionary.

When I read the above passage to W, whose eyes were bothering him greatly—another ailment on the mounting list—he chuckled in appreciation. "Maurice is a monster boomer," he said. "He can make you feel a lot too big about yourself if you don't look out. Dear Maurice!"

Bucke and I, both of us realizing that we needed a deep understanding of each other in our efforts to prolong W's life and uphold his work, decided to do some traveling together, even though this meant being away from W's bedside for one long day. Our assignment was to pay a visit to William O'Connor, who was possibly W's oldest friend he was still in contact with, someone he first met in Boston in 1860:

one of what seemed the few momentous relationships formed *before* and not *during* or *after* the war. When the conflict came, O'Connor too became a clerk in Washington City. Like Burroughs, he worked at the Treasury but continued clerking when the peace came. Now, still in Washington, he was dying. Cancer was the culprit that was stealing his life, and W was eager for first-hand unseasoned news of its terrible progress, however fearful he was of what information might be produced. He thought of making the journey himself in the company of a doctor, but of course was unable to. So it was that on a heavily over-cast day Bucke and I crossed over to Philadelphia and took the 8:31 for Baltimore so as to change there for Washington. I had never been in the capital and was startled to see the monuments and buildings I was familiar with from photographs only, and surprised as well by the high percentage of Negroes in the population, much higher than Camden's or Philadelphia's, and the curt relations with them pursued by whites.

William and Nellie O'Connor lived in a well-maintained house no bigger than Mickle Street but brick, not frame, and in a respectable neighborhood, absent both fertilizer manufactory and railroad tracks. Nellie went alone to pave the way for us upstairs, where the patient lay. Then we were summoned. The sick man sat in an armchair, for after being stricken with the ongoing disease he had suffered a brain incident somewhat like W's, denying his limbs the use for which our bodies intend them. The resulting absence of exercise had caused him to put on considerable weight, no doubt despite a diminution of appetite. The extra pounds notwithstanding, you could not look into his eyes without appreciating the extreme gravity of his condi-tion. His good nature, though, had not entirely deserted him, and his ironic humor still functioned. He asked if we had come to view the remains, and smiled.

He told Bucke how often and with what affection W spoke of me in his letters. I was touched. When Missus O'Connor stepped out of the room, he bade me come close, and hugged me and kissed me on the lips and on my eyelids and on the forehead. When he did so, I suddenly smelled the death we had already seen. I knew that I was the pale proxy for W but that I would have to do, and that I would be required somehow to transmit the love to the other sick man back in Camden. He then said that he and W were in constant touch by telepathy.

Some dying men are tight-lipped. They have only silent conversations with those they hope can hear them through the obstacles of time and distance and perhaps via the agency of faith, for them that have it. Others talk a blue streak. O'Connor was in the latter camp. He evidently had had few visitors, and confronted with our presence decided to uncork the bottle. The need for beneficial company and plenty of it, as well as additional care and strong young men to lift him when necessary, is probably what led Bucke, in his usual tone of unintended authority, to tell O'Connor that he should ask to be moved to a proper hospital. Other than such remarks, we did not speak of his illness and certainly not of the specifics of the disease, which in any case were all too apparent on his countenance. Bucke asked him if he was writing, for all agree that he was a writer of surpassing prose.

"I cannot," he replied, a little plaintively, and tears began to seep from the corners of his eyes.

Bucke replied by saying, "Nonsense. You mustn't give up on your gift, not when you most need its benefits." I wonder to what degree, if at all, such statements were part of the vocabulary he used in conversing with the saner sort of lunatic. O'Connor showed no visible reaction, but the subject did lead to talk of other writers.

To my delight, he reminisced about the young W, whom so few were left to remember, and he recalled for me the dark atmosphere of government offices in wartime when, he said with a smile that was brief but broad, W was a fellow member of the notarial class. He said his own approach to surviving the repetitive work in the face of emotional peril and bureaucratic terror was to throw himself into it purposefully, like a horse that must continue trotting because the blinders circumscribe its awareness of the other possibilities. By contrast, he went on, there was W, whom he described as a charismatic fellow who cut a memorable figure. W was then a healthy man of forty-three or -four, "narrow at the flanks," O'Connor said, and with a beard that was still more dark than not, as on the frontispiece of the 1860 *Leaves*. "The red of his face was not bloat (I know that well) but a sort of sun-flush." All I could think of was Eakins's photograph of the sick and aged W as fully and unashamedly naked as the day he was born.

In time, O'Connor had suffered a seemingly sudden and certainly dramatic nervous attack owing to the strain. I asked how W had avoided the same development, as their situations were very near identical.

"Oh, by not working hard," he said, a discernible smile reappearing where a few tears had held sway only minutes earlier. "He would come in of a morning, sit down, work like a steam engine for an hour or so, then throw himself back in his chair, yawn, stretch himself, pick up his hat and go out." Had this not been his apparatus for neutralizing the chaos and sorrow around him, O'Connor said, he would not have had the inner strength left to help all those boys laid out in the wards like railroad ties. Nor, in O'Connor's view, would he have continued to write poetry.

Turning to W's reputation as an artist, he suggested that his friend, while increasingly the recipient of honor and esteem in the nations of Europe, and in the northern Dominion (nodding at Bucke), he was still far from fully appreciated, or often not even tolerated, in his own country.

The dying man now looked me squarely in the face, his eyes level with my eyes, his nose seemingly in contact with my own, his mouth telling my mouth words it implored my entire body to remember.

"Horace," said the transfigured lips, "you must return as my delegate to Walt. Take my body and take my soul with you. Set them down on his doorstep, under his feet, across his pillow, anywhere, so that he may know I have survived whole and entire in the Old Faith. To this message I consecrate your journey back to Camden."

This will sound odd, but for a second I wondered whether Pete Doyle, a direct son of the old country over the ocean, had ever managed to free himself from his own theater of candles and incense or had turned back to it, if he had ever truly left, to seek expiation for what nearly everyone save convicts, soldiers and sailors without recourse to females, and certain poetry-writing Englishmen who have such access but refuse it, evidently considers a heinous sin and a soul-destroying terror. You are a forthright woman, sensitive but devoid of most forms of nonsense and not given to squeamishness or timidity, so I trust that I can be frank with you, even bald in my way, when I mention such things. If I have made an error in judgment in doing so, I will implore you to harass me by the use of spirit mediums once I am gone, perhaps even before completing my *cri de coeur*, if that indeed is what I am writing for you now! You see, I jest.

Bucke and I stayed for two and one-half hours in all before leaving to catch the three-thirty train. That was on March second. William Douglas O'Connor deserted life on May ninth, aged fifty-seven, thirteen years younger than W when he learned of the news and only four years younger than I am as I write this. W was sadder than I had ever seen him. How did O'Connor's departure compare with other dark cataclysms? With Lincoln's murder? With his mother's death? With what I was coming to sense may have been a violent separation from Pete the Great? I didn't know the answers to such questions, and I lacked the means of improving my judging ability.

Another of my duties was to be what I believe is now called a press agent. Formerly W had performed this task for himself, and no one could have done it better. Such was my impression from what had become my rather bulky file of newspaper cuttings. Once, when we were working on *Complete Poems and Prose*, he told me that the previous evening, after I had left him, when Missus Davis had gone to bed and the house was dark, he was moved by an urge to go downstairs. I did something I virtually never did: I upbraided him. Didn't he realize how dangerous and foolish that was? Why did he ignore advice from me, Missus Davis and his impressive complement of doctors? Why did he ignore even what his own body was imploring him not to do?

He looked contrite and said he had made the descent unaided because he suddenly needed a book from the parlor and didn't wish to disturb Missus Davis. "I'll never again attempt to make the trip alone," he said. "Never. I promise." He said that he spent so much effort slowly navigating the staircase in the blackness that he had exhausted himself, and that he continued to be exhausted even now, a fact that was obvious. For some reason I suddenly had a vision of W the young schoolboy, the one who, or so his adult incarnation claimed, had been part of the crowd welcoming the aged Marquis de Lafayette to Long Island in Twenty-five. This was at the commencement of the old Revolutionary gentleman's triumphant tour of all twenty-six states, where he might easily have died from being fêted and fed so often and so grandly. One end of life and then the other, with too short a string between them.

In any event, as W's health worsened still more, it fell to me to make certain that his name continued to be laid before readers' eyes without permitting them to believe that the famous man was dying. Here, for example, is a piece I prompted the *Ledger* to publish by imposing on my acquaintanceship with one of the newspapermen across the river, who came to the house but was denied a meeting by

W, thereby unwittingly providing me the opportunity to steer the reporting in a certain benign direction without much loss of prominence in the paper as printed:

> Walt Whitman, the "good gray poet," of Camden, was reported last week to be suffering from a severe cold, necessitating his confinement to his room. This report was denied at his home, 328 Mickle-street, last night, and it was stated that his health has remained about the same for several weeks past, and that he has not left his room, except at intervals for a short time, since the recurrence of his old illness, several months ago. It was also stated that no serious danger at all is apprehended by his present condition.

I cannot lie to you by claiming that I wasn't lying then. W was terribly ill with a malfunctioning of his lungs and chest, some sort of severe failure in his left leg, and what he confided to me in a meek voice was discomfort and even pain deep within the reproductive regions. My supposition was that the last item on the list would have affected him the most, as it would do with anyone but especially so him, as the author of all those hymns to the body that brought him so much in the way of scandal and rejection. These ailments were in addition to his growing shortcomings of memory and vision. These were simply attendants of old age, though Doctor Osler would inform me that they were nonetheless opportunistic ailments that had taken root only because other divisions of the body had broken down.

Short of the immediate aftermath of the brain seizure that had stolen his mobility, W was now in the worst condition I had seen him suffer through. I find it difficult, however, to remember this fact now, looking back, for the story of his icy slide toward death was doled out a day at a time. The ligatures that joined each day to the next were usually so tenuous that it was difficult to observe the general trend at first hand while retaining a sense of which way the story's big arrows were pointing. That is the way history is. Like the Chinese water torture, it is released one drop at a time, in a steady *pling pling pling*, designed to limit our comprehension of the deluge overall. That type of understanding is the job of later historians and of the next generation as a whole.

I did not always find W in his bedroom, lying either in or across the bed (the sign of a day of weakness) or reading in his chair by the windows (compared to the other, an indicator of a more positive state). Sometimes he would greet me from the front parlor once Missus Davis had taken him firmly by the arm and shoulder and eased him down to the main floor, a task that on other occasions I would be called on to perform. Sometimes I would catch him emerging from the second-floor bath-room, carrying a towel or belting his trousers. His lengthy visits there were audible to all, as he enjoyed singing arias, loudly, while sitting in the zinc tub. Seeing him navigate Missus Davis's well-worn runner in the hallway gave me a still more accurate sense of the hesitation and difficulty with which he propelled himself along. At the end of the shortest such journey, he would be glad of a rest in the chair or a return to his bed.

Knowing the difficulty I was having raising money to pay for nursing, Bucke had somehow persuaded a young man named Nathan Baker, who worked at the Canadian asylum, to come down to Camden. When he left in order to pursue medical studies (Doctor Osler gave the address to his graduating class), Bucke sent Eddie Wilkins, a fine young man, selfless and intelligent, with a companionable personality as well as a strong physique. Most likely it was Osler who brought in

Doctor Daniel Longaker of Philadelphia to examine W on a regular basis, recording the many diseases and their symptoms, relieving the suffering that attended them and throwing impediments in their path where he could. Doctor Longaker was a worthy of the Society for Ethical Culture. I am not certain whether the Ethical Culture doctrines found favor in your own country. If they did, Doctor Bucke would surely have been at the forefront, I imagine. In the United States such groups formed in all the great cities. Their common basis was the belief that ethical behavior lay at the heart of all the organized religions and that the pursuit of such an approach in all departments of life was the proper substitute for what goes on in churches, synagogues, tabernacles, gospel halls, Quaker meeting-houses, and any number of temples and mosks. I need not say that W, though he was not a joiner and said he never had been, found such non-theistic views agreeable. He was true right to the end to whatever combination of non-beliefs he held dear, though he may have been wavering. Once I came upon him sitting in his chair reading a big old leather-clad Bible. He looked slightly embarrassed, telling me that he read it frequently as the source of so much of our literature rather than as insight into God or the Lord (or even as a source of comfort for its familiar and reassuring words, which is what I imagine he was seeking).

One evening when I arrived at the house, his first question was, "Where have you been to-day?" I believe he took a vicarious pleasure, the only sort he could practice by then, in my hum-drum traipsing from a chair at the library to my stool at the bank, from post office to grocery to newspaper stand.

I told him that I had gone for a pleasant walk across the river with a friend of mine.

He pressed for the details.

Then he responded by telling me what I already knew. "I walked great walks myself in the Washington days. Often with Pete Doyle.

"Pete was never a scholar," he continued, reconfirming the blatantly obvious. "We had no scholarly affinities. But he was worldly, an everyday workingman."

In those photographs of him that I had seen, Pete looked no different from the other thuggish Hibernians found everywhere in the country. I have never visited the island nation whence they originate, but I knew the statistics showing that they had been the main practitioners of immigration and new growth to America until overtaken somehow by the clearly less fertile German migrants, such as the Traubels. Even the German Catholics bred far fewer children than the Irish with whom they shared dogma. I suppose this is because the Germans are industrious and gifted in business, so it is constantly said, and thus stand in contrast to the Irish, whose great contribution to civilization has been the whiskey they distill but whose main exports to America's shores are young men so full of the stuff that work suffers when it cannot be avoided altogether.

Continuing on, W pronounced Doyle a companion who was (and still is?) "full to the brim with the real substance of God." This statement almost left me prostrate. He then contrasted the abundant perambulations he and Pete shared with the relatively infrequent ones he engaged in with his friend O'Connor during the same period. Of course in the latter case there was clearly an intellectual bond being forged, based upon their shared interest in books and writing. Its continuation on the additional grounds of shared ideas in other areas was a later development. So W explained, adopting the tone of crystalline candor that he took to whenever the spirit moved him to truly open up instead of merely reminiscing or recounting events. These moments became the real joy of all the Camden conversations I came to cherish.

"At that time," he said, "for the first two or three years of the war, William O'Connor was warm, earnest, eager, passionate—warrior-like for the anti-slavery ideas. He was immersed, suckered in. This in some ways served to keep us apart, superficially apart. I can easily see now that I was a good deal more repelled by that sentiment, by that devotion in William, than was justified, for I am not temperamentally suited to having any truck or trade with fashionable movements. With these latter-day confirmations of William's balance, of his choice, of his masterly decisions—the fruit of later eventuation, the later succession of events—there has come to me some self-regret, some suspicion that I was extreme or at least too lethargic in my withdrawals from William's magnificent enthusiasm." He paused, looking spent. "Years have added luster to the O'Connor of that day."

I wished I could induce him to apply the same honesty to the subject of Pete Doyle and whatever others like Doyle there may have been and must have been, though clearly Pete was a special case. There is only one such attachment in a single lifetime, or so sentimentalists tell us. Mine was and is Anne Montgomerie, just as his, I have not the smallest doubt, was Peter Doyle, late of the Confederate army and who knows what other rightly maligned and constantly misunderstood associations.

It may be, I thought, that there will never come a time when I can put to W the questions that now occupied such a prominent place in my mind. In any event, I knew that this was not that moment. This, rather, was a time for comings and goings. It was a time of frequent visitors who, by being briefly present, worked in favor of his spirit even as they further eroded his strength, and of contemporaries, some of them long-time compatriots, whom he saw drop away, snapped up by death in a manner that could not help but make his last days all the sadder.

THIRTEEN

BUCKE, THE MERCURIAL bombastic Bucke, so mysterious because he was mystical, so overpowering because he was enthusiastic to a degree ordinarily found only in Hell's-fire preachers and underhanded stockjobbers, was promising (or threatening) to come down from Canada for another visit. Every few days a postal would arrive, announcing his imminent arrival, followed quickly by others that cited inevitable delays. "He has been coming every day since last September," W said with a lightness of tone that could not obliterate the bed of anxiety over which it was lain.

That Bucke's life was busy there was absolutely no doubt whatsoever. Doing good for the weak-minded remanded to his care was enormously difficult and demanding, particularly if one was forever evading censure, as I imagined he was, for introducing new techniques and ideas. And possibly, but I'm not certain, for being associated with the notorious libertine W, whose very name, as the libertine himself enjoyed remarking, would sometimes be invoked to frighten small children into behaving themselves.

Bucke of course was at all times minutely aware of conditions at Mickle Street, for he sent letters as well as cards. He kept W engaged in the longer exchanges of the sort the old man had gotten in the habit of maintaining. As he did so, however, he also wrung news from the other members of W's—what is the proper term? Not *circle*, for though I have used that description often enough, it sounds far too literary and genteel for the intended purpose. Not *coterie* or *band*. Truth to tell, *gang* is nearer the mark, though the newspapers' love of sensational crime has given the term an unhealthy cast. Or perhaps the German *Ring*. In any case, Bucke finally arrived in a frenzy of compassion in February of Eighty-nine, and when I was alone with him, he was extremely candid as to W's chances. We both knew that the situation was bleak and its termination near, but Bucke's dark vision had greater power than my own, as he could back up his assertions with medical reasoning and all the terminology that attends it, including generous outbursts of Latin and even, when extra emphasis was warranted, of Greek. He was one of W's comparatively few friends who were highly educated according to accepted principles, though it was obvious that he filled his days with living as well as with mere learning. In that way, he stood proud of the other gang-members.

Previously I had usually confined my visits to the hours after supper, by which time the food had lifted W's energies a bit and he was feeling most rested. Yet following Bucke's departure, I added morning calls as well. It was remarkable how his condition, rather than simply his disposition or alertness, varied from one end of a day to the other. I do not know whether or to what extent he feared death. He seemed no sadder to be going than he was weary of lingering, but that was sorrow enough for anyone to feel or even, as I did, to experience by direct witness. Perhaps he found some true comfort in the knowledge that his pain was about to end. I hope so. Not to compare myself to him in his condition, but I myself was finding it hard to adjust to his pending absence and the sheer awful permanence of it. My life until that time had been devoid of tragedy, but I knew full well what to expect. I did not know how I might react, then and later; how I might bear up under the grief that events made me practice for, every day, twice a day.

Bucke's energy, while perhaps not contagious, did linger in the air for a while following his visit. W had grown to depend on some form of communication from him. He needed the certainty of this communication as well as that of my visits, and other things, to serve the function of little rituals to which he could hitch himself on his last earthly journey, now so surely in its final miles. Even with the benevolent fumes of Bucke's personality still in our nostrils, he became agitated with worry when days and days went by without any word from Ontario. Looking back, I wonder now, as I did then, why Bucke, who was so well informed, had allowed his friend's supply of reassurance to be interrupted in this way. I tried to palliate the prevailing atmosphere by repeating that Bucke had taken to cultivating an appearance as much like his hero's as possible. He had groomed his beard to closely approximate the famously tangled garden of gray that obscured W's breastbone, had disciplined his hair, if that is a correct verb, to place as much emphasis on his bare pate as possible. He was also dressing in clothing of the color (black) and cut (slightly homespun looking) that had always distinguished W's own. He was even aspiring to the young W's deliberately lackadaisical manner, quite singular for someone other than, as W said, admiringly for once, "a Negro tramping along a railroad right-of-way in such a suit of clothes, carrying himself in a free, easygoing, unpremeditated and joyous manner even when no cause for joy was apparent but quite the opposite."

I did remark to W, however, that on seeing Bucke, people sometimes asked me whether he was related to the Good Gray Poet. "A long-lost sibling perhaps, come back to claim an inheritance," I said.

"Might he not more reasonably be mistaken for one of my children out of wedlock?" W responded in kind. "He is some two decades my junior"—eighteen years actually—"and could well be the fruit of one of my missteps in love. Let's see, I would have been teaching country school on Long Island about then. But he has traveled in this country a great deal, as you know, just as I have lingered with such easy pleasure in his own."

Even as I watched my own head start to become frosted with white like the panes in a shop-window at Christmas, I was always to remain, save for Anne, the youngster of this tight little gang of rogue spirits, for while I myself was born some twenty-one years later than Bucke, I was, at the same time, W's junior by thirty-nine. This fact caused me to carry on the playful charade.

"Might not I be another of the unintended ones of whom you have been known to brag with such unselfish shame?"

I took W's chuckle as a sign that at this last or at least penultimate extremity, our relationship had reached a fresh plateau of candor. Just as I articulated this thought, silently to myself, he began to cough uncontrollably, a horrible tearing cough from some place near the center of his skeletal framework and deep within his girdle of vitals. Had it persisted with such violence, I realized, I wouldn't have known what to do, but I was able to stem the deathly noise with a slap on his now sadly convex back and a few sips of water. A man is in a sorrowful state when his own laughter causes him pain.

When he recovered his bearings, he returned to being morose, and spoke feelingly of the way so many of his old friends had lost their final struggle with the dark angel. This euphemism had been used commonly among his beloved boys in the hospitals so long ago, boys who by the time he said this were men in their forties, their bodies, however well they survived the rebellion, far from the young specimens of W's constant recollection.

He spoke of how death had reshaped his world. He saw the numerous fatal casualties just within his own family as the opening of a drama on which his own non-existence would bring down the curtain. And then there was the fact that some of his wartime contemporaries specifically, his fellow non-combatant veterans you might almost say, had also begun disappearing, although most were younger than he was. I don't believe he knew anyone his own age who had participated in the conflict in ways so profound as his own. Wounded and maimed men certainly, but not ones who emerged from the conflict with a change of spirit in ways that Grand Army of the Republic parades could never fully express. All too soon he and these men would be history together, imperfect as history always is.

When this thought welled over me then, it remained unexpressed. Yet I knew without saying so that this was another signal that W was enlarging his trust in me. Especially so coming on the heels of all the harmless banter about his children who existed only as a device for deceiving and deflecting the naïfs, the suspicious ones and those who were far too curious. Language always had been the food of his non-bodily existence, but precious little talk was expended for the rest of the day.

He was certainly living far longer than anyone, medical people and members of the laity alike, had expected. Some elderly persons are too ornery to die when others suppose they should. You must have known instances of this, just as I have. Then there are artists who often must hang on against all the bookmakers' predictions until they have finished some great work that not only concludes their lifetime of labor but symbolizes and indeed actually completes, with a satisfaction impossible for us to guess, one entire human consciousness (oh dear, I'm sounding like the late Doctor Bucke).

There was to be one more edition of *Leaves*, the ninth one not counting piracies, though it was really no more than a needless fattening of a life's-work that had reached its state of fullness long ago and increasingly was accepted by the world that once reviled it, though W for sanity's sake still clutched at its rebellious bent and flavor. Although the book seemed to have created him as much as he had created it, I believe it was far from the only thing keeping him alive. Another one, as I steadily came to realize over time, was Anne: a statement that will probably surprise you but I hope will delight you as well.

How shall I put this? There is a stage, the highest and most profound one, I believe, at which a black man and a white man lose their respective histories of degradations and prerogatives. Without diminishing their pride in what they are—on the contrary, in fact—they become, quite simply, two men who have moved beyond what so obviously separates them and have located the knowledge that they— and we, all of us—are in the same boat, trying to survive while straining to figure out what is so good about the "good life," that elusive abstraction of the philosophers.

With the races, so too with the genders. What I learned from W, and also, to give him his due, from Bucke, is that there is a place in our collective existence that lies on the other side of biology, where propagation and pleasure are not the only purposes to which love and desire may be put. There is an attenuation of our sexual beings that can, in persons of sufficient openness and exalted understanding, subsume the mechanical and emotional differences between the male and the female, resolving them in the universal name of humanity, by which I mean the state of being human—and humane. One gender requires the other if it is to transcend the differences that only disunite without enriching. One needs an opposite in order to reach one's potential, whether alone or in harness. Anne became his opposing pole and made his last years even more trying, and of course more rewarding as well. Just as she was swept away by his magnetism

when she first laid eyes on him on a lecture platform, so he himself, I think, was instantly infatuated with her ease and charm. In time, he truly came to love her, without the corrupting carnal need that underlay his relations with the men he loved as well, especially Pete— as I sensed early on and accurately enough but without too much conscious thought. For knowledge in that area came to me slowly, if steadily, as my relationships with W and then with Anne and finally with both of them together as well as singly—relationships of the heart alone in the one instance, of heart-and-body in the other— developed as they did. Do you know the term *ménage à trois?* It is a coarse and distasteful expression in French, referring to the situation that obtains when two men are attached to the same woman, or, I suppose, when two women share the same man—and, whichever is the case, do so under the same roof. W, Anne and I found ourselves with a similar dilemma (or ecstasy) but with important differences. We all loved one another, though perhaps not equally, and of course only two of us were united in the marital sense, as the third was so far along in his physical decline and so high above us in the almost empyrean way he had transcended mating. Otherwise, it was much as one might read about in the prurient flash sold, rather furtively, by Parisian news-agents. Certainly it was not without its jealousies, at least not on my part, I'm sorry to admit.

Or, to put the matter in quite a different way, he was ennobled by an inventory of kindness so large that he had yet to dispense it all, and by romantic wounds that he had prodded and examined until they became his finest group of poems, the "Calamus" ones, which healed some of the enormous hurts he had endured. That he found it necessary to keep the circumstances of his creating them away from the broad public was a hideous irony. On the surface he may have betrayed no hint of these large lashing affronts to tranquillity. But to visit him as so many did, and see him trade the companionship of living people for another spoonful of the precious energies he needed to conserve like a miser, was a glum and piteous experience at times. To look in on him and listen to him twice daily as I did, seeing his unabated hope in the face of grimacing reality, was to believe, mistakenly, that he was continuing to die in the orderly fashion that he believed the world expected of him.

John Addington Symonds and other London and Oxford admirers, sitting at inlaid writing-tables in their clubs, persisted in asking him for confirmation of the sexual propensities—I choose that phrase, hoping it is properly neutral—they found encapsulated to perfection in "Calamus." W ignored them just as he did mere autograph-seekers. Or I should say, in the case of fellow writers, did so to the extent consistent with the simple courtesy that educated overseas readers, in sympathy with the author's perceived intent, quite reasonably expected to be shown. At least they didn't usually show up at the door unannounced, as did many other visitors, whose courtesy calls left him enervated to an unusual degree.

Of course, W's dissembling didn't strike me as an especially satisfying explanation, but only as a failed effort at being disingenuous when in a tight jam, logically speaking. Such were the individual fears of us both, about the near future, the very near future indeed, that loomed above us a day or a week or several weeks or a month ahead, that I felt I had little to lose if I pressed him. I believed that the closeness we had arrived at through surviving various adversities and reverses together allowed me to understand him so much more deeply than I had done early in our curious partnership. The situation emboldened me to be devilish just to see what would happen.

"And what would Pete Doyle from Limerick"—which W had once told me casually was the correct place of origin—"say about your lines in honor of the Queen who had mercilessly and criminally oppressed his people, perpetuating the conduct of queens and kings back through the long history that the two races of people shared so uneasily—and tragically?"

I tried to utter the words in a more or less conversational tone, and showed, I believe, no trace of either humor or anger, neither of which I actually felt in any case. Yet my words, springing so unexpectedly out of what began as polite chat, seemed to echo in a way that added urgency, and possibly rebellion or defiance, to what otherwise might have been closer to the innocent interrogative that I had intended, whether or not I believed in it.

To the quiet that followed my question, W responded with a silence of his own. He looked at me for one terribly long instant. I could see none of the many possible responses in his melancholic, worn-out and half-dead eyes. He stroked his whiskers with his right hand as though combing them before a mirror.

"Horace, we each of us have reasons to hurry, for the hour grows painfully late, as I do not have to tell you."

I waited for more words to follow.

He opened his meek and sweet old mouth, now much misshapen by time, and through the aperture in his rapidly thinning whiskers, the good gray beard of the man who had made himself a figure of legend with generous assistance from his motley coalition of madmen, visionaries, charlatans, geniuses, inverts and occasionally some man's bored wife, said that while each of us had reason to act in haste, we should not cease to cultivate assiduity and evenness of effort.

"Be patient, my fine young friend. Be patient."

In the quiet that then recurred, in that bedroom with all its jumble and perfectly preserved disorder, we could hear that Mickle Street was receiving a fresh coat of rain.

FOURTEEN

B Y 1888, WHEN I FOUND my true place in W's orbit, he
already had an extraordinary array of doctors and other
medical people attending to his health, or rather to his aston-
ishing lack of it. Sitting atop the roost of course was Doctor Osler,
who took him on as a patient when he came down from Montreal to
Philadelphia in, I believe, Eighty-four. In those days of course he had
yet to be given the noble title he continues to enjoy over there in
Oxford or London. I use the present tense, for surely I cannot have
somehow missed news of Sir William's passing. The press, even the
Camden Courier, would have made quite a story of that event. Like W
himself, as it gives me a shiver to realize now, I cling to the newspapers most doggedly. They are my link to the world of the active,
the mobile and the robust, people who can look at the future and see
more than their own extinction.

I don't know when Osler was first called the Father of Modern
Medicine, a distinction I understand he has disputed, or indeed
when he became the single most famous physician in the world,
but even when he had W in his care he was already far famed as a
singular individual, destined for greatness if indeed not already
invested or infected with it. I recall him as a small-boned man; his
feet in particular were tiny. By contrast, his forehead, protecting all

that brain, covered quite an expanse. He was most neat and orderly. W was the first to admit how fortunate he always had been in his doctors, yet he found the depth of Osler's humanity even greater than the breadth of his learning. To W, who said this to me one evening, Osler was someone who, "though a Canadian, is yet Southern and French. He shows indications of both." All attempts to elaborate on this observation for my benefit left its meaning no less obscure.

There was strangeness about W's pronouncements on the northern origins of those who had them. He asked once whether I had observed "the Canadian" that underlay the features of Doctor Bucke's face. Again, I questioned what he meant.

"I cannot say, but it is there," he said. "You will know it someday. You'll get up there, tramp about, see the Doctor, then come to know what I mean."

Even after accepting a far higher position at Johns Hopkins in Baltimore, Osler, who himself became quite a literary figure as well, still saw W from time to time, though others assumed his function once the Good Gray Poet's diseases and afflictions tightened their conspiracy against him during the three years and a bit that I served as (in Anne's phrase) his recording angel. Doctor Longaker I believe I have mentioned. There was also Doctor Henry Cattell, a friend of Eakins, who taught at the university, and then, in Camden itself, Doctor McAlister—Alexander McAlister. All good men, good men indeed. W needed all such help he could attract and muster.

❖

In May Eighty-nine, Ed Wilkins took W for a long push in the wicker-seated invalid's chair. Returning from this, his first outdoor adventure since the previous June, W announced that he would try to duplicate the activity each day. I and others tacitly assumed, though none of us spoke directly of such a motive, that he was adopting the practice in order to build up his endurance for the big do scheduled to take place on his birthday. On the thirty-first of the month he would turn seventy. That was the event for which he had no doubt been anxiously preparing long before he and I had entered each other's lives in any meaningful way. With eight others, some of them members of the gang, others political and business friends of Tom's, I organized a large banquet in Camden to celebrate the anniversary that W feared he would never attain (and he was not the only one). The event was to be called the Feast of Reason (a compromise title) and would unfold at Morgan's Hall at Fourth and Market, a former Odd Fellows meetinghouse that had become, after enlargements and extensive renovations, what young people to-day would term the ritziest place in town.

Here is a terrible admission for a Socialist to make: I had learned that committees seldom function at acceptable levels of efficiency and moreover that I am rarely at my best as a member of one, or at least not of a large one. In some ways, the dinner that resulted from this assembly of worthies resembled what might have come to pass if God, rather than barking an order, had assigned Moses the task of striking a board that would entertain the possibility of proposing a list of possible Commandments, no fewer than eight nor more than twelve.

For example, Anne was radiantly furious with me for days afterward once she discovered that she was to be the only woman seated with two hundred men at the enormously long linen-draped tables arranged in neat ranks. I first tried to pass the blame to Tom's banker friends on the committee, saying that they were not aware they were being rude but were simply not accustomed to dealing with women in the exercise of their daily business. When that didn't wash, I switched to Tom's Republican Party colleagues. "They do not value women," I said accusingly, "because women do not yet exercise the franchise, though let us hope that this tyranny of denial will end soon, as seems to be in the cards."

Her gorgeous blue eyes narrowed as though she was squinting at me through a gun-sight on the firing-range. For indeed I was properly to blame because I was after all the convener and the chairman. To be sure, I never repeated the mistake. The greater lesson I took away from the experience, however, was how even a slight rebuke from Anne pained me more than if a bullwhip had turned my flesh to raw meat. It was not simply that I couldn't live without her but rather that I could not even understand how I had done just that for so long. The slightest tremor in our arrangements, of the sort that I imagine *all* couples must experience from time to time, sent me tottering until I felt I might tumble over the edge. I all but literally worshipped her, and worship her still. It is one thing to turn your back on your religion, a practice not unfamiliar to the Traubel family. It is quite another to realize to your horror that your religion may be, if only temporarily, turning its back on you.

Rather than try to transfer blame to others, I might have enhanced my apology by enumerating all the chores and charges with which I had had to deal in preparing for the occasion, in addition to earning the money we needed—calling at Mickle Street for hours each day, being an errand-boy, editor, proofreader and printing-house foreman ex officio, and all the rest. But did I really need to point this out? She saw the banners I had had made stretched across the wall, high above the head table. She saw the bill of fare, tasteful in its typography and perfectly printed on the best card-stock, and, looking at it, could not have been unmindful of the agony of decision-making that went into choosing each dish in consultation with Morgan's Hall's accomplished head cook. There were little-neck clams and jellied consommé to begin, followed by either beef or lamb on the one hand or fish on the other, the last of these alternatives recognizing that some of W's admirers were rather more Pythagorean, and right-eously so, in their dietary habits. And so on, descending the list of courses, as though down a flight of lushly carpeted stairs, until one stepped on the landing below to be offered coffee, pressed in the French manner, and cigars (fine ones, not Walt Whitman Cigars, though it was claimed these were hand-rolled in Havana—Havana, New Jersey, perhaps).

Moreover, I had filled the room by selling tickets at five dollars apiece, a price intended simply to recoup expenses, for profit would have been the unseemly residue of such a tribute. Or, that is to say, I sold tickets to the literary gents at least, who ranged from Hamlin Garland, the enormously popular novelist who idealized the farms of the Midwest, to Julian Hawthorne, the flamboyant Harvard-educated newspaper correspondent and literary jack-of-all-trades. What's more, I had secretly solicited, from literary worthies in every quarter, messages of congratulations and praise to be read aloud during the ceremony. They arrived by post and by wire. My inside breast pocket had a thick packet of them, from Mark Twain, Howells, Whittier, Rossetti and no less than Tennyson. I had taken care of everything. What I had not done, for it was not possible, was to guarantee that the guest of honor would appear.

People in Camden, and no doubt in other places that imitate Camden in their civic deportment, prefer to dine on the early side, and the crowd was largely assembled by five o'clock, enjoying their apéritifs and scuttlebutt. Rather than make a formal announcement and risk being the object of a massed stare of disappointment or even a chorus of boos, I quietly went from prominent person to prominent person, saying that when I had popped in on W only a few hours earlier, he was mightily ill and not ambulatory in any way I could visualize. He felt dead of spirit as well as body, for here I had invested so much effort—so many of us had—to realize this epochal evening that I knew had existed in his forward imagination for such a long time. He was disappointed for his own sake and also for mine. It made for a poignant and disheartening scene. I told everyone in whom I confided the news, expecting them to tell others, that we would carry on regardless, with first the fine meal and then speeches, telegrams and other encomia (including one from Bob Ingersoll, delivered to me by messenger as I was entering the hall). Certainly we displayed all the warm sentiment and sense of occasion that we could wear on our faces. I imagined that W would have difficulty getting there even if he were feeling better. A very strong westerly wind, the kind that steals hundreds of hats and makes horses stand stock-still and plant their hooves on the bricks as firmly as they can, was blowing across the city, accompanied by a pulverizing rain.

Everyone enjoyed the meal, and I remember thinking how thoughtless I was to have ordered up so many rich dishes, as Bucke was forever concerned that spicy foods were another source of W's intestinal distress. But of course this would not be a problem if the hero failed to appear.

As the waiters were bussing the soiled plates &cet., a strong voice at the back, near the double doors, shouted to us: "He's coming!" I looked across to see one of the two Camden coppers whom Tom had persuaded his friend the chief of police to post at the function (warning me, for he was wise in such matters, to see that the head cook fed them lavishly in the kitchen, "as much as they want of whatever they want"). The cop then disappeared into the corridor. The crowd fell silent, like, I imagined, the Millerite brethren who for years would gather at certain spots on particularly portentous dates, waiting in utter silence for the Rapture that never came. In a moment, the doors flew open and the two Irish coppers, the shouting one and his equally burly colleague, gently set W's wheeling-chair and its passenger down on the floor, having carried it up the long flight of steps.

Ed Wilkins, who had followed behind them after shepherding the chair from Mickle Street in a hack, resumed his grip on the handles and pushed W slowly toward his empty place at the main table, near to the podium. As he did so, the guests, every last one of them, rose to their feet in a single motion, applauding, cheering and whooping hosannas. In the case of those who had not seen W in an age or perhaps had never laid eyes on him before, as with some of Tom's businessmen who were present because they never missed a chance to give a boost to Camden, the fortissimo greeting may have masked shock at the storied poet's appearance.

I surely more than anyone else had seen W in all stages of ill health, but I must say he looked especially terrible: wobbling from side to side in his seat, his head appearing to bob up and down, his frame, growing thinner by the day, looking as though it was constructed of *japonais* rice-paper, his fingers clutching the sides of the chair for dear life. He looked startled, as though he had just heard an unfamiliar noise in the middle of the night. That he was soaking wet certainly did not help the overall impression. But his dress and grooming did. Draped around his shoulders was a blue overcoat that a well person would have found far too heavy for the end of May, even in such inclement weather. Beneath it was a black jacket, not his old gray one of the same cut, and beneath that a fine white shirt, brand-new would be my guess, open at the neck in the way he favored. Inevitably perhaps, he was wearing his familiar sloucher, tipping it slightly to acknowledge the ovation and not taking it off until he was positioned in the place of honor. The dining chair there had been removed, enabling him to continue to sit in his mobile one, as he preferred. His trousers bore a crease and had obviously, like his beard and hair, been vigorously brushed. Someone, Missus Davis I presume, had blackened his boots. There was a bouquet on the table in front of him, and he leaned forward to savor its aroma.

There were eight speeches, each quite excellent in its way. Tom, for example, was forcefully eloquent yet cogent and to the point, as though the trial in the case of *United States v. Whitman* were nearly at an end and he was winning over the jury by infusing his closing arguments with equal measures of logic and charm. Another set of remarks came from Julian Hawthorne, another good friend to W, who, in acknowledging the kind oration, paid tribute to the memory of the speaker's father, the author of *The Scarlet Letter* and other tales and romances, who had died during the war, though not of it. W had made certain that I had reporters from the Camden newspapers there and that I gathered up copies of the tributes being delivered, for he certainly had not abandoned his fight for authorial survival by any means necessary, including press-agentry.

Tom whispered in Ed's ear to run over to the Harned homestead on Federal Street, only a short distance away, and ask Gussie (another female I had snubbed! good grief!) to give him a bottle of champagne. This was quickly done.

Rising from his wheeled contrivance seemed an especially difficult feat for W to accomplish. I suspected it was so low that it was hard for him to decamp without becoming dizzy enough to lose his balance. With assistance from Ed and me, however, he stood up, fortified by small sips from his champagne glass, to join in singing "Auld Lang Syne." Then he had to sit down again, quite unsteadily. He took one of the fresh flowers from the vase, inhaled its scent once again, and placed it in his lap.

Everyone present seemed to be pressing in, hoping to shake his hand. With cold weak fingers he was acceding to their requests, however tiring all the shaking was proving to be, but at the same time he signaled for Ed to begin the homeward procession. Progress toward the doors was slow, as the people with hands still unpumped surrounded his vehicle. He did his best to give them all what they sought and to acknowledge their congratulations and best wishes. But then suddenly he asked all these cigar-wielding men to step aside that he might give precedence to another hand-shake petitioner standing near the swinging doors of the kitchen. They dutifully parted like the Red Sea and the colored woman who supervised all the cooking at Morgan's Hall, she with whom I had conspired to devise the menu, came forward slowly. She was clearly excited by the opportunity and spoke so that all the men standing there, the ones saying their good-byes to W with their eyes but not their words, the banking cabal, the members of the Camden bar and the large patchwork of Bohemians and bibliophiles, could take in the full meaning of her words.

I will never forget even one syllable of what she said: "I am sorry to see you looking poorly, Mister Whitman, sir, for you are a great and good soul, and it is the pleasure of my own long life to touch your hand. During the war, when my man went and got himself wounded, you nursed him back to health. The love in your heart was the medicine you used. And Jesus has not yet called him home. He walks the streets of Camden still—cause you treated him no different than you would any *white* boy."

W drew her close. I sensed that he would have preferred to stand, but his body insisted he retain his place in the chair that was also his cage. He gave her the flower. The cook's eyes became moist. So did W's. So did mine. There was another burst of clapping and a further murmur of acclaim.

***

Once he had achieved the momentous birthday, outside events, even longer-term subjects of concern such as the tariff, could rouse his voice to a level of fervency and ardor that his body had long since ceased being able to match, for he, perhaps more than anyone, knew what a big slice of biological existence the passions account for. He had looked so wretched at the big banquet, and in front of all the most prolific gossips of Camden's commercial and professional classes, that rumors about his condition started to spread quite widely. In the aftermath, he found himself in the unprecedented position of receiving more newspaper publicity than he might have wished. There was a headline in the *Philadelphia Record* that ran

WALT WHITMAN ILL
The Poet Stumbling to Old Age
and Feebleness

HE'S CONFINED TO THE HOUSE

A Familiar Face Missed in the Streets of Camden—
Preparing for the Final Scene.

The story began: "That Walt Whitman, 'the good, gray poet,' is failing—and rapidly, too—is a fact patent to all of his intimate friends." Noting a drastic decrease in wheeling-chair sightings, the piece went on to report that "Lawyer Thomas B. Harned, the poet's close friend and counselor, recently admitted that Whitman is failing rapidly, that a marked physical change has come over him, and that his friends are just beginning to realize it. Whitman was never of a robust physique [how W hated that particular 'blasted calumny'], and of recent years he has been feebler than ever. Dr Buck [*sic*], his biographer, is spending a good deal of time with him now, and he, too, admits that the famous man is nearing the end."

The famous man was not in the least amused.

Such bulletins (there were others) only increased the number of visitors hoping to shake his palsied and sepia-spotted hand. We

guardians kept many of them away, but there seemed to be no lessening in the volume of correspondence, leastwise not of the incoming
portion, as·I struggled as best I could with the outbound. Some days
W would declare that he felt so-so, not bad, all right, good, or even,
on one occasion I recall, moving right up to the top of the scale,
jaunty. Most days it was quite otherwise, though here too there were
many gradations, most of them discernible by the strength or weakness of his voice and, on close examination, the condition of his eyes:
clear or cloudy. Still other factors figured into the general picture. For
example, the state of his deafness varied considerably one day to the
next, though the overall direction was downward; but the real deter-
minants were deep inside his own body, in his lungs and limbs and
in whatever was causing the terrible pain in his side. Ed Wilkins
thought it could be nothing else but the kidneys, as W said he sometimes found himself unable to pass water when the need to do so was
upon him, particularly in the night.

But at least his voice always seemed to pick up when he spoke of
his latest project, a pamphlet to be made from the speeches delivered
at the birthday banquet, with an assortment of other pats-on-the-
back thrown in. He thought such a thing would be of the greatest
possible benefit to the sale of his books, including this new and still
larger edition of the *Leaves* that he had in the works for me to engineer. At the time I thought there was something too blatant even
for W in the notion of this publicity booklet, which I nonetheless
managed to have appear that Autumn under the title *Camden's
Compliments to Walt Whitman*, but of course I kept my opinion a
private one. Later, I acquired a better understanding of the idea's
importance. He saw us noticing that his deterioration continued
unchecked. He needed new endeavors, including ones as small as
Compliments, so modest in size if not in conception, as much as he
needed one so enormous and vitally important as the new *Leaves*,

which was to be in two fat volumes. He needed them, as he needed Anne's constant affectionate mindfulness, to keep himself breathing. If he ceased doing what writers do, which is to write and publish, then he ceased to be one and his end would come all the more swiftly. He believed this; so did Anne and I.

Even so, soon after the banquet, any repetition of such an event as that, with all its physical stresses, was rapidly becoming unthinkable. But W was nothing if not tenacious. In fact, he carried tenacity well beyond the point at which it ceases to be bravery and is left to sit as a monument to folly. That Summer, when it was so hot that he had to make his outings in the chair only after the sun had retreated, he managed to visit Philadelphia. A photographer there, Gutekunst by name, wished him to sit for the lens, and sealed the deal by sending a carriage for him, promising the same for the return journey as well. But this show of will on W's part was dwarfed by another, early the following Spring, when he again crossed the river to deliver his Lincoln lecture. On returning, he found the additional bit of strength needed to write out an anonymous account of his appearance for one of the Boston papers. He was the busiest sick man I had ever seen, but likewise the sickest busy one, though I myself may be breaking the first of these records right now. Either way, there was a note of desperation to his actions that was unbearably sad but also somehow admirable.

The search for other matter to supplement the banquet tributes led him to sift roughly through some of his floor-level files again. On mornings when he never rose at all, or got up intending to breakfast but instead spent the entire day lying on the bed fully dressed, he would ask me to gather up great double armfuls of letters and documents, much as one gathers up dead leaves in the Autumn, and deposit them on the bed next to where he lay. This refortified his habit of showing me things from his past, giving them to me to take away forever, and the practice went on at this rate virtually until the end (but, strangely, without making a significant dent in the mounds that were scattered all about—I seemed to be witnessing some miracle on the order of the Loaves and Fishes). I kept hoping that he would again find the original letter from Emerson about the first *Leaves*, hoping indeed, but never aloud, that he would present it to me. Each time he had a different excuse for not locating it.

He did, however, unearth, and bade me read to him, a letter written to an acquaintance from his Bohemian days in New York, I believe. It was dated "Camden, Nov. 26, '75" and told of W's struggle to recover from the first debilitating "whack" while still attempting, after three years, to properly set himself up in the latest, and what he seemed to sense was also the last, of his adopted towns. It was no Brooklyn, no Mannahatta, and no New Orleans. With one dipping of the pen, he declared himself "at the end of my rope, and in fact ridiculously poor." With the next, he was feeling "about as cheerful and *vimmy* as ever," though he knew his paralysis was for keeps. This was either a draft of a letter he may then have touched up as he wrote it out for mailing, or else the fair copy that he retained for his files, duplicating the text from the original. Hard to say. But it was written on the backs of six scraps of various sizes, one of them the first page of a letter from Pete Doyle on the letterhead of the Baltimore & Potomac Railroad, where he was evidently working back then. It revealed nothing new.

W was not a sentimentalist about his own manuscripts once he could replace them with a book or a cutting from a paper or magazine containing the same piece in more permanent and more readable form. He once confided to me that he thought he had used most of the original manuscript of *Leaves* for other purposes after the first edition was safely in his hands back in Fifty-five. I think it most likely that the leaves of *Leaves* became separated from one another and were used as scratch paper over the course of some years, being mixed up with scraps and strays from other sources. But I didn't know just what inference could be drawn from W not preserving one of Pete's letters, given that he seemed to have preserved most everyone else's.

About two weeks later, he had me rooting through the tumuli for something when my claw happened to pull up that photograph of Pete and him posing in two chairs facing in opposite directions, W looking especially nondescript, yet mysterious behind his curtain of facial hair, P displaying a condescending little smile. I hadn't lain eyes on the thing in quite a while, and Tom, who happened to be with me, had not known of its existence.

W laughed the moment I held it up. Tom then tried to reproduce Pete's expression. This made W laugh some more (which was good for him, I thought).

"Never mind," he said, "the expression of my face atones for all that is lacking in his. What do I look like there? Is it seriosity?"

Tom answered. "Fondness," he said. "And Doyle should be a girl."

I said nothing, but W emitted another laugh. "Now don't be too hard on him. That is my Rebel friend, you know. We were true comarados in our time." He added, "Tom, you would like Pete. Love him, in fact. And you too, Horace—especially you. You and Pete would get to be great chums. I found everybody in Washington who knew Pete to be loving him." W called him "a master character."

In fact, I had been so curious about this master character from the past that I had long since been asking W's older friends, when I had them alone for a minute, to recall of Pete whatever they could. It was clear to me that Burroughs was the only one who could stand him in the least.

"One of your powerful uneducated persons," I said to W.

He shot back jovially, "Just that, a rare man, knowing nothing of books, knowing everything of life. A great hearty full-blooded

everyday divinely generous workingman, a hail-fellow-well-met."
Then he went too far. "Maybe too fond of his beer now and then, and
of the women, but for the most part the salt of the earth."

I kept my tongue in my firmly shut mouth, having no wish to
upset W or perplex Tom. W meanwhile kept right on.

"Most literary men, as you know, are the kind that the hardy and
genuine man would not go far to see, but Pete fascinates you by the
very earthiness of his nobility. Yes, you fellows will know him. You,
Horace, must particularly make it your point to come into relations
with him. You will know him, both of you, and then you will understand that what I say is wholly true and yet is short of the truth."
His coyness had achieved a new plateau; I wasn't sure what to think
or believe.

"When *shall* I ever meet him?" I asked in an absolutely innocent
tone of voice.

"Oh, there will come a time," he said.

At which point I changed the subject to the late war, a topic calculated to keep W going for however long he had the strength to do so.

I believe he probably would have been more candid with me on the
Pete business if Tom had not been along. Such at least is what my
instinct told me, for he did, in his fashion, feed me tiny tastes of what
he knew I wished to know—knew but would not acknowledge, if
I was reading him correctly. For example, during another visit not
long afterward, he began by saying that he had found something else
that might interest me, as indeed his discoveries always did.

"Do you know who this is?" he asked, handing me a horizontal
photograph, evidently recent. It showed a boy or young man with
cropped hair shaved high above the ears, lying on his belly, stretched
on the floor in a state of nudity, contemplating a flower vase that he
held in one hand. The central fact of the picture was not the lad's
face, which was turned away from the viewer at a slight angle, but

rather his bare posterior looking like two perfectly round melons sliced down one side and spliced together. I shook my head.

"Look again. Do you not remember the buggy that was precursory to the wheeling-chair?"

"Bill Duckett!" I said, first in triumph, then in mild confusion.

"Indeed it is. This is another of the photographic studies Eakins makes for his students or for himself alone, I'm not certain which it is in this case, as the pose is not anatomical in the way of others I have seen. Not one of his standing figures for demonstration purposes, you see, but a complete work in itself, artfully arranged and lit."

I acknowledged that this was so, that this was art and not an entry made for one reason or another in a visual note-book. I handed it back. He laid it beside him.

"Eakins was kind enough to strike a copy for me, knowing my interest in fellows who work vehicles, all kinds of vehicles."

I thought this was a reference to the outings he used to make with Duckett. I can see them yet, Duckett, wearing a derby, holding the reins loosely in one hand, W, in his sloucher, beside him on the seat with a blanket athwart his lap.

Flora, do you know what in German is called a *Fetisch?* Originally, as I understand it, the word referred to a Negro talisman. Certainly it most usually implies the excessive and perhaps irrational worship of an object, and not, as in the case of W and his young transportation-men, of a profession and those who practice it. Yet I felt then that W's decided preference was a devotion carried to extremes and might be squeezed in under the same heading. Would he have wished such a photograph if the model had not been, as W and I knew him, a buggy driver? Admittedly the job hardly ranks with those of railroad engineers or seamen aboard steamers, but it does involve forward movement for some commercial goal, and that was one of the characteristics W favored. Doubtless I would learn of others later on.

These days of course I see myself in my own memories of Mickle Street. When I called in the mornings, I usually found him eating his breakfast, eagerly expecting its delivery or waiting for Missus Davis to come and retrieve the bowl, plate and cup. At other times he had next to no appetite, and the afternoon did not make good on the morning's promise. Sometimes I was able to call at mid-afternoon and often found him sitting contentedly in the wheeling-chair outside the front door. He would be taking the sun and conversing with Missus Davis's mongrel or with neighborhood children. Later, indoors, he might complain of the noise in the street or, even on warm days, of the chill. Early one evening I arrived to find him absent, and waited until I heard the approach of Ed, pushing the chair. The passenger asked to be deposited at the window in the front parlor, where he could go on observing his fellow citizens at their own eye level rather than from above, in his bedroom.

He had been taking the fresh air down by the river, which he called his oldest friend. I suppose he meant that rivers in general were his oldest friends, for how could he sit on the busy banks of the Delaware, watching the ferries come and go, staring across the way to the big inviting metropolis, without being reminded of the view from Brooklyn toward Mannahatta?

Ed, who had been one of Bucke's protégés, returned to Canada to pursue the study of veterinary medicine. I then spread the news of the sudden opening to Bucke and to all the other doctors who were nearer to hand. After some fumbling, the job was bestowed on Missus Davis's foster son, Warrie Fritzinger. "Warrie" was affectionate for "Warren," and he had been an able-bodied seaman. The able-bodied part proved useful in lifting and sometimes carrying W, who however no doubt placed greater emphasis on the other part of the description. The match was a sound one. At one point Warrie even went to the Philadelphia Orthopedic Hospital to learn the science of massage, to improve the way he administered what W, who found in them some temporary relief, referred to as "pummelings." Warrie was also a student of the violin. W found his playing salubrious as well. (I found it less so, and once had the misfortune to be present when the dog joined in.) Warrie also did much-needed jobs of carpentry around the house. I believe he might have apprenticed as a ship's carpenter, for his skill was at making what was very strong rather than attractive to look at.

Now that I see these words, I realize that they might describe W just as well. His muscles had turned to India rubber long before, as was bound to be the case since he lacked the strength, agility and most of all the wind necessary for exercise. His hearing, particularly on his "bad elevation," was a hit-or-miss thing, but more so out-doors than in his room, where the walls contained and thus focused the sound. His eyesight, too, became even less than it had been. Formerly he had asked me to read letters and things to him because he enjoyed experiencing the words that way (as poets perhaps often do); now there was no doubt an additional and more practical reason. What was most strange was the way his beard was thinning dra-matically, giving his face, indeed his head, an entirely new outline, revealing a countenance that had been hidden from the world for decades. I was reminded of the ghostly outlines of those no longer extant chimneys and staircases you often see on the side of a sur-viving house when the one that once adjoined it is pulled down in some money-making scheme. Yet despite all this, and I know that I dance with cliché here, his spirit retained its strong pulse most of the time. When I think back on that Autumn and Winter of Ninety, I confront a torrent of images and little episodes that make me, and dear Anne as well, smile at their proof of his contradictions even as they also recall the depth of his justifiable melancholy.

Not only was he dying, but others he loved were dying with him or, all too often, a little in advance of him. First came Charlie Pfaff, owner of the beer hall on lower Broadway where the healthy young poet of yore jousted and sparred with fellow writers and artists, including the actress Ada Clare, to whom an unknowledgeable person might suppose he was romantically appended. Charlie was a last link to a past that likewise had not survived. And where there was not actual death, there was more sickness aplenty. Hannah, his favorite sister, took ill (though she outlived W by nearly a decade), and W wrote often to comfort her.

A much different and unknowable case was that of Harry Stafford, he of the piercing look from underneath dark eyebrows. In his youth he had shared a close but, so it struck me, closely guarded relationship with W, who performed the paternal rôle and Stafford the filial. *Père et fils.* My understanding is that when W, in need of fresh air and the other commodities of Nature, stayed at the farm of Harry's parents, much communal swimming took place. Harry was now a married man with children of his own, and on occasion he called at Mickle Street, once after a severe if also somewhat mysterious sickness had debilitated him. He reported that his condition had caused him to quit his railroad job (as W's vaunted Quakers would have said, he was a transportation-man "by convincement"). W advised him to rent a property where he could take up farming in place of railroading. The labor, while much harder, was also perforce far healthier, he said. Stafford did so, and recovered. I suppose one can't help but absorb some medical wisdom if brought down by as many diseases and ailments as W had been hard done by for so long. Once recovered, though, Stafford wished to continue in agriculture, maintaining the health of his newly restored body, but the lease on the farm expired and he lacked the means to renew it. Left without resources, he returned with his wife and their two young ones to his parents' home. Whereupon some break occurred between him and W, I don't know what or how. After Stafford left following his next visit to No. 328, W chastised Missus Davis for letting "every specimen of riff-raff" into the house. Scolded her with the lightest possible touch, of course, given that the recipient of this displeasure was so demonstrably gentle and kind a woman. (When later, at Christmas, he presented her with a simple gold ring, you'd have thought that no one had ever before behaved toward her with such thoughtfulness.)

I watched all such fluctuations from a distance and in a state of puzzlement, and while continuing to perform my duties, was also able to keep pursuing my curiosity, hoping that the time for a discussion franker than any W and I had shared previously would come before Death commenced rapping at *his* door. I feared this was meant to be a closely run thing.

⁂

I was charged, but truthfully had charged myself, with the formidable task of keeping all the key figures in the drama of W's decline, and equally in the wonderfully inspiring story of his persistence, in touch with me and, through me, with one another.

So it came about that I heard that, yes, Pete Doyle was indeed living in Baltimore, though whether working for the same railroad as before, or working at all, I did not know. I thought of going there to track him down. How difficult could it be? But I hesitated, of course, knowing that W would feel that I had stepped outside my boundaries.

J.W. Wallace was, with his friend Doctor John Johnson, leader of the Whitmanite study circle in Bolton over in England, the group that prefigured the various Whitman cells and fellowships, including of course your own Canadian one and excluding, naturally, the

fraudulent effort planned by Sadakichi Hartmann, whom W continued to regret having ever met with. Like Doctor Johnson, Wallace
seemed to me a perfectly congenial fellow from the provinces, a
person of laboring-class stock. In Ninety-one he was over in America
to extend his researches into W's past doings. I found him easy to talk
with, and one day I let slip what I knew of Pete's whereabouts in
vague terms. As I had not thought to pledge him to secrecy, Wallace
later passed along the information to W, who was eager to interro-
gate me about the matter.

He contrived to be off-hand about it. Turning from friendly
remarks about Wallace and his group, he said: "And before it passes
out of my mind, Horace, let me ask you something. Wallace says you
report Pete Doyle is in Baltimore. This is entirely new to me. I did
not know of the change. The noble Peter! I hear but little from him.
Yet that is not to wonder, for I never did hear much."

"Did he not at one period write you often?"

"Oh no, his letters were never frequent. He is a mechanic, an
instance of the many mechanics I have known who don't write or
won't write and are apt to get mad as the devil if you ask them to.
But I always humored Pete in that respect. It was enough for me to
know him, and I suppose for him to know *me*. I did most of the writing.
He is a train-hand, and like all transportation-men, he is necessarily
a wanderer."

I took this in.

"Wallace wants to see him," he continued. "He is a collector, collecting not simply scarce copies of my books but the acquaintance
of most everyone I have known. You must put your heads together
and see if a meeting with Pete can't be arranged."

His voice was unruffled and convivial, but I did not take these words
literally, for I comprehended the threat that was hidden in them at no
great depth, embedded like sharp bits of iron baked into a cake.

On his death-bed, W executed a codicil to his will. In it, he revoked the bequest of his gold watch to Pete and the silver one to me. Now the gold went to me and the silver one to Harry Stafford, with Pete the Great receiving nothing. I take from this several suppositions. First, that perhaps W and Pete had some final contact of which I never learned, some correspondence exchanged and quickly destroyed in the new stove, perhaps even some unsuccessful reunion, carefully held when I was not around and of which I was never told. Another conclusion, which I am now in the unfortunate position of being able to confirm from my own present experience, is this: that the body outlives, what shall we say?, physical amativeness, but desire in turn outlives the body.

⁂

The double-decker *Leaves* on which I labored at W's direction was in large part a stereotyping of the previous one. In that sense it was not a true edition at all, not as genuine bookmen would see it— that is, no fresh setting of type. It was, however, to have appended to it a sequence of new poems, written over the past two years and continuing into the present. He decided to call this section "Good-Bye My Fancy." I was staggered when I first read the title piece with which we are all now so familiar, the poem in which he bids farewell to his creative life, the soul of his existence that he was watching go dark—except that the lines themselves had been pushed up from the deepest and most fertile part of his imagination in a way that perhaps (I hoped) gave lie to their literal intent. This time he did not tarry in having the new writing ready for me to mark up for the plant. There was none of the agony of finishing his essay on Hicks. This time the agony was in what the writing was actually saying.

He had a headache much of the time now and was going through a rough patch of deafness. The pains in the lower belly and, most obviously, his constant difficulty breathing, were further unwavering indications of the curtain about to descend. Before the end of the year he had a bad fall when his game leg gave way as he was making a transit of the hallway. Fortunately, he wasn't on the stairs. But then he could never have been on the stairs without assistance from Warrie, who was quite protective of him and quite considerate as well, sometimes bringing him flowers for the room.

I marveled at what I saw, just as I marvel at the memory of it now. Despite what he said at times, W wasn't simply waiting to die. He would, to the best of his capabilities, carry on being Walt Whitman and let Death surprise him as to the exact timing, shutting him up in mid-sentence and stilling him in mid-motion. In the interim, he would write as best he could and show himself to still be part of the world.

❦ FIFTEEN ❧

OCTOBER OF NINETY was the worst month to date, and not only for W but also for those who cared for him. The statement is not meant to contradict Dickens's famous assertion that the worst of times are often the best of times as well. After all, we are alive, and what else matters, especially if, like me in those days or W's atheistic friends, one carries no brief for the afterlife, at least not for our own. Flora, I apologize if this offends, but I am beyond mere etiquette, lurching toward some type of truth, I hope.

W's influence on me was so overpowering that I sometimes felt like a minor colony of his existence, designed to enrich him while leaving me with traces of his personality and a strong desire to emulate his style in all things. It was in this situation that I turned to writing poetry, reams of it as collected eventually in books such as *Chants Communal* and *Optimos*. I struggled hard to make it my own but, as I have only recently been able to admit, it came out sounding like W's poetry retold in prose—possibly in prose translated from the German! It seemed always to declaim rather than reveal or imply. I convinced myself that my poetry was helping to disperse W's ideas and philosophies to certain small audiences that his may not have reached, owing to the intolerance that still covered his name in some quarters. At this late hour all I can say is what most people in the circle were too considerate to state at the time: that I was blinded by hubris even in thinking that I served such a modest good by steering a handful of uninformed readers to the genuine article.

A greater contribution, one for which I was more fitted, was the *Conservator*, the monthly magazine that I founded that same year and edited in partnership with Anne. We called it the *Conservator* because it would gather together what needed to be saved before it could be disseminated: the ideas and doctrines of Walt Whitman primarily, but with other content as well, writing on progressive political and economic matters, which W was always too courteous to grumble about in my hearing (or, as far as I know, to complain about at all).

I taught Anne the California case. She picked up almost at once what had taken me months to learn as an apprentice. Her long graceful fingers plucked the leaden characters from the cabinets with the utmost speed and precision. When I praised her for this as we stood side by side setting the type—she wearing a work apron with great aplomb, though it was too big even for me and made me look and feel like a disenfranchised schoolboy—she replied that her nimbleness was "the only surviving residue of all those years of piano lessons." She pretended to shiver at the recollection. When we think back over decades of love, oftentimes what we remember is not the impassioned pronouncements but such small moments of unaffected joy in the company of the other person (who most likely recalls totally different examples, or possibly none at all). Through our hard effort, the *Conservator* attained enough subscribers to help us pay the greengrocer and the butcher.

I have already said something, something brief, about our wedding. Let me now tell you of the love it codified. I wanted Anne to live under the same roof with me, whether as husband and wife or as a couple who followed "the custom of the country," as I believe the expression had been on the old Western frontier. She would not dare contemplate the latter option. She knew what violent anger the very suggestion would ignite in her father, perhaps the only person alive who could terrify her. Just why she was so frightened of him I was never certain, though he was, I grant you, a forbidding personage. As for matrimony, what can I say except that he envisioned—demanded—a better match for her. Anne and I did not discuss his wishes in detail. From the very avoidance of the subject, however, I concluded that he would almost rather have her (and certainly me) dead than see her become the bride of someone he appeared to think of as a little immigrant Jew. That I was born in New Jersey made me no less of an immigrant in his eyes. And of course it has long been my fate to be considered both a little Jew by those I wished to accept me on other terms and a non-Jew by fully fledged adherents to the faith.

This was the Autumn that John Burroughs came to town to visit with W. The essayist on Nature was younger than the poet of Democracy by perhaps twenty years but seemed to be catching up to him in appearance if not in chronology. He dressed much as W did, with only a slight variation in the shape of the soft felt hat. He too had a big nose (though smaller ears than W's) and wore his white beard to the center of his chest. But none of this, or so I sensed, was done with an air of calculation equal to Bucke's. Why did so many of W's most ardent admirers end up resembling him? I too was becoming like W, but in other ways that were both more disturbing and less noticeable if not necessarily less comic (read *Chants Communal*—no, on second thought, please don't). Sometimes I felt that I had no individuality except that which I copied from W or picked up from Anne whenever I embraced her.

My sister, Gussie, she who was born to be a hostess, invited Burroughs to dinner along with Anne and me. She wanted W, assuming he was able to convey himself there with Warrie's help, to enjoy comfortable surroundings when he conversed with his old friend and admirer. It always amazed and delighted me that Tom, a man of no overwhelmingly obvious literary bent, threw himself so whole-heartedly into these endeavors. Perhaps he wished to learn, or perhaps he simply hoped to hear the authentic table-talk of great men. All of us but Gussie, who was checking on progress in the kitchen, were enjoying ourselves in the parlor, Tom, Burroughs and I on chairs and W on the horsehair sofa with Anne inches away, holding his left hand tenderly in her right. He gazed at her for the longest time, even longer than usual, and then uttered—uttered in a clear voice—words that seemed to turn the air to ice. "I know you, my dear, don't I? Haven't I known you somewhere?"

Tom and Burroughs looked horrified, and I must have appeared the same way to them. Anne, however, did not change expression except in that, as she looked over at us, her eyes widened, like two blue wild-flowers suddenly blooming. Tom punctured the terrified pause in the conversation with an opinion, a piece of news or a pat of gossip. W took in what was being said and even nodded in acknowledgment, but he kept readjusting, re-intensifying, the silent question he put to Anne, as though, given sufficient concentration, he could recollect the precise nature of their acquaintance. She continued to hold his hand, not one bit more tightly than before, but probably, I remember think-ing, with a gentle and reassuring current passing from her fingers into his. Cogitating on this later, for the scene obsessed me with its poignancy, I guessed that this was perhaps the same method by which W had raised the pitiable hopes and eased the suffering of wounded soldiers. Bucke, Burroughs and the others could wear their Whitman costumes as they wished, but a part of me had become W. An unde-tectable breeze had carried a spore from his body to mine, where it had taken root, and now I could see the process repeating itself between the man I so admired and the woman I loved more than speech or written language could possibly say.

Gussie entered, cognizant that there had been lightning in the room but unaware just what had taken place, and called us to the table. When we sat, with Anne drawing her chair closer to W's, it was apparent that the episode had not led to worse. I knew that much when the rest of us laid our linen napkins across our laps and W tucked his into his shirt collar with democratic frontier gusto. Anne and I later determined that she felt the threat retreat even before I did, and Tom was not more than a second behind me.

"I made the meal myself," Gussie said to W as she introduced several good sized roasted chickens to her guests. "I am mindful of Doctor Bucke's comments about the ill effects of too much richness in your diet."

"Bucke is a typical scientist," W replied without a second's hesitation and obviously in full possession of his senses. "He knows all about things that are knowable, but forgets about the existence of some others that defeat his principles."

Burroughs, uncharacteristically, could be heard chuckling softly from deep within his whiskers, and Anne and I smiled in relief. W interpreted our reactions as an ovation, and so began a series of conversational encores on various topics. Everything was back to normal, yet nothing was ever quite the same again. The paradox might have appealed to the man who wrote *A Tale of Two Cities*.

⁂

No sooner had Burroughs, the equitable and soft-spoken apostle of Nature, concluded his visit towards the end of October than Bucke, the human steamroller, arrived on a whirlwind mission of his own. I found the rapid transition difficult to adjust to. But then, W's apprehended stroke, a volcano that spit out sparks and emitted some smoke but did not erupt—not this time—was playing harshly with my nerves. Such was what I kept telling myself, using this quite true but simplified explanation to cover, or cover up, a number of other agitations. Some were straightforward: money worries, or the work of getting the *Conservator* off the ground. Others were deeper, more nebulous, even frightening and dark. Was W's comradely adhesiveness, though obviously no longer physically lustful, limited to friendships with other males, as many had surmised despite his statements to the contrary? And if it was, had the extraordinary Anne Montgomerie, fearing no one and nothing (save her father) and willing to go anywhere experience might take her—an explorer, you might say, who never set foot in Africa, indeed never left home— inspired him to exempt her from all the restrictions he usually placed on his preference? Obviously, if she for her part loved him, it was a love totally different from that which existed between us as man and woman. But what effect might it have on the relationship she and I shared? or, for that matter, on my association with W or his interconnection with me?

Reassured that W had eluded further disaster to his health, Bucke was returning to Canada, and asked me if I wished to travel there with him and be his house guest. He must have sized up my predicament, for whatever else he may have been, he was chock full of wisdom and intuition. I asked Anne if she wished to come along, but she said that she should remain in Camden to oversee W's care while I was away, a matter, barring a real spurt of magma, that consisted of coordinating his assorted doctors and being a sympathetic pair of ears. She seemed sincere in telling me that, yes, I should go, but not for long—no longer than necessary for me to accomplish the thinking I required.

I then called on W. The day was damp but not cold, so I was surprised to find him in the bedroom wearing his overcoat completely buttoned and the collar turned up. I told him that I needed a rest, as he had needed one when the wounded in the hospitals threatened to overwhelm him. I told him I was going to take his advice about seeing some of Canada but would return soon enough. If he needed me urgently, he could always send me a message at Bucke's home.

"In that case," he said, "you will be in the finest pair of hands." And with those words, as huge piles of papers were turning to compost at his feet, he gave me one of his secular all-purpose blessings and wished me a safe and restorative trip.

The evening before Bucke and I caught our train, Anne and I attended a lecture by "Colonel" Bob Ingersoll at the Horticultural Hall in Philadelphia. The event was a benefit for W, who was persuaded to attend, though he was as pale as an eggshell and all too frail-looking up there on the stage where Warrie had positioned him. A large crowd listened to Ingersoll orate on "Literature and Liberty" for an hour and three-quarters; it was easy to lose oneself in the rhythms of his eloquence. The house was full, resulting in a net profit of nearly nine hundred dollars. No doubt the turn-out owed much to the controversy that preceded it. The spectacle of America's most despised agnostic agitator raising money to help America's most immoral poet naturally led to an effort to deny them the use of the auditorium; the attempted eviction failed, but not before triggering considerable publicity. Anne and I had been asked to join a very small number of people sitting on stage with W. I felt slightly ridiculous seated there in a straight-backed chair, but Anne was the very picture of radical poise.

<hr />

I noticed right after boarding the train that Bucke traveled, and I suppose long had done so, with a copy of the immortal *Leaves* to consult for its beauties and profundities and also no doubt the visionary properties that interested him even more. I picked it up for a few moments when he had nodded off to sleep for a short time somewhere in the state of New York, and turned to "By Blue Ontario's Shore" and "Summer Days in Canada," two of the poems that W had returned with from his spell at the Buckes' a decade earlier. "Summer Days in Canada" is the less magnificent of the pair though magnificent all the same, but I could not match their images of high Summer with what I was seeing in late October, when the trees were scarlet and the sky slate-gray.

We pushed on until reaching the region whose center is the grandiloquently named London, from whence Bucke conveyed us to the asylum by carriage, and we arrived at the superintendent's home in time for dinner with the gracious Jessie Bucke and their children. The Doctor showed the same white-hot energy in being the host that he seemed to bring, in my observation and experience, to all and any tasks or functions. The next day, a Saturday, he let me into his office to admire the shelves and cabinets of W's manuscripts and published writings. The collection was immense, occupying the entirety of a large wall and extending even into several closets.

He asked me if I knew what W thought of this treasure hoard.

"You doubtless know," I said, "that the handsome prices some of his early books fetch as rarities drive him around the track, for not one cent of the increase in value is returned to his own pocket. I once tried to use this to illustrate a point about Capitalism, but he was deaf to my parable."

Bucke smiled and said, "I have heard him rag the collectors all right. But of course he has been very generous with me as he has been with you, and with the boys from Bolton as well, as he knows that we have higher motives than bookselling and that, in our different ways, we are scholars and curators—preservers."

He told me that his goal was to turn the collection, which takes in photos, albums, letters and so on, as well as books and the manuscripts that fathered them, into an annotated bibliography. He owned some of W's letters to Harry Stafford and to Pete Doyle. I would have valued a look at the former, for to me Stafford was a minor mystery within the greater mysteries of W's life, but Bucke was highly protective of his collection. As to whether this attitude arose out of some fear that I would steal secrets he was saving for his proposed bibliography or jealousy over my being able to speak with W every single day, I cannot say. Still, I was of course actually quite excited to get a look at the Pete letters, though I had to content myself with an all too brief and closely observed peek. Bucke let me hold them while he stood there. I was able to take in only a little of the content. What I could discern was only that the letters were as W had said or suggested: erratic in content and not particularly revealing of much beyond the unlikelihood of so intense an association between two such dissimilar individuals. To distract me, Bucke continued to chatter the whole time, before whisking me away to tour the grounds and examine what he called his *other* collection. He was referring to the lunatics and madmen gathered together from various institutions elsewhere in Canada. I was permitted to look into several of the cells, as I suppose one must call them, housing some of the most seriously deranged patients. I found everything settled and in good order, with the walls freshly calcimined.

The next day, Sunday, I was dragooned by the distaff side into attending a Presbyterian service in the town, a tidy and resolutely undemonstrative place, while Bucke himself underwent a Catholic Mass, which surprised me. How did he know I was not one of the German Catholics so numerous in my own country and presumably present in his own as well? What had W told him of my background? I was most eager to be the proper house guest, well mannered, enthusiastic and favorably impressed, so I kept my questions to myself, which is to say, I kept the truth of the matter to myself as well. The truth was that in those days, when I did not protest the practice of religion, I was doing so out of respect for Anne, who clung to at least the appearance of Christian worship as a courtesy, or peace offering, to the savagely Protestant Montgomeries of Philadelphia, especially her father. My own father was somewhat appalled at my caving-in to these niceties, just as his own parents, and their parents before them, would have been horrified at his, and my own, evident abandonment of Hebrew beliefs and traditions. In any case, the following day, being Monday, I felt sufficiently cleansed of sin to bring up the more serious matter of Doyle.

Bucke of course knew vastly more about him than I, not only as a protective guardian of far longer standing and better provenance than I, but also as a medical man whose decision to take one form of "abnormality" as his specialty might have steered him to some theory of "abnormality" more broadly defined. I know now to surround the word with quotation marks, not to call undue attention to it and most certainly not to sneer, but only to emphasize the truly educational nature of a question in need of answering; one about which I could find no help in books, not English, German or French, and was resigned to never hearing W—the prolific father of all those native New Orleanians!—speak of candidly.

"What is it, do you suppose, that formed the basis of the friendship between W and Pete?" I asked with a naivety that might have sounded real enough.

To-day, at the tail-end of the second decade of the twentieth century, having seen whole societies come through the unspeakable horrors of the great European war whose treaty details are only now being negotiated, you, I or any other sophisticated individual with a smattering of psychological knowledge would answer the question simply: "Homo-sexualism." A modern person who has lived in Greenwich Village as I have will be familiar with some of its characteristics and representative personalities, for it is a way of living that is no stranger to the arts, connected as it somehow is with the creative temperament, as I have read and been told.

In Ninety, however, the term was unknown to popular usage and probably to learned speech as well. The few who spoke of the matter at all, the British in particular, generally used the term *Uranian*. Bucke began to talk instead of what he called "anomalous love." He defined it as the situation in which one person might show a carnal propensity, as well as mere affectionate regard, for another individual of the same sex as himself. He was of course a scientist, albeit an unorthodox one, and he spoke freely of these matters, paying me the compliment of knowing that I would not be repulsed, as most people are, or titillated, as some, but only a few, apparently become.

"Are they not just more feminine, then?" We had left the building that was both his office and family quarters and were strolling past the asylum's impressive gardens.

"That is a common perception, occasioned partly by the fact that this type of behavior is never spoken of openly by anyone outside human-science, and only seldom by professionals of impeccable credentials in clinical research. Yet it is well known in places and organizations that are peopled exclusively by young men without recourse to women, and sometimes by those not so young as well. Prison warders, if they were guaranteed immunity from scorn in trade for their candor, could tell us much of it, I believe. Military and naval commanders too."

My mind jumped instantly to W's work in places like the Armory Square hospital, but also to his love of ships and those who sailed— transportation-men! I needed time to contemplate this information that only Bucke would give me. But I could not do so just then, interrupting his generous and impartial conveyance of this rare learning.

Lest I stanch the flow of his talk, I dared not even acknowledge receipt of his gift.

"The word most often used in connection with such practices," Bucke went on, "is of course sodomy, the type of intimate congress that the overwhelming majority of people condemn by rote as a result of their Bible study. I've never been convinced that union of this type is necessarily any more harmful to the body or mind than what passes between husband and wife. I am certain that in some though by no means all cases it would disappear if women were introduced into situations that are now exclusively male. But I am mindful that in most of the world it remains a capital crime, which would be absolutely ludicrous if it were not so horrible."

I continued to do little but nod attentively.

"I have strayed from your original question," he went on. "To be sure, some inverted men are effeminate in manner or even dress. But this means only that they do not wish to appear as proof of the exclusively masculine part of our civilization. No, they do not wish to be women. They wish only to be who they are.

"Such men are usually the more passive of any pair. Many share a particular physique that draws the notice of their eventual inamoratos. They are often short and slightly built, and compared to the general run of men you see in the streets, neither so broad in the chest nor so narrow as to the hips. More like birds than mammals, you might say, and like male birds rather than the females, they use their plumage to entice a mate."

I confess that a startling fascination I felt assisted me in keeping my mouth closed, which Anne will tell you is not my customary way. I did manage, however, to interject another question. "The molly-boys, you mean?"

"That and many other terms. For safety in a world so hostile to their existence, inversionists, if I may coin or claim a term, have constructed a colorful and complex nomenclature and other trappings that allow them to communicate among themselves in ways incomprehensible to the majority, or better yet in ways simply of no interest to the majority at all. As with the Gypsies, as indeed with your religious forebears and other groups in similar circumstances, their world is difficult for outsiders to penetrate."

(So W *had* told him of my family.)

"They are almost more secretive," he said, "than the Rosicrucians of the late Paschal Beverly Randolph . . ." My expression must have betrayed my ignorance of the figure being referred to. " . . . the Negro occultist and what is called a trance medium, who did so much for members of his race during and after your civil war."

He continued to lecture as we walked, crushing fallen leaves with our boot-steps.

"Then there are those others, like the Good Gray Poet, our exquisite acquaintance, who incline differently from the aforementioned mollies. They seek the companionship of men still more masculine in appearance and attitude than themselves. By such means they hope to join the dominant body of opinion while preserving their minority conduct. They try to anchor themselves in a society from which they must nevertheless always stand apart. Like immigrants from a country where English is not spoken, you might say. Their tastes lean toward younger men who commonly are muscular examples from a lower station in life, often to be found working in rough occupations. If one of these older and perhaps, even in Walt's case, somewhat better off men should happen to be an American and educated, he might well consider such a physical companion to be, bluntly, the more inherently democratic alternative. Our friend epitomizes this."

"Hmmm." I'm afraid that's all I could offer by way of thanking him for giving me this newfound understanding. I urged him to carry on with his ideas.

"You know as full well as I what our friend wrote in 'Song of Myself' most of a lifetime ago. That he was 'Walt Whitman, an American, one of the roughs, a kosmos, disorderly, fleshy and sensual, eating, drinking and breeding, no sentimentalist, no stander above men and women or apart from them, no more modest than immodest.'"

Bucke then apologized if the quotation so long in his memory did not come out letter-perfect.

I will never forget the little thing that happened next. There was a bird-sound in the tree nearest to us. We glanced up distractedly just as a male blue jay, like an actor on stage who is flawless in the timing of his exits and entrances, took flight and disappeared.

"Those lines from the poem were more than a description of their author as he wished to be seen," Bucke continued. "They were a setting-down of the ideal he needed to become in order to inhabit the other half of himself. In picking the words he chose, he was, without necessarily being aware that he was doing so, summoning, beckoning, what the words were naming. They were a sort of advertisement, a flash of colorful feathers aimed, unknowingly of course, at attracting the person with whom he would build his nest and make for both of them a sanctuary in a world so full of predators."

"He was advertising for a Pete Doyle?"

"Quite so, my friend."

We walked back to the superintendent's house, silently at first.

"Did your study of these matters," I asked, "arise in the first instance from your admiration for Walt or from a different or an additional source?"

I was wondering, mistakenly of course, whether his own interest went beyond the clinical. I can admit this now that he is dead, now that I am following behind the departed so closely that it is pointless for me to be guarded. But in an instant, his talk switched from the expository to the more discursive.

"You will not believe how much conditions at this institution have improved in the time I have known it," he said. "This is not a boast but a fact. When I arrived, for example, patients caught practicing onanism had their arms pinned behind their backs for days, weeks and even months. Such cruelty. What became of those few who engaged in acts of sodomy I cannot say. Records were never kept or else were neutered or destroyed. The nearest I could come to the truth was the statement that what helped the patients to reform their ways also protected the institution from scandal and from retribution, both public and bureaucratic."

"What did you do?"

"I ordered an end to harsh treatment, whether named or unnamed, and policed enforcement of the new direction."

"Have there been subsequent instances of this inversionistic behavior?"

"A few."

"Tell me, do you believe that this inversionism in men is carried in the blood of families or learned, perhaps through mimicry and by force of the different values of cultures very unlike our own?"

"Geneticism or acquisition? Involuntary or consciously chosen? That is a good question, but no one has the answer to it."

"What way does your instinct incline you? From having observed and studied the relevant inmates in your care?"

"What I have seen provides no such answers," he said. He nodded toward the enormous building where I had seen the unfortunates' living quarters. "And in any case, these people are all as crazy as wild monkeys."

The smart-aleck Bucke had returned, forcing the other back into his hole. I much preferred the latter.

I was hoping to return from Canada having written poetry about it as W had done in his day, but Canada did not speak to me the way it did to him. He loved the land if not the nation built on top of it. He loved those of its people who worshipped him without asking too many difficult questions, but he found the others very un-American (except perhaps the Canadian transportation boys—there must be many of them, though I saw none and wonder now whether he had).

Considering the question at this late date, I believe W must have felt threatened by whatever was foreign. This is a trait I often notice in my fellow native-born Americans especially. Nonetheless he was always drawn to the exotic. As he was not, however, a widely traveled man, he found such exoticism in what were in fact the most humdrum localities. For this is the essence, I think, of his few months' stay in New Orleans when he was already drawing a bead on his thirtieth birthday. The city had been part of Spain and then of France before the United States bought it for cash on the barrel-head, an event still clear in the minds of many older residents in W's time there. I think he was aroused to still be safely within America while easily imagining that he was actually elsewhere. Maybe in one sense he was right to see New Orleans as a special case, for it became a piece of the United States for a second time after the Confederacy collapsed, and I don't know but whether people there may take such matters in their stride, thinking to themselves that one day this too shall pass. Thirty-some years after his tropical passade, he must have had almost the same reaction to Bucke's town up in Ontario.

As someone who was reared in a European family, I by contrast saw the whole continent of North America as exotic, uniformly so, all of a piece, and yet with, if I may be permitted this confusing contradiction, every part different from the rest. The circles printed on the map appear to me as prospects, places to survive in, ones to change and improve upon (an indication perhaps of what Father called *socialisme* beliefs, evidently believing that their origins are French), busy little outposts of their own in which to blend without surrendering completely, lest one become just another bolt or bushing in the whole contraption. One selects a city as one's bodily address, the spot from which to attend to quite different matters, ones that are no less urgent than they are timeless.

Flora, I know of all the great and good performed by the Caledonian tribe that boasts of you as one of its members. But I do not know what *socialiste* distance you enforce between your origins and your intentions. I trust and hope, and in fact know, for I have an eerily accurate sense of these matters, that you still have many years to live. As my own tenure has shriveled, I have found myself resuming conversation with the Jew who lives inside me. I only hope that my dear late father, should he somehow be absorbing these scratchy lines of mine, will either forgive me or confess that he underwent a similar experience that he thought best to withhold from me at the time.

All of which is to say that I can look back on the events outlined in this private narrative with a clarity denied me at the time I'm now describing and also with a charity that I lacked back then. I am far enough along on my journey to accept incongruity for what it is and then draw correspondences from it. I recognize full well that I have grown more conservative as I have grown more radical. The one does not controvert the other, much less diminish it; it merely illustrates the mechanism. In coming to understand this, I also realize that W was precisely the same. I can know these things without prejudgment of him or fault-finding in light of all the days that have followed in merciless lock-step sequence. To repeat certain facts about him in any other way would be wrong. I devoutly wish you to hold this in mind when, if I have the strength to bring this narrative to its close, you should be tempted to assess my own limitations.

Such was the confidence of the still somewhat young and relatively healthy man I used to be that I felt it possible to participate in some fashion in W's genius. Instead, I merely parodied it and pilloried myself while doing so. This continued, unwittingly and for the longest time, until about ten years ago, when *With Walt Whitman in Camden* was well under way, the green cloth of its binding a tip of the hat to the immortal *Leaves* as originally published. I felt that this would be my best gift to W's memory. Anne of course helped me to arrive at this conclusion, whereupon she and I decided to suspend the *Conservator*.

When I digress in this manner, I betray my age as fully as I underscore your patience, my dear audience-of-one. Nevertheless these days my thoughts do tend to stray, until the stream becomes a delta with countless fingers. In this if not in many other ways I can truthfully claim to be just as W was. I flatter myself that, like him, I always manage to guide my travelers back to the main channel—in this case, my trip to Canada. The topic is an important one.

My visit there was much more successful than I ever could have hoped. It was a roaring success, as W liked to say, throwing his head back in imitation of a certain elderly lion in the Philadelphia zoo with which he was on familiar terms. When the British-Canadian border agent asked me whether I was bringing into the country anything that should be declared, I said no. When asked the same question by his American brother on crossing back, my reply was identical, but I was lying. The brain formulating my deceitful words held a fortune in undeclared intellectual treasure, albeit a kind that could not be spoken of openly.

The war was the greatest event ever to take place on the outskirts of W's body during the seventy-two years he inhabited it. Everyone understood this, for it was a truth common within his generation and more especially to the younger ones who did most of the fighting and dying. But I believed that the speculations that Doctor Bucke had entrusted to me so unselfishly would help me to identify, and perhaps even understand, that W's greatest internal event, originating in the mind and merely influencing the body, was unrelated to war except in superficial chronological terms.

Bucke, bless him, was an impossible man. He became an unstoppable spouter of mystical nonsense whenever you needed him to use plain and monotonic language, as when answering some query concerning practical or physical science. At other times, when speculation about mystical and unknowable magic was the subject appropriate to the moment and to his visionary speculations, he would change completely, talking like a shopkeeper who knew little of life on the other side of the counter. Of course, I hardly need to tell you about the Doctor.

Returning to Camden, I resolved to write him a letter that would serve a dual purpose. Superficially, it would be what I had heard W refer to as a meat-and-potatoes letter, thanking the host and hostess for their hospitality. On another level, my letter would employ appropriate circumspection. Draping myself in language clear to the Doctor but pleasantly meaningless to Missus B, I would beg him to point me toward whatever small amount of research had been undertaken, however remote from the main thrusts of scientific inquiry, on the subject of inversionism.

I knew just enough of the scientific world to suppose that such papers would likely be in German. I would no doubt need to conquer many unfamiliar German scientific terms. Possibly, I thought, some inversionistic research might also have been published in French. For someone to whom this tongue is not native, I read and speak it easily enough. I always had to be cautious, however, when dealing with the correspondence, articles and news cuttings sent to W from France or its colonies, as he only pretended to understand the language. Once he even went so far as to dissect the work of his French translator in some detail! I imply nothing underhanded. He also loved to warble arias, ones from Italian operas in particular, but like most opera singers, or at least those who found their way to the fabled stages of Camden, New Jersey, he understood few of the words (though all of the emotions). He was funny this way. For all the confidence he showed to the world, he was shy and vulnerable in such matters as these. One evening, when I was reading the day's mail aloud so as to spare his tired reddened eyes, he stopped me at a spot where the writer, whoever he was, referred to the recipient, in a most positive and complimentary way, as an autodidact.

"That is the euphemism, thought polite enough for the parlor, for someone who, miraculously, turned out to have a brain after all even though his father had no money."

He said this in what sounded almost like a snort.

"Whenever I hear *autodidact*, I think of *auto-da-fé*. Both are sentences that cannot be appealed."

He pronounced the latter term something like Otto Dufy, so that I first thought he was referring to a person, possibly some Alsatian saloon-keeper from his long-ago Bohemian days.

⁂

Oftentimes retrospect plays us false, giving us absolute confidence in our memory of events and conversations that in fact did not take place as we remember them, and maybe never existed at all. Certainly, I was eager to engage Bucke in an extended private discussion of the most delicate kind. Just as certainly, I never expected that the meeting would go so well as it did. Until just recently, however, my mind had rubbed out all trace of my second reason for the trip to Canada.

I had become intrigued, and puzzled, by W's decision to leave the hospitals for an extended stay in New York in June 1864, when the end of the war was not yet in sight and the wounded were no less numerous. Certainly there were family difficulties with which he was obliged to deal, but then the Whitmans were one of those families whose crises were so continuous that one could join in the upheaval and distress at any moment, and leave at any moment, as easily as one could climb aboard a traction car and get off again at the next stop. He chose to remain there for a number of months. Then, in late March, he got a further two weeks' leave, returning to the capital in mid-April, a couple of days after the president's murder.

The common explanation, which W implied to his early biographer-friends O'Connor, Burroughs and Bucke, was that he had undergone a debilitating disturbance of the mind, a deadening disruption of the spirit, after such a long time spent tending to his boys and watching helplessly as so many of them lost the struggle with their terrible wounds and afflictions. But I found the tale of this episode, particularly the extension of his visit, difficult to credit as it seemed so out of character. I was never quite able to muster the same faith in the truth of it that others did, not even after I had accepted Bucke's invitation because I too was suffering a mental exhaustion that, while in no way comparable to W's wartime one in its intensity, was perhaps of similar design. I had much on my mind, far too much. My labor had been ceaseless, and every day I watched my spirit-father die a little more. The process was continuous and cumulative, the outcome inevitable and hideous. And I worried so about Anne's reciprocation of my love for her. I wrote her from Canada several times but received only one letter, albeit a long and affectionate one, in reply; it arrived just as I was planning my return home. But my assorted troubles did not banish my—*suspicion* is too strong a word, so let us say my *intuition*.

The Canadian trip did what it was intended to do, as I came back feeling more rested; I had repaired, though perhaps only temporarily, the breach in my emotional fortifications. Once again, I was visiting with W once or twice each day, but I looked upon him with eyes that were no longer so well accommodated to watching the vitality leak out of him as gas hisses out of a balloon. I also plunged back into the tasks associated with publishing the new *Leaves*, which of course we all knew would be the last he would ever see.

"I have had a visitor from Harleigh Cemetery," he said one day. "We had quite a talk." It seemed that he was being offered a free burial plot in exchange for writing a poem enumerating the beauties of the cemetery in question. The proposition struck me as tawdry as well as macabre, even for a poet grown accustomed to whipping up emergency elegies and topical odes on receipt of telegrams from editors in New York. I thought the scheme probably redundant as well, since I distinctly recalled his telling me of a plot in another cemetery he had bought and paid for long ago. He said he remembered as well.

"I am very careless of my possessions." Those were his exact words. "I have a farm somewhere which I have never seen. And lots, the Lord knows where. I am, as you see, a much more *possessing* man than you have supposed."

I rejoiced a little at this reappearance of good humor, a sign that his pain was not too severe that day and his lung power not so limited as usual. Of course, I was also making silent wise-cracks to myself: "Perhaps you will be bequeathing these imaginary properties to your many illegitimate children."

The day before Christmas, a cold and miserable one, Warrie took W and the wheeling-chair out to Harleigh by carriage, a journey of which I had not thought him capable. He looked the place over and selected a large lot, twenty feet by thirty, on a small wooded hill, and was soon designing a stone mausoleum for himself, using a pencil and what scratch paper had come to hand. When he returned with Warrie that day, he looked as though all life had been siphoned from him. Missus Davis was apparently having the same thought, but she gave it voice. She told me that W could not look any worse when he finally did die than he looked right then. I could only nod. Both Doctor Bucke and Doctor Osler were now of the view that their friend should give up Mickle Street and move into a hospital. Nothing came of this, however, partly because he had long ago selected the room in which to die, the one with which I was so familiar.

Because W had so many old friends on the newspapers, and because he used the newspapers to inform the world of himself, his condition was destined to become the kind of ongoing melodrama that editors enjoy. But now stories appeared about the celebrated local author's plans for eternity. I saved this example from the *Philadelphia Press*. It has never been reprinted and I suppose never will be, as the publishing world long since lost interest in bringing out further volumes of *With Walt Whitman in Camden*, in one of which I had hoped to include it.

WALT WHITMAN'S GRAVE

—

The Aged Poet Picks Out a Burial Lot on the Outskirts of Camden

Walt Whitman has chosen a spot for the final disposition of his body, when his life is ended. The place is characteristic of the man. It is located in Harleigh Cemetery, about a mile from Camden, and in the prettiest part of the grounds. It is a natural mound, beneath majestic oaks and chestnut trees, while about 200 feet below a stream of water flows over a precipice from an artificial lake. A driveway, which leads through the woods, winds within a few feet of the spot, and the boughs of the gnarled oaks are spread like arms over the hillock, and touch the greensward on the sides. Back of this piece of ground is the woods, where a footpath leads to the entrance gate.

Walt Whitman has been in poor health of late, never having fully recovered from his serious attack of the grip. Yesterday he was able to take a drive, but upon his return home was prostrated with the exertion, and was unable to see anyone last night. He confirmed the report of the selection of the site and the informant said that many persons had called upon him to make his selection of a burial place at Washington, Philadelphia, New York City and London, but he preferred to rest under the trees in New Jersey, where his friends might visit the grave unfatigued.

So many errors in so few sentences, but even the errors flattered him.

❧ SIXTEEN ❧

WKEPT REVISING HIS WILL. Then he would revise the revisions with a codicil. Tom undertook all the paperwork good naturedly and without charge, having, I suppose, become W's official counsel, so to speak, the moment he married my sister.

Tom's friends in the Republican Party and others of like mind couldn't understand how W could have been, since the beginning of his authorial life, so relatively poor while also being at the same time so famous and notorious. This state of affairs gave even greater meaning to the way he wished to remember his helpers and supporters (such as yours truly and Bucke), his surviving family members and that troublesome third category: his special sentimental friends.

You will already have seen that this hurried manuscript I am writing is informed by the straightforwardness that often characterizes fading fools such as myself. Many view such a forum as one of the compensations (or privileges, or responsibilities—or time-killers) of age. If I am being more candid about W here than in all my published writings on the subject, it can be put down to the hope that as I approach the end of these hasty reminiscences, I am coming to the point of them as well.

As I sit here writing these words, W has been dead scarcely more than a quarter-century. During this time, however, a new generation of critics has begun to explore the motives and meanings of his work with an exactness and freedom not possible earlier. New biographers are appearing who never knew him personally and thus have been beyond the reach of his gentle but artful sleeve-tugging and persuasion. My first reaction to such people was to say to myself, "They weren't there, they can't have known." But of course I was not there in Brooklyn or Washington either, yet I believed I understood. My certainty about such comprehension became stronger as Bucke and so many others have died off, leaving me to suppose somehow—but only for a brief period—that I had inherited their own wisdom just as surely as I did W's watch. The little waves of corrective honesty, which likewise found expression only in my head, led me to look even more deeply into *Leaves*, the "Calamus" poems especially, learning to read not between the lines so much as behind them. Having done so, I compliment myself on now having gained a bit of comprehension that I lacked previously. In essence, this is my own little bequest to those of you I so often see described as "the Whitman cult," the chairmanship of which, mostly unwanted as time wore on, I now relinquish.

From this new kind of reading and from some external experiences of my own in recent years, I have learned from W's posthumous example that secret alliances of the heart are often accumulative, not sequential. One of them does not entirely supplant another. It is quite possible and indeed quite common to love more than one person simultaneously, though not equally perhaps. Residual feelings for the past always affect the present. All nature is a process, not a delineated fact. So it was that in his last months W would decide to eliminate this beneficiary, restore that one and change the pecking order of the others. He was grappling with the fact of simultaneity as well as with the fact of cumulativeness. The latter, I can see at this late date, is why he continued to publish *Leaves* in so many different editions, most having new poems but with some of the older ones revised or retitled.

I am of course no critic of literature, only a publicist of that part I personally have found most important, but what I take from the "Calamus" poems, at which I have now squinted so intensely for such a long time, is that they address three individuals, not one nor a group or type. The first I figure to be Fred Vaughan, the car conductor who would lose himself in Canada, seeking invisibility perhaps. W spoke of him hardly at all, certainly not to me. But something of him remains in the poems like the impression of an extinct creature found in a fossil. Then of course Pete the Great, the other streetcar man. I have no smidgen of doubt whatever that when their eyes met on that horse-car in Washington nearly five and a half decades ago, it was the announcement of W's great love of a lifetime and possibly of Pete's as well. Vaughan I never saw. Pete I got a look at only after W's death; he was always unknowable to me and even to Bucke, with whom he had dealings, as well as to all those amateur Walt-detectives from England.

The third ghost is Harry Stafford, at least subordinately a transportation-man, an agricultural one otherwise. I had perfectly cordial relations with him for years, but in many ways know him the least of all. W had watched him grow to maturity and was on terms of intimate friendship with his parents, to whose farmstead he often went, as he put it, to freeload. The whole business was complicated in ways I can't imagine. It can only have been made more so by the fact that W's period of greatest affection for young Harry overlapped with his lingering and anguished regard for Pete. In the course of W's incessant will-making, Harry fell in and out of favor. He survived, however, in the version that truly became the *last* will and testament (and which also, for the first time, remembered Susan Stafford, his mother).

You of course recall what Emerson wrote to W about the first *Leaves*, for I suppose all of us have committed the letter to memory:

"I greet you at the beginning of a great career, which yet must have had a long foreground somewhere for such a start."

The two were not then personally acquainted of course. Therefore I risk imputing to the sage of Concord greater percipience than becomes the memory of even Transcendentalism's founding father. Still, I speculate as to what in this instance Emerson might have been referring to, on an intuitive plane, as his pen moved across that sheet of paper, the one I continually pestered W to let me read again and whose survival as a document I hoped he would entrust to me. Without actually knowing any but the few facts W had given him, Emerson might, I put it to you, lady of the jury, have been alluding to a mystery. The mystery of how a less than totally distinguished newspaper drudge, one who had left positions under circumstances that were cloudy rather than clear, could have emerged as such a surprising poet—or as a poet at all, given that so many of the world's other great ones lapse into redundancy or silence by thirty-six. That was W's age when he raised his head so high above the democratic crowd to yell that he was indistinguishable from it. There is no answer to this conundrum except perhaps accepting the "long foreground" as one of emotions as well as experiences. Beyond that there remains only acceptance that we do not possess the particulars or have need of them. What we do have is the proof of his courage, and this is of course more significant.

W understood that he had no useful rôle to play as a soldier; the valor I speak of was of a different order than that revered by fighting men. It is one that continued to be tested long after General Lee's surrender at Appomattox, in fact for the rest of W's life. Given his vast body of work, the emphasis on the "Calamus" poems is undeniably greater than it ought to be, even though these are certainly among his greatest writings. At first I was merely intrigued by them. That is the word. In time, as my own life has sometimes taken unanticipated turns and twists, I have come around to seeing them as the final and indisputable proof of W's brand of gallantry, a far rarer sort than that seen on the old American battlefields or even on our own ones in Europe, where grass has scarcely begun to hide the scars inflicted on the landscape.

Throughout his poetry-writing years, he tried to distract people from a nature that combined adhesiveness with what his old phreno-logical friends called amativeness, both prerequisites, I suppose, to Bucke's idea of inversionism, or at least a way in which it might be better understood. To avoid the tar-bucket or the lynch mob's noose, he was reduced to tales of children born out of wedlock and a certain flexibility as to whether pronouns should be masculine or feminine. But just as he had to limit the hatred of those who reviled him, he had also to repel offers of acceptance from those most certain to love him for what he was. Such was the case especially with the London aesthetes. I believe that he thought, but would never say aloud, even to me, that the damn English were just too smart for their own (and certainly *his*) good, that their society was more intelligent than ours over here, and that its members knew how to read in a way that Americans did not.

All of this made his public existence as extra-troubled as his private one. But he never ceased to practice the point he understood so well: that while an author may fairly try to limit the acid effects of negative reaction, he must never allow fear of unpopularity and worse to distort his purpose in creating. He must write what he knows must be written. I don't believe W was ever really of much account as a newspaperman or magazinist. He was not a vendor of facts. He was a seeker of truth.

From the day Anne suggested that I keep a record of W's conver-sation to the day of his death was slightly less than three and a half years. What I would give to have been born in, say, Forty-eight rather than Fifty-eight. That would have made me old enough, barely, to have participated in the war, if only as a drummer-boy. Then I could feel the war in somewhat the same way W's generation, and none more deeply so than he himself perhaps, understood it. I would have been his contemporary and hence his equal. My spirit-father and I were merely coevals, two people who happened to be alive at the same time. I regret these facts just as I regret that I was able to depict him for my readers only as he was during his last phase, when his condition mocked the booming health and bounding vitality he bragged of in the first *Leaves* and made such essential parts of his entire view of the world.

As I sit at this table glancing over these pages, I see that they too sometimes seem cruel for the same reason. W in his years of prime creativity was the person whom I, like virtually everyone else alive to-day, know only from his books. The actual man with whom I spent so many hours, weeks, months and years was long past his peak. He was holding on to life because he loved it so—well, that plus a strong and surprisingly undiminished strain of stubbornness, which he called "cussedness" and regarded as quite a virtue. The gods were unkind to him in his final years, and I suppose I may be seen as equally unkind in my portraits of him in the three volumes of my published journal and now in this eleventh-hour memoir, which has become yet another somber study in decline and decay. What was I to do, and what am I to do now? I tried to aim for the right thing, the true thing. Not knowing how else to act, I shall simply continue until my own flame is snuffed out between two quick wet fingertips, leaving me in eternal darkness.

※

One visitor to whom W was willing to grant an audience, any number of them in fact, was Doctor John Johnson of the Bolton Boys in the

North of England, as the Boltons were enthusiasts, not critics in either sense of the term. They collected W's works in every conceivable edition and language they could find and made a huge archive of even the most ephemeral newspaper articles by and concerning him. How proud they were of their vast array of Whitman autographs, jots, doodles and stray proof sheets that had been corrected, or not, in some long-ago time and faraway place. Good grief, they had a lock of W's hair (which he might have wished returned, given his spreading baldness, if he hadn't by this point gotten way beyond such worldly vanity). Now they decided to interview as many of W's friends, relations, acquaintances, associates, antagonists and former army-hospital patients as possible. The initiative showed an admirable determination to extend their knowledge. To W's understandably suspicious mind, however, their plan was potentially revelatory in a way he once feared so much, but less and less with each additional year of his survival. In the event, these people did him no harm with what amounted to the literary equivalent of philately or amateur watercolor painting. I'm sure W thought they were a useful counterweight to the Londoners and, in their purblind enthusiasm for his every line and utterance, probably good for business over there. Besides, they were working-class folks, the kind of Englishmen W got on with, quietly admiring the manners and unadorned accents that would doubtless have been totally incomprehensible to the Queen. If they were American rather than British, they would be from New Jersey.

Doctor Johnson was actually a Scot. He was a powerful-looking youngish man with thick dark hair and thick dark clothing. He had a pointed nose below which hung, like a signboard on a storefront, a long and luxuriantly droopy moustache. I should say *has* not *had*, for at last report he was still alive, part of an ever-decreasing number whose most prominent member, other than Doctor Osler, I suppose is the ancient Burroughs. W liked Johnson, as did Bucke, as did I, as did Anne (who as a reader of people's character was far superior to any of the rest, individually and perhaps even collectively). Johnson was almost disturbingly knowledgeable about the whos, wheres and whens of W's life and career. He solicited a trunkful of reminiscences and impressions, and visited every building in which W had ever worked or resided, or such of them as had survived. He retraced, so to speak, the Stations of the Cross, and then said farewell and went back home.

⁂

As Ninety gave way to Ninety-one, I had the feeling that W sometimes seemed to know exactly, possibly to the very day, when his life was going to end, but, like his doctors and nurses, he did not know precisely what he was to die *from*. There were so many possibilities. Doctor Longaker and Doctor Bucke were not in agreement on whether his circulatory system or respiratory one was the weaker. Other candidates were his digestive and disposal mechanisms, and W believed that his heart was losing strength all the while. All of these, or any one of them, made his problems with vision and hearing seem unimportant, for he was dying of something greater than "old age." One of the many things for which Doctor Osler became so famous was his theory that when a person has two equally serious diseases at the same time, the one is usually the result of the other. W's case was certainly found to illustrate the point. As a patient, he also showed that the number of simultaneous diseases needn't be limited to just two.

Certainly Ninety-one, W's penultimate year, is the period I remember most vividly. So much so that I hardly need glance at my old notes. (Which is just as well, as I have finally lost patience with my own penmanship—a crabbed mess of scribbling and squiggles that only Anne, alone among inhabitants of our planet, can make out as though it were printed from clean type come straight from the foundry. Naturally, I am forming these lines with all the care I can muster lest I vex your own tolerance even further and compel you to hire her as translator!) Yet I do have here before me the text of a memorandum that I copied out for insertion before leaving Camden, feeling that it should be quoted with the strict accuracy that critics often have found wanting in my work.

It is a note of something that Anne said. The occasion was one of W's last outings. Of course, we always feared that each would be his final such venture, but this one came closest yet to being so. It was a small gathering at Tom and Gussie's, not a supper or a dinner but something closer to what people now call a cocktail party, with the guests milling about the house, conversing volubly. I can see Anne there yet, sitting halfway up the front staircase, taking in everything and missing nothing, in her usual manner. I can picture the way her knees were drawn up near her breast and her elbows rested on her upper legs so that she could use her hands to cradle her head in a relaxed and informal way. I even remember what skirt was covering her delicate ankles. I can usually remember what she has worn on any given occasion back through time, though I've never told her this lest she mistake this small expression of my vast love for a *Fetisch*.

From her perch, she saw W being assisted along the hallway below, and she experienced what I imagine must have been somewhat similar to the epiphany she had the first time she ever laid eyes on him, that night in Philadelphia, when he balled up his sloucher, rammed it into his pocket and crossed the stage to capture the lectern.

As soon as we left the party, she described the sight of him as he shuffled down the corridor with such difficulty. "It was the most beautiful face I ever saw," she said. "An expression I have never seen in any other human being. I wished then we might sit there in simple silence, that nothing at all might be said." That is, nothing to ruin the impression formed in and of that moment. She understood, even better than I could do, that although he was continuing his ragtag skirmish with death, he was also at peace with the amount of time remaining. I was much moved. I suppose I am an emotional man. But on this occasion, as on so many others both earlier and afterward, I kept my reaction in check so that I would appear to be (as W was so fond of saying) manly. My love for Anne was so strong and finely made a thing that I had a recurring fear that its beauty might render it fragile, like an exquisite porcelain teacup or some similarly precious piece of *chinoiserie*. In this particular case, another factor served to make me withhold my thoughts even from the silent friend, my journal: I was simply too busy in my capacity as W's jitney. Even as I struggled to scratch a livelihood from the *Conservator* and the bank, I was still deeply involved in producing what has come to be called the Deathbed Edition of the immortal *Leaves*. With the utmost difficulty and the ticking of the clock loud in my ears, I managed to have finished copies in my hand by the middle of December, though the book bore the publication date of Ninety-two, the following year.

<hr />

Events were bubbling all around W's recumbent form. Eakins paid several calls, needing to retrieve his portrait of W, as it was to be shown in the annual exhibition of the Pennsylvania Academy of Fine Arts. Such an odd man, not least in the way his lustful energies performed so important a function in his life as an artist. One result of them was how, like W, though hardly to the same extent, he was visited by scandal now and then. Whereas W at least had tried to contain the public's perception of his long-ago dramatic adventures by placing so much emphasis on manliness and such, Eakins by contrast had few front-parlor skills. In particular, he also lacked one of the talents so useful to W in both his private and professional existences: the ability to give the press something it would like to publish, thus keeping his name before the readers while also preventing reporters and editors from giving him a more intrusive form of attention that, however well intended, was certain to be harmful. Poor Eakins knew only his classroom and his studio, in both of which I believe he tended to barricade himself. Perhaps he feared making friends lest they break his concentration or force him into conversation that might depend on the use of what's now called small talk, of which he possessed none whatsoever. In fact, he had no middle-sized talk either.

He was a married man, his wife of many years being one of his frequent models, but Bucke explained to me that he was also what is known in the relevant branch of academic inquiry as a *bi-sexualist*, the noun whose adjectival forms are *bisexual* and *bisexed*. Bucke said: "Such individuals appear to be fervently mistrusted by both genders, each of which evidently believes itself sufficiently interesting as to deserve attentions that are undivided." Yes, Bucke was in and out of Camden frequently that year, fretting over W. And also, as he always did, explaining the mysteries of medicine and science. Such a talent is rare and most useful, though in his case it coexisted with its exact opposite. I mean the eccentric impracticality of his mystical beliefs, which often seemed to me so much codswallop, leavened, he must have thought, by his snappy and sarcastic asides, at least in private conversation. I've long suspected that he knew far more about humanity—the mass of it, but also its humaneness—than he did about real individuals. Once again, pardon my frankness.

The sense everyone had, that the long drama, at times melodrama, of W's life was finally and surely approaching its conclusion, was confirmed by a surge of invitations to symposia and other events, none of which he could accept, and the arrival of ever more visitors. More ominous were the honors. Another portrait of W, the one by John

Alexander, was purchased by the Metropolitan Museum in New York. From that same city came William O'Donovan, an Eakins colleague or acquaintance, who wished to sculpt a bust of the dying man. This proposal meant repeated appearances. Later, O'Donovan engaged a student of Eakins to take a series of photographs of W in his rocker. They still make for sad viewing to-day.

W complained that the callers were giving him headaches and aggravating his deafness. But when he forced himself to rally enough for a spin in the wheeling-chair with the ever-loyal Warrie as navigator, Warrie reported that the passenger found life in the street confusing and that the unfiltered daylight weakened his vision even more. I understood the significance of the fact that, as testimonials and trophies continued to pour in, W, for perhaps the first time in his life, tried to ignore them.

Never had so many of his poems been published in so many different prestigious journals in so short a time. Some editors ran special sections on him. These read well enough, but I thought they were suggestive of the ribbons made by the local mill at which Anne eventually had to take a position (writing the firm's advertising copy and causing sales to increase, I need hardly say). The company specialized in those long, broad and tastefully fancy ribbons that are attached to funeral wreaths and bear such sentiments as "From a Friend" or, what's more in the style of my home state, "So Long Our Pal Walt From The Brotherhood Of Hod Carriers And General Laborers Local No. 17 Newark New Jersey."

⁂

To return to my original point in the way that sick old men must always discipline themselves to do, it was at this exact moment, smack in the middle of all this crepuscular terror, that I experienced the single happiest day of my life. I have mentioned it some pages back, but I am feeling a bit stronger this morning, so permit me to elaborate upon it. In a change of heart not far short of a brazen miracle, Anne announced that she no longer had any doubts about our becoming married. Indeed, she felt we should have the ceremony quickly, "as our engagement, at least in the less formal sense of the term, has now gone on so long."

My delight blocked out all other concerns and kept me from trying to understand this volte-face. She had been looking pale and tired of late, a fact I put down to the Mickle Street situation, which was jangling the nerves of all of us who were witnessing it up close day after day. I nonetheless understood that the agent of her decision was her father across the river. They were still fundamentally at odds on almost every matter. Perhaps while continuing to fear him she had also wearied of doing so, and in that way stepped up her defiance to the point of saying to herself, "I shall marry Horace, just as my heart urges me to do, and Father be d——ed." She told me that she didn't wish him to give her away or even be invited to the ceremony. Strangely, though, she did desire that a minister officiate. To me, this illustrated how her increasing defiance went hand in hand with her ongoing ambivalence about the Montgomeries, Philadelphia, allegiances based upon the class system, and everything that went with them; sometimes, surely, such an extraordinary woman could hardly escape being complex beyond the comprehension of us less remarkable men. She and I agreed that I would ask my father if we might have the event take place in the Traubel home (where the suggestion was of course received with cries of joy and, to my well-hidden amusement, what I interpreted as a sigh of relief).

When I told W the news and how it had come up so quickly, like the most benevolent Summer storm you could possibly imagine, he was happier than his condition had allowed him to be for—actually, for as long as I had known him. What a pity, he said, that he himself could attend only in spirit, not in body, given the general agreement by everyone with day-by-day knowledge of the situation that his numerous ailments (the word is hardly satisfactory), which previously afflicted him in an orderly sequence, a few each day or each week, had now combined all at once. Before I could react intelligently, he insisted we hold the ceremony in his room, where, he said, all would be welcome. He offered to draw up a wedding document to which all those present, perhaps twenty of us all told, could affix our signatures. He would try to revive the unaffected and democratic beauty of the copyist's script by which he had earned his bread in Washington, he said. Anticipation of the event as well as the event itself perked him up to the extent that he was able to pay a weekend visit to his tomb, ordering changes to the stone lettering above the massive door. I went along. So did Bucke, who had just arrived.

Father suggested, and I, Anne and then W all agreed, that the only possible choice of a minister was the Reverend John H. Clifford of the Unitarian church in Germantown. He often built his sermons around lines from *Leaves* and was as close as possible to not being a clergyman at all while still meeting all the legal and institutional requirements. With that resolved, the pace accelerated even more. Anne seemed just as delighted with the progress as I was, though she hoped, she said privately, that Missus Davis might find some method of at least moving the paper residue of a long and busy life to one side of W's room or the other. "Otherwise there will be no place for people to sit," she said. "Or to stand, for that matter."

She was nearly correct. The only one who sat was W. In my mind's eye, I see him there yet, assisted from bed to rocker, decked out in his best suit of democratic clothes, both serene and highly animated (as much of either as a sick person can be), seeming to consolidate within himself the rôles of best man, maid of honor and both proud parents. All the while he smiled so broadly that I thought I saw the tip of his beard curled upward like the toe of an elf's shoe. Beneath our happiness, though, we knew that he was exhausting one of his last reserves of energy.

Bucke's visit was partly to confer with Doctor Longaker and others about the state of W's health. They pooled their observations to essay a prognosis with which, sadly, no one familiar with the patient's precipitous decline could disagree. Bucke had to get back to his asylum soon, and Anne and I accepted his invitation to accompany him so as to have a wedding trip, albeit a quick one: our wedding night would in fact come a few days after the wedding itself. I was as nervous as all those bridegrooms in flash fiction are said to be.

The night before Bucke, Anne and I boarded the train together, he to his berth and we to our compartment, I was visiting Mickle Street, where I became somewhat terrified by a horrible suspicion. Something hinted at by a new look in W's eyes suggested that perhaps he thought it his duty, as a spirit-paterfamilias, to whisper to me about the things new husbands are supposed to know relative to how they should conduct themselves in—how shall I put this?— "the boudoir." That would have been at once rather more than merely risible and also the signal for buffoonish laughter, given that, as Anne and I had long since been doing business as a fully fledged couple, I possessed more understanding of such relations than he could possibly have dreamed of having. That is, unless, by some magic, his unwed mothers in New Orleans should turn out to be more than mere characters in his own unwritten fictional account of his various doings on Earth. I swear I do not believe that my hunch and fore-boding misread his intention, one that, if carried out, would reinforce the claim to the manliness that he pursued through the corridors of his imagination. What saved me the embarrassment but otherwise scared me greatly was the fact that he accidentally set fire to some of the papers on the floor, unaware that he had done so until I managed to stamp out the flame with my boot. Naturally, this increased my remaining apprehension—my concern about leaving him. But Anne and I had responsibilities to ourselves.

For the whole trip, she and I were scarcely ever out of each other's sight. So, once we were settled in at the Bucke residence in London, I had no opportunity to continue my earlier conversation with him on the subject of inversionism. I got only one brief additional look at Pete Doyle's letters, and it did little to further my understanding of either their author or recipient.

⁂

We were delighted to find on our return so many notes and letters of congratulation from near and far, including one from Doctor Johnson in Bolton and another from his co-leader there, James William Wallace, known as J.W. It was evidently the latter's turn to sail over to America to pursue more of the field research that Doctor Johnson had undertaken during his own stay. Wallace was about five years older than me. Pardon once again, I should say *is;* it is my bad but understandable habit to assume that everyone from the past has predeceased me. He looked as English as he sounded, and I suspected that his speech would have seemed almost as curious to a sophisticated Londoner as it did to people in Camden. His elliptical face was very narrow, yet he seemed to have the beginnings of a second chin. He was clean-shaven except for sideburns (or *burnsides* as W still called them, a reference to the wartime general with whom the vogue originated); they extended the whole way to his lower jaw. He wore small wire spectacles for his large eyes to peer through, and was seldom seen without a derby, pronounced *darby*, worn squarely on the head, not aggressively askew like Pete Doyle's in that old photograph.

I think of the comparison because I had virtually no opportunity to speak with Bucke about Pete the Great during our honeymoon, honeymoons being what they are. I looked forward to showing my bride Niagara Falls, but the weather was so foul on the first attempt that we could hear its roar but see very little. We had better conditions the following day, having stayed on in any case so that our baggage, which the railroad had misplaced, could reunite with us. At the Buckes', all was well. Anne got on splendidly with Missus Bucke and her children, but confessed after a few days that she had overtaxed herself and was once more feeling run-down. And of course both of us were distracted by our worries about W, though I received communications from Warrie and others almost daily and these suggested no further decline.

Wallace had seemed a likable fellow in his earlier correspondence with me and, like Johnson, proved to be so in person as well. Anne and I got back to Camden two weeks after the wedding and learned that he would be arriving in late August or very early September (perhaps having learned of the notorious mugginess and misery of Summers in New Jersey). He arrived bearing gifts for the strangers he would soon turn into friends. These were presented in the name of the entire Bolton group. They included a beautiful red coverlet for Anne. Being one of those people who could talk himself into the good graces of anyone he wished to see, and get them to impart the information he sought without making himself sound like an interrogator, he proved just as dogged a researcher as his friend Johnson, though he spent most of his time with W. Assuming his means to be as modest as our own, Anne and I were putting him up at the brand-new matrimonial apartment we had rented, where I was astonished to learn that he was intending to keep a literal transcription of every word that came from W's lips. He spoke of his plan quite freely, unaware of what I'd been doing since March of Eighty-eight. I said nothing.

Such was his frankness that he kept mentioning what a poor memory he had. On days when he and I had been in W's presence at the same time, he would ask afterward, "What was that word he used in answer to my question about . . . ?" or "Can you remind me of his opinion about" such and such. One evening I found him busily engaged in working up his day's notes. Again, he chided himself for not having the type of recollective powers required to set down speech in an accurate fashion. While we talked, he asked if I would like him to read some of his entries, and they were quite good. Don't think me arrogant if I say they were much as I would have done them, except that he lacked a natural affinity for the American idiom.

Not long afterward, I was taken aback when, over a cup of tea, he said, "I read some of my notes to Missus Traubel and she thinks them quite like Walt, I believe. But she tells me also that you are doing this same sort of work, and have been for a long time."

Motivated by her helpfulness and her openness of heart, Anne had let the cat out of the bag. I resolved to think of the matter that way, rather than in terms of worms that could not be put back in the can. I told him about my manuscripts in some detail and later even read him some patches. I suppose I thought at the back of my mind that the length, breadth and depth of what I was doing would deter him from trying to beat me into print. Two years ago, *With Walt Whitman in Camden* having come to a halt with changes in the public's reading habits and the rise in government repression of dissent during (and since) the war in Europe, the Johnson and Wallace collaboration finally appeared. It was entitled *Visits to Walt Whitman in 1890–1891 by Two Lancashire Friends*. I was happy to see the book for its worthwhile qualities, but honesty compels me to say that I was just as pleased, if not more so, to observe that it found no wider audience than it did and came to light long after my own.

Sadly, this shows that there was Capitalist competition as well as Socialist co-operation amongst the Whitman circles, a fact that eventually snapped shut the correspondence between Wallace and me, which extended into the present century. Looking back, I am alarmed to see how competitive I myself was about Emerson's 1855 letter to W. I told myself that I was eager only to rescue it from accidental loss or destruction; I couldn't admit that I was just as eager to prevent it becoming a part of Bucke's collection. "No, I haven't forgotten," W would say. "It shall be yours when I see it next." He often claimed to have misplaced it. My hunch was that he knew exactly where it could be excavated with a few seconds' drilling. I could not restrain my pleasure when I visited one day and found Wallace at the bedside getting W to autograph a stack of photographs. W greeted me with, "Here it is!" The original envelope was all nicked and soiled from so much shuffling around the floor, but inside was folded the communiqué beginning with its famous greeting, with its wise prediction of a long career and its prescient understanding of W's long foreground. Not only that, but it was in fine condition. Someday had arrived after all.

❧ SEVENTEEN ❧

As W's end came ever nearer, finally at a canter rather than a creep, he himself became more sentimental in his love. I am remembering one day at the end of November Ninety-one when Anne and I visited and they kissed each other heartily yet tenderly with the full measure of whatever connected the dying inversionist with the vibrant woman forty-four years his junior. I do not believe that this was merely a proof that she saw him as the father she would have preferred over the one she had been assigned. Beyond that, however, I don't know what, if anything, it is that I do know as a certainty. As she and I were about to depart, he kissed her again, saying, "Come often, darling. Come often." As we descended the stairs, he was straining his feeble voice to call out similar sentiments after her.

As I entered the house on December seventeenth to make my regular suppertime visit, Warrie warned me that W had experienced a terrible day. I went in and found him unable to raise his head from the pillow. But his humor was fit enough, for he dismissed what was clearly a general malfunctioning of the lungs as "premature rigor." I was greatly worried, and sent for Doctor Longaker. The next day's *Camden Post* carried the headline

WALT WHITMAN'S ILLNESS.
The Aged Poet Unconcerned as to its Outcome.

Without giving their names, the reporter who came calling described being met at the door by the "hearty and hospitable" Missus Davis, followed by Warrie, "Mister Whitman's faithful and courteous attendant," bearing a note from W. The note read: "I may get over it and I may not. It doesn't make much difference which."

Doctor Longaker came on the scene, Doctor Bucke hurried down from Canada and John Burroughs arrived as well, as did W's niece Jessie, the first of the family members to reach the house, followed by W's brother George, to be followed by his wife, a more difficult person. Longaker vouchsafed to me that W's odds of survival were very poor indeed. The congestion was internally crippling. None of the great amounts he coughed up from the depths seemed to reduce the total; his chest was like a magic well in a children's storybook. He was often thirsty and sometimes a bit disoriented with fever. With Missus Davis and Warrie, there were more than enough of us to stand watches, like sailors at sea. The Bolton Boys sent me a list of code words to be used to wire them any news without incurring big charges. A message reading only *Ontario* would mean "No alarm at present," while *Prelude* would be "Much worse." *Starry* was the cipher to be used for "Likely to be fatal." *Triumph* would signal that W had died.

Doctor Longaker's prognosis soon became the standard of opinion, for no one, including the patient, was even guardedly optimistic. Bucke, for example, said just after midnight on Christmas Day that he doubted W would make it to sunrise. Of course, when W did in fact meet the morning, he did so in even worse condition and with a slowed heart rate.

I will not impose the burden of much further graphic detail so as to keep myself from having to relive those weeks and months and to spare you the necessity of reading much more of my prose. I will say only that Doctor Longaker told me in early January that it was a mystery how W continued to cling to life in the face of all medical knowledge. My own theory concerned the part Anne's presence played in steering him away from defeat, but I kept it to myself lest it be discounted as unscientific. Three days later W and I had our single most important conversation.

I came into the room to find him sitting up in bed, his head clear, his spirits not at their worst and his voice rough and scratchy, sometimes perfectly understandable but other times on the level of a mumble. On the counterpane lay a pine box about a foot long and perhaps four inches high and five wide. It was well constructed, joined without resort to nails, and looked rather old.

He asked after my health and Anne's, and I after his, though we both already knew the answers.

"I feel somewhat more nearly hale to-day," he said. "As for hardy as well, perhaps that is gilding the lily." We talked about *Leaves* for a moment and followed with trivialities such as the news.

Then he got more serious. Not solemn or lugubrious, but sober.

"Horace, my boy, you of course know of my most recent will. There is one more bequest I must make. It is a bequest to you, as it may complete your work with me, in the same sense of the phrase that I am completing my own labor on this Earth. I have not bothered Tom this time to make a new document for me, because I want this gift to be a private matter between us. No one else is to know of it. No one else *can* know of it. What I'm giving you doesn't even belong to me in the strictest legal sense of ownership, but I have been storing it for a great many years, hiding it in fact. I brought it with me to Camden when I first came here. Yesterday I got Warrie to retrieve it from its hiding place."

Well, this certainly sounded intriguing; he surely did know how to tell a story. I sat attentively and said nothing.

"Where shall I begin? Where *can* I begin?"

In general terms, I knew now what must be coming. W was tidying up all his unfinished business and I was part of it. "Pete Doyle?" I asked.

There was a pause.

"Yes, Pete."

He told the story everyone now knows of the Washington City horse-car on that snowy night during the war, and how he would continue to take the same car other evenings, hoping always to engage Pete in more conversation. That led them to drink together at the Union Hotel in Georgetown, a place that had returned to its original use, having been transformed into yet another hospital for the wounded at some stage. When not in the tap-room, they would cross the Navy Yard Bridge to tramp along the Maryland shore of the Potomac and even take the ferry—W and his love of ferries!—to Alexandra, on Virginian soil. Flora, forgive me, I don't know how much of this geography you're familiar with.

"Whether we were getting half-loaded, as I confess we did on occasion, or marching along country roads, we would talk. Our talk was endless, back and forth it went, freely exchanged. Someone overhearing us might have said our conversation was incessant, which it was—when we weren't singing instead. Sometimes I would recite passages from Shakespeare or sing snippets of arias. Pete with his natural honesty of statement said he liked hearing the music of the first but enjoyed the 'tunes' of the other, while understanding nothing of either. Ours wasn't a great intellectual sympathy, but a great unaffected one of a much rarer and more important kind."

His voice was starting to lose the clarity of only a few minutes earlier, becoming a low rumble, the result of lingering fatigue. I didn't want to wear him down or tire him out. He wasn't telling me what had happened between the two of them, but I was uncertain whether I should interject any questions less I scotch the feeling of the moment. I decided to take the risk.

"Was yours what might be called an *intimate* association?" I asked.

"An intimate *friendship* to be sure." A pause in such a way that the momentary silence became another species of question. "I understand the direction you are taking. While I don't wish to be coy—and before not very long I will have no further need to be—I can say that such intense fellowship as Pete and I had, during the war especially, often ripens quickly into an ever greater bond. Those are the best friendships, in fact."

"I have read some of the letters that passed between you that Bucke got from Pete."

"Well, then you know. In the main, they are not letters on lofty subjects. They are bits of news and what you might call domestic gossip."

"The Lincoln murder. We know of the happenstance that put Pete in the theater that night. What more did he tell you of it than you were able to make use of for the Lincoln lecture?"

His voice sank further and he coughed and floundered for a few moments. Was it his voice I was overtaxing with these questions, or something else?

Again he sounded growly, but not from meanness. I sensed that he had begun to feel the relief of impending weightlessness, as the secret was about to be lifted from his shoulders.

"Horace, you would have made a fine inquisitive lawyer, just like Tom. I can see how you would break the resolve of an elderly witness, trying to force a confession of guilt but not wishing to appear to be doing so, posing instead as just an honest counselor attempting to get to the bottom of things." He said this, however, in a wry tone, unmistakable even with his voice in its present condition. "Or a reporter of the very first rank, which I suppose you are."

I said nothing (a lawyer's trick or a reporter's?), so he was forced to resume.

"Lincoln saved These States from disintegrating and ultimately disappearing from the map of Liberty. Its location at the center of that map is after all what brought your own family here escaping oppression."

(I thought to myself, "We can debate that another time." Then I realized there would of course be no other time.)

"No one exceeded me in admiration for Lincoln," he went on. "By which I mean, not even in the all too brief periods when he was enjoying his topmost level of support. I was vocal about it. You've never lived through a war, my boy. You can't imagine what the reality of it was day upon day, the politics, the whole atmosphere and feel of it, not simply dispatches from the battle-fronts. You might say it assumed its own form, as both religion and disease. It entered every conversation just as it filled every newspaper. The District was a city besieged, as well as the besieger of its nemesis. Of course you already know all this from what I later wrote.

"Now Pete had all the virtues of very young men: manliness, quickness, a reckless disregard for his safety based on the belief— until it was proved wrong, as it was for my hospital boys—that he was invincible. But despite the hard life he had led, his responses were not yet always tempered by his experiences: the corresponding *weak* spot of the young. He was prone to sudden floods of temper. I could picture him entering into brawls with his fellow Rebel soldiers from time to time, and perhaps doing likewise with the patrons of Northern saloons. To see him in his town clothes he was not especially athletic looking, but he had a powerful chest and strong arms."

I had to move my chair closer as his voice was curving downward again. I could see the way he was expending his energies, and it moved me deeply, as it does now to recall.

"He was given to periods of stationary blackness as easily as to ones of touchiness, when he could not be approached without caution. I was one evening speaking of Lincoln, talking of the war and political affairs of the day, when he seemed to erupt in flames."

Here he paused to let more breath accumulate in his damaged lungs.

"He was accusing me of loving the president more than I did him. He was being absurd of course, in the grip of an angry fit. Lincoln was an impressively tall and straight-backed man whose face made an art of homeliness, but those were my only opinions on his physical person as distinct from his convictions and philosophy. Pete stormed out of my room. More than once in a single evening, in fact. I resolved to show greater grasp of his piques and vexations. But some damage had already been done, and more was to follow.

"Horace, I won't be able to talk much longer. I don't have the wind and am unsure even of my will. So I will come to the head of the matter. When we resumed our bond, but on a slightly less happy and less constant basis, he let me know, by dribs and drabs, that he had become acquainted with Edwin Booth's brother, the darkly handsome one. When he was in the right state to tell me, but wishing to tell me so as to do me no injury, he revealed that he had, in a way, rejoined the Struggle. Booth had recruited him for a conspiracy to kidnap the president and hold him hostage. The way in which he revealed this to me, with his head almost bowed, suggested to me that his being raised in the Roman faith, even though he no longer subscribed to its precepts or dogma, had left him with the idea that any form of transgression was erasable with enough confession and penance.

"Naturally, I advised him never to repeat to anyone else what he had told me in the confessional of my boarding-house and with all swiftness to distance himself from J.W. Booth. I presume he took the first advice, but evidently he didn't accept the second.

"I was unwell at the time with the lingering consequences of an unusual fever I seemed to have contracted from the wounded. I was in my latter forties, but this was the first time my body had let me down in such a way: a warning of what was to come, I would learn to my sorrow. Also, my family in Brooklyn was experiencing difficulties once again. What's more, I wanted to find just the right printer for stereotype copies of *Drum-Taps*. Leaving Pete in what I hoped, and what certainly seemed to be, a calmer state of mind, I therefore went to New York.

"Four years after the whole glorious hell began, I was on my leave, up in Brooklyn again looking after family matters, when I read the first news of Lee's surrender. And so too, a week after that, getting ready to address the cooked breakfast Mother had prepared, I picked up the paper and saw the telegraph news of Lincoln's murder the previous evening. For the rest of the day I went up and down the old streets, watching shopkeepers tacking up black crepe. I grabbed newspapers. I brought home every morning and every evening edition. The boldest, blackest headline in one of them was A TERRIBLE TRAGEDY!, which indeed it of course was. There was a feeling of tragedy in my heart as well when I read that Booth was the killer, though I did not know how an abduction had become an assassination or what part Pete might have played and what the condition of his mind must be."

He began to cough and asked for some water, which he drank quickly. Some of it spilled down his front. It looked to me that his under-lip had gone numb, for it appeared scarcely to move at all when he spoke.

"I was back in the District two days later. I couldn't locate Pete anywhere; he had gone to ground. You have read about the events that followed the murder. There was found to be a large conspiracy. Many were jailed, from the surgeon who set Booth's leg to those who had made disparaging remarks about Lincoln and people who just happened to resemble Booth. It was a bad time for good-looking black-haired young men with a certain bearing to them. Of the actual assailants, three were hanged: Payne, who stabbed Seward, Herold, who fled with Booth into the swamps, and the feeble-minded Prussian, Atzerodt. Missus Surratt, who participated in no violence, was hanged with them. Her son, however, escaped to Canada and from Canada to Europe, and when brought back for trial was let go because of a hung jury. He is still among the living.

"In short, the country was in an uproar of retribution. Even a fellow named Spangler, I believe it was, one of the stage-hands at Ford's, was sent to prison, because he may or may not, absentmindedly or with deliberation, have left open the rear door through which Booth fled. Everyone believed that there were a great many other small fry, and no doubt some bigger fishes as well, who dispersed widely in the hours after the event and were never identified, have not been identified even yet."

He took another gulp of water and closed his eyes, resting for less than half a moment. His voice was still more hesitant and muted when he resumed.

"Pete burned the one piece of paper that would have connected him to the assassin with criminal certainty, a brief note Booth had sent him. Then he fled the capital, sensibly enough. He was still in a state of justifiable fear in the Autumn of Sixty-eight when he wrote me that he was considering taking his own life on account of a bad case of barber's rash. Of course I knew the genuine agony that hid behind that flimsiest of ciphers. He was wounded and needed me. In my letters I sent him every affection. We even undertook a brief trip together. He accompanied me to Mannahatta and to Brooklyn, where I introduced him to Mother, though we were careful to stay in New Jersey. It was here in Jersey that he gave me the details of April the fourteenth Sixty-five and what he was doing at Ford's.

"Booth had obviously planned the murder to take place at a moment when the stage was least populated with actors. He also depended on the fact, or the hope, that the response of those in the audience would be slowed down by the jolt to their nerves. He believed that he could make his histrionic leap, utter his line like the player that he was and escape across the stage—but only if there were no overly heroic soldiers in the house who were armed and were quick enough of wits and hands to prevent him from effecting his exit. Booth asked Pete to rise the instant the commotion began, survey the rows carefully and shoot down anyone who might himself get to his feet and begin to point a weapon. He sat on the left-hand side of the house, the actor's stage-right, up quite a ways so that there would be few who could in turn shoot him in the back. But not so far away as to preclude him from discerning the Lincolns clearly. He had to get his quarry, if there were to be any, before they could clamber awkwardly onto the stage from below and step over the foot-lights, becoming, for that one brief but crucial moment, other than fully upright and then silhouettes with blurry outlines.

"I was astonished. If this had been known, poor Pete would have been hanged for certain. I asked what plans Booth had made for Pete's own escape from the theater. Apparently there were none. Fortunately, no armed soldiers jumped up before Booth disappeared, and Pete didn't even touch the pistol hidden beneath his long coat. He just took his sweet time, as shocked as everyone else, and walked out of Ford's seeming to be exactly the thing he was not, another follower of the theater, slightly fazed and confused."

W paused once more, overcome by emotion this time and perhaps by the necessity of having to re-enter the one part of the past he feared reliving. He got control of himself and tried, unsuccessfully, to clear his throat.

"Later, in my own silent analysis of what he had told me, I could conclude only that Pete's lack of ease, or do I mean his disease?, must somehow have entered a new period. The two hemispheres of his problem—the extreme melancholia that weighted his step and dulled his thinking, and the blind anger that became actual violence; two states that until then had alternated with irregular frequency— were now, briefly, operating in unison. Bucke is the expert who would have the better explanation, but of course I have never told him of Pete's part in the tragedy, have never told another soul until this instant. And you must never do so either, on your word to God or whatever you hold most sacred, for Pete too is still among us on Earth, weighted down with guilt. Whether at this late date he might still be hanged or at least imprisoned, I cannot say, but he would be destroyed all the same."

W's eyes opened and closed rapidly a number of times, as though he were trying to clear some obstruction from his idealized vision of those war-weary days. Or perhaps he was fighting to keep from weeping.

"After that, I resolved to break off our relations, though another part of me wished not to. The process was neither quick nor neat. Both of us had grave doubts about our abilities to go on as previously. There was much recrimination, to be followed by attempts at renewed affection, themselves succeeded by still more recrimination. Knowing myself the pressures brought by family difficulties, I tried to help and console Pete in Seventy-one when his brother, the policeman who had barely escaped dismissal from the force, was shot to death while performing his duties.

"Pete needed a fresh start. He quit the horse-cars and became a railroad brakeman. As I had tried to comfort him when first restoring contact and then during the unfortunate business with his brother, so he helped to nurse me when I had the first stroke in

Seventy-three, which as you know brought me here to the city from which I am about to take my leave."

By this time, I believe I myself must have been in tears.

"He quit the brakeman's job too, and got work as a baggage master in Philadelphia. We wrote each other still and even visited. It was always awkward. I wished my heart to be free of him, yet could not cease to worry about him, which inevitably meant continuing our communication. He gave me this box, telling me he wished never to set eyes on it again, though why he didn't destroy it I don't know. I suppose that, like me, he was now trapped in his past while trying to persist through each new day."

He stopped once again, for his lungs' sake, I believe.

"And that is the sad story, abridged to meet the requirements of my waning strength. For now I have made myself very tired. You see how my hands shake. I must rest."

With his eyes he pointed to the box, imploring me to take it with me when I went, which I did but only after opening it, to see what I was letting myself in for. Inside, wrapped tightly in a big square pillow slip, was a very old pistol of some kind.

He had talked far too much and at far too great a cost. His voice was barely functioning at all. I believe what he said was, "Colt, thirty-six caliber. Not large."

I resealed the lid and left with the box under my arm, like a large loaf of bread. Going back across to Philadelphia, I threw it over the side of the ferry when I thought no one was looking.

❧

Still stunned and about to become more so, I entered the front parlor at mid-morning to find Tom sitting there with the painter Eakins and two of Eakins's assistants, all of them looking purposeful and somehow serene. Sitting opposite were W's brother George and his fearsome wife. Missus Whitman looked cross. W had died the previous evening, March twenty-sixth, Ninety-two. Even now I can barely write even a sentence about what I had seen take place the previous evening, not with any assurance that my face will not soon be streaked by tears. I was at the bedside with Tom, Doctor McAlister, Missus Davis and Warrie. Once the end came, all of us dispersed to our individual sorrows. And to our tasks, as with Tom and me frantically sending the news by telegraph far and wide to those who most cared for him. Missus Davis washed the face and Warrie the body. Then the room was darkened. Later I returned alone and gazed down on the still form, which looked sweet and innocent of trouble. I bent down and kissed his forehead. He was stony cold of course, but I caught the scent of his hair. Later still I went in a second time just to take another look. I kept my composure but barely. Now I took Eakins and his apprentices up the worn stairs and opened the shutters on the three windows. It was raining hard yet there was good light, which they needed in making the death mask. Tom helped them. I can't imagine what use a lawyer could actually be, but he too was quite attached to the person who had resided in the body, and so he wished to participate as best he could.

I had to go over to Philadelphia again to meet with Doctor Longaker and Doctor Cattell, and was surprised to learn that W had given permission in December, when he so very nearly died, for a post-mortem examination to be performed in the name of scientific inquiry. Why had he told me nothing of the matter? George objected strenuously when he too learned of this for the first time, and continued with his protests throughout the day. The formal instructions of the deceased, however, trumped the wishes of the next of kin, and the autopsy convened in the back parlor at about supper time. I was present in my familiar rôle as amanuensis, writing down Doctor Cattell's commentary as he spoke it. Doctors McAlister and Longaker were part of the team as well. Also present at least some of the time was the undertaker, a man named Simmons, who had brought the body down from the bedroom on a stretcher and transferred it to a mortuary table that had been carried in once all the normal furniture had been removed. Also there in the beginning was a reporter from the *Camden Post*, who rejected common decency to the extent that I had to have him thrown out. My numbness of spirit was evidently lessening, or my awareness of its cause finally affecting me, for I had a difficult time controlling my feelings, not to mention my stomach.

W was stretched out neatly with his arms at his sides, a cloth draped across his loins. I was suddenly reminded of the unclothed photograph that Eakins had made for the purposes of art study. I kept thinking of Doctor Osler as well, for he had long been one of the most important advocates of autopsies. I once read that he had personally performed well over eight hundred of them just in the years when he taught in Montreal, long before moving to Baltimore and thence London.

The tools and other instruments being used were terrible to see and to hear, and their effects far worse. The doctors sawed around the upper portion of the skull, its entire circumference, and extracted the brain, which was placed in a gupsack brought along for that purpose. Except for being slightly deficient in weight, due to age and illness, it did not, on cursory inspection, seem abnormal. So I was told, and so I duly wrote in the note-book I had been given. When the chest and abdomen were opened and spread apart, the remarkable things to be seen there were obscure to none of the medical men. W's left lung had collapsed like a punctured bellows and the right one, they estimated with apparent precision, had been performing at only sixteen per cent of its intended volume. Abscesses had deformed some of the bones in the chest, and small hard protuberances called tubercles were visible in the stomach, intestines and liver. A stone almost filled the space inside the gall bladder. Oddly, his heart, which W thought was betraying him as well, had been the soundest part of him. It weighed nine ounces.

I wrote all this down, but the jottings I turned over to the doctors at the end of nearly four hours were fragmentary and telegraphic and full of words such as *oedematous* and *athermatous* whose proper spellings I did not know, much less their meanings. Nonetheless my notes, written as legibly as I possibly could make them when working so quickly, provided a kind of outline for the write-up done by the doctors who later subscribed their names to it. This final report made some remarkable statements about W's physical tenacity that seemed to complement what those of us who knew him best had always seen reflected in his spirit. If I may, let me quote from their findings. "The cause of death was pleurisy of the left side, consumption of the right lung, general miliary tuberculosis and parenchymatous nephritis." I'm not certain precisely what the last of these is. The document went on to opine that any other man "would have died much earlier with one half of the pathological changes" that W had endured for so long.

The organs that had been removed, all except the brain I mean, were placed together in the chest cavity, and the incision that was the trap door to the body's mysteries was stitched closed. I then re-admitted Simmons the undertaker to begin performing his own magical work.

The viewing was held at 328 Mickle Street, and thousands of people snaked their way along the sidewalk in a line-up that extended around the corner. I was later told that one of those slowly shuffling past the coffin was Pete Doyle. He had at first been turned away by a policeman engaged in managing the crowd but had made it inside and solemnly walked through with all the others. I don't know why he should have been singled out that way unless he had arrived too late or was being belligerent or was acting otherwise disturbed.

During the entombment ceremony at Harleigh Cemetery, Burroughs nudged me and directed my eyes to a little hilltop nearby where a solitary figure stood, holding a switch from a tree, swishing it back and forth absent-mindedly.

"Peter Doyle," he said.

I would not have recognized him from the old photographs, for he had grown much heavier. As we were returning to the city, we saw him again, strolling along the road, still with the switch in his hand. We stopped the carriage so that Burroughs could renew their acquaintance and I could be introduced. At closer range, it struck me that his entire physiognomy had undergone some fundamental alteration that gave him the general appearance of a splendidly moustachioed Irish bartender who had recently come to know a modest degree of prosperity. I later learned that he was working for yet another railroad and was active in the Elks club and the United Confederate Veterans. He was not unpleasant but had little enthusiasm for saying much, and seemed unmoved by his old comrade's end. Perhaps his own numbness of spirit had not begun to wear off. Who can say? Certainly not I.

❧ EIGHTEEN ❧

FLORA MacDONALD HAS long been divorced from Howard Denison of Detroit when Horace encounters her at a Toronto dinner party in 1916. Even at this first meeting, in the home of some fellow Whitman disciples, they address each other by their first names. Such is the common practice among the small but incessantly vocal group of Whitmanites, anti-monarchists, Socialists, single-taxers, theosophists, atheists, spiritualists, communalists and Americanized cranks who, if you were to see them in a shopping crowd on King Street, would be indistinguishable from normal God-fearing Canadians, the ones who march in the Orange parade and read the *Evening Telegram*, atop whose front page every day sits an engraving of the Union Jack, unfurled and benevolent.

Nonetheless, in the early years of their acquaintance Horace always calls her Missus Denison when speaking of her to others. She learns of this but never corrects him. Such usage does not contradict her suffragist beliefs or even the democratic principles implicit in the use of forenames (advanced people do not endorse the term *Christian name*). No one can quite explain why she is so forgiving, except to say that Horace, whom she has long hoped to meet, is one of the last important links to the living human being who wrote the immortal *Leaves*, in the pages of which a new generation has found validation for its every cockamamie belief. Even if he were not the last, Horace would still be one of the most important. Knowing the man who was Walt's closest confidant for the final three and a half years is suffused with special meaning. How could one possibly explain this to other Canadians except by saying that it is analogous to meeting Paul of Tarsus?

Horace compliments the hostess on the "damn nice spread" with its damn nice vegetables and such, and Flora immediately sizes him up. With his casual tweed clothing and his wild white hair and droopy white moustache, he is obviously, she believes, a gentleman of learning and European refinement who nonetheless has so embraced the memory of his late spirit-father that he revels in the use of slang, with all its inherent democratizing.

"I have heard Mark Twain speak and know what real cursing is," she later tells her local Whitman group, one of the most active of the many such organizations. "It is usually a way for the speaker to show his disdain for the listener. Horace's was just the opposite."

Following the dinner, he offers to walk her home to Carlton Street so that he can hear more about Bon Echo, the resort property she has acquired in the eastern part of Ontario. She had been a private dressmaker, it seems, but later became head of the ladies' custom-tailoring salon at the Robert Simpson Company departmental store at Yonge and Queen streets. She still finds it necessary, however, to do a certain amount of dressmaking at her residence. She needs the extra money because Bon Echo costs her slightly more in taxes and the manager's wages than it returns in fees from campers. Hence her plan to turn the place into a permanent memorial to Walt, as outlined at dinner. As it isn't making money anyway, it should be made to serve a higher purpose. Who knows but that in time it might prove self-supporting or even turn a small profit, as the number of Whitman pilgrims will only grow as his spiritual doctrines seep even more deeply into the texture of society, as she believes is beginning to be the case.

They stroll through the wartime streets. At one point a constable walking the beat approaches from the opposite direction, and Horace tenses a bit. But when he gets closer, the policeman says, "It's a nice night" as he passes them by, not taking them for radicals but only as an elderly gent and his somewhat younger companion.

At Carlton Street, they sit and talk in the front room for hours. She describes the property generally and Mazinaw Rock in particular. This is a granite outcropping cast up by the glaciers. It is more than a mile long and, at its zenith, three hundred feet high, accessible by small boat on Mazinaw Lake, which laps demurely at its base.

"It was a sacred place to the Indians," she says. "You can see their paintings of beasts and birds, hundreds of them, faintly on the steep granite face."

Horace nods approvingly. He remembers how, when Walt was a government clerk in Washington, he actually saw genuine Indian chiefs, in their full ceremonial get-up; they had come in from the West on treaty business. Walt always regarded himself as a commiserative white man. This connection would make Horace even more sympathetic, as though greater sympathy were wanted, with Flora's wish to, as she explains at length, dedicate the Rock to Walt on the occasion of the centenary of his birth, in 1919, and eventually to build a Whitman Library there where scholars and ordinary enlightened people could come to study and reflect.

"Flora, go right ahead," he says at the close of the evening, while warning her of the obstacles in her path. "You will be up against snaps," he says, taking silent delight in keeping alive one of Walt's terms for his many critics. "Your best friends will desert you or be indifferent to your work."

He sounds as though he is speaking from long and bitter experience gained while spreading the Whitman gospel.

"But go right ahead, and I will help you," he continues. "Why, the whole thing is magnificent. Canada's Gibraltar a monument to Walt! Don't let anything switch you."

She gives him gifts to take back to his wife and their daughter, Gertrude.

Later she receives a warm note of thanks from Anne that makes her feel as though they are already friends and confidantes, as indeed turns out, magically, to be the case when they meet the following year at the annual Whitman Dinner held in New York on May thirty-first, the great man's birthday.

Over the years, Horace has spent many short periods in Canada without being able to explain exactly why but only to note that the country, slowly and eventually, gripped his imagination as it had Walt's, though Walt supposed it to be a natural paradise unspoiled by industry and Horace likes it for its cities. He has even holed up in Montreal to do some of his writing.

It is August 1918, four years exactly into the Great War that in Europe is being fought against the Germans but in America is being fought against dissent, and less than a year since the Bolshevik revolution of which Horace excitedly approves. He is in Hamilton, Ontario, a place that he thinks has some characteristics in common with Camden, visiting a Whitmanite couple there who are old friends of his. Flora arrives after a very brief train ride from Toronto to share in his company but is shocked, horribly shocked, when she lays eyes on him again. Horace is ill—sallow-looking, with a slight yellow cast; cheeks sunken; somewhat hesitant and stooped in his movement. She tries to keep from betraying her concern, because Horace himself is speaking as though nothing is amiss.

"Flora," he says, "I'll be at Bon Echo and do anything you want me to do next year except make a speech."

She hopes that she can get him to give any number of addresses or lectures, if he is well enough to be present at all and, if so, well enough to speak.

⁕

Anne tries to alter Horace's unhealthy existence but cannot. Typically he sleeps only four hours out of twenty-four and spends eighteen writing and editing at his small dark office in Philadelphia. The place is in and of itself unhealthy, a rat's warren of obsolete pieces of paper, including a great many of the very same ones that littered 328 Mickle Street decades earlier. Usually he does not eat with Anne and Gertrude at the house on Elm Street in Camden but snatches a bite at a cheap and brightly illuminated little place before heading back down to the ferry a couple of blocks away. Philadelphia and the other large cities have many more all-night diners than places like Camden possess. In any event, he doesn't eat on a fixed schedule. Indeed he is reminded of the necessity to eat only when the rumbling of his stomach threatens his concentration. As the Traubels have next to no money, Gertrude wears second-hand clothing, Anne shops at the day-old counter of Camden's biggest bakers—and Horace will seek out one of the places (it hardly matters which) patronized by taxi-men, soiled doves, coppers, and workers setting out for another day on the seven-to-three shift or just coming off the eleven-to-seven. He will carefully read the menu cards, correcting typographical errors when he finds them, and order the largest amount of the cheapest offering that the coins in his pocket will provide. He has had many a fine meal whose various courses have all been bean or barley soup, a little watery but excellent for the purpose when consumed in volume.

When he was fifty, he prided himself on having much the same blooming vitality as W crowed about so loudly in his earliest poems.

But gradually the situation began to change. In O-nine, while crossing back to Camden on the ferry, he was knocked off his feet by a nervous horse. The frightened animal trampled him, breaking a number of his ribs. While hardly so severe a misfortune as W's initial brain-attack of Seventy-three, the incident has the same power to foretell the direction the future will take. Horace was a suspiciously long time recovering, with Anne nursing him at home as he chafed to return to his office. From that point forward, he has never had full confidence that his body isn't planning something else. So there is at least a bit of relief to be found amid all the dread and fear when, in the year the European war breaks out, he is found to have a leaky valve in his heart.

As he recuperates, Anne tries to keep him from seeing the newspapers, thinking that the news is terribly bad for him, as the war has defeated all hope of a peaceful Socialist world. But his friends visit constantly and they recount and recite the day's events. Soon, however, some of these same visitors are being hounded by the authorities.

Almost out of the blue, one evening he says to Anne, "If Father were still alive, he'd probably be rounded up as a German-born radical, though he never harmed a soul in his life."

In one way, it is perhaps all to the good that Horace will not be around to share in the strange triumph of his friend Eugene Debs. Debs is the unionist agitator sent to prison in Ninety-four on a charge of inciting the great Pullman strike that paralyzed all railroad traffic west of Chicago. He served his sentence in Moundsville, one of the most hellish prisons in the country, but was at least permitted to do some reading and writing there, and made himself a crude desk for his cell.

Debs has been the Socialist candidate for president of the United States in 1900, 1904, 1908 and 1912. Horace and his circle are proud when, in 1918, Debs makes a speech urging American men to avoid the draft. They are horrified when, in retaliation, he is tried under the Espionage Act and sent to the Atlanta penitentiary. In 1920, while incarcerated there, he runs for the presidency again, as a write-in candidate. In the country of fifty-four million people, he receives an astounding 913,664 votes, a feat made possible partly by the fact that this is the first national election in which women enjoy the franchise. Horace does not live to see this.

America has waited out the first part of the war until Britain, Canada, Australia, France and others weaken the Germans at staggering costs to themselves. But then in 1917 the U.S. enters the conflict for the final phase. The exact cause and effects are of course impossible to state scientifically, but Anne believes that this development is what has made her husband's heart condition not only recur, not only worsen, but become permanent.

Washington enlists itself in the war in April and Horace has a heart attack in June that very nearly kills him. A coincidence? Horace is alone at the time, for Anne and Gertrude have gone to New York to finalize arrangements for Gertrude's wedding, scheduled to take place there two days later. One day after the heart episode, Horace is feeling strong enough to put in another all-night appearance at the office. When his stomach reproaches him for neglect, he eats a big plate of beans at a lunch-room he knows, where he has a lively but disturbing discussion about the war with the waiter, a German who has lost two brothers in the fighting. Then he catches the ferry, only to discover when he gets to Camden that he has just missed the last streetcar. The night is clear and warm, so he decides to walk. Late that evening, he has a second attack similar to the first. Breathing becomes quite difficult and he suddenly finds himself so weak that his arms remain at his sides.

His friend David Karsner, who is the biographer of Debs, has been staying at Elm Street the past little while, and the following day the two men leave for the ceremony in New York, Karsner convinced that his comrade has had another heart attack but Horace refusing to entertain the idea, much less admit how damaging it was. Looking back, Karsner and Anne will find it incredible that Horace survived the trip. He does his clearest thinking when away from home. So when visiting New York he is able to sort out his honest thoughts. There he comes to terms with the terror he has been trying to avoid and realizes that when the Traubels return home, he must go to Philadelphia and close his office. Shut the place down. Turn out the lights. Lock the door.

Thus it comes about that he takes his seat at the desk for a final time, and spends a couple of hours letting various Mickle Street relics find their place in his hands. He allows his mind to play over the course of his relationship with W, applying clear reasoning, he hopes, to the question of to what extent, and how and why, his own life was changed forever by their association.

The overwhelming majority of his Mickle Street notes aren't written up yet but still sit, and most probably will forever do so, in these cabinets and cartons, wherever they may end up. If he is going to truly follow W's example, he too must be a seeker after truth. With whatever writing energy might remain to him—perhaps more will come once he has rested for a significant period—he will begin a memoir of everything he still remembers but deliberately has never committed to paper. He doesn't know how long such a document will be, only that, given the actuarial circumstances that prevail, it must be written quickly; but then he always has been a fast writer, as, in his experience, authors who work through the night usually are. Whether such a thing could be published, at least during what remains of his own lifetime, or perhaps ever, who knows? That will depend on whether tolerance ever returns to America or continues to be chipped away. Perhaps for that reason one of the Canadians or the English should become its guardian. In any case, it should go to someone who loves what W stood for but never made his acquaintance, a natural teacher but a discreet person all the same, someone who is a confident personality without being a censorious or condemnatory individual, someone who might be willing to accept the truth and then understand it—and proceed from there in one fashion or another, basing decisions on whatever conditions may be current at the time. He settles on Flora MacDonald. So resolving, he packs up whatever material he knows he will need to freshen his memory, making a note to have it delivered across the river. Then he takes one last panoramic look at the old place, pulls the chain that operates the green-shaded lamp overhead, and makes his way back to the ferry with the most prudent and conservative slowness.

Month after month, he takes it easy physically while building up the muscles of the mind. Most of the words come easily enough once he gets into the swim, but the actual act of composition is tiring, particularly as his eyesight is now poor and he must write less quickly than in the past and in a large hand. He works an hour a day, possibly an hour and a half. He has made very substantial progress by the time the leaves have fallen from the trees and the winter of 1918–19 approaches.

When he needs another big shot of new surroundings to get him through the wrenching details of W's own last illnesses and diseases, he and Anne accept an invitation to visit radical friends in Connecticut. There another attack strikes him, one the doctors are convinced comes closer to stopping his heart altogether than the previous ones combined. He has walked with a slight limp to his left leg ever since that horse fell on him, and the latest heart episode had made the stiffness more pronounced. He must now drag the leg behind him as he pulls himself forward with a cane, this man who used to race up several flights of stairs to reach the office, for the building has no elevator. His mind goes back to Doctor Bucke's crippled limb, and this helps him remember still more. Despite the fact he is getting far less exercise, he loses weight rather than gains it. Perhaps this is the effect of his diet. The doctors back in Camden all tell him that he must ask the heart to carry around as light a load as possible without becoming so thin as to compromise his system in some new way.

Two important tasks remain. He and Anne move to New York for a few weeks to bask in the presence of their infant grandson and lift some of the burden from the boy's parents, Gertrude Traubel Aalholm and her husband, Malcolm Aalholm, both musicians. They move into a rooming-house on West Twentieth, around the corner from the Aalholms. A week into their stay there, Horace suffers— no one knows what to call it. Not a heart attack in the sense of pain or even discomfort, nothing to do with the left side as distinct from the right, but just a sudden and deep weakness that leaves him facing a new level of disability. His mind, however, remains vigorous. His manuscript moves forward.

He and Anne accept the kind invitation to share the Karsner living quarters, the basement and ground floor of an apartment building on Beekman Place, right on the East River. Horace is delighted to be able to write at the very desk that Debs made in prison. It occupies pride of place in the front room, where Horace can look out directly onto the life of the river and the Brooklyn waterfront in the distance. The similarities between past and present are becoming eerie. Worse than eerie—frightening. Especially at night when he lies in bed next to Anne, when fear of dying in his sleep keeps him awake, and alive, until some force delivers another morning right on schedule. Writing through lameness and weakness, always fearful of new outrages against his body yet accepting of them as well, remembering the old days, seeing Brooklyn when his eyes open and likewise when they shut, thinking about the war, he wonders whether some angel, or devil, has taken hold of him, forcing him to end his own days as W ended his. The room actually looks a bit like Mickle Street, except that it's clean and neat as a pin. In whose past is he being held prisoner, his own or the other person's?

He even finds himself beginning to sound much more like W than he had years ago when he used to consciously attempt such mimicry, producing an approximation of the strange juxtaposing of suspicion and admiration that W himself so often provoked in people of both classes. For example, the verb *to freeload*. The Traubels are acutely aware of freeloading on the Karsners, and embarrassed by it. One day, after the freeloading enters its fourth week, Horace is playing with Walta Whitman Karsner, who is three going on four, when without warning the feral dogs attack once again and bite into his heart with their sharp white teeth. But he survives one more time. Barely, but he survives.

⁂

The Brevoort Hotel at Fifth Avenue and Eighth Street is where the leading Whitmanites gather for a dinner each May thirty-first. This time, two hundred people will be celebrating W's centennial, and Horace is determined to be there, however much further damage he might do himself in the process. He knows almost everyone at the tables; from the gossip network that is even more efficient than telegraphy, they know that he is dying. As if to reinforce the point, he eschews the head table and sits at the back, by the door, in case he should have another meeting with the snarling mastiffs.

The event is taking place immediately prior to passage of the new Espionage Act and the Palmer Raids, in which American citizens such as Emma Goldman are forcibly deported (in her case to Russia, where over the next decade she will lose many of her radical admirers, temporarily at least, by exposing the horrors still taking place there routinely, long after the Revolution). Even that young man named Hoover in the Treasury Department is a few months away from compiling lists of thousands of Reds and radicals. The atmosphere in the country is such that matters similar to these, rather than the literary and spiritual small talk of past years, dominate most of the speeches. Only one guest, someone with whom Horace has corresponded for years but meets now for the first time, speaks with eloquence of W's views on writing and society: Helen Keller. At the apex of the evening there is a lengthy tribute to Horace, who replies to the compliments as best he can, though by now his voice is low and muffled, as though W's voice, as it was at the very end, were being superimposed over his own.

Flora's dedication of the Rock at Bon Echo does not follow hard on the celebrations in May, for she has planned the event for August, one of only two months on the calendar when tourists foreign and domestic can take good weather for granted in that part of Ontario. For Horace, though, this will be the climax of everything. Rough as it is, his manuscript is three-fourths finished, and he has got through the night at the Brevoort without incident. His spirit and mind are peppy even if his corporeal self is not. Some friends headed for the same destination go with him and Anne to Grand Central. Lest any dull-witted people miss the gods' irony, he is wheeled to the platform in what's now simply called a wheelchair. He has a slight heart attack en route to Montreal.

The reason Bon Echo is as unspoiled as Flora's literature promises is that it is terribly remote and difficult to get to. At Windsor Station in Montreal, you leave the Canadian Pacific from New York and take a westbound train about two hundred and fifty miles to a place called Napanee, which sits a few miles north of Lake Ontario. From there you wait for a train to take you straight north to Kaladar, a distance roughly equal to that between Kaladar and your destination. The country is made of granite, limestone and thin soil, the lakes look cold and deadly. God help the people who farm here, but many do.

In late afternoon on the third day out of New York, Horace and Anne arrive at Flora's rather primitive establishment in an auto from Kaladar driven by another pair of Whitmanites. Flora has decorated the "inn" with a Welcome Home sign and is flying both the Stars and Stripes and the Union Jack. Horace writes to Missus Karsner: "Here safe. Tired. Hopeful. I'm yours in all real senses of the spirit. I hope to come back but not so helpless. Can be of more use to you. I recall the hours with you and Dave and the dear child as a furlough in paradise."

Horace, the soul of affability, performs all the reminiscing that is expected of him. For many of the Whitmanites, and there is a good crowd of them, promising a small profit for Flora, he is the only person they've ever met who was a proven friend of the great man. When he is not earning his supper this way, he is nudging his manuscript to its summation, working either in his room or out on one of the verandas.

Flora is constantly busy as the hostess and manager of the event, but makes time to get to know Anne better. Anne is intelligent and serene and deeply committed to social justice. She is also one of those thin women in whom you can still see the beauty of youth beneath the equal but different beauty of experience. They discuss suffragist issues. In a somewhat patchwork fashion, Canadian women were given the vote partway through the war.

Over the days and weeks, they exchange personal confidences. Flora tells how she went to Detroit when her son, Merrill, was about to be born so that he would be an American citizen, and relates the story of her failed marriage to the boy's father.

"I assume the people in Canada view divorce much as Americans do," Anne says.

Flora nods assent, but explains how much more difficult it is obtaining a Canadian divorce, what with the King's Proctor and the requirement that a private member's bill be passed as an act of Parliament.

"The failure is always claimed to be the fault of the wife," Anne says. "Some inadequacy or other, and then she is kept at a distance, viewed with the sort of suspicion that, I suspect, once greeted those vaguely suspected of witchery. But believe me, no sensible woman would blame you in the least. Only moralistic snobs."

"You and Horace must be a true love match," says Flora. "To look at the two of you, one would think you stand together on some geological formation like the one this place is built upon."

Anne smiles, shyly and perhaps a little wanly. "People assume that," she says, "but there are always compromises to be calculated and weighed. Is an offense that is too big to be overlooked also too big to be forgiven? In the longer run, no. But there are difficult times in every marriage."

"I find that hard to imagine with the two of you."

"Oh, the things I could tell you."

"Please. You know my own failures."

Anne lets out a miniature sigh, one of fatigue rather than exasperation. "Where can I begin? I have always, as far back as I can remember, been praised for my disposition or temperament or whatever others have wished to call it. I was the best-liked girl in the class."

Flora immediately forms the familiar image in her mind, though she herself was hardly a person ever singled out for such a distinction.

"I did always smile and try to put others at ease. But what others took to be my great social gift became, at times, more of a curse. I felt that my father, even more so after he became a widower, was using me as a young business accessory. When he invited associates or rivals to our home, as he seemed to do constantly, I was the hostess. I was there to supply the diverting conversation and poise of which he himself was so obviously incapable. Then, once the meal was polished off, I was expected to withdraw to what our mothers would have called the withdrawing room, leaving fat men to bite off the ends of their equally fat cigars as they got down to serious politicking and capitalizing. The hostess sat alone reading a novel or hid in the kitchen with the cook."

As she says this, she cannot help but show a bit of the same soothing smile that, by her account, helped give rise to so much misunderstanding and mistrust. "I was in the strange position of being the center of attention that no one took seriously. Walt was the first important intellectual who befriended me, followed by Horace. The three of us became inseparable. Walt became more and more affectionate the closer death approached on tiptoes. I understood that, in looking at me, Walt was looking back on youth (I speak in relative terms of course), casting his eyes over the past as it was and as it might have been. But I did not feel that I was used for strange emotional pleasure. It is too simple, the kind of simple thinking I hate, to say that he needed an imaginary daughter as I needed a replacement father. It was more than that, and less than that.

"Horace was so euphorically happy when, after long months of my being evasive on the subject, I gave in and suggested that we marry—the sooner the better. Well, Walt Whitman was not the only musketeer in our trio to sometimes keep secrets. I trust you, Flora. Trust you to the point that I can tell you what I've never told Horace, not that it matters much now. We had conceived a child, if indeed he or she could be called a child at that first stage of existence, and it—in the circumstances, I think I am more comfortable using the neutral pronoun—died in the womb in a matter of weeks, its father in ignorance of its existence. Why did I not tell him? Many reasons, I suppose, including concern for how he would have reacted, for he is such an emotional man, you know. Also, concern for what Father might have done if and when he learned of it. To him, the only thing worse than sharing my life with Horace Traubel was to have a child with him out of wedlock. Marriage came to seem an option that would give some comfort to the people involved.

"But the wedding, I must tell you, was ludicrous, though I can see the rich humor in it now. Horace and Walt arranged all the details. Need I say more than this? Well, I suppose I shall. The bedroom on Mickle Street was our chapel. In honor of the occasion Walt had evidently permitted Missus Davis, the housekeeper, to change the linen and make the bed, which he had vacated, probably not without difficulty, for his reading chair only a few feet distant. She had blackened the stove, beaten the rug and washed the windows. She was powerless, however, to do much about Walt's 'files' beyond throwing out the comparatively recent newspapers. She dared not disturb the order in which the senior papers were piled atop one another, along with all the old letters, documents and manuscripts. She stuffed as many stacks as possible either in the closet or under the bed. Even with this unprecedented tidying, there was scarcely enough space for the guests and us to stand shoulder to shoulder. I did not have a bouquet, but if I had, I could only have handed it to the person next to me as there wouldn't have been enough clearance for me to toss it in the air. The service, which made no reference to any divinity and may not even have mentioned marriage as such, was conducted by a perfectly kind but bumbling man. He was not simply a Unitarian but, I believe, a *lapsing*, or perhaps I should say *col*lapsing, Unitarian, finding the strictures of that sect's virtually nonexistent doctrines too harsh and confining for him to bear. He was dressed like a man applying for a position as a cigar-roller. As he spoke, Horace and Walt became rather weepy. And then our wedding trip was with Bucke, who not only traveled with us but, once at our destination, followed us everywhere with such overpowering closeness that Horace and I scarcely had a waking second alone together. Such was life with Horace and Walt.

"Despite the concern of my doctor, the second pregnancy, which began not long after I was declared fit, was without incident, and our lovely Gertrude was born a little more than a year after the previous experience and a little less than a year after Walt's death. Horace certainly greeted his daughter's arrival with all the joyousness it deserved, but otherwise he wasn't himself after Walt died. Understandably enough, witnessing that slow death at close range every day affected his equilibrium. He was forced to grab life by the coattails lest he undergo a somewhat similar future but without having first lived to the fullest. He was often away in either New York or Boston, especially Boston. When he was not, he still worked through the night. I felt he was meeting someone else or at least trying to avoid me."

Flora listens closely.

"Sometimes we quarreled. Or rather he attempted to quarrel and I refused to take part. He began giving voice to his resentment that I had never accepted an allowance from Father. 'Now we have another mouth to feed,' he would say. I grew weary of explaining yet again how any such arrangement would have been a collar and chain stricter than the household budgeting we must practice without it. This argument, which ran like an underground stream, out of sight but gurgling sometimes, ended when Father was ruined, absolutely and completely, down to selling the house and all its contents, in the great Panic of Ninety-three. It seems he had every cent of his money, what he had made or inherited plus whatever he could borrow, invested in railroad and bank stocks. When the railroads began failing, there were runs on the banks, many of which closed. Some men caught in the situation killed themselves. Father did not, though I cannot but conclude that the humiliation of his newfound poverty hastened his own end.

"I was expecting once again while the Panic unfolded, and Horace's anxiety grew. Little Wallace Traubel, named after our friend the Whitmanite from Bolton in England, was underweight at birth, and was always a sickly child. We were both devastated, as you might imagine, for I cannot describe the extent of such sorrow, when dear little Wally was carried away by scarlet fever shortly before what would have been his fifth birthday.

"My response was a great aching of the spirit that went on and on. Horace's reaction was rather different: he went and had a child by another woman. When I learned of this, he suggested in effect that such was his right. Those were not his words but that was his meaning. He was distraught and not himself at all. We came to terms with the situation in time."

Flora is flabbergasted and thinks she will never be able to look upon Horace again in quite the same way, not that much time remains for anything other than posthumous judgments.

"Have you ever come across the name Gustave Wiksell?" Anne asks. "He is from Boston. Another quasi-holy person."

"I would remember a name such as Gustave Wiksell," Flora answers.

"He was Horace's *other* lover. I felt myself quite inadequate of course, but in the end this revelation was much more easily digested than the other had been, and all was fine. The three of us all learned to share ourselves, which is no bad thing."

Flora is shocked anew. "I don't know what to say, because I suppose I don't know what to think."

"Like the other, it goes back to Walt in some basic way that is so much easier to see from the outside looking in than it is for Horace to see on the inside looking out. You know of Walt's bastard children, all phantoms of course, and his relationship with Peter Doyle and doubtless others, which he sought to hide by lies and evasions while also burning to express his joy in them."

Flora doesn't know how to react to the things she is being told. She fumbles, betraying her astonishment. "I didn't know that Walt and Doyle were actually practicing homo-sexualism, if I am correct in taking that to be your meaning and if this is the correct term for it."

Anne again shows Flora her patient-suffering smile. "Walt was a very important person indeed in my life, in all our lives, in various ways," Anne says. "I believe that I loved him in a way that was of course shy of the physical but nonetheless powerful, and that he loved me as much or more than he did any other woman after his mother. But still and all, sometimes one has to admit that dear old Walt was a bad influence on the world that had mistreated him."

⁂

For the first while, Horace seems at least somewhat less frail and certainly in good spirits but continues to put off the day when he and Flora will cross the lake by boat and consecrate the monument to Walt's memory. He will be ready tomorrow, he says each day. Flora has many reasons to urge him on, including the fact that the room he and Anne occupy, the only one free for them to use, is unheated. He might still be there when the weather starts to turn cooler, as it commonly does in early September but can do so even in late August.

August the twenty-fifth is the day when the weather is still warm enough, the lake still enough and Horace feeling well enough for them to act. He walks down the path to the large rowboat as others carry his empty wheelchair behind. Flora is in the stern with Horace, Anne in the prow. There are four or five others, including the volunteer oarsmen. Another party follows them in a smaller rowboat, followed in turn by still others in a canoe. The little flotilla moves through the Narrows into North Lake, the larger of the conjoined bodies of water, and crawls along the base of the Rock. When they come alongside the spot where the inscription is to be carved, the first boat is maneuvered up close against the cliff and held steady. Standing up precariously, Horace and Flora place their palms against the Rock and, by prearrangement, say "Old Walt" as they dedicate the site to, as they say, the Democratic Ideals of Walt Whitman. Then Horace begins to sob, as does Anne. Seeing them crying together this way, Flora, who has been avoiding Horace since hearing Anne's revelations, is reassured that all is well between the two of them. Horace, who believes his years with Walt have helped him locate and sharpen a latent talent for personal diplomacy, tells Flora that evening that the ceremony opened a door into his spiritual consciousness and flooded him with invisible light. He always knows just the right thing to say to believers.

When the party returns to the inn, Horace is taken to the proposed site of the Whitman Library that will never be built and turns the first spadeful of earth. He gathers up the loosened dirt and gives each person a handful. Writes "Walt" on the bare spot and then, strangely, empties his pockets of coins and covers them with soil. This exhausts all the deeply moving symbolic gestures that his imagination, tired from writing, is able to come up with on short notice. Having thus acquitted himself honorably, he goes to lunch in the dining hall.

There Flora speculates idly as to whether she can convince the Dominion government to contribute some financing help to make Bon Echo a permanent Whitman memorial. Why she even considers such a notion is a mystery but for the fact that Flora is an enthusiast and a mover. Horace speaks right up with his own view.

"You cannot trust governments," he says emphatically, suggesting perhaps the extent to which illness has weakened his Socialist outlook as well as his body. "No governments and no railroads!"

That night he takes a turn for the worse. Anne, who is herself on the verge of collapse with unstated sickness, probably a complaint of the nerves, looks after him tenderly, uttering endearments. There the situation remains for several days, as various other guests leave for the city. Their departure frees up a warmer room for the Traubels. One night Horace claims that Walt has appeared out of the lake and spoken to him. He has a similar experience, but one that takes place in the daytime and is entirely auditory, on September third, when it seems he might give up.

"I hear Walt's voice," he says to Flora, who is paying a bedside courtesy call. "He is talking to me."

"What does he say?"

"Walt says, 'Come on, come on.'"

After that, he is quiet for a while but breaks the silence by saying, "Flora, I see them all about me. W and Bob Ingersoll and Bucke and the rest."

Restless after so long in one position, he says, "Turn me." None of the Whitmanites knows or recalls that these were Walt's last words, spoken to the faithful Warrie.

Then he adds, "Why is it so difficult to die?"

Doctors have been sent for, but it takes two days for the first one to get there. He pronounces that a cerebral hemorrhage has left the patient completely paralyzed. Anne is sitting at his side when Horace dies at five in the morning on September eighth. He is sixty-one.

Flora suggests that Horace might be happy to rest eternally at Bon Echo, but Anne smoothly counters that she will return with him to either New York or Camden. Merrill Denison, a young writer of twenty-six, dresses the body as Flora rushes to the nearest likely town, a scribble on the map called Flinton, to buy a coffin in which the body can be transported. It is an ugly thing that is delivered that evening, when there is an impromptu funeral service before Horace's boxed corpse is taken across the lake by boat, then transferred to Flora's rattletrap Ford for a wild dash to Kaladar station so that Anne and her husband of twenty-eight years can catch the Montreal train. The motor trip covers more than twenty miles in a rainstorm so intense that the road, at the best of times little more than a deeply rutted trail, is being obliterated, or so it seems. The two women arrive with only moments to spare.

Anne, Flora and the mortal remains arrive in New York, where the body is embalmed and placed in a fancy coffin. There is considerable discussion as to where the New York funeral should be held. Anne of course has the deciding vote and chooses a community church known for its liberal views and general avoidance of theology. Mourners and curiosity seekers are beginning to select their seats early, for the body has not even arrived from the undertaker's as yet. Suddenly a woman enters to say that the building is on fire, as indeed seems to be the case. The hearse and the fire reels appear simultaneously and could have collided. Anne, whose long marriage to Horace has instilled in her a certain flexibility, scurries to find a new venue: a school auditorium. Flora keeps her shock to herself on learning that the service will be conducted by Gustave Wiksell.

The next day the body is taken to Camden by motorized hearse as Anne and Flora take the train, and Horace is buried in Harleigh Cemetery, not far from the Whitman tomb.

❈

Nearly two years have gone by, during which Flora has agonized over what to do with the manuscript found with Horace's effects at Bon

Echo. Anne has read it and pronounces that it contains little new except the exposure of Pete Doyle, which is of no interest to anyone, he having died in O-seven. In any case, it was a gift, albeit an odd gift, from her late husband to Flora, and so properly belongs to its intended recipient, not to the widow. Flora considers perhaps deleting some of the material that casts Walt in an unfair light, the result no doubt of restricted vessels in Horace's brain that were forewarnings of his eventual stroke. But what would be left? What would propel the great Whitman Fellowship, and perhaps the Whitman Library at Bon Echo, and what would impede them? On a more ethical level, she wonders whether imposing censorship could ever be the proper reaction, given how poor Walt, so misunderstood until the Whitmanites came along, suffered at the censor's hand during his earthly life. In the end, she takes all the pages and burns them in the furnace at Carlton Street.

This destruction in no way impairs her own pursuit of an answer to what has become for her the central question. Was Horace Traubel the actual spirit-child of his spirit-father Walt Whitman in more than a symbolic way? Or might their two souls have crossed or mingled? Might Walt's *living* spirit, after years of wandering, have found another home, inside Horace's shell?

She has pursued her research with Canadian mediums but without satisfaction. She has, however, heard of a medium in Buffalo, New York, who is spoken of so highly by seekers and admirers that she invites him to Toronto in the hope he might be able to put her question to the author of the immortal *Leaves* directly. So it is that two Americans come to her door, a small bald-headed fellow fretting inside his celluloid collar and carrying a flat parcel wrapped in oiled paper, and another one, who is younger, taller and faithful to the gospel of the firm handshake. She shows them into the surprisingly large front room, saying, "Welcome, gentlemen, to 22 Carlton Street.

Although both of you *are* gentlemen, I am sure you won't be intimidated to know that I have entertained Missus Pankhurst herself in this very room."

The short one nods in meek fashion and says little thereafter. The tall one smiles and says, "Ah, the famous Missus Pankhurst. Of course."

They look around the square room, whose main furnishing is an oaken table. The walls are papered in a French pattern above the wainscots and there are pillows everywhere, encased in fabrics bearing what appear to be various Oriental designs. The alert one of the pair notices a rod running across the ceiling midway down the room.

Flora sees him shoot glances at the unusual drapes of rough linen and the tassels used as wall decoration.

"Do you like my Bohemian style?"

"Very much so," he replies.

She regards her guests again. "Do either of you have any notion why so few of the people with your gift are female?" As she says this, she looks directly at the short man, who says, "No." The answer collides with the other one's response.

"I don't believe that is the case at all," he says. "You see . . ."

But she is off on a different topic, the persecution, as she calls it, of spiritualism by the church-going officials of Toronto. In a few minutes she winds down, and silence threatens to reassert itself until the taller man rushes to fill the gaps in conversation that his companion has left unclaimed. He compliments his hostess on the cleanliness of Toronto's streets. She replies by denouncing the city again, as an oligarchy of Capitalists and clergy, dividing her opprobrium equally between the two categories.

"I cannot abide their ignorance—no, that is the wrong word, their contempt—for Democratic Ideals," she says. She rants against the misguided fools at moderate length, allowing thin splinters of her own story to poke through the invective. She lets drop that she is no longer married and earns her living doing dressmaking at home. The vocal American thinks: That explains the curtain, which can be drawn to divide the space in two, creating one chamber with only the chairs and the big table, the smaller one with abundant cushions, a clothes tree and a painted screen.

He politely offers to bring her up to date about the spiritualist progress being made in Buffalo, again trying to compliment the Canadians, going so far as to make mention of the famous Fox sisters, who gave the modern movement its first push by their remarkable communications with the Other World almost a century earlier. "Were they not born in your own state?" he asks unnecessarily. "Or am I thinking of Quebec?" When the hostess does not respond to this attempt to inject the relevant history with female participation, he pushes right into the present and the great regard in which the work of Doctor Albert Durrant Watson is held across the border.

Missus Denison replies: "One might say that indirectly he is what brings us together at this time. Those of us who have been associated with him in Progressive Thought and Psychical Research Work have such confidence in him, and love for him, that I can barely convey it to you with accuracy. I remember how I gasped when I first read *The Twentieth Plane* and came upon the words that Walt spoke to him from the Other Side. One sentence in particular is preserved exactly in my memory." She shuts her eyes for a moment and changes her voice slightly to indicate quotation. "'What a solemn tread I had when on Earth, as I walked down the corridors of that too short time on the Fifth Plane, but, by God, I sent echoes of Truth flying, which will resound to the end of time.'" Her eyes open. "You will find that on page sixty-four."

The tall man is impressed; the short one wears an unfocused gaze as though he were in a trance already, though he suddenly jumps slightly—a shiver suggesting that he expects something to happen.

But it is only the sound of the day's post, bills no doubt, falling to the floor through the letter-slot.

"Doctor Watson is indeed an asset," says the talkative one. "I have naturally studied his work with admiration for its voluminousness and sincerity. In short, his messages are lofty, though I confess that I sometimes find them vague and unevidential."

"In what way?"

"In his excessive inclination toward the sheer illustriousness of those made contact with. This avoidance of the spirits of ordinary people greatly disfigures his work." He can see the remark is somewhat disturbing to his hostess, and adds, "At least, this is my own view. I grant that this may have less to do with the control than with the mediumship being employed." (The other guest betrays no reaction.)

"No, you are correct in one quite real sense," Flora says. "Being himself a poet of such superb sensitivity, Doctor Watson is naturally attracted to his peers who have passed. Thus the transcripts of his communications with Shelley, Coleridge and so on."

"I confess it, Madam, I know very little of verse myself."

"But you know our beloved Walt?"

"Certainly the name and the"—he seeks the proper word— "standing. But I cannot claim to have read his work at length." He fumbles about for other names but trails off amid the sounds in Carlton Street, where motorcars have suddenly grown louder.

"Then you still have ahead of you the pleasure of the immortal *Leaves* in its magnificent entirety!"

The man avoids replying, but asks whether she herself had ever met the poet when he was on Earth.

"Alas, I did not. But I have had the benefit of knowing many who did, including the one who knew him best: dear Horace Traubel, his spirit-child, chronicler and amanuensis, who died while visiting with our Canadian circle at Bon Echo. You have not asked, however, whether I have met with Walt since his crossing—for I have done so, at the Watson home. It was one of the most profound moments of my life, if not indeed the most meaningful one of all. Ever since then I have reflected on it almost daily, and have concluded that he wished to address me individually, privately you might say, so as to entrust me with information that for some reason he did not feel could be given me in the presence of the particular group gathered at the Watsons'. That is what led me to extend the invitation that you have accepted so kindly."

At this, the tall man smiles while the short one, who is beginning to look mighty uncomfortable in his stiff collar, nods in the affirmative. "Within our means, we will go any distance to seek the truth," says the spokesman of the pair.

With that, Flora quickly stands up, causing the two men to do likewise. "So, then," she says heartily. "Let us see if Walt Whitman is receiving callers."

She draws the linen window draperies just as a streetcar totters out of sight. Then she extinguishes all the electric lights, puts candles around the room and pulls the curtain closed so as to divide the room in two. The three figures gather their chairs round the table. The taller man, known as the control, says, "The medium will now enter into a trance state."

As though on command, his partner immediately shuts his eyes and begins breathing deeply in a slow rhythm. After a minute or two, the sound of his respiration starts to fade until it becomes inaudible and he himself motionless. At that point the control withdraws his billfold from his inside breast pocket and reveals a piece of card to which four pins are affixed. He extracts one of the pins and jabs the point into the medium's left hand. The puncture seems to have no effect. Then he sticks in a second pin and finally, switching his attention to the medium's right hand, does likewise with the two remaining ones, before withdrawing all four. The medium's eyes remain closed and he makes no move or sound. A thin trickle of blood on the left hand is the only sign that the pins have actually penetrated the flesh.

The control unties the parcel, revealing a small sheet of ordinary plate glass. "We are ready," he says. Flora and the outgoing one sit with their palms on the tabletop. The medium for his part rests his fingertips on the glass, to which a Ouija pointer has been affixed, and begins with a sort of incantation that is in effect an attempt to find the correct address. This is the first time so far that he has spoken more than a word or two. His voice is deeper than those brief previews have led Flora to expect, and there is an odd quality about it: not ethereal but certainly distant, as though the sound being received in this room, as on a crystal set perhaps, indeed originates on a different plateau of reality. He speaks of such matters as the love of all beings for one another, and continues speaking until a sudden change comes over him. It is as though someone else whom the others cannot hear has joined in, allowing two spirits to converse with each other through a single mind.

The medium's eyes are open now and his finger takes direction from the Other World, making the pointer alight on one letter after another, quickly but in clusters of movement, as though its animating force were pausing normally between words and at the ends of the sentences. The medium utters groups of words aloud as he sees them formed, letter by letter, on the apparatus.

"To dare is the thing I have always enjoyed most," the spirit is telling him through the letters—telling them all. "I wrote free verse because I could write no other. Did not have that kind of education. Technique failed me when I desired it most. I am not sorry that I wrote in the pure, native, glistening state as it came from the mine of my mind, and lived as poetry that the world, in some cases justly and in other cases unjustly, has immortalized."

Flora is excited the second she recognizes whose spirit is communicating with them, even though she is mildly surprised at the spirit's point of view with respect to what had been his earthly labor. Coming as it does, character by character, the process allows various levels of meaning to be appreciated.

She knows that she is expected not to speak during the encounter, but her heart is crying out to learn the great animating answer to her theory about Horace that only Walt can provide, as Horace has never yet responded to her summonses (perhaps it is still too early, as he may not have completed the transition). It is this very secret about the state of Horace's spirit that she knows must flourish somewhere within Walt's. The event, however, concludes too soon, after it becomes apparent that either the medium or the subject is not fully open and that some countervailing force might be impeding free transmission of the natural currents.

To Flora certainly and perhaps to the two men as well, an hour and a half feels like only a few moments. The last utterances that the pointer can signify so haltingly are heavy with melancholy. "I feel the solemnity of the moment greatly, and in parting I will say a few words to the soul of the Universe: Father, lover of all children, though we are encased in physical garments that obstruct the wider, more intense and clear light with which we hear and see, bend a little closer to all of us. Never have I seen, from this pale existence, more serene and worthy souls than those who hear my words at this moment, so beneath the fitful light of yonder star, as it enmeshes itself in the substance of the children who are sons and daughters of Yours, Father, be with them so that they may know that at the helm of life is a Captain whose name is Love. Amen."

Then the subject seems to change abruptly, and Flora becomes increasingly aware that the spirit is speaking to her directly, without reference to the others present.

"I am certain that all you have done thus far is like the music of Niagara . . ."

This comes through even more slowly, the letters widely spaced, as though the voice were rapidly losing strength or perhaps even the will. Then comes this: "Good-bye."

The medium's face, which during the trance seemed almost featureless and free of anxiety or worldly attention of any kind, slowly resumes its original appearance.

There is a moment in which the three people look straight ahead and then glance at one another silently. Then come thanks and other courtesies, and Flora finds herself resenting the reassertion of earthly demands.

She asks the gentlemen if they wish a taxi to return them to the station, but they have only to walk the few steps to Yonge and board a southbound streetcar. They find places near the back and sit in silence until they are past Dundas Street. Then the outgoing one says, "That was odd, wasn't it?"

"I don't understand what you mean," his friend replies.

"She is far from being a reticent woman, but there is much that she is not telling us, don't you think?"

The other man says nothing.

❧ ACKNOWLEDGMENTS ❧

THIS BOOK IS THE REVERSE OF A NON-FICTION NOVEL in that it is fiction that exploits some conventions of non-fiction, rather than vice versa. It borrows from *With Walt Whitman in Camden* by Horace Traubel, published in nine volumes between 1905 and 1996. In a great many instances, the dialogue I attribute to Whitman and Traubel was actually spoken by them, though in many or most places I have changed it either slightly or fundamentally, and of course have tried to match its tone the rest of the time, when writing without benefit of Traubel's jottings. Anyone seeking to know Whitman owes an incalculable debt to Traubel and his posthumous editors and publishers down through the years, and perhaps none more so than me. But I have re-imagined the whole range of principal characters and given Walt, Horace, Pete, Bucke, Anne and Flora, as well as the group that conspired against Lincoln, new or at least greatly altered personalities.

As this is indeed a novel, with all such attendant liberties, conjectures, transpositions and imaginative untruths, it will be of no interest or use whatever to Whitman scholars, which I regret, for I found many of their books to be indispensable. I have relied especially on two of the latest biographies, *Walt Whitman, A Gay Life* by Gary Schmidgall (1997) and *Walt Whitman: The Song of Himself* by Jerome

Loving (1999). Also particularly useful were *Walt Whitman's America: A Cultural History* by David S. Reynolds (1995) and *Freedom Rising: Washington in the Civil War* by Ernest B. Furgurson (2004). With some major exceptions and a number of minor ones, the facts concerning the man whose friends called him Wilkes are much as set out in Michael W. Kauffman's groundbreaking analytical study *American Brutus: John Wilkes Booth and the Lincoln Conspiracies* (2004) and James L. Swanson's driving narrative *Manhunt: The 12-Day Chase for Lincoln's Killer* (2006). I also gained much from *Dixie & the Dominion: Canada, the Confederacy and the War for the Union* by Adam Mayers (2003).

When I was at work on this book, many of my literary colleagues were writing essays on the American invasion and occupation of Iraq. *Walt Whitman's Secret* is my own modest if now somewhat belated contribution to this discourse.

Walt Whitman's Secret is George Fetherling's third novel and fourth book-length fiction. He has also published many works of poetry, travel narrative and memoir. He lives in Vancouver and Toronto.

A NOTE ABOUT THE TYPE

Walt Whitman's Secret is set in Monotype Van Dijck, a face originally designed by Christoffel van Dijck, a Dutch typefounder (and sometime goldsmith) of the seventeenth century. While the roman font may not have been cut by van Dijck himself; the italic, for which original punches survive, is almost certainly his work. The face first made its appearance circa 1606. It was re-cut for modern use in 1937.